WRITTEN BY
JOHN HARRIS DUNNING

ART BY
RICARDO CABRAL

COLOR ART BY
BRAD SIMPSON

LETTERS BY
JIM CAMPBELL

DARK HORSE BOOKS

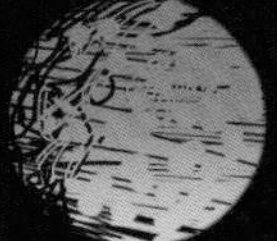

PRESIDENT AND PUBLISHER
MIKE RICHARDSON

EDITOR
BRETT ISRAEL

ASSISTANT EDITOR
SANJAY DHARAWAT

DIGITAL ART TECHNICIAN
SAMANTHA HUMMER

COLLECTION DESIGNER
MAY HIJIKURO

Published by Dark Horse Books
A division of Dark Horse Comics LLC
10956 SE Main Street, Milwaukie, OR 97222

First edition: November 2022
Ebook ISBN 978-1-50673-341-8
Trade Paperback ISBN 978-1-50673-340-1

10 9 8 7 6 5 4 3 2 1
Printed in China

Comic Shop Locator Service: comicshoplocator.com

FSC www.fsc.org MIX Paper from responsible sources FSC® C169962

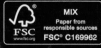

Library of Congress Cataloging-in-Publication Data

Names: Dunning, John Harris, writer. | Cabral, Ricardo, 1979- artist. | Simpson, Brad (Bradley Darwin), 1975- colourist. | Campbell, Jim (Letterer), letterer.
Title: Wiper / written by John Harris Dunning ; art by Ricardo Cabral ; color art by Brad Simpson ; letters by Jim Campbell.
Description: First edition. | Milwaukie, OR : Dark Horse Books, 2022. | Summary: "Lula Nomi is a Wiper-a private detective who guarantees complete discretion. A memory wipe after every job sees to that. When she's hired by enigmatic robot Klute she thinks the case is the answer to all her problems. But there's something oddly familiar about Klute-and the more she investigates the disappearance of journalist Orson Glark, the more she suspects that he's somehow connected to her own past..."— Provided by publisher.
Identifiers: LCCN 2022011325 | ISBN 9781506733401 (trade paperback) | ISBN 9781506733418 (ebook)
Subjects: LCGFT: Science fiction comics. | Graphic novels.
Classification: LCC PN6737.D86 W57 2022 | DDC 741.5/942–dc23/eng/20220325
LC record available at https://lccn.loc.gov/2022011325

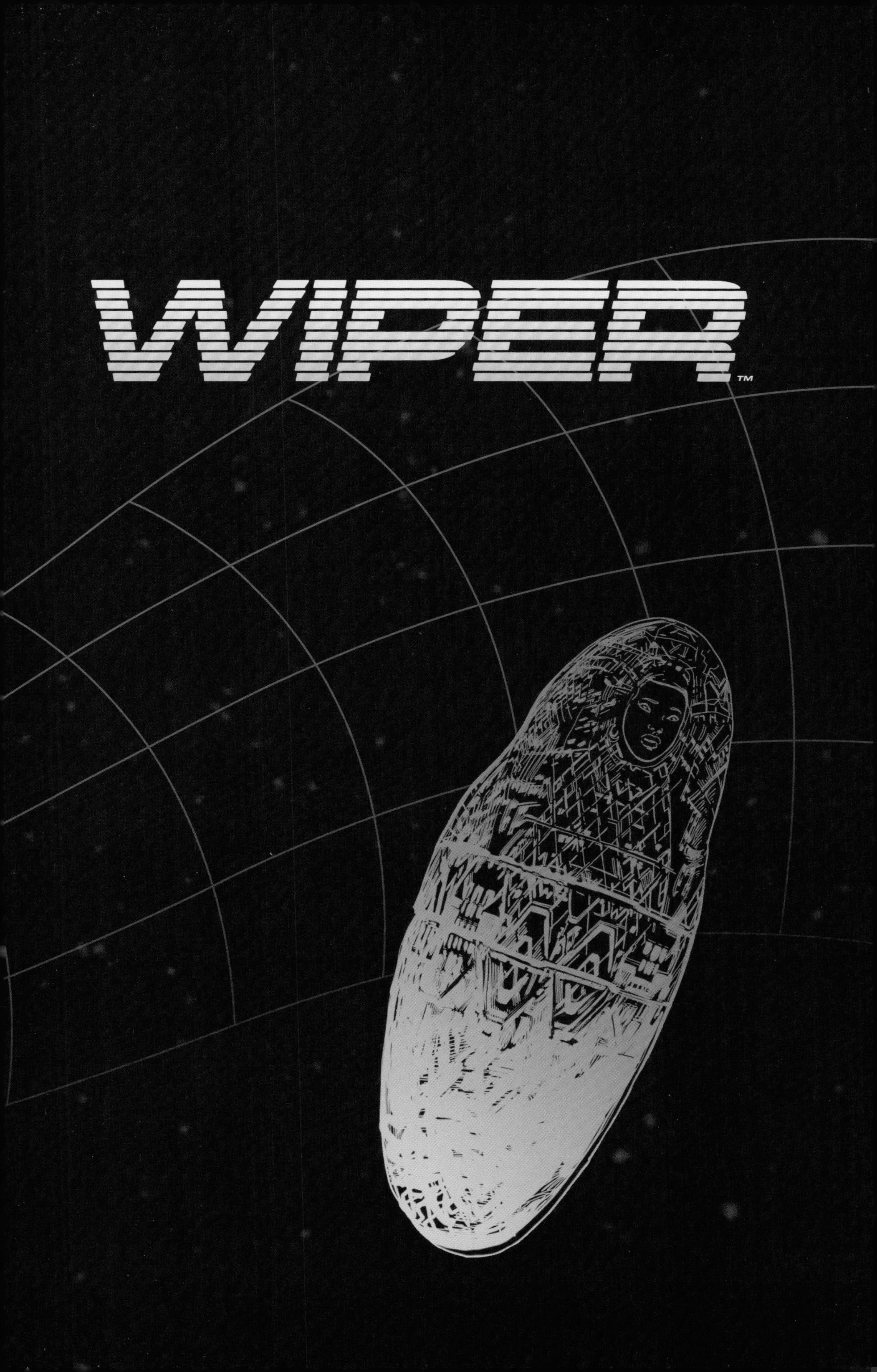
WIPER™

I AM GETTING SO FAR OUT ONE
DAY I WON'T COME BACK AT ALL.

—WILLIAM BURROUGHS

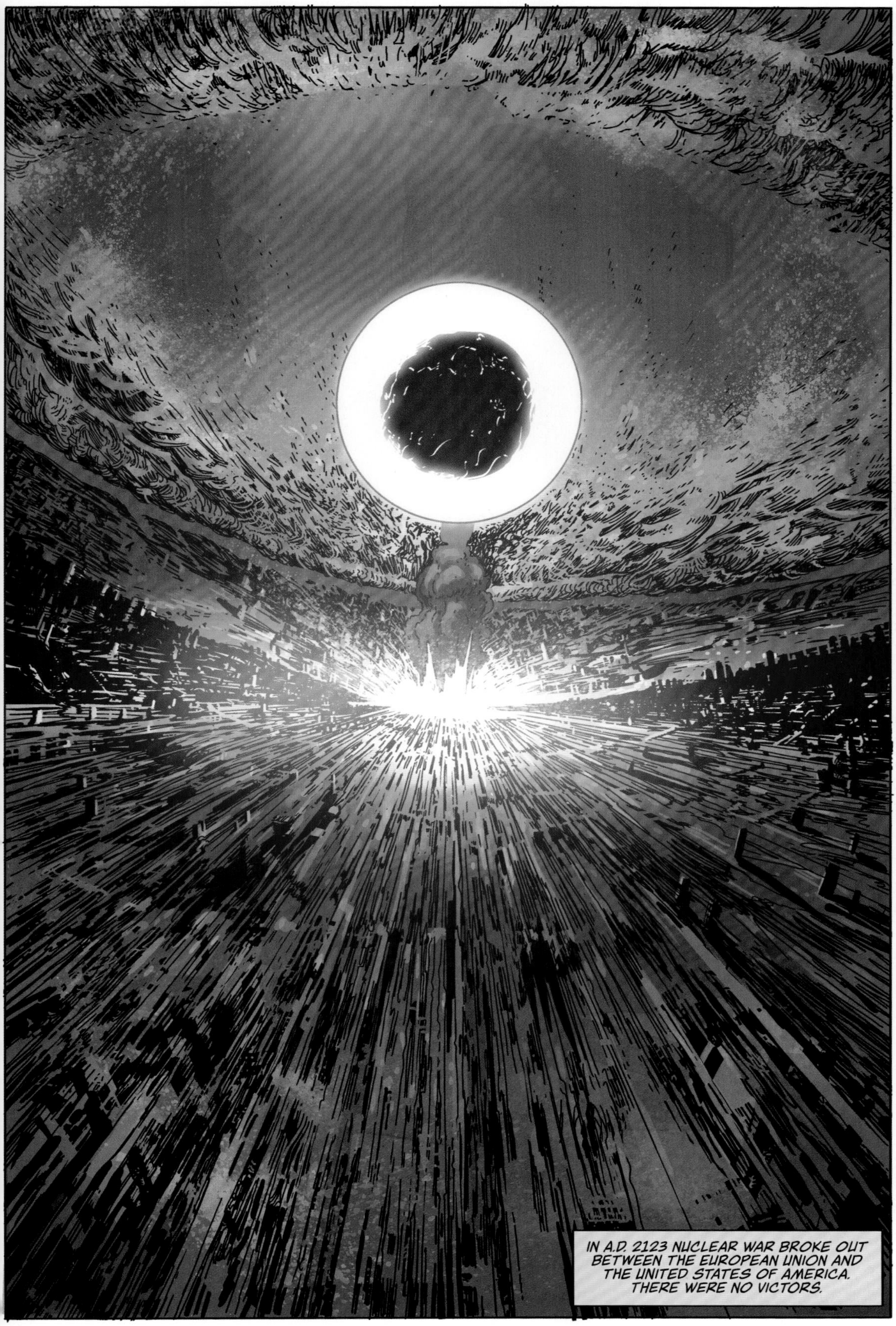
IN A.D. 2123 NUCLEAR WAR BROKE OUT BETWEEN THE EUROPEAN UNION AND THE UNITED STATES OF AMERICA. THERE WERE NO VICTORS.

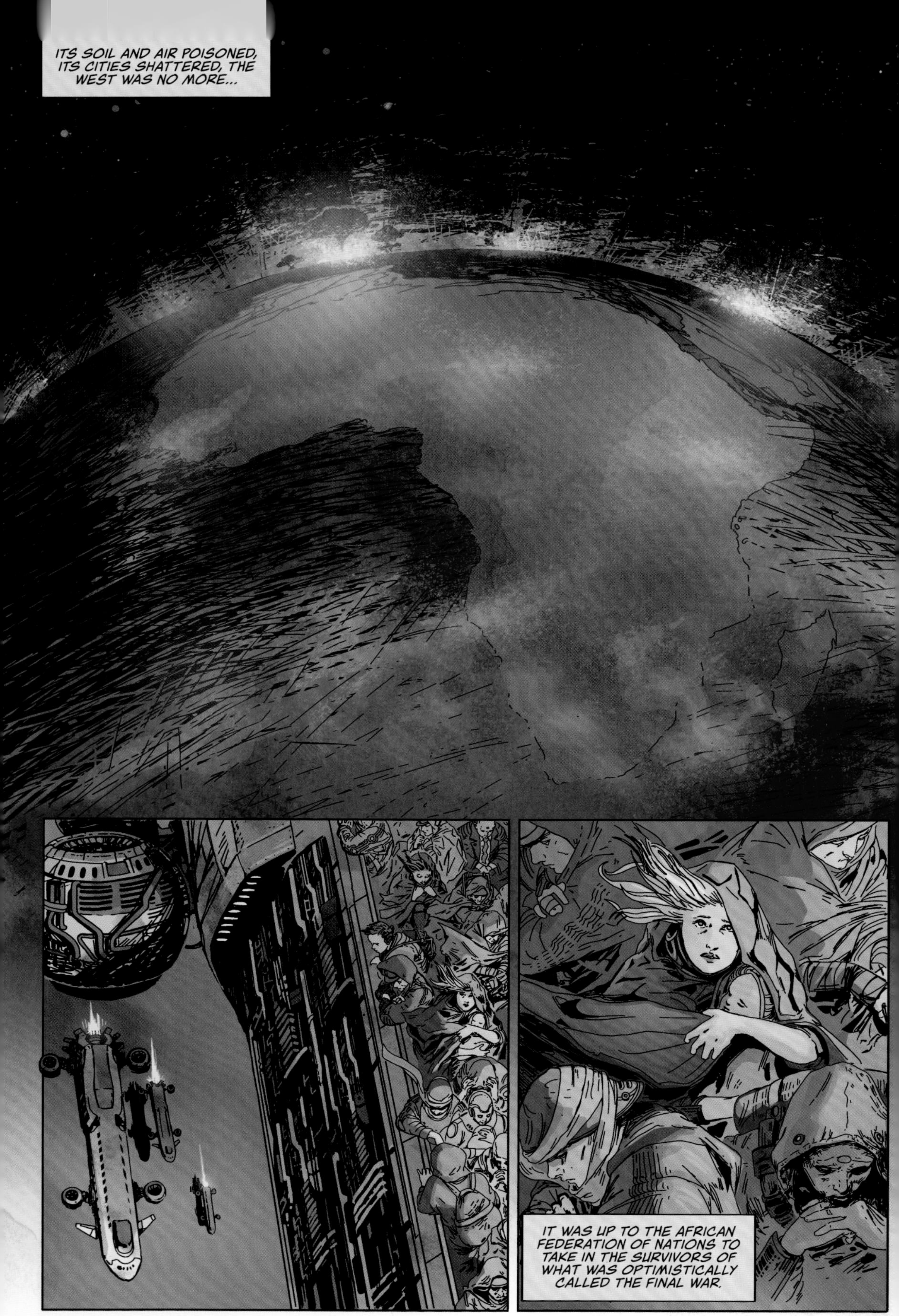
ITS SOIL AND AIR POISONED, ITS CITIES SHATTERED, THE WEST WAS NO MORE...
IT WAS UP TO THE AFRICAN FEDERATION OF NATIONS TO TAKE IN THE SURVIVORS OF WHAT WAS OPTIMISTICALLY CALLED THE FINAL WAR.

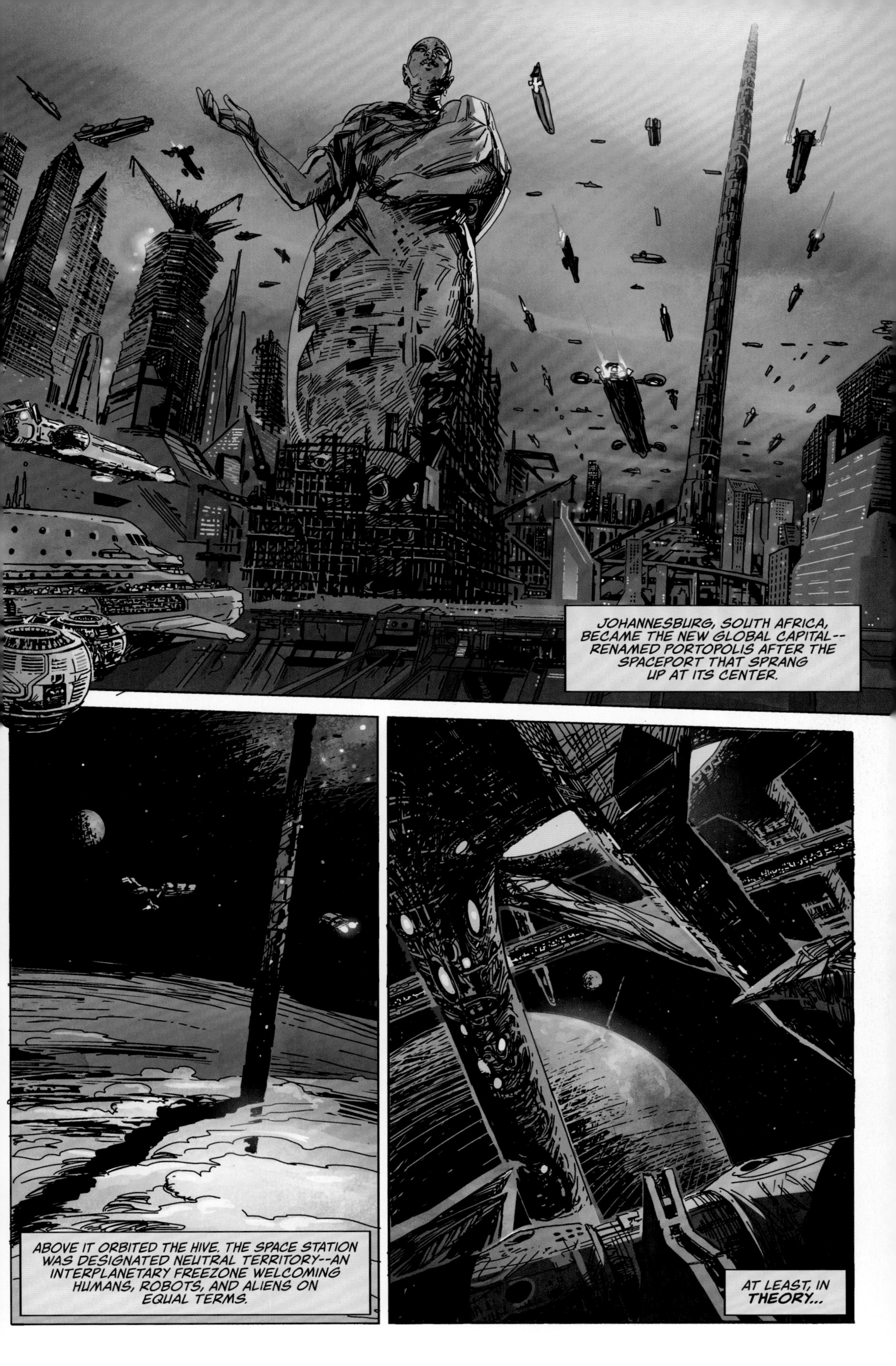
JOHANNESBURG, SOUTH AFRICA, BECAME THE NEW GLOBAL CAPITAL--RENAMED PORTOPOLIS AFTER THE SPACEPORT THAT SPRANG UP AT ITS CENTER.
ABOVE IT ORBITED THE HIVE. THE SPACE STATION WAS DESIGNATED NEUTRAL TERRITORY--AN INTERPLANETARY FREEZONE WELCOMING HUMANS, ROBOTS, AND ALIENS ON EQUAL TERMS.
AT LEAST, IN THEORY...

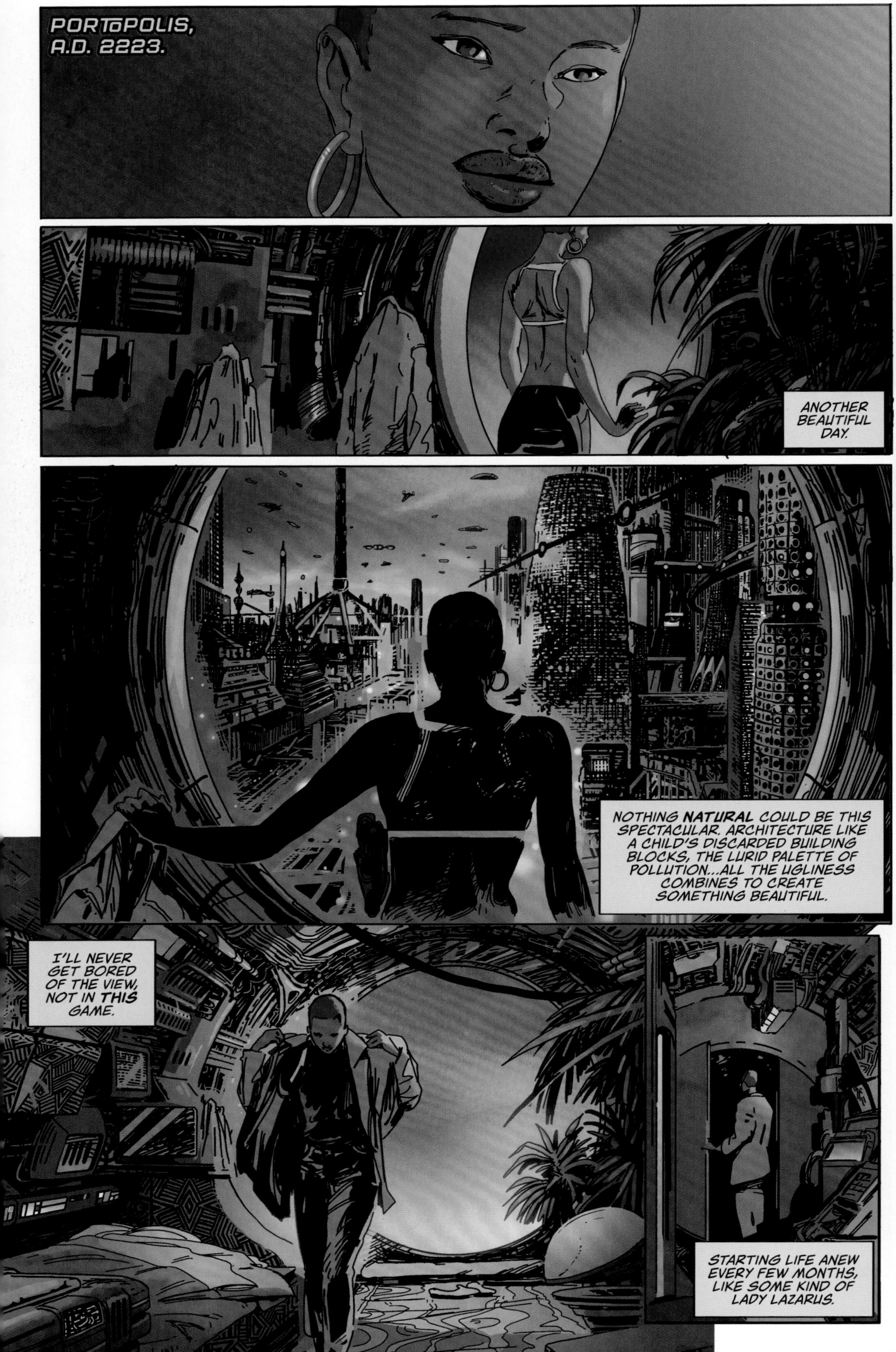
PORTOPOLIS, A.D. 2223.
ANOTHER BEAUTIFUL DAY.
NOTHING NATURAL COULD BE THIS SPECTACULAR. ARCHITECTURE LIKE A CHILD'S DISCARDED BUILDING BLOCKS, THE LURID PALETTE OF POLLUTION...ALL THE UGLINESS COMBINES TO CREATE SOMETHING BEAUTIFUL.
I'LL NEVER GET BORED OF THE VIEW, NOT IN THIS GAME.
STARTING LIFE ANEW EVERY FEW MONTHS, LIKE SOME KIND OF LADY LAZARUS.

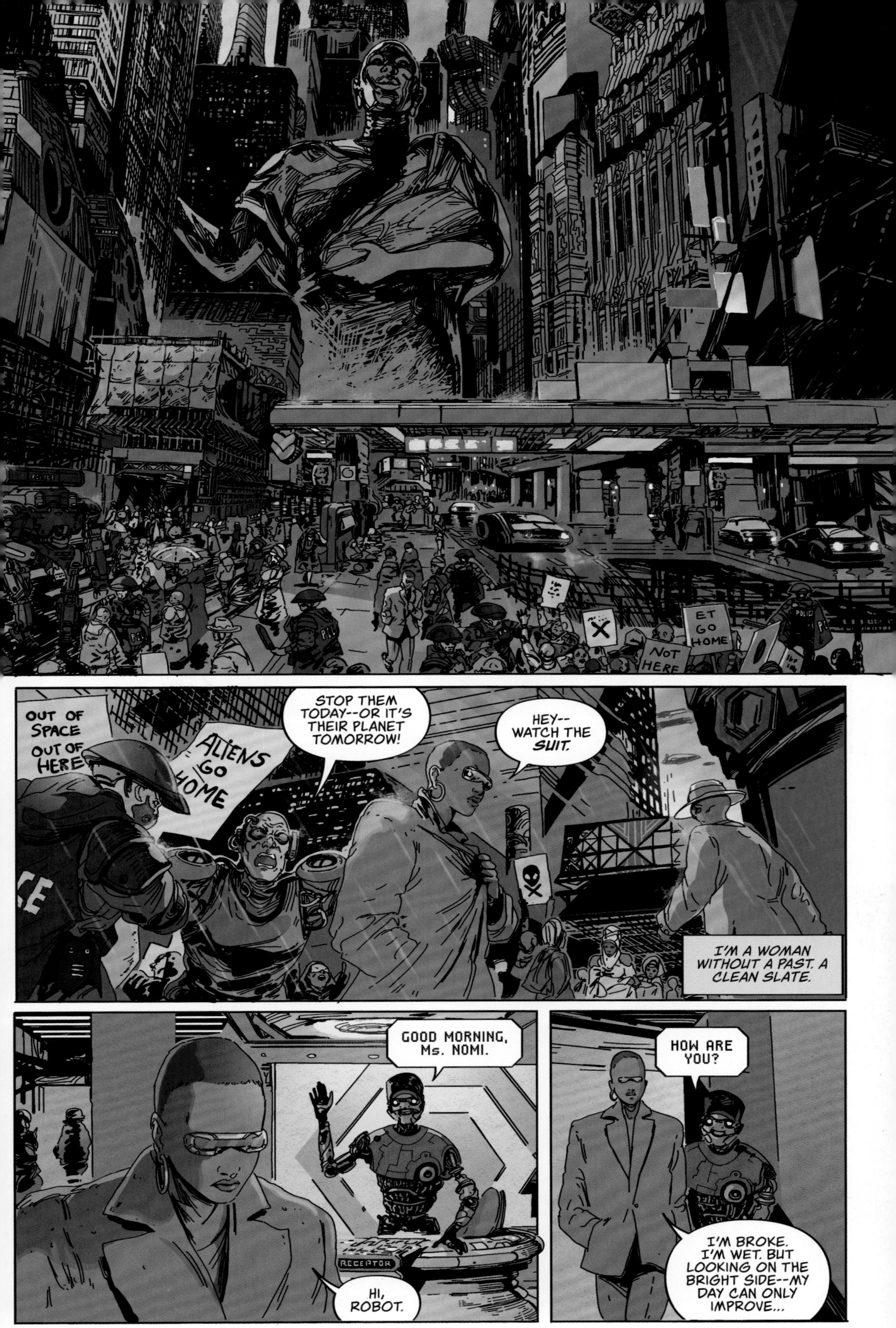
ET GO HOME
NOT HERE
OUT OF SPACE OUT OF HERE
ALIENS GO HOME
STOP THEM TODAY--OR IT'S THEIR PLANET TOMORROW!
HEY-- WATCH THE *SUIT.*
I'M A WOMAN WITHOUT A PAST. A CLEAN SLATE.
GOOD MORNING, Ms. NOMI.
RECEPTOR
HI, ROBOT.
HOW ARE YOU?
I'M BROKE. I'M WET. BUT LOOKING ON THE BRIGHT SIDE--MY DAY CAN ONLY IMPROVE...

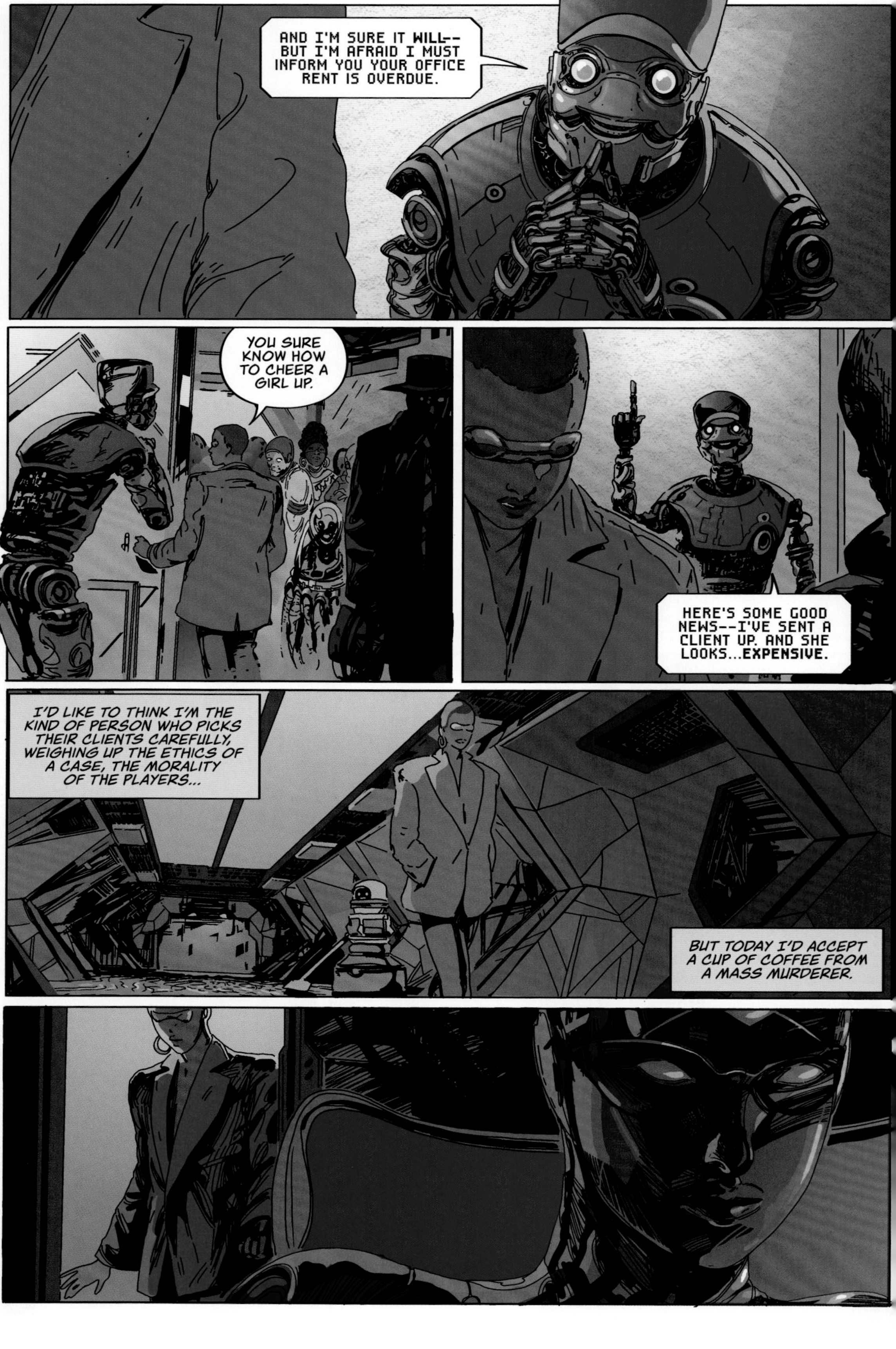
AND I'M SURE IT WILL--
BUT I'M AFRAID I MUST
INFORM YOU YOUR OFFICE
RENT IS OVERDUE.
YOU SURE KNOW HOW TO CHEER A GIRL UP.
HERE'S SOME GOOD NEWS--I'VE SENT A CLIENT UP. AND SHE LOOKS...**EXPENSIVE.**
I'D LIKE TO THINK I'M THE KIND OF PERSON WHO PICKS THEIR CLIENTS CAREFULLY, WEIGHING UP THE ETHICS OF A CASE, THE MORALITY OF THE PLAYERS...
BUT TODAY I'D ACCEPT A CUP OF COFFEE FROM A MASS MURDERER.

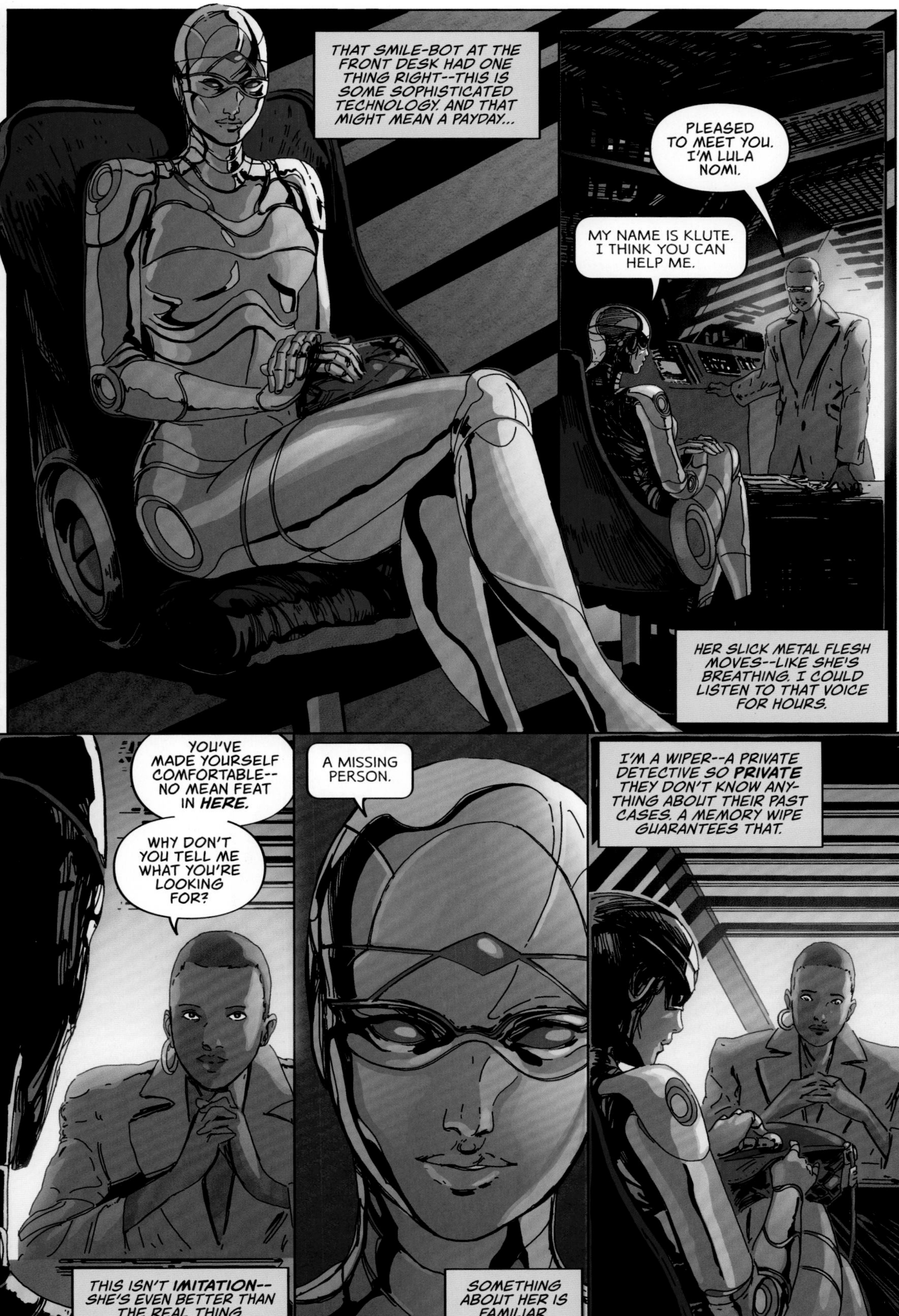
THAT SMILE-BOT AT THE FRONT DESK HAD ONE THING RIGHT--THIS IS SOME SOPHISTICATED TECHNOLOGY. AND THAT MIGHT MEAN A PAYDAY...
PLEASED TO MEET YOU. I'M LULA NOMI.
MY NAME IS KLUTE. I THINK YOU CAN HELP ME.
HER SLICK METAL FLESH MOVES--LIKE SHE'S BREATHING. I COULD LISTEN TO THAT VOICE FOR HOURS.
YOU'VE MADE YOURSELF COMFORTABLE-- NO MEAN FEAT IN HERE.
WHY DON'T YOU TELL ME WHAT YOU'RE LOOKING FOR?
THIS ISN'T IMITATION-- SHE'S EVEN BETTER THAN THE REAL THING.
A MISSING PERSON.
SOMETHING ABOUT HER IS FAMILIAR.
I'M A WIPER--A PRIVATE DETECTIVE SO PRIVATE THEY DON'T KNOW ANY-THING ABOUT THEIR PAST CASES. A MEMORY WIPE GUARANTEES THAT.

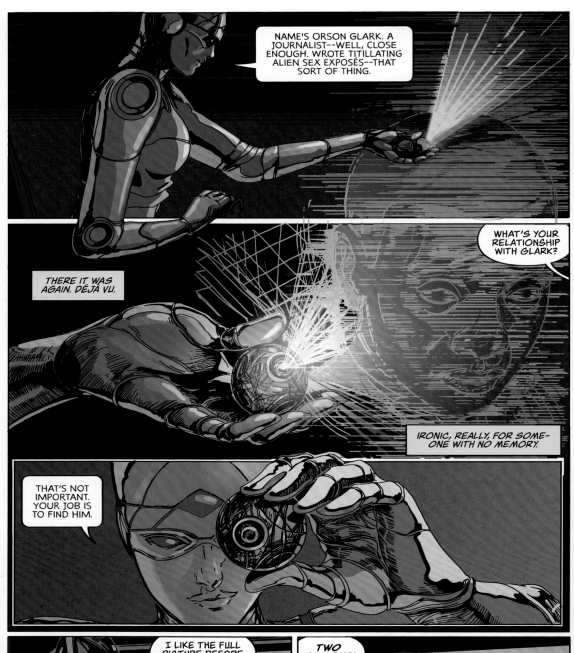

NAME'S ORSON GLARK. A JOURNALIST--WELL, CLOSE ENOUGH. WROTE TITILLATING ALIEN SEX EXPOSÉS--THAT SORT OF THING.

WHAT'S YOUR RELATIONSHIP WITH GLARK?

THERE IT WAS AGAIN. DÉJÀ VU.

IRONIC, REALLY, FOR SOMEONE WITH NO MEMORY.

THAT'S NOT IMPORTANT. YOUR JOB IS TO FIND HIM.

I LIKE THE FULL PICTURE BEFORE TAKING A CASE.

YOU'LL LIKE TWO MILLION CREDITS MORE.

TWO MILLION?!

HALF UP FRONT TO SECURE YOUR SERVICES. EXPENSES ON TOP.

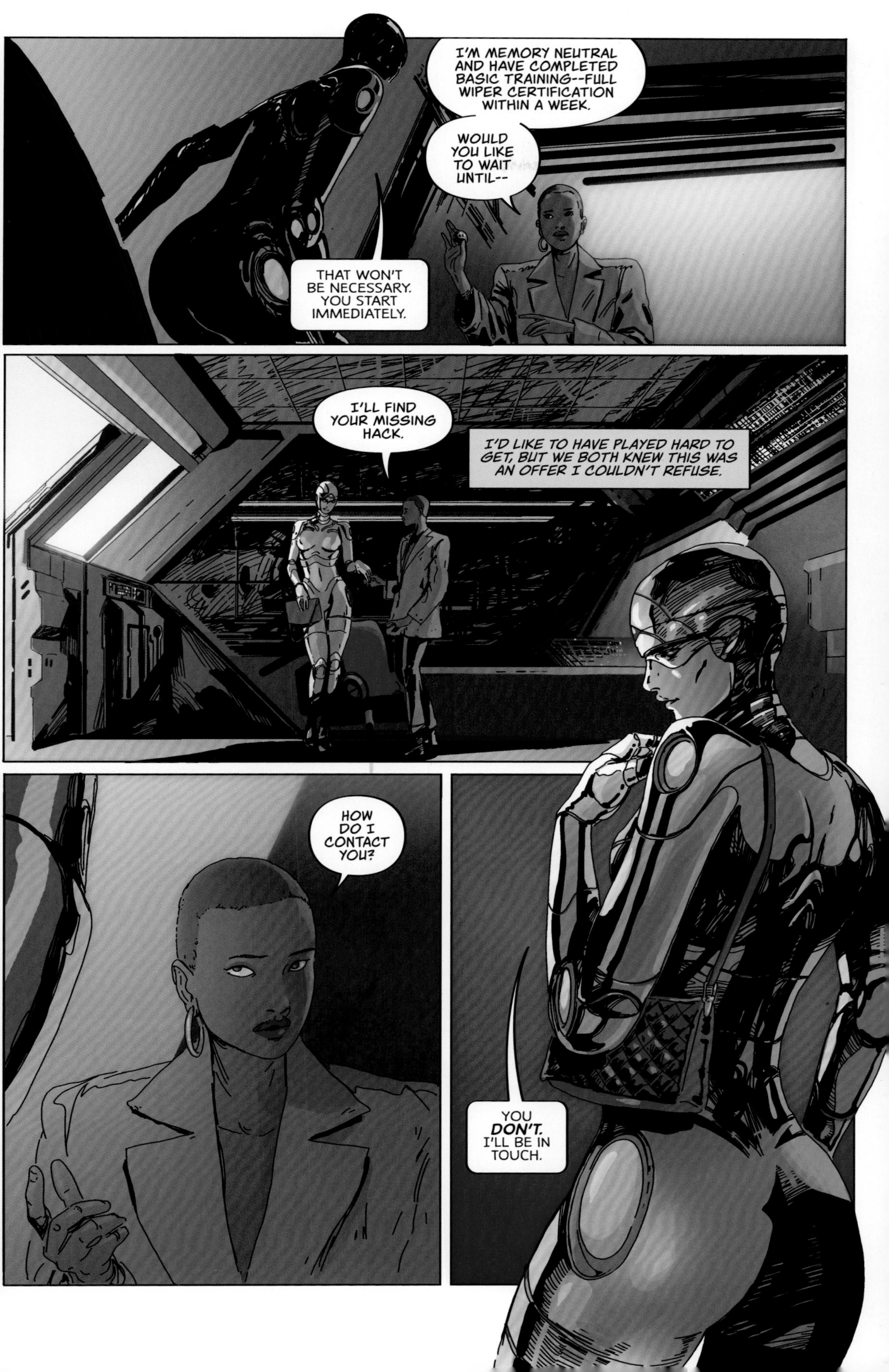
I'M MEMORY NEUTRAL AND HAVE COMPLETED BASIC TRAINING--FULL WIPER CERTIFICATION WITHIN A WEEK.
WOULD YOU LIKE TO WAIT UNTIL--
THAT WON'T BE NECESSARY. YOU START IMMEDIATELY.
I'LL FIND YOUR MISSING HACK.
I'D LIKE TO HAVE PLAYED HARD TO GET, BUT WE BOTH KNEW THIS WAS AN OFFER I COULDN'T REFUSE.
HOW DO I CONTACT YOU?
YOU DON'T. I'LL BE IN TOUCH.

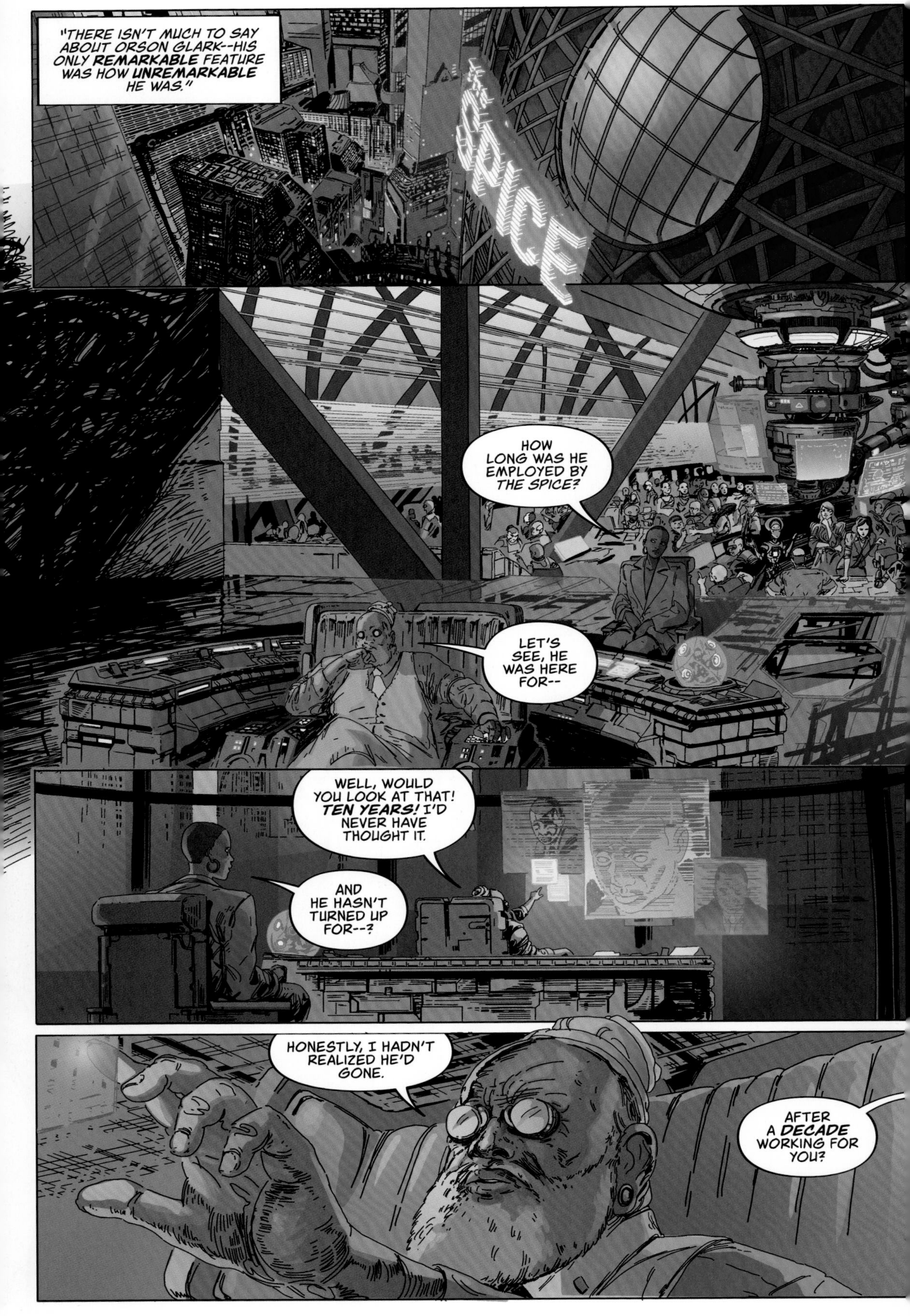
"THERE ISN'T MUCH TO SAY ABOUT ORSON GLARK--HIS ONLY REMARKABLE FEATURE WAS HOW UNREMARKABLE HE WAS."
SPICE
HOW LONG WAS HE EMPLOYED BY THE SPICE?
LET'S SEE, HE WAS HERE FOR--
WELL, WOULD YOU LOOK AT THAT! TEN YEARS! I'D NEVER HAVE THOUGHT IT.
AND HE HASN'T TURNED UP FOR--?
HONESTLY, I HADN'T REALIZED HE'D GONE.
AFTER A DECADE WORKING FOR YOU?

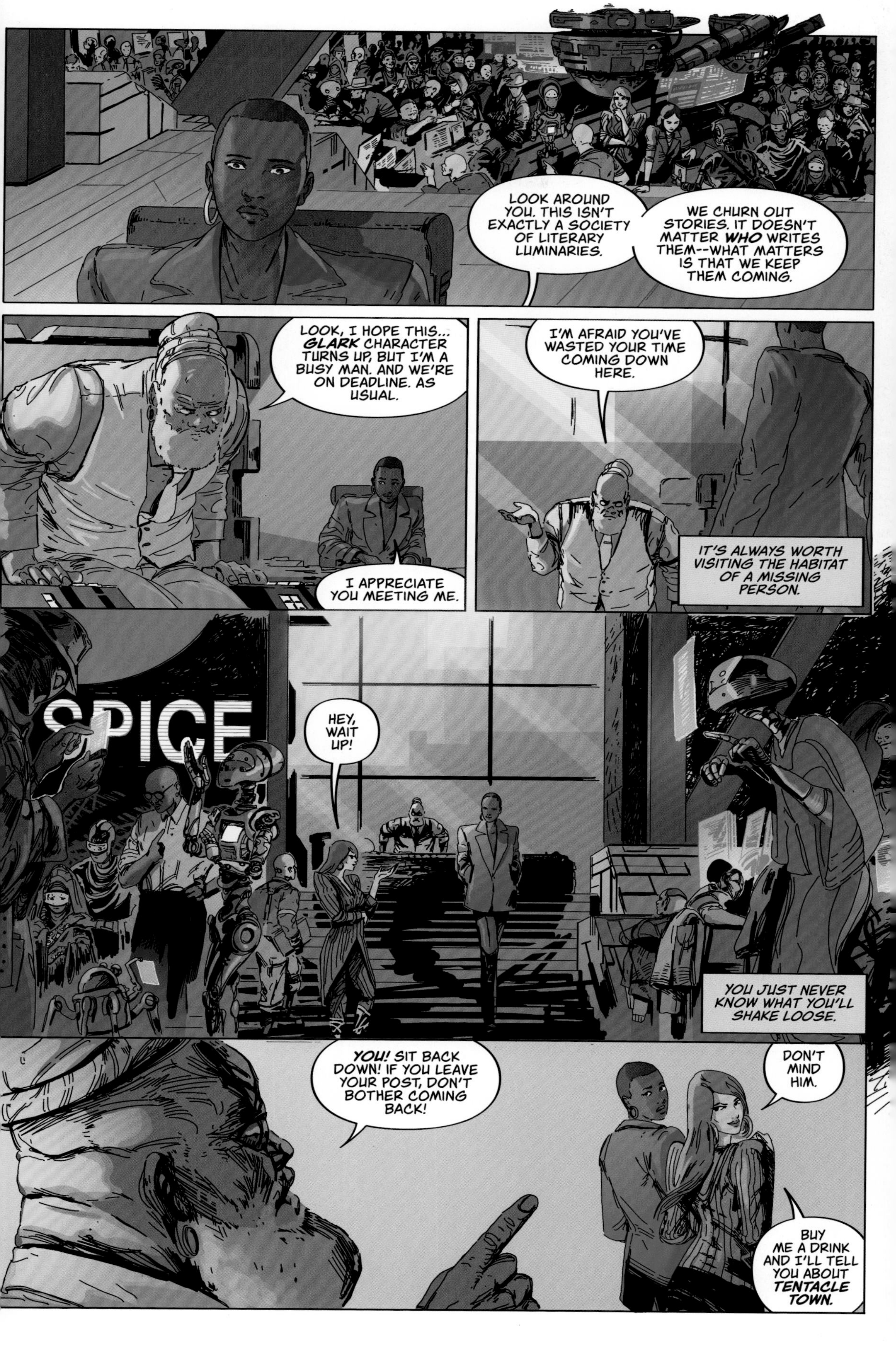
LOOK AROUND YOU. THIS ISN'T EXACTLY A SOCIETY OF LITERARY LUMINARIES.
WE CHURN OUT STORIES. IT DOESN'T MATTER **WHO** WRITES THEM--WHAT MATTERS IS THAT WE KEEP THEM COMING.
LOOK, I HOPE THIS... **GLARK** CHARACTER TURNS UP, BUT I'M A BUSY MAN. AND WE'RE ON DEADLINE. AS USUAL.
I APPRECIATE YOU MEETING ME.
I'M AFRAID YOU'VE WASTED YOUR TIME COMING DOWN HERE.
IT'S ALWAYS WORTH VISITING THE HABITAT OF A MISSING PERSON.
SPICE
HEY, WAIT UP!
YOU JUST NEVER KNOW WHAT YOU'LL SHAKE LOOSE.
YOU! SIT BACK DOWN! IF YOU LEAVE YOUR POST, DON'T BOTHER COMING BACK!
DON'T MIND HIM.
BUY ME A DRINK AND I'LL TELL YOU ABOUT ***TENTACLE TOWN.***

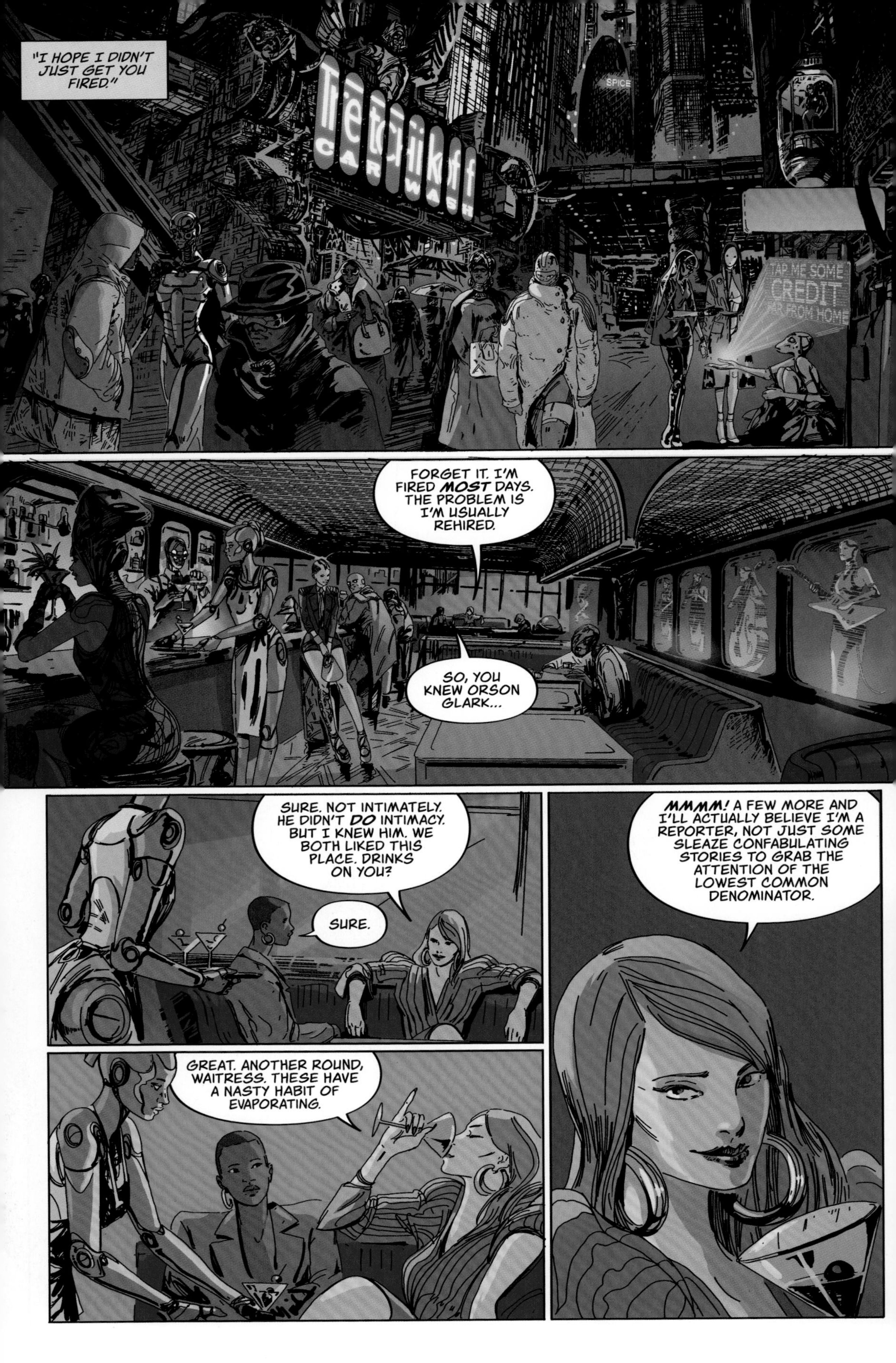
"I HOPE I DIDN'T JUST GET YOU FIRED."
CAR WASH
SPICE
TAP ME SOME CREDIT
FORGET IT. I'M FIRED MOST DAYS. THE PROBLEM IS I'M USUALLY REHIRED.
SO, YOU KNEW ORSON GLARK...
SURE. NOT INTIMATELY. HE DIDN'T DO INTIMACY. BUT I KNEW HIM. WE BOTH LIKED THIS PLACE. DRINKS ON YOU?
SURE.
GREAT. ANOTHER ROUND, WAITRESS. THESE HAVE A NASTY HABIT OF EVAPORATING.
MMMM! A FEW MORE AND I'LL ACTUALLY BELIEVE I'M A REPORTER, NOT JUST SOME SLEAZE CONFABULATING STORIES TO GRAB THE ATTENTION OF THE LOWEST COMMON DENOMINATOR.

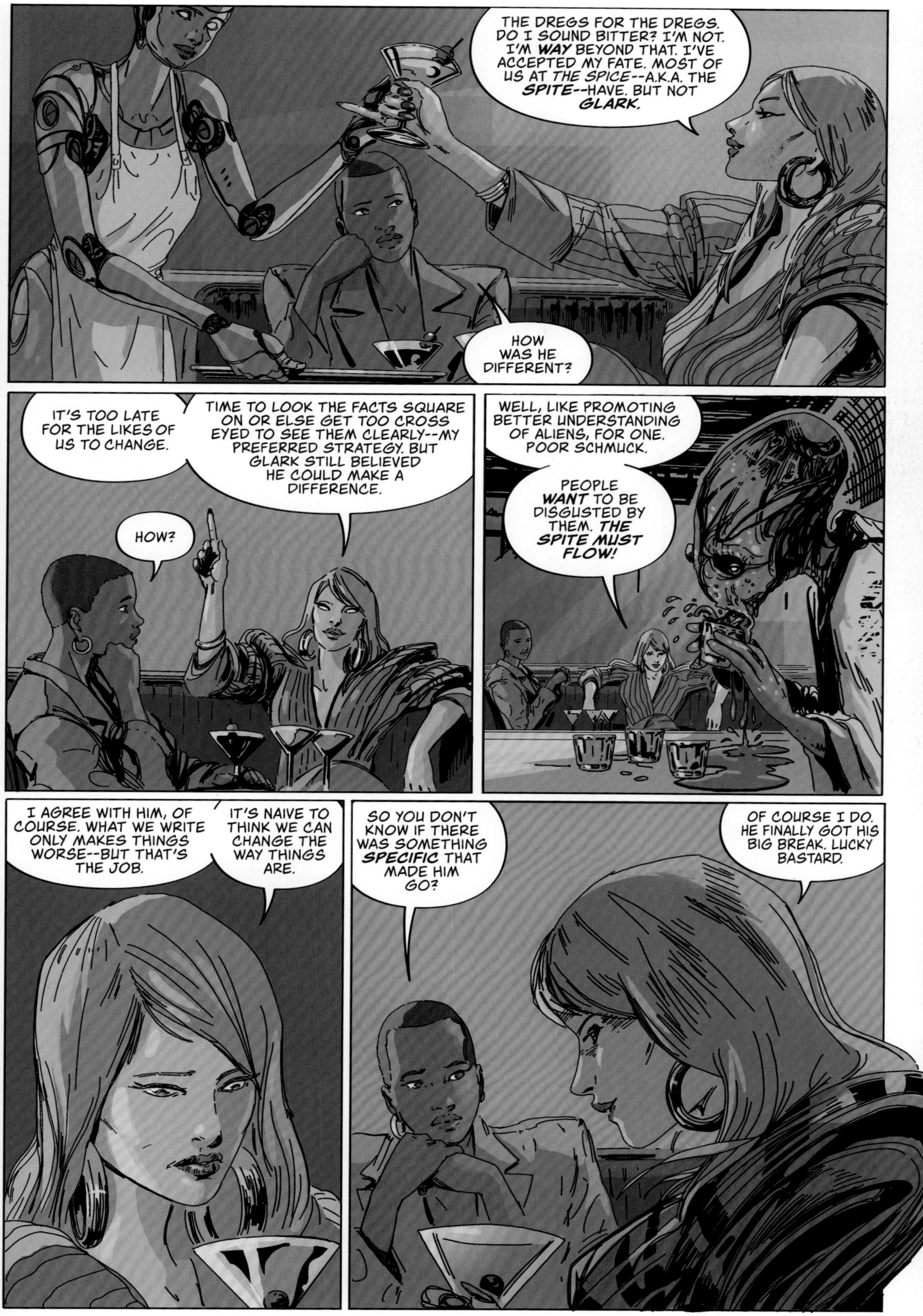
THE DREGS FOR THE DREGS. DO I SOUND BITTER? I'M NOT. I'M WAY BEYOND THAT. I'VE ACCEPTED MY FATE. MOST OF US AT THE SPICE--A.K.A. THE SPITE--HAVE. BUT NOT GLARK.
HOW WAS HE DIFFERENT?
IT'S TOO LATE FOR THE LIKES OF US TO CHANGE.
TIME TO LOOK THE FACTS SQUARE ON OR ELSE GET TOO CROSS EYED TO SEE THEM CLEARLY--MY PREFERRED STRATEGY. BUT GLARK STILL BELIEVED HE COULD MAKE A DIFFERENCE.
HOW?
WELL, LIKE PROMOTING BETTER UNDERSTANDING OF ALIENS, FOR ONE. POOR SCHMUCK.
PEOPLE WANT TO BE DISGUSTED BY THEM. THE SPITE MUST FLOW!
I AGREE WITH HIM, OF COURSE. WHAT WE WRITE ONLY MAKES THINGS WORSE--BUT THAT'S THE JOB.
IT'S NAIVE TO THINK WE CAN CHANGE THE WAY THINGS ARE.
SO YOU DON'T KNOW IF THERE WAS SOMETHING SPECIFIC THAT MADE HIM GO?
OF COURSE I DO. HE FINALLY GOT HIS BIG BREAK. LUCKY BASTARD.

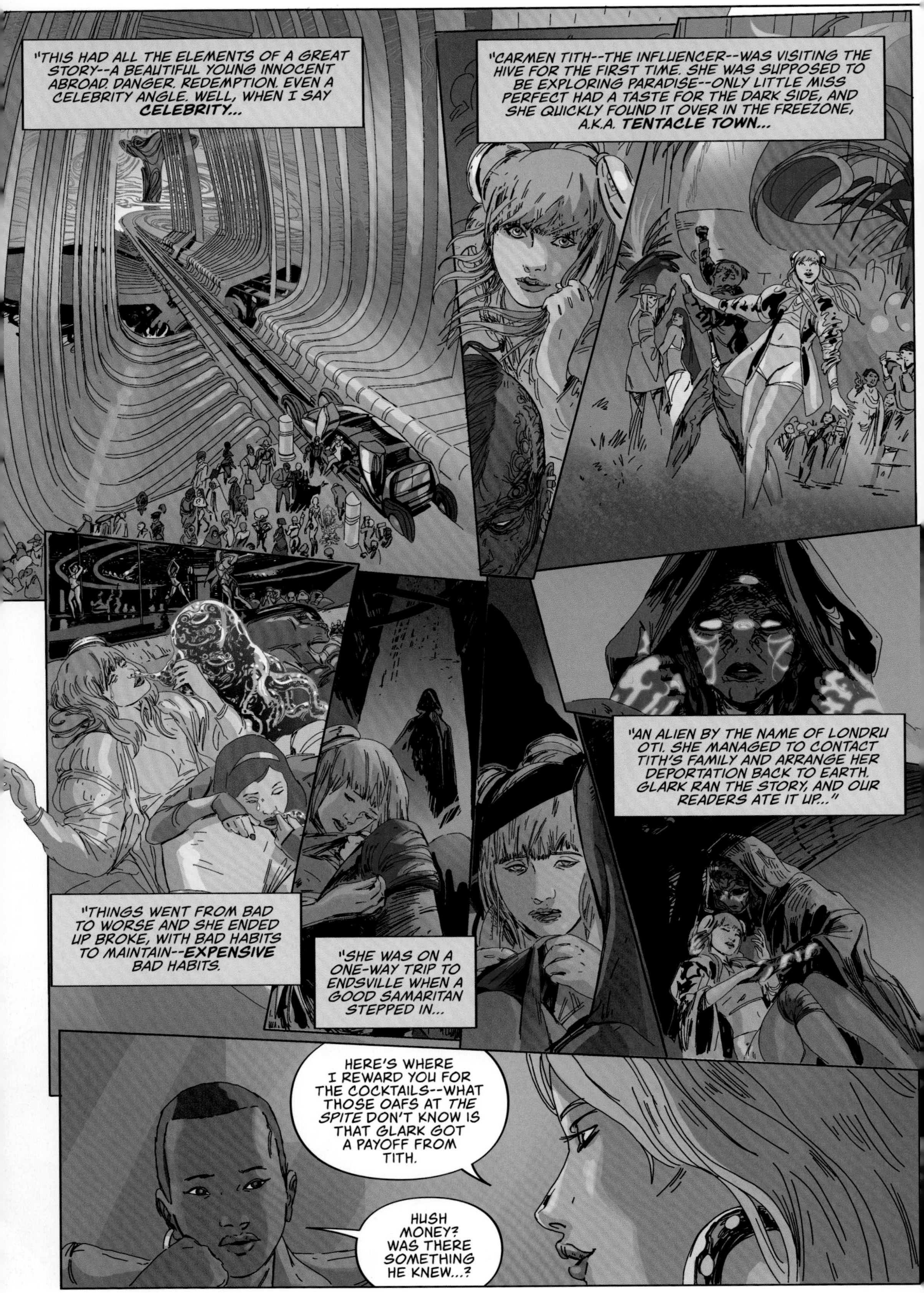
"THIS HAD ALL THE ELEMENTS OF A GREAT STORY--A BEAUTIFUL YOUNG INNOCENT ABROAD. DANGER. REDEMPTION. EVEN A CELEBRITY ANGLE. WELL, WHEN I SAY CELEBRITY...
"CARMEN TITH--THE INFLUENCER--WAS VISITING THE HIVE FOR THE FIRST TIME. SHE WAS SUPPOSED TO BE EXPLORING PARADISE--ONLY LITTLE MISS PERFECT HAD A TASTE FOR THE DARK SIDE, AND SHE QUICKLY FOUND IT OVER IN THE FREEZONE, A.K.A. TENTACLE TOWN...
"THINGS WENT FROM BAD TO WORSE AND SHE ENDED UP BROKE, WITH BAD HABITS TO MAINTAIN--EXPENSIVE BAD HABITS.
"SHE WAS ON A ONE-WAY TRIP TO ENDSVILLE WHEN A GOOD SAMARITAN STEPPED IN...
"AN ALIEN BY THE NAME OF LONDRU OTI. SHE MANAGED TO CONTACT TITH'S FAMILY AND ARRANGE HER DEPORTATION BACK TO EARTH. GLARK RAN THE STORY, AND OUR READERS ATE IT UP..."
HERE'S WHERE I REWARD YOU FOR THE COCKTAILS--WHAT THOSE OAFS AT THE SPITE DON'T KNOW IS THAT GLARK GOT A PAYOFF FROM TITH.
HUSH MONEY? WAS THERE SOMETHING HE KNEW...?

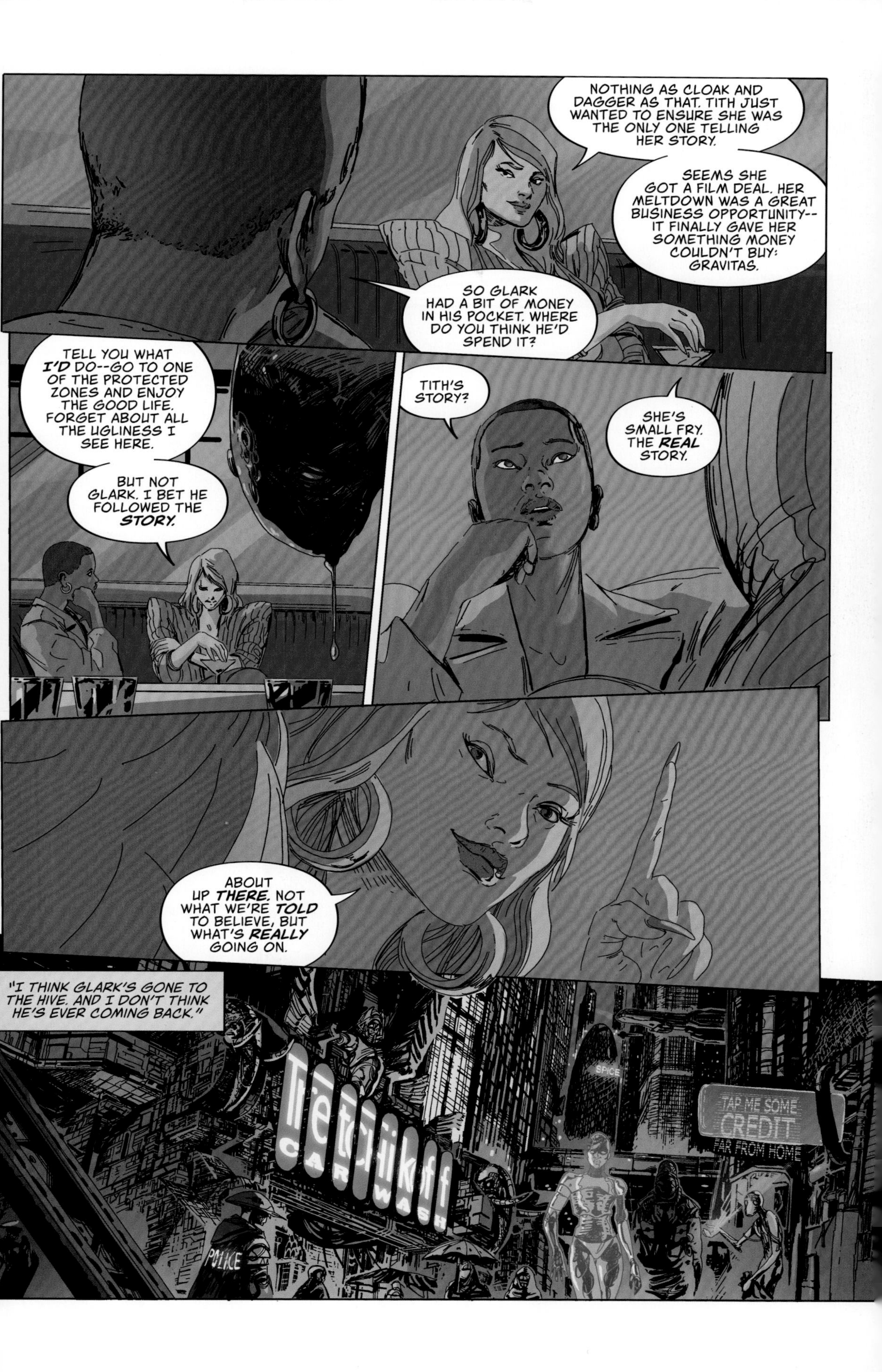
NOTHING AS CLOAK AND DAGGER AS THAT. TITH JUST WANTED TO ENSURE SHE WAS THE ONLY ONE TELLING HER STORY.
SEEMS SHE GOT A FILM DEAL. HER MELTDOWN WAS A GREAT BUSINESS OPPORTUNITY-- IT FINALLY GAVE HER SOMETHING MONEY COULDN'T BUY: GRAVITAS.
SO GLARK HAD A BIT OF MONEY IN HIS POCKET. WHERE DO YOU THINK HE'D SPEND IT?
TELL YOU WHAT I'D DO--GO TO ONE OF THE PROTECTED ZONES AND ENJOY THE GOOD LIFE. FORGET ABOUT ALL THE UGLINESS I SEE HERE.
BUT NOT GLARK. I BET HE FOLLOWED THE STORY.
TITH'S STORY?
SHE'S SMALL FRY. THE REAL STORY.
ABOUT UP THERE. NOT WHAT WE'RE TOLD TO BELIEVE, BUT WHAT'S REALLY GOING ON.
"I THINK GLARK'S GONE TO THE HIVE. AND I DON'T THINK HE'S EVER COMING BACK."
CAR WASH
SPICE
TAP ME SOME CREDIT
FAR FROM HOME
POLICE

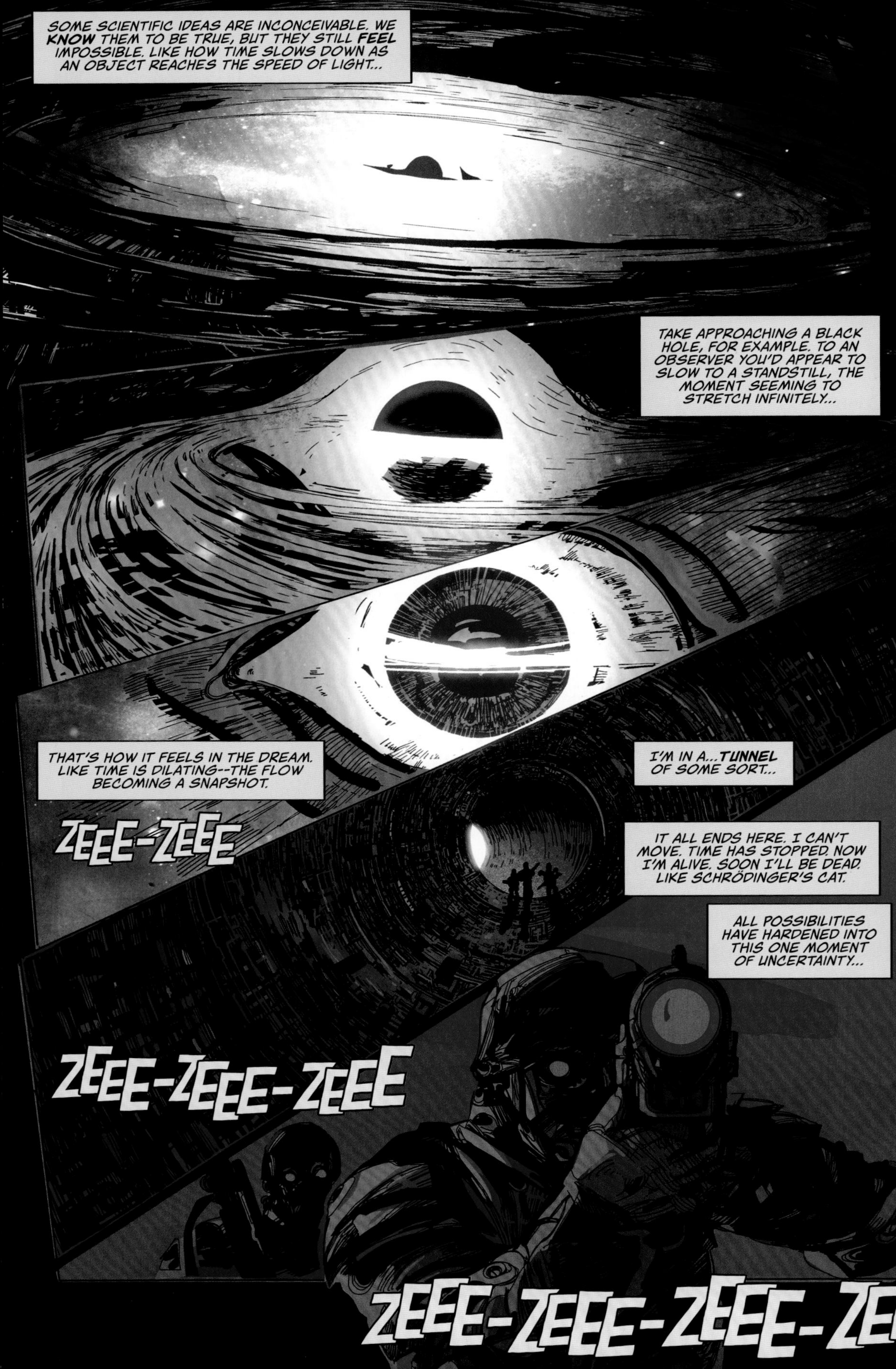
SOME SCIENTIFIC IDEAS ARE INCONCEIVABLE. WE **KNOW** THEM TO BE TRUE, BUT THEY STILL **FEEL** IMPOSSIBLE. LIKE HOW TIME SLOWS DOWN AS AN OBJECT REACHES THE SPEED OF LIGHT...
TAKE APPROACHING A BLACK HOLE, FOR EXAMPLE. TO AN OBSERVER YOU'D APPEAR TO SLOW TO A STANDSTILL, THE MOMENT SEEMING TO STRETCH INFINITELY...
THAT'S HOW IT FEELS IN THE DREAM. LIKE TIME IS DILATING--THE FLOW BECOMING A SNAPSHOT.
I'M IN A... **TUNNEL** OF SOME SORT...
ZEEE-ZEEE
IT ALL ENDS HERE. I CAN'T MOVE. TIME HAS STOPPED. NOW I'M ALIVE. SOON I'LL BE DEAD. LIKE SCHRÖDINGER'S CAT.
ALL POSSIBILITIES HAVE HARDENED INTO THIS ONE MOMENT OF UNCERTAINTY...
ZEEE-ZEEE-ZEEE
ZEEE-ZEEE-ZEEE-ZE

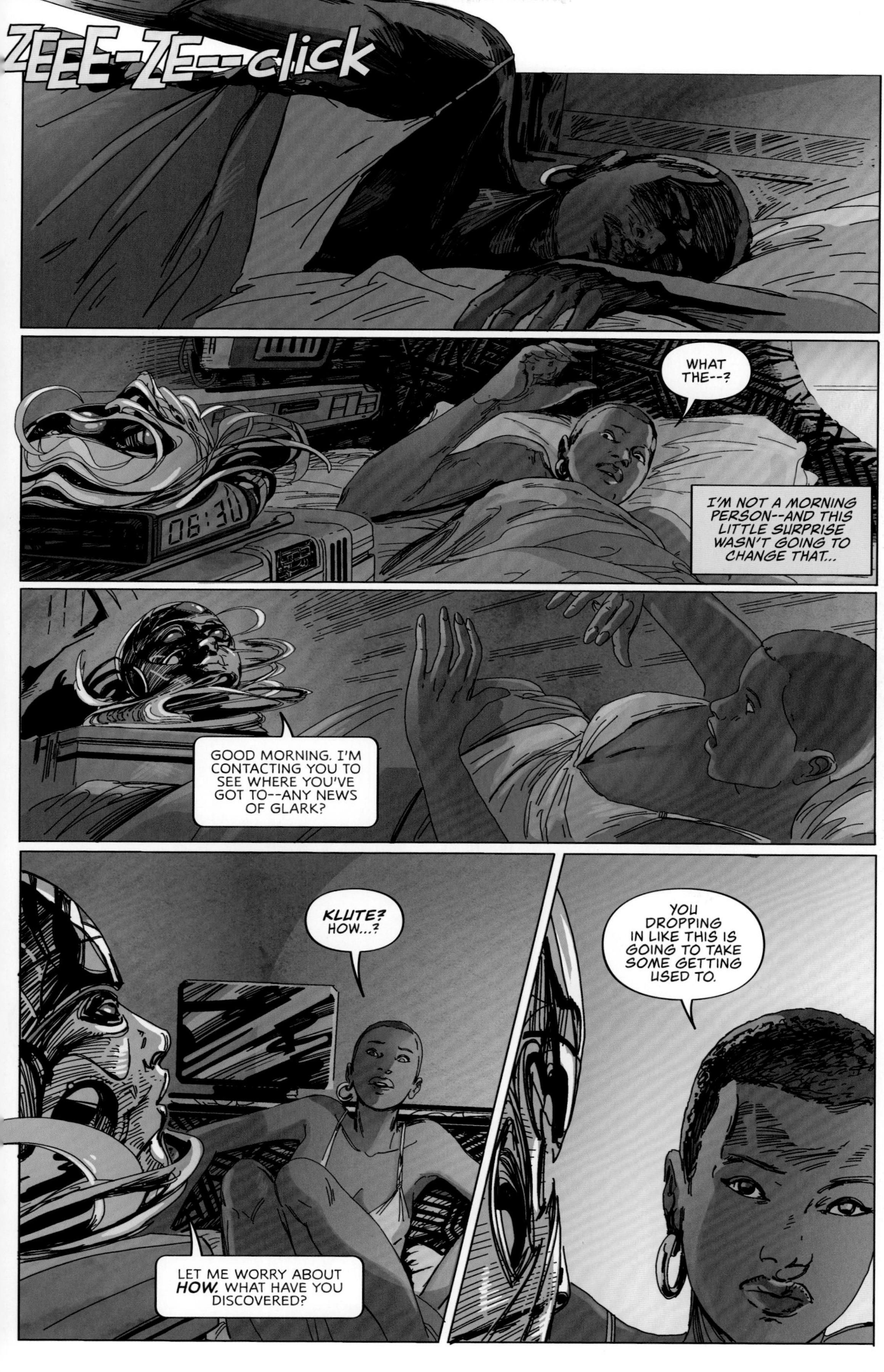
ZEEE-ZE--click
WHAT THE--?
I'M NOT A MORNING PERSON--AND THIS LITTLE SURPRISE WASN'T GOING TO CHANGE THAT...
06:30
GOOD MORNING. I'M CONTACTING YOU TO SEE WHERE YOU'VE GOT TO--ANY NEWS OF GLARK?
KLUTE? HOW...?
LET ME WORRY ABOUT HOW. WHAT HAVE YOU DISCOVERED?
YOU DROPPING IN LIKE THIS IS GOING TO TAKE SOME GETTING USED TO.

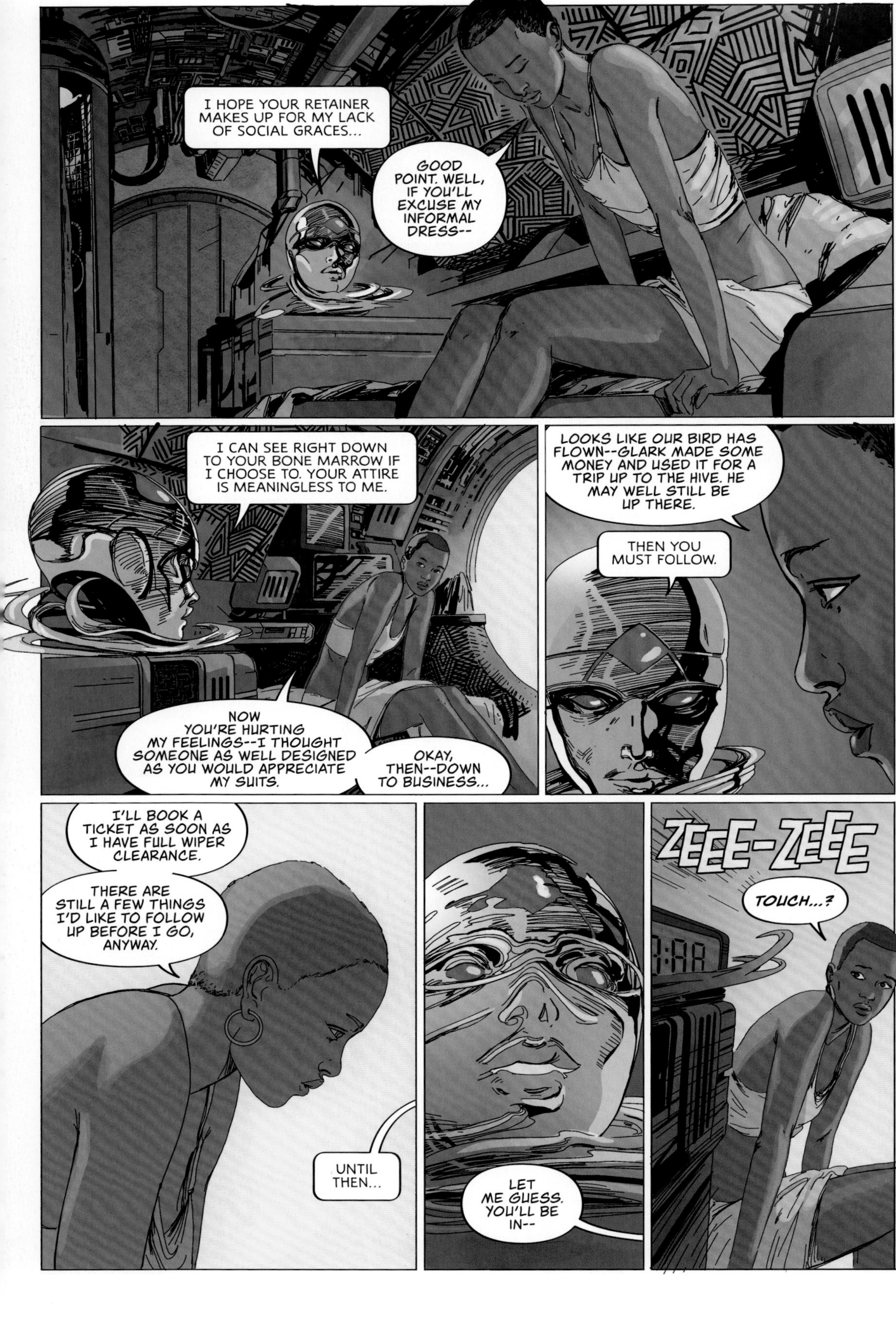
I HOPE YOUR RETAINER MAKES UP FOR MY LACK OF SOCIAL GRACES...
GOOD POINT. WELL, IF YOU'LL EXCUSE MY INFORMAL DRESS--
I CAN SEE RIGHT DOWN TO YOUR BONE MARROW IF I CHOOSE TO. YOUR ATTIRE IS MEANINGLESS TO ME.
NOW YOU'RE HURTING MY FEELINGS--I THOUGHT SOMEONE AS WELL DESIGNED AS YOU WOULD APPRECIATE MY SUITS.
OKAY, THEN--DOWN TO BUSINESS...
LOOKS LIKE OUR BIRD HAS FLOWN--GLARK MADE SOME MONEY AND USED IT FOR A TRIP UP TO THE HIVE. HE MAY WELL STILL BE UP THERE.
THEN YOU MUST FOLLOW.
I'LL BOOK A TICKET AS SOON AS I HAVE FULL WIPER CLEARANCE.
THERE ARE STILL A FEW THINGS I'D LIKE TO FOLLOW UP BEFORE I GO, ANYWAY.
UNTIL THEN...
LET ME GUESS. YOU'LL BE IN--
ZEEE-ZEEE
TOUCH...?

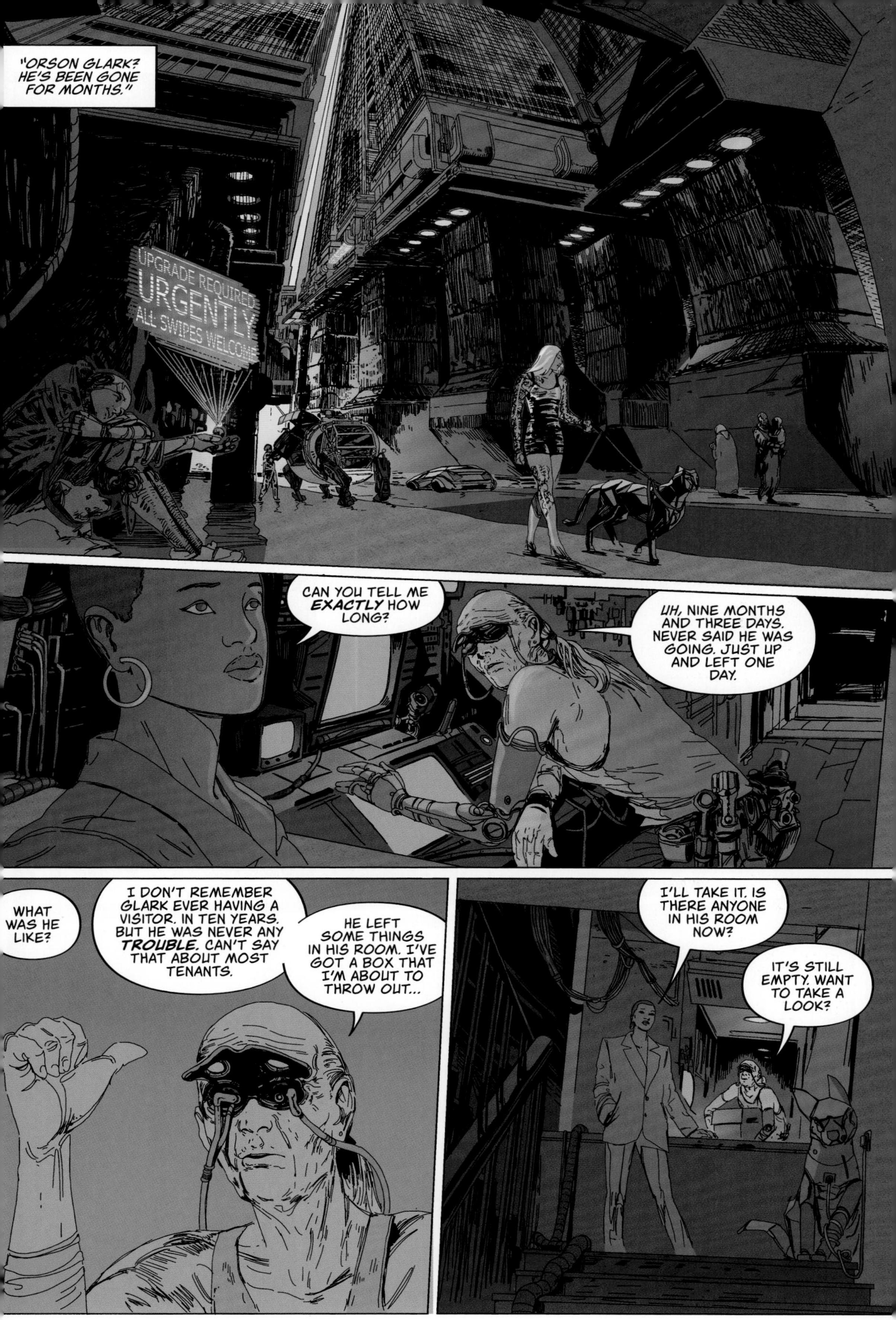
"ORSON GLARK? HE'S BEEN GONE FOR MONTHS."
UPGRADE REQUIRED
URGENTLY
ALL SWIPES WELCOME
CAN YOU TELL ME *EXACTLY* HOW LONG?
UH, NINE MONTHS AND THREE DAYS. NEVER SAID HE WAS GOING. JUST UP AND LEFT ONE DAY.
WHAT WAS HE LIKE?
I DON'T REMEMBER GLARK EVER HAVING A VISITOR. IN TEN YEARS. BUT HE WAS NEVER ANY *TROUBLE*. CAN'T SAY THAT ABOUT MOST TENANTS.
HE LEFT SOME THINGS IN HIS ROOM. I'VE GOT A BOX THAT I'M ABOUT TO THROW OUT...
I'LL TAKE IT. IS THERE ANYONE IN HIS ROOM NOW?
IT'S STILL EMPTY. WANT TO TAKE A LOOK?

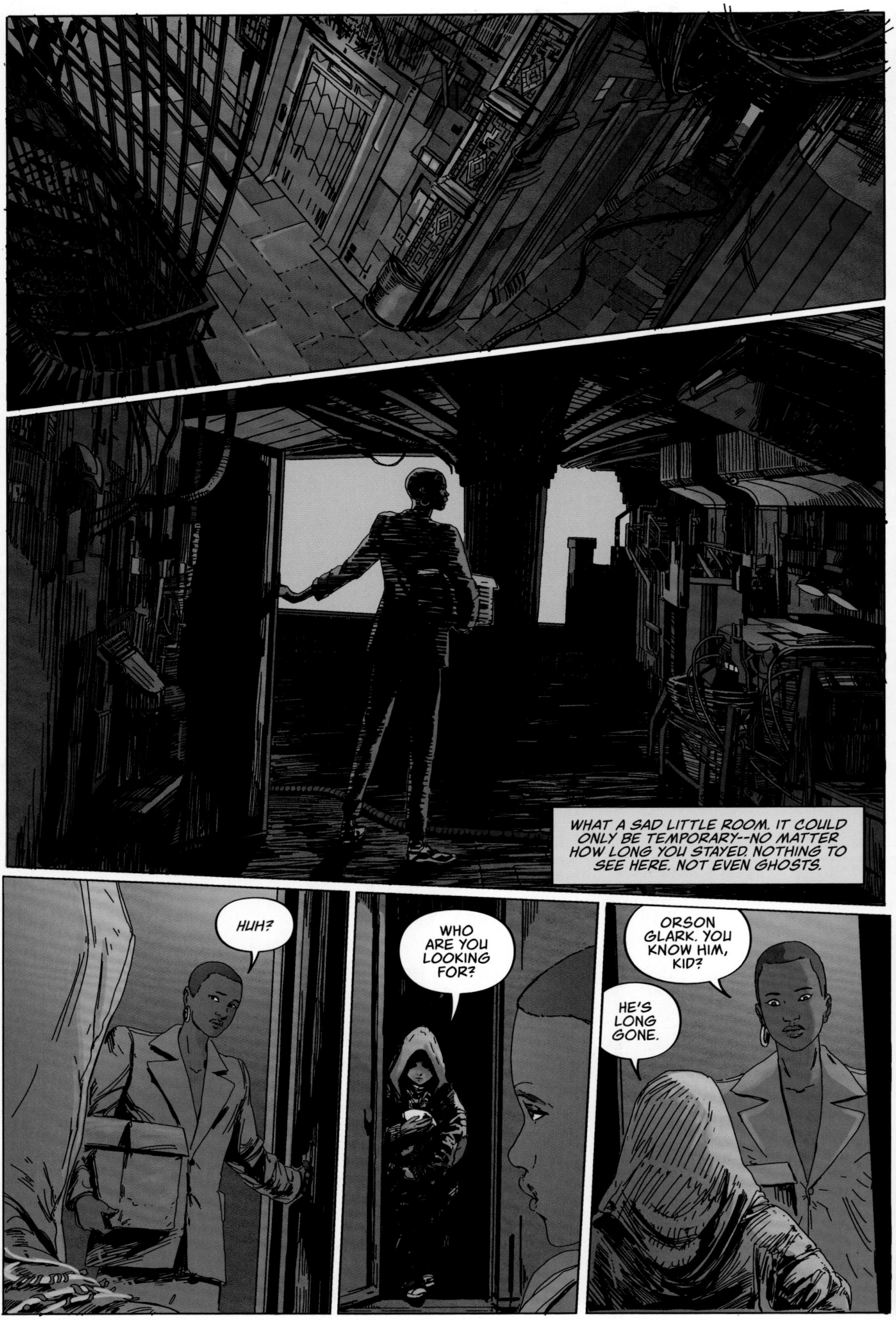
WHAT A SAD LITTLE ROOM. IT COULD ONLY BE TEMPORARY--NO MATTER HOW LONG YOU STAYED. NOTHING TO SEE HERE. NOT EVEN GHOSTS.
HUH?
WHO ARE YOU LOOKING FOR?
ORSON GLARK. YOU KNOW HIM, KID?
HE'S LONG GONE.

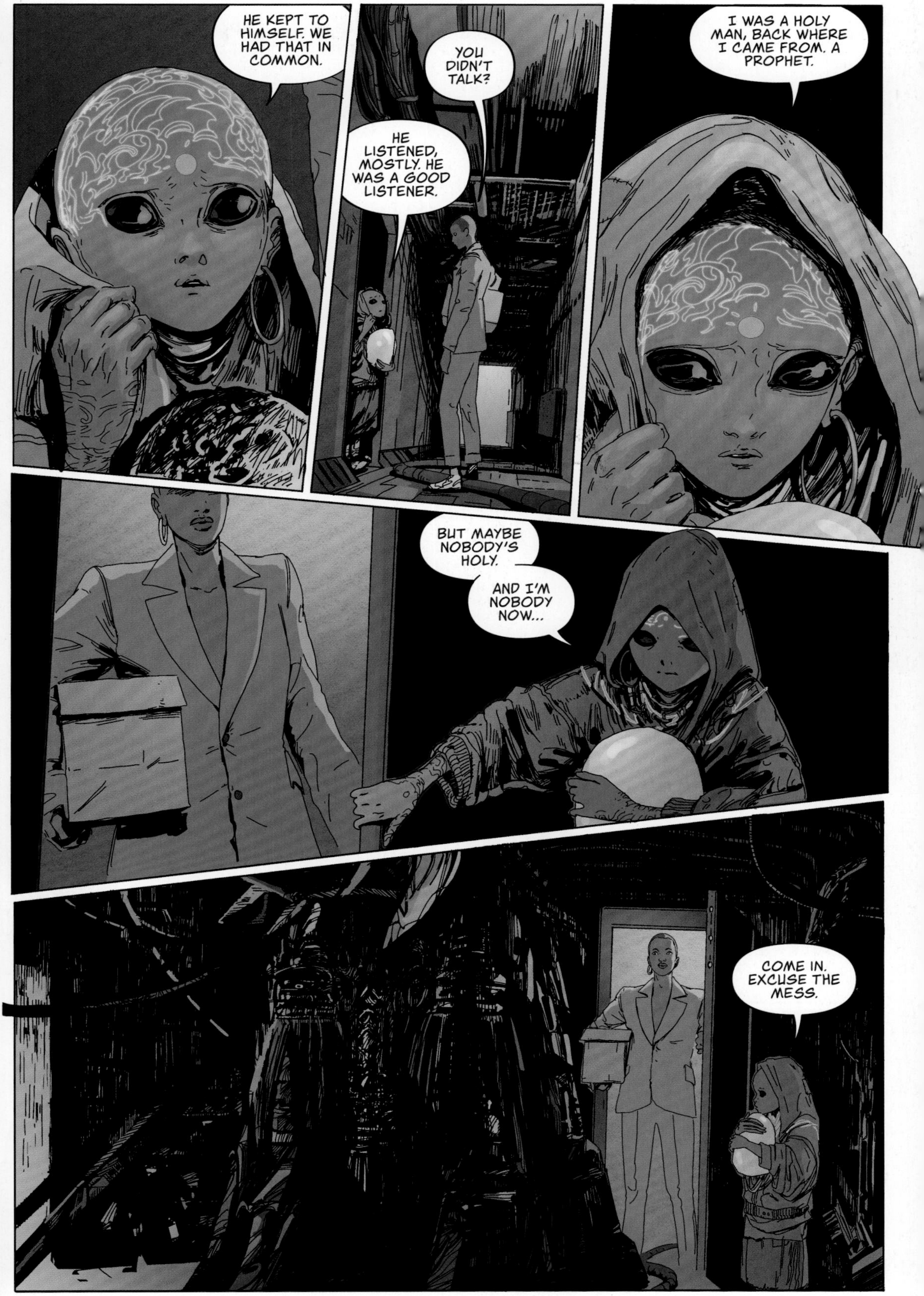
HE KEPT TO HIMSELF. WE HAD THAT IN COMMON.
YOU DIDN'T TALK?
HE LISTENED, MOSTLY. HE WAS A GOOD LISTENER.
I WAS A HOLY MAN, BACK WHERE I CAME FROM. A PROPHET.
BUT MAYBE NOBODY'S HOLY.
AND I'M NOBODY NOW...
COME IN. EXCUSE THE MESS.

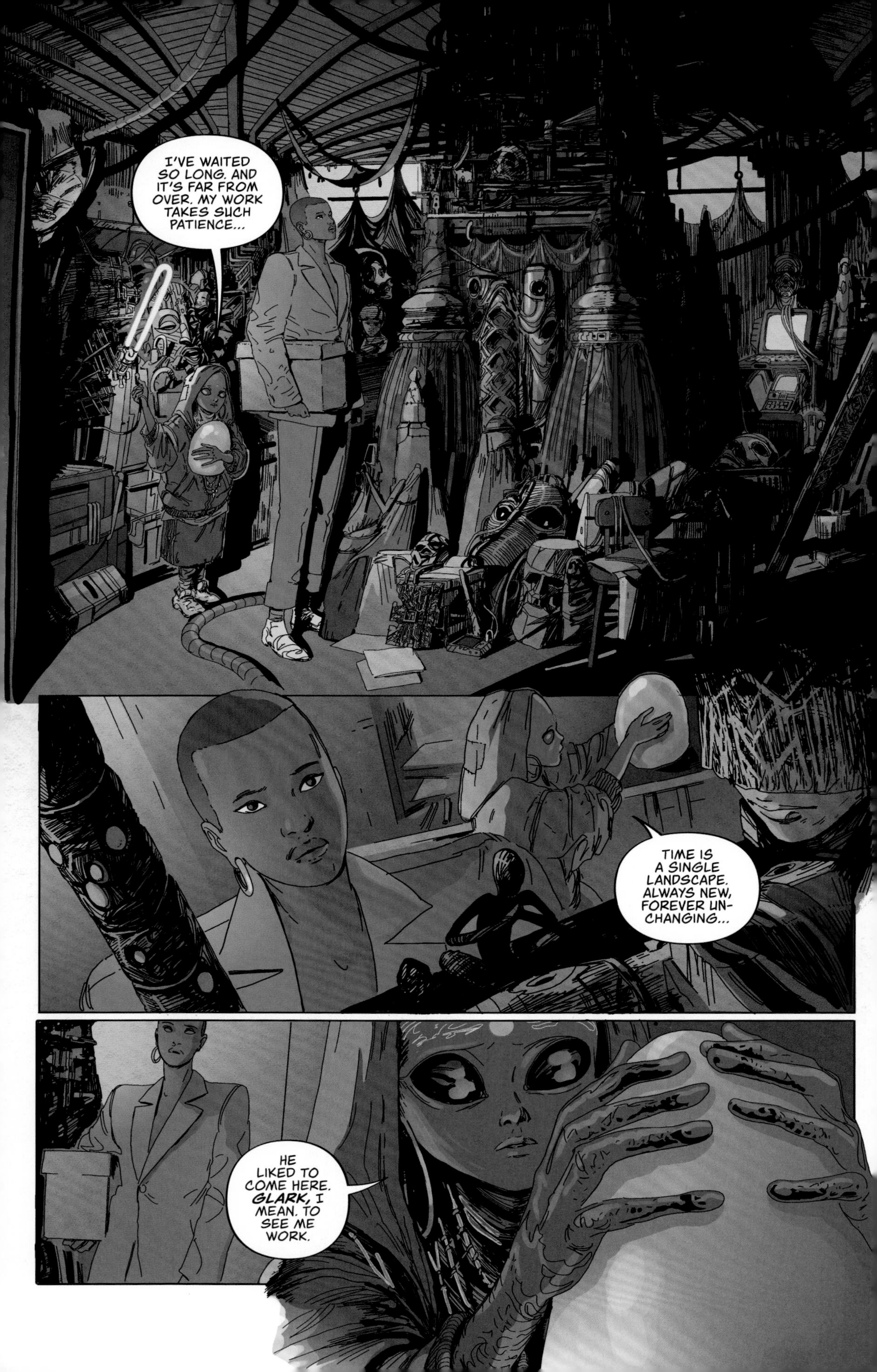
I'VE WAITED SO LONG. AND IT'S FAR FROM OVER. MY WORK TAKES SUCH PATIENCE...
TIME IS A SINGLE LANDSCAPE. ALWAYS NEW, FOREVER UN-CHANGING...
HE LIKED TO COME HERE. GLARK, I MEAN. TO SEE ME WORK.

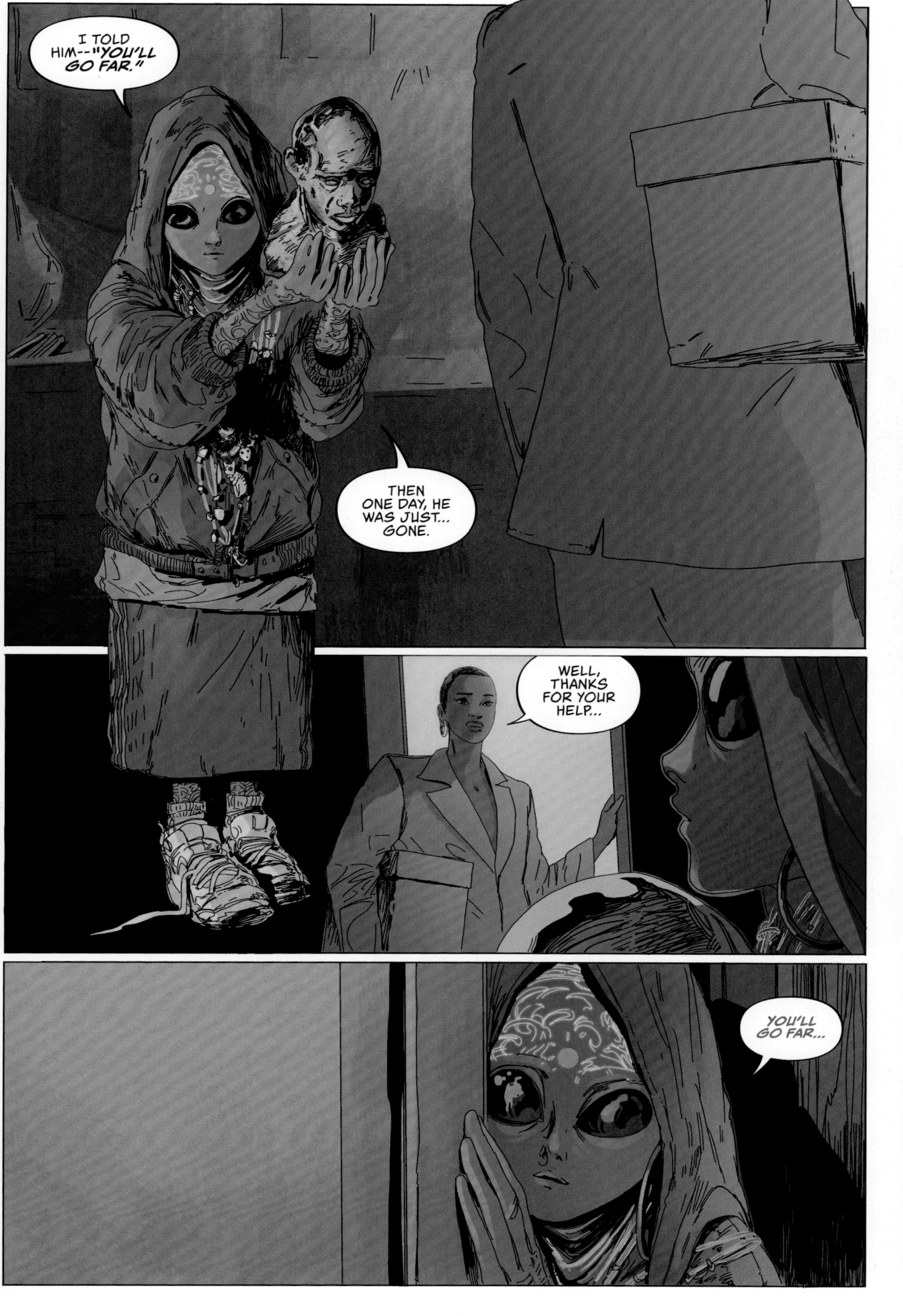
I TOLD HIM--"YOU'LL GO FAR."
THEN ONE DAY, HE WAS JUST... GONE.
WELL, THANKS FOR YOUR HELP...
YOU'LL GO FAR...

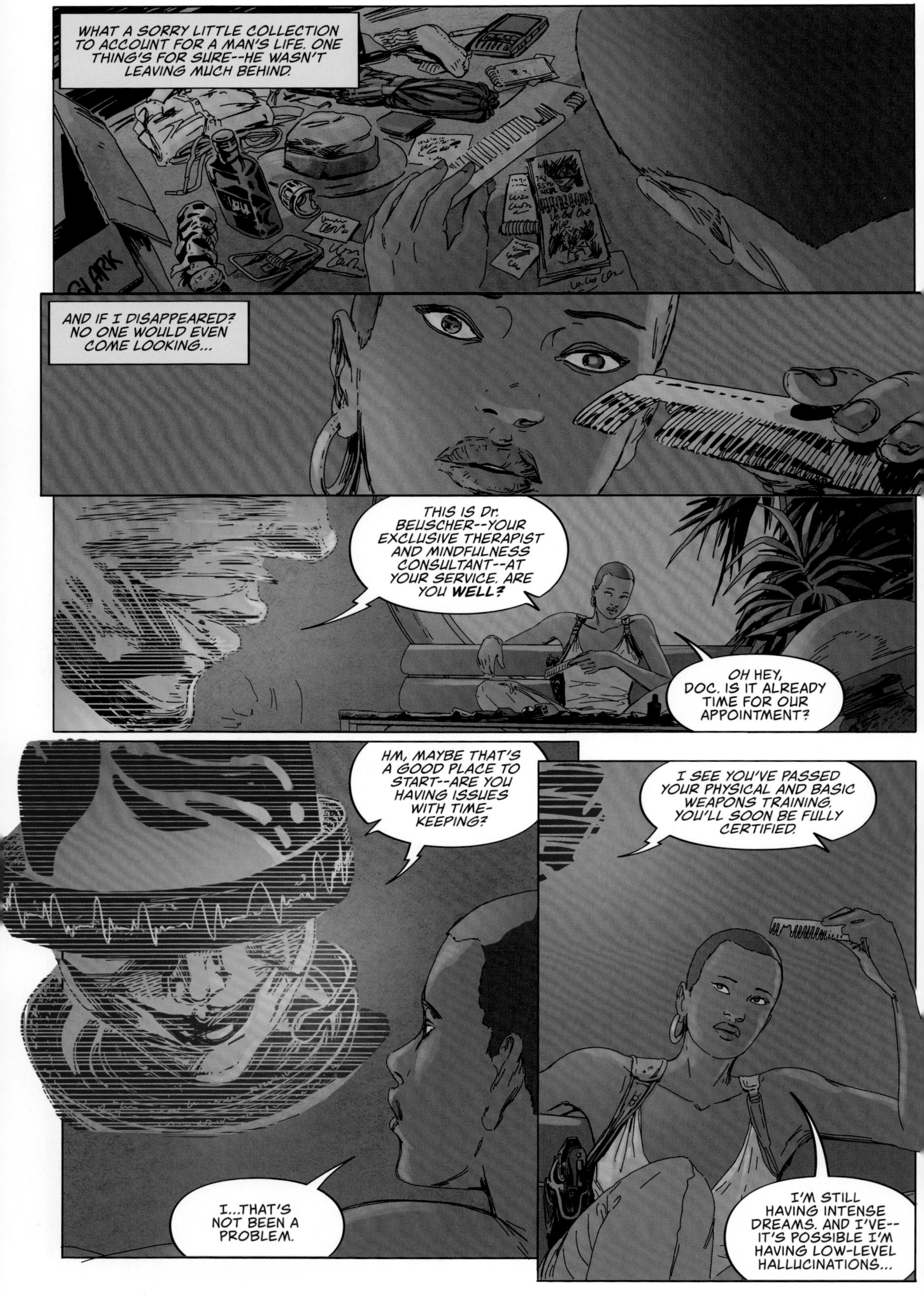
WHAT A SORRY LITTLE COLLECTION TO ACCOUNT FOR A MAN'S LIFE. ONE THING'S FOR SURE--HE WASN'T LEAVING MUCH BEHIND.
AND IF I DISAPPEARED? NO ONE WOULD EVEN COME LOOKING...
THIS IS Dr. BEUSCHER--YOUR EXCLUSIVE THERAPIST AND MINDFULNESS CONSULTANT--AT YOUR SERVICE. ARE YOU WELL?
OH HEY, DOC. IS IT ALREADY TIME FOR OUR APPOINTMENT?
HM, MAYBE THAT'S A GOOD PLACE TO START--ARE YOU HAVING ISSUES WITH TIME-KEEPING?
I...THAT'S NOT BEEN A PROBLEM.
I SEE YOU'VE PASSED YOUR PHYSICAL AND BASIC WEAPONS TRAINING. YOU'LL SOON BE FULLY CERTIFIED.
I'M STILL HAVING INTENSE DREAMS. AND I'VE-- IT'S POSSIBLE I'M HAVING LOW-LEVEL HALLUCINATIONS...

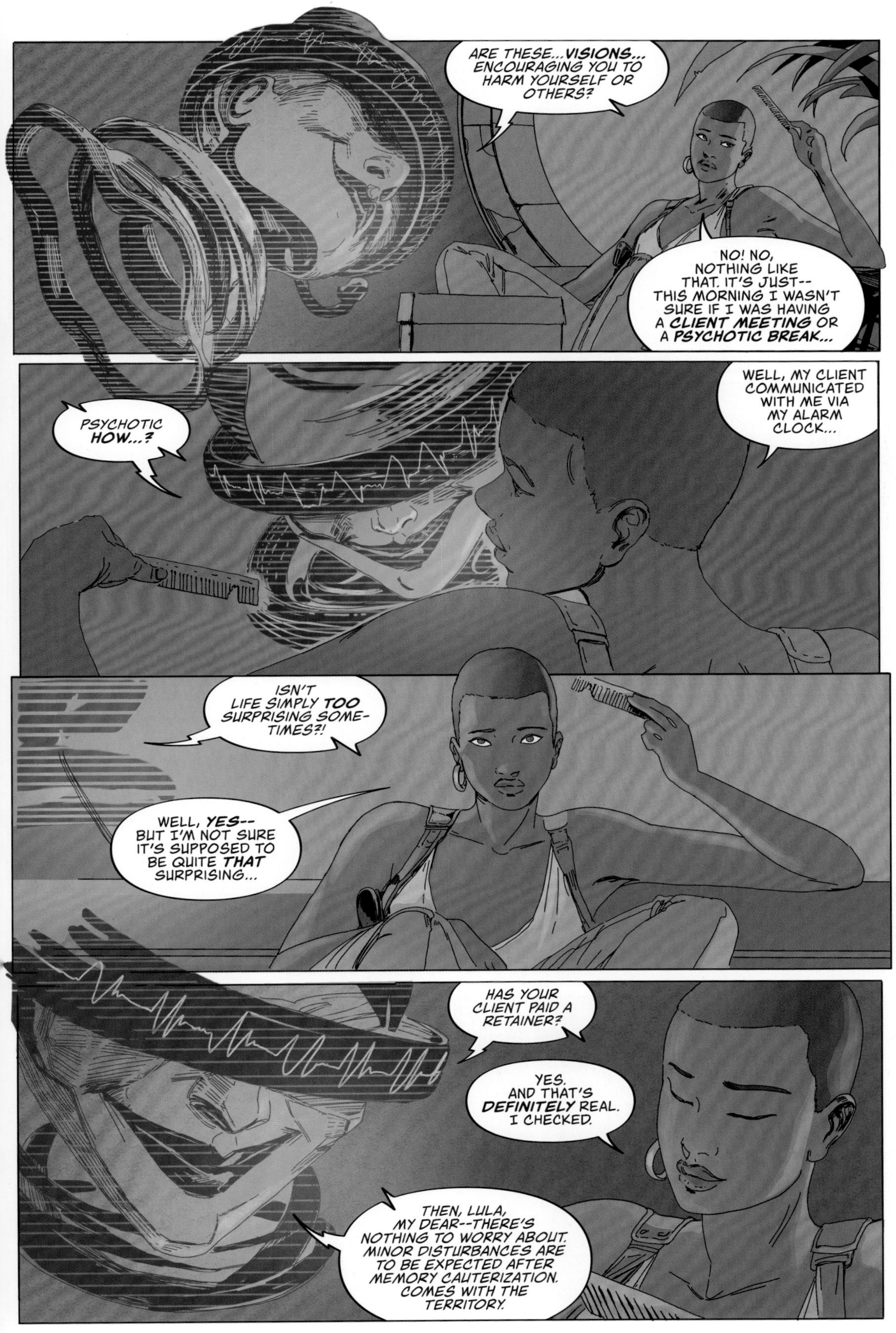
ARE THESE...VISIONS... ENCOURAGING YOU TO HARM YOURSELF OR OTHERS?
NO! NO, NOTHING LIKE THAT. IT'S JUST-- THIS MORNING I WASN'T SURE IF I WAS HAVING A CLIENT MEETING OR A PSYCHOTIC BREAK...
PSYCHOTIC HOW...?
WELL, MY CLIENT COMMUNICATED WITH ME VIA MY ALARM CLOCK...
ISN'T LIFE SIMPLY TOO SURPRISING SOMETIMES?!
WELL, YES-- BUT I'M NOT SURE IT'S SUPPOSED TO BE QUITE THAT SURPRISING...
HAS YOUR CLIENT PAID A RETAINER?
YES. AND THAT'S DEFINITELY REAL. I CHECKED.
THEN, LULA, MY DEAR--THERE'S NOTHING TO WORRY ABOUT. MINOR DISTURBANCES ARE TO BE EXPECTED AFTER MEMORY CAUTERIZATION. COMES WITH THE TERRITORY.

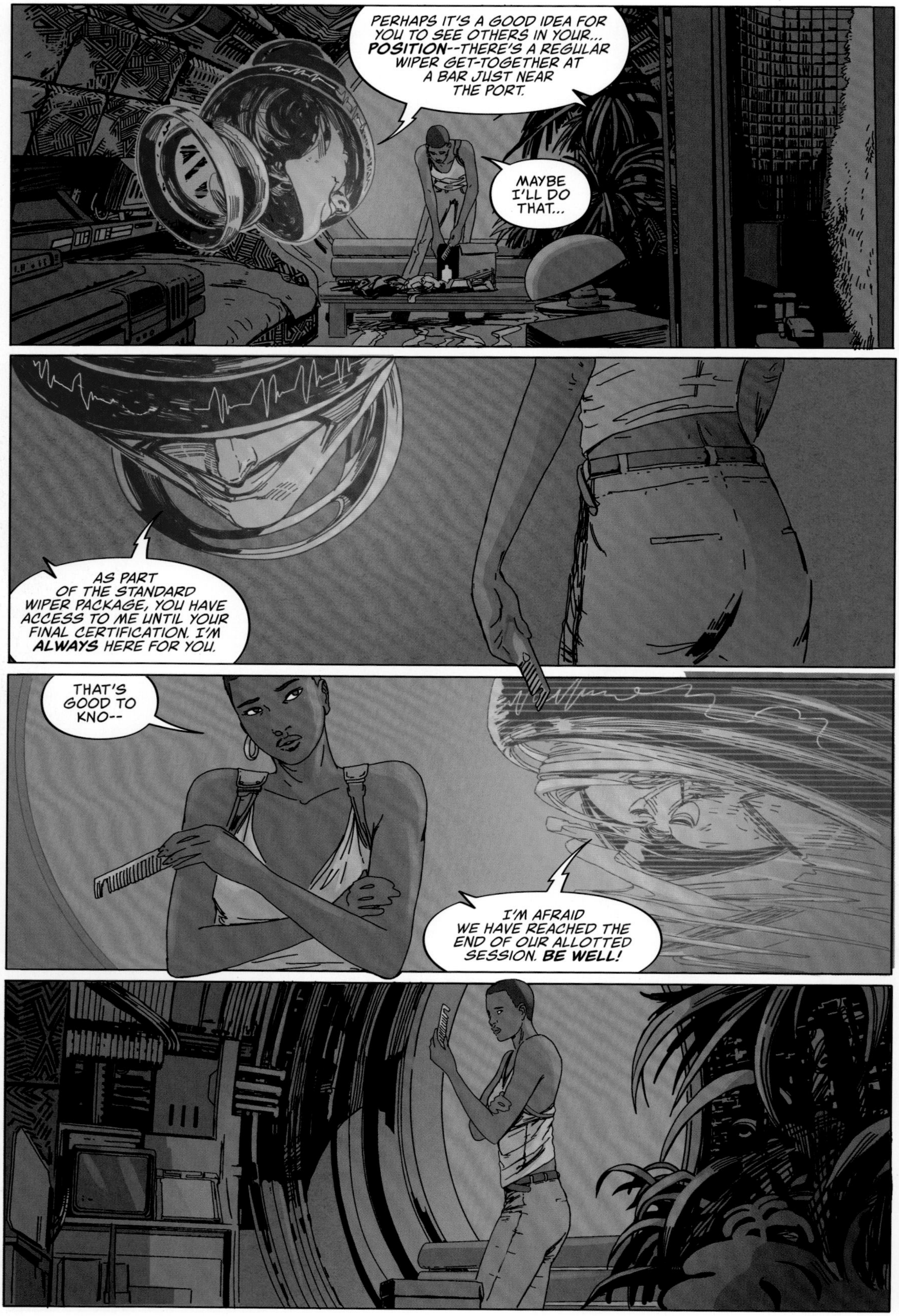
PERHAPS IT'S A GOOD IDEA FOR YOU TO SEE OTHERS IN YOUR... **POSITION**--THERE'S A REGULAR WIPER GET-TOGETHER AT A BAR JUST NEAR THE PORT.
MAYBE I'LL DO THAT...
AS PART OF THE STANDARD WIPER PACKAGE, YOU HAVE ACCESS TO ME UNTIL YOUR FINAL CERTIFICATION. I'M **ALWAYS** HERE FOR YOU.
THAT'S GOOD TO KNO--
I'M AFRAID WE HAVE REACHED THE END OF OUR ALLOTTED SESSION. **BE WELL!**

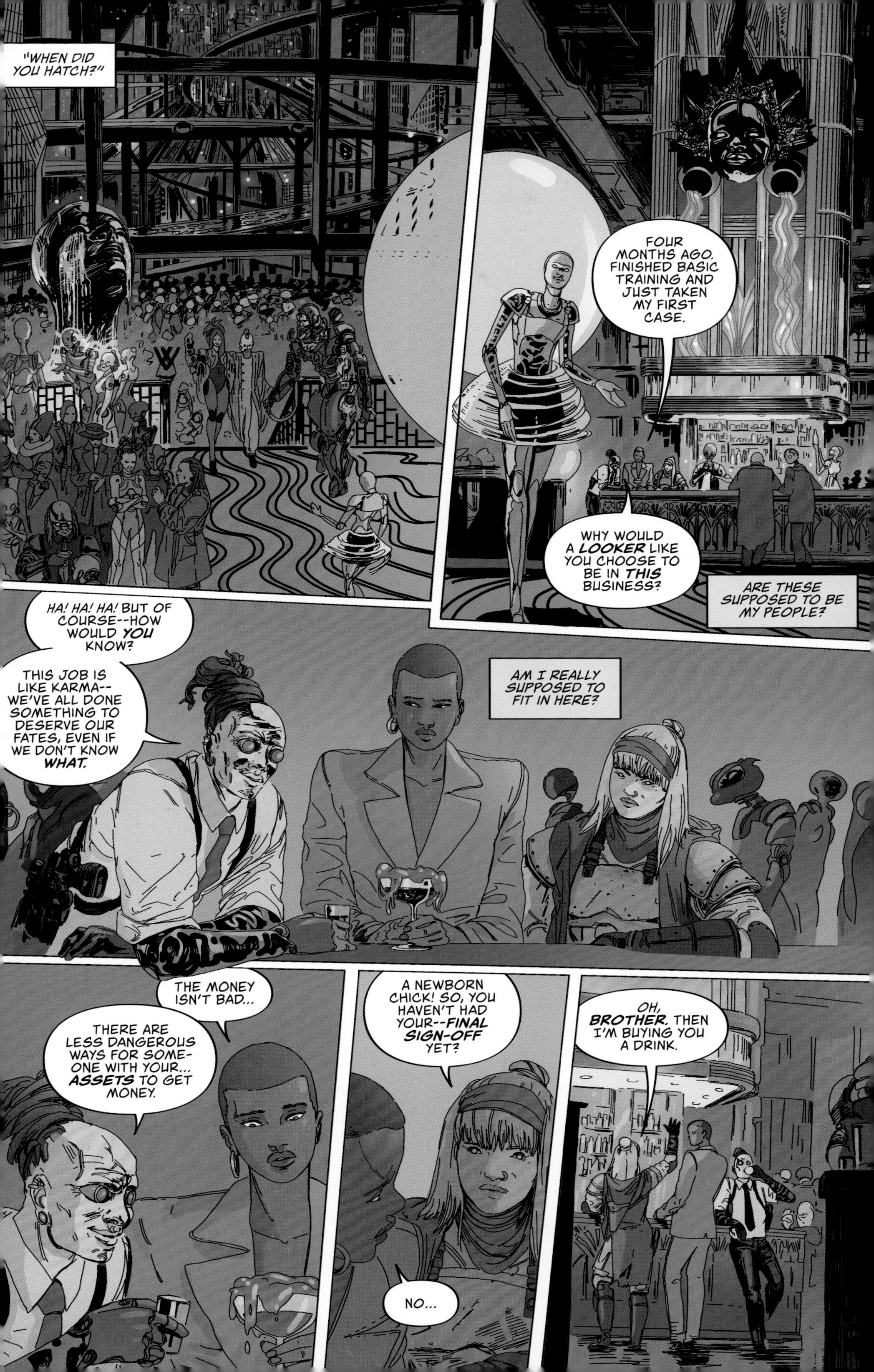
"WHEN DID YOU HATCH?"
FOUR MONTHS AGO. FINISHED BASIC TRAINING AND JUST TAKEN MY FIRST CASE.
WHY WOULD A LOOKER LIKE YOU CHOOSE TO BE IN THIS BUSINESS?
ARE THESE SUPPOSED TO BE MY PEOPLE?
HA! HA! HA! BUT OF COURSE--HOW WOULD YOU KNOW?
THIS JOB IS LIKE KARMA--WE'VE ALL DONE SOMETHING TO DESERVE OUR FATES, EVEN IF WE DON'T KNOW WHAT.
AM I REALLY SUPPOSED TO FIT IN HERE?
THE MONEY ISN'T BAD...
THERE ARE LESS DANGEROUS WAYS FOR SOME-ONE WITH YOUR... ASSETS TO GET MONEY.
A NEWBORN CHICK! SO, YOU HAVEN'T HAD YOUR--FINAL SIGN-OFF YET?
NO...
OH, BROTHER. THEN I'M BUYING YOU A DRINK.

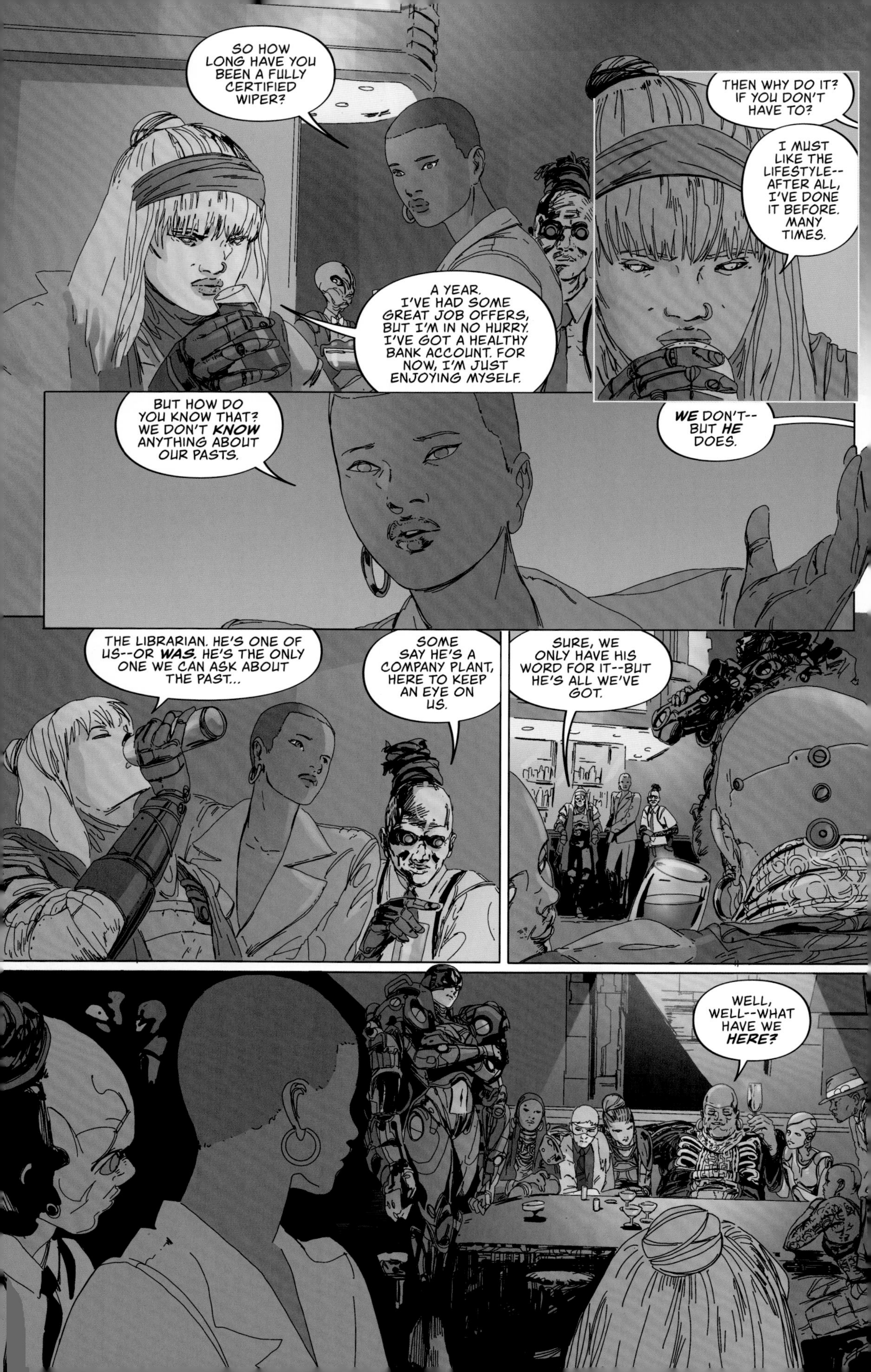
SO HOW LONG HAVE YOU BEEN A FULLY CERTIFIED WIPER?
A YEAR. I'VE HAD SOME GREAT JOB OFFERS, BUT I'M IN NO HURRY. I'VE GOT A HEALTHY BANK ACCOUNT. FOR NOW, I'M JUST ENJOYING MYSELF.
THEN WHY DO IT? IF YOU DON'T HAVE TO?
I MUST LIKE THE LIFESTYLE-- AFTER ALL, I'VE DONE IT BEFORE. MANY TIMES.
BUT HOW DO YOU KNOW THAT? WE DON'T KNOW ANYTHING ABOUT OUR PASTS.
WE DON'T-- BUT HE DOES.
THE LIBRARIAN. HE'S ONE OF US--OR WAS. HE'S THE ONLY ONE WE CAN ASK ABOUT THE PAST...
SOME SAY HE'S A COMPANY PLANT, HERE TO KEEP AN EYE ON US.
SURE, WE ONLY HAVE HIS WORD FOR IT--BUT HE'S ALL WE'VE GOT.
WELL, WELL--WHAT HAVE WE HERE?

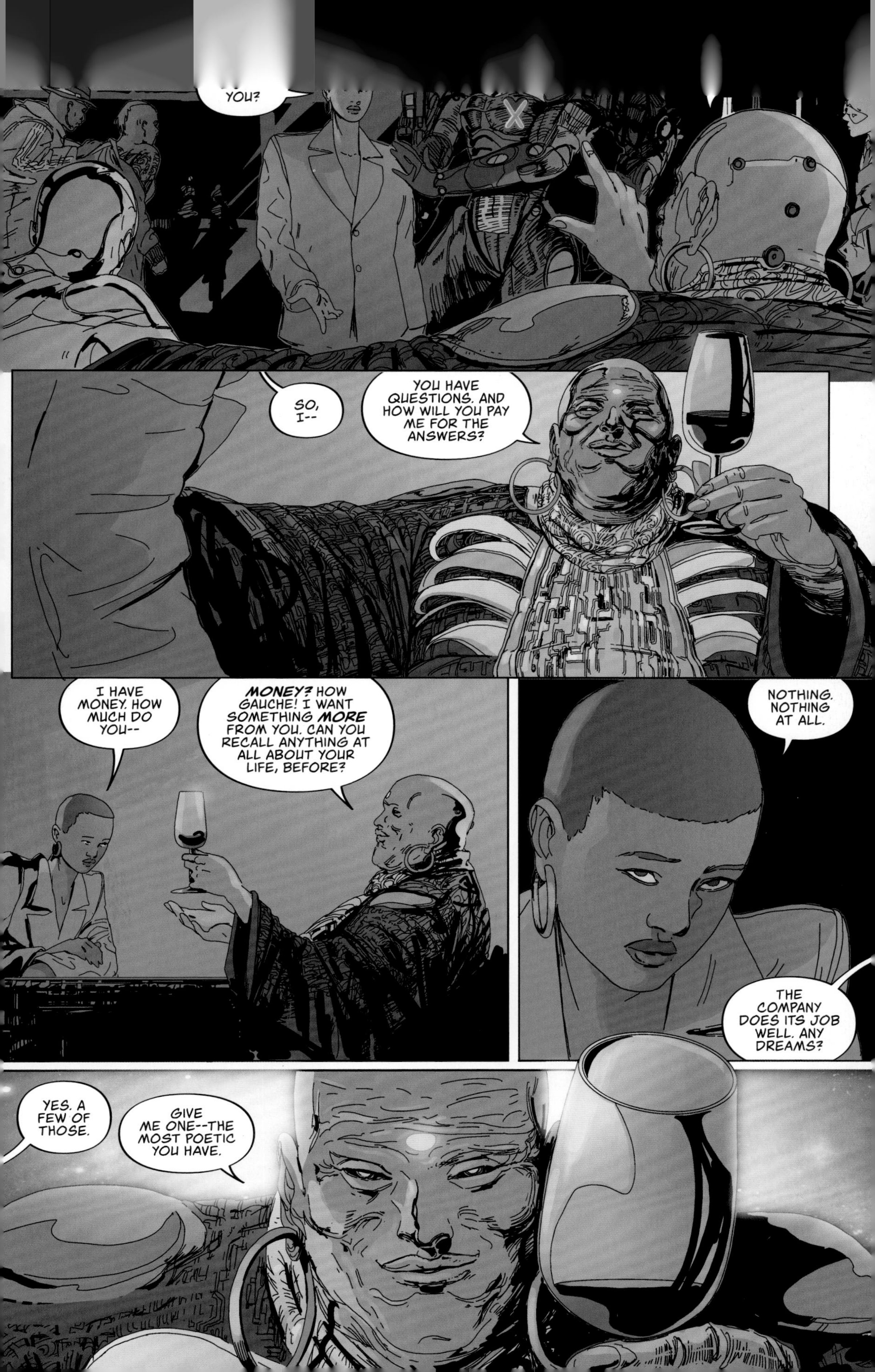
YOU?
SO, I--
YOU HAVE QUESTIONS. AND HOW WILL YOU PAY ME FOR THE ANSWERS?
I HAVE MONEY. HOW MUCH DO YOU--
MONEY? HOW GAUCHE! I WANT SOMETHING MORE FROM YOU. CAN YOU RECALL ANYTHING AT ALL ABOUT YOUR LIFE, BEFORE?
NOTHING. NOTHING AT ALL.
THE COMPANY DOES ITS JOB WELL. ANY DREAMS?
YES. A FEW OF THOSE.
GIVE ME ONE--THE MOST POETIC YOU HAVE.

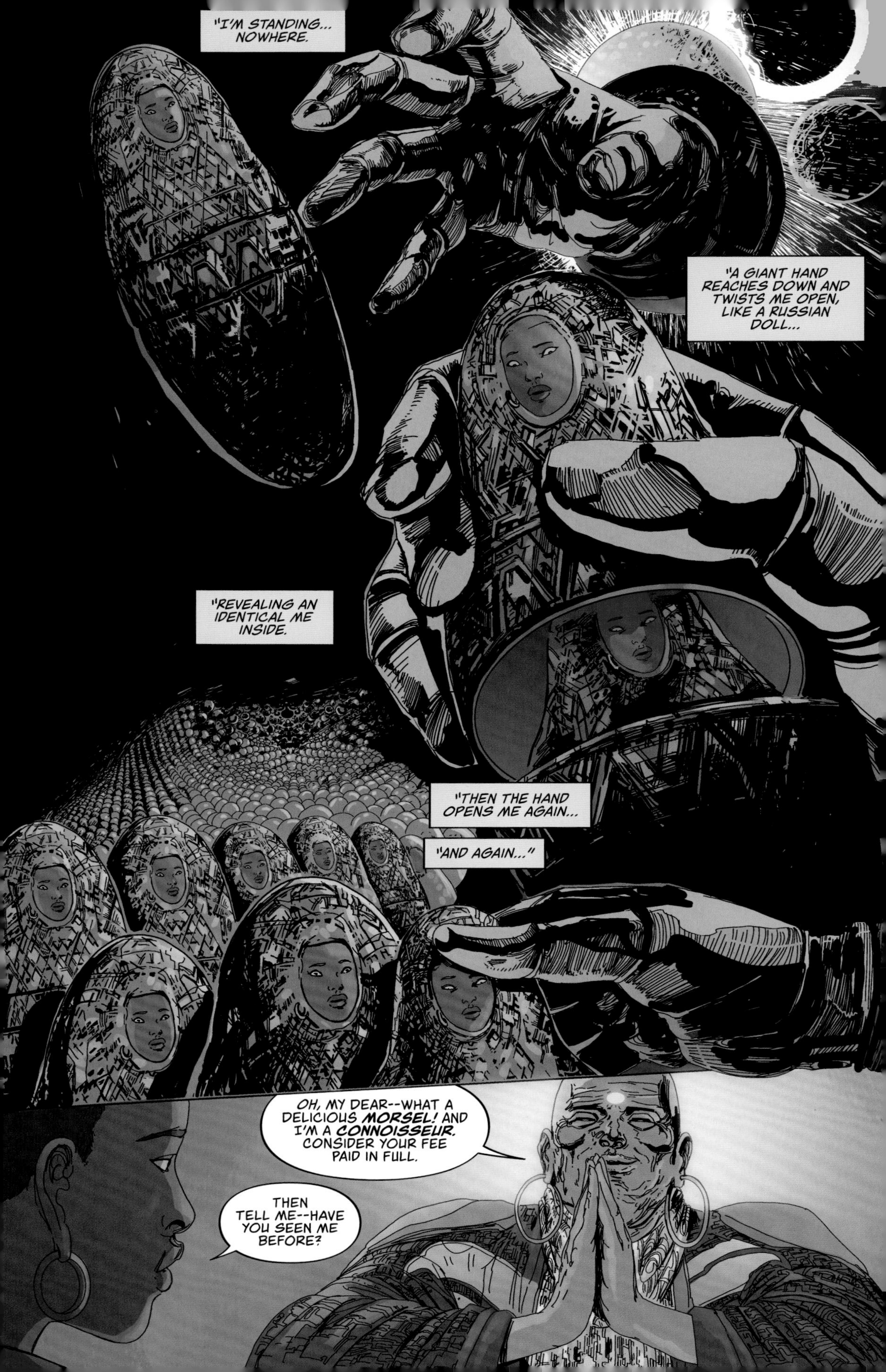
"I'M STANDING... NOWHERE.
"A GIANT HAND REACHES DOWN AND TWISTS ME OPEN, LIKE A RUSSIAN DOLL...
"REVEALING AN IDENTICAL ME INSIDE.
"THEN THE HAND OPENS ME AGAIN...
"AND AGAIN..."
OH, MY DEAR--WHAT A DELICIOUS MORSEL! AND I'M A CONNOISSEUR. CONSIDER YOUR FEE PAID IN FULL.
THEN TELL ME--HAVE YOU SEEN ME BEFORE?

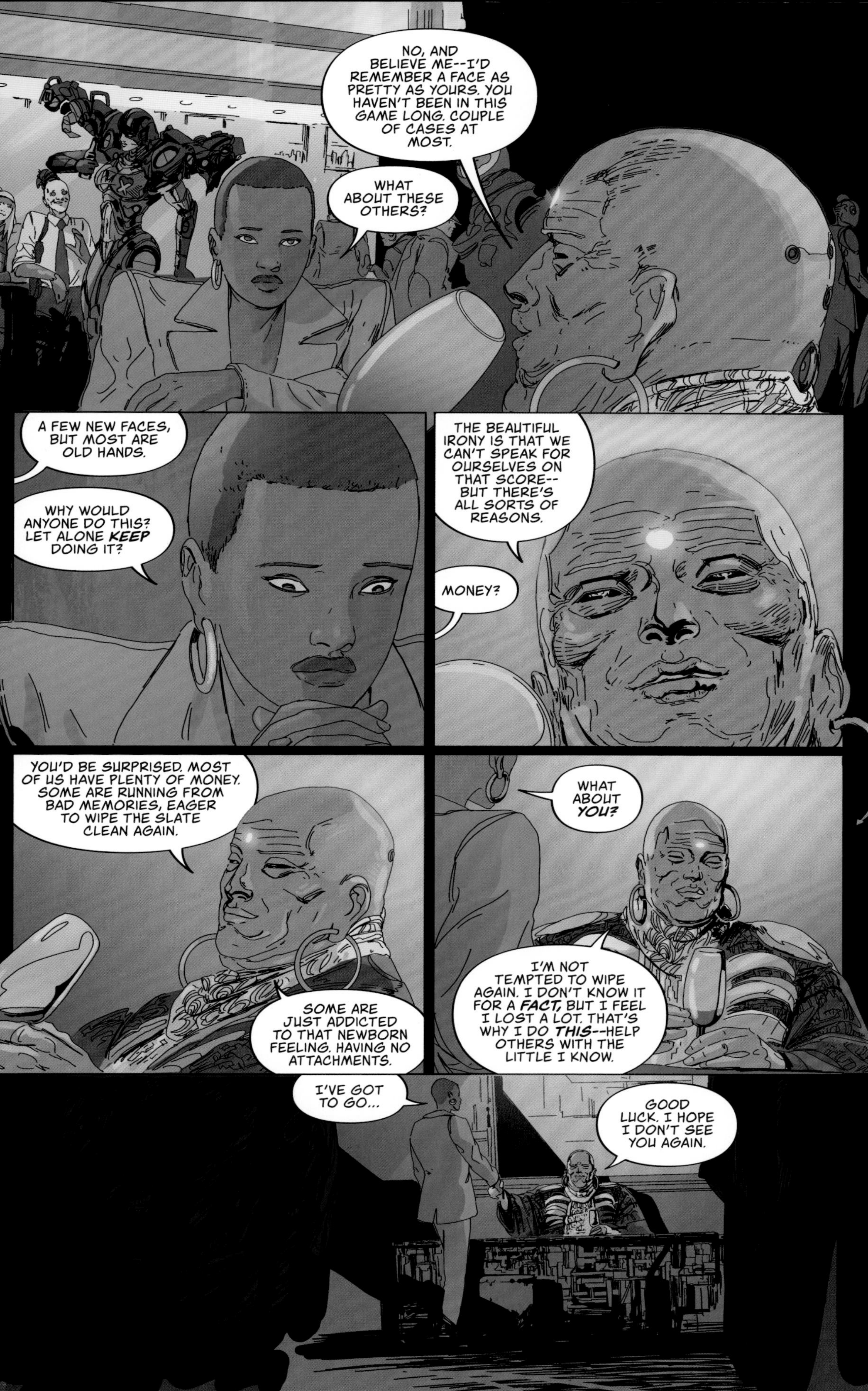
NO, AND BELIEVE ME--I'D REMEMBER A FACE AS PRETTY AS YOURS. YOU HAVEN'T BEEN IN THIS GAME LONG. COUPLE OF CASES AT MOST.
WHAT ABOUT THESE OTHERS?
A FEW NEW FACES, BUT MOST ARE OLD HANDS.
WHY WOULD ANYONE DO THIS? LET ALONE KEEP DOING IT?
THE BEAUTIFUL IRONY IS THAT WE CAN'T SPEAK FOR OURSELVES ON THAT SCORE-- BUT THERE'S ALL SORTS OF REASONS.
MONEY?
YOU'D BE SURPRISED. MOST OF US HAVE PLENTY OF MONEY. SOME ARE RUNNING FROM BAD MEMORIES, EAGER TO WIPE THE SLATE CLEAN AGAIN.
SOME ARE JUST ADDICTED TO THAT NEWBORN FEELING. HAVING NO ATTACHMENTS.
WHAT ABOUT YOU?
I'M NOT TEMPTED TO WIPE AGAIN. I DON'T KNOW IT FOR A FACT, BUT I FEEL I LOST A LOT. THAT'S WHY I DO THIS--HELP OTHERS WITH THE LITTLE I KNOW.
I'VE GOT TO GO...
GOOD LUCK. I HOPE I DON'T SEE YOU AGAIN.

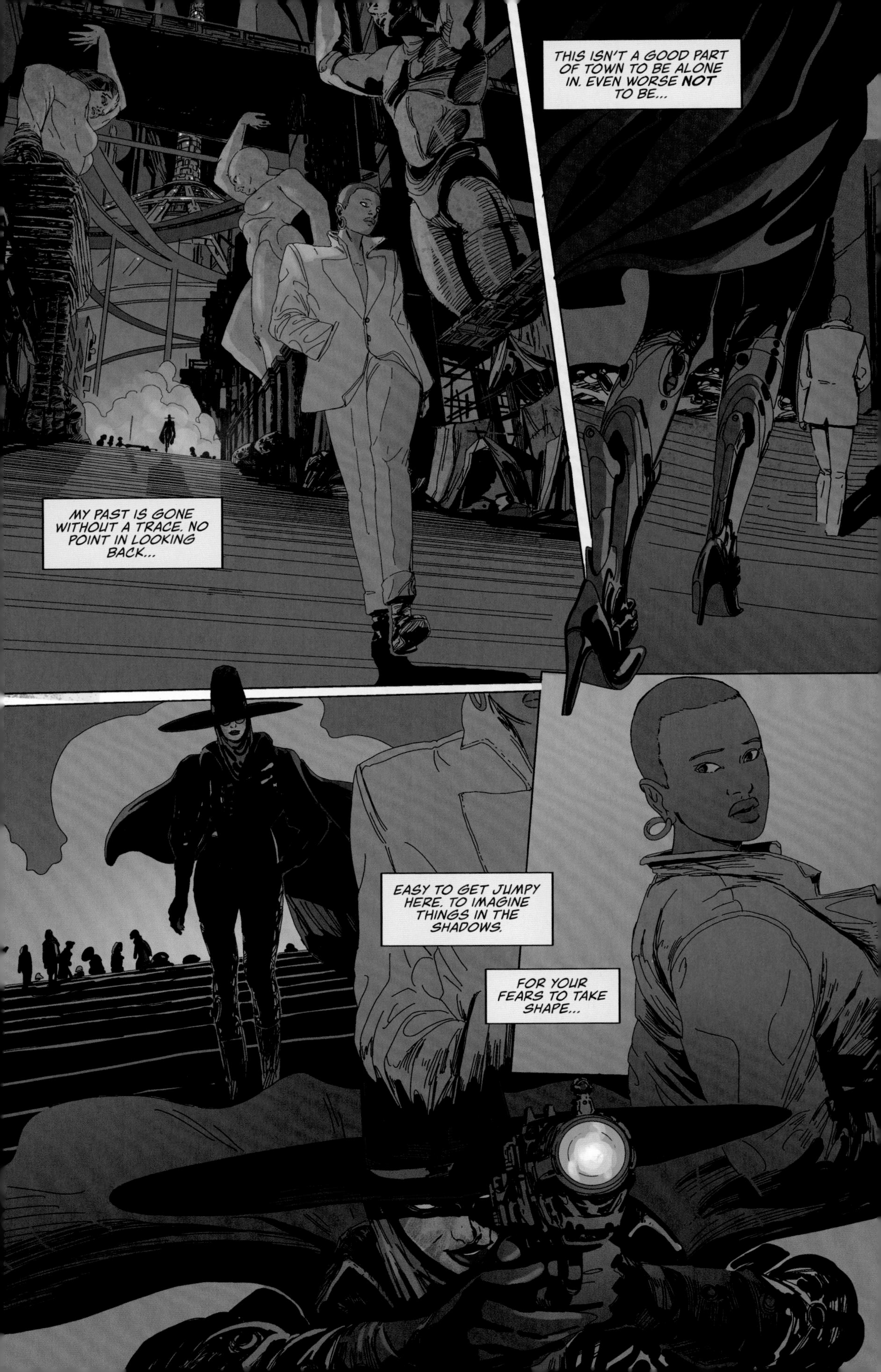
MY PAST IS GONE WITHOUT A TRACE. NO POINT IN LOOKING BACK...
THIS ISN'T A GOOD PART OF TOWN TO BE ALONE IN. EVEN WORSE **NOT** TO BE...
EASY TO GET JUMPY HERE. TO IMAGINE THINGS IN THE SHADOWS.
FOR YOUR FEARS TO TAKE SHAPE...

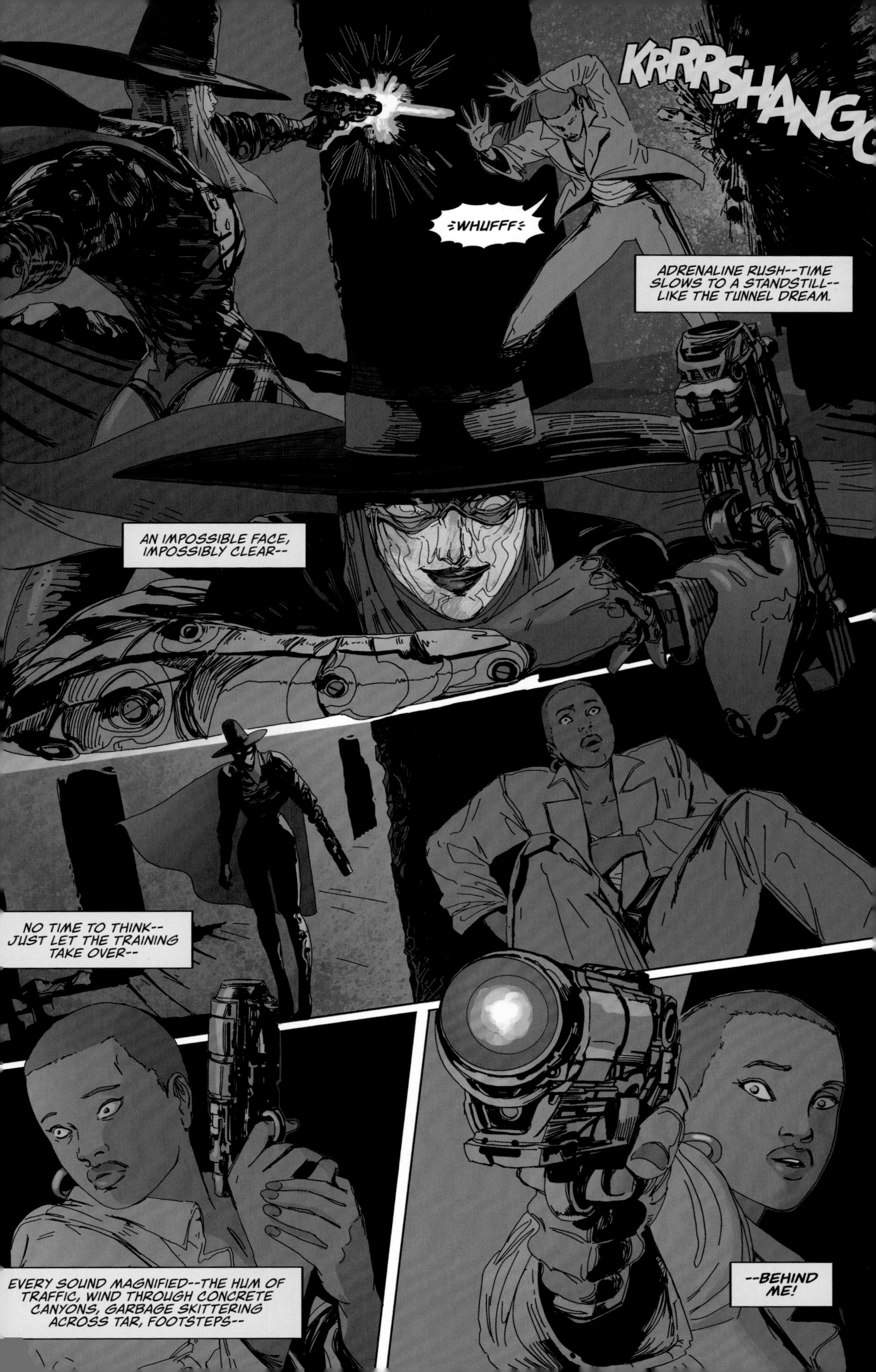
KRRRSHANGG
WHUFFF
ADRENALINE RUSH--TIME SLOWS TO A STANDSTILL--LIKE THE TUNNEL DREAM.
AN IMPOSSIBLE FACE, IMPOSSIBLY CLEAR--
NO TIME TO THINK--JUST LET THE TRAINING TAKE OVER--
EVERY SOUND MAGNIFIED--THE HUM OF TRAFFIC, WIND THROUGH CONCRETE CANYONS, GARBAGE SKITTERING ACROSS TAR, FOOTSTEPS--
--BEHIND ME!

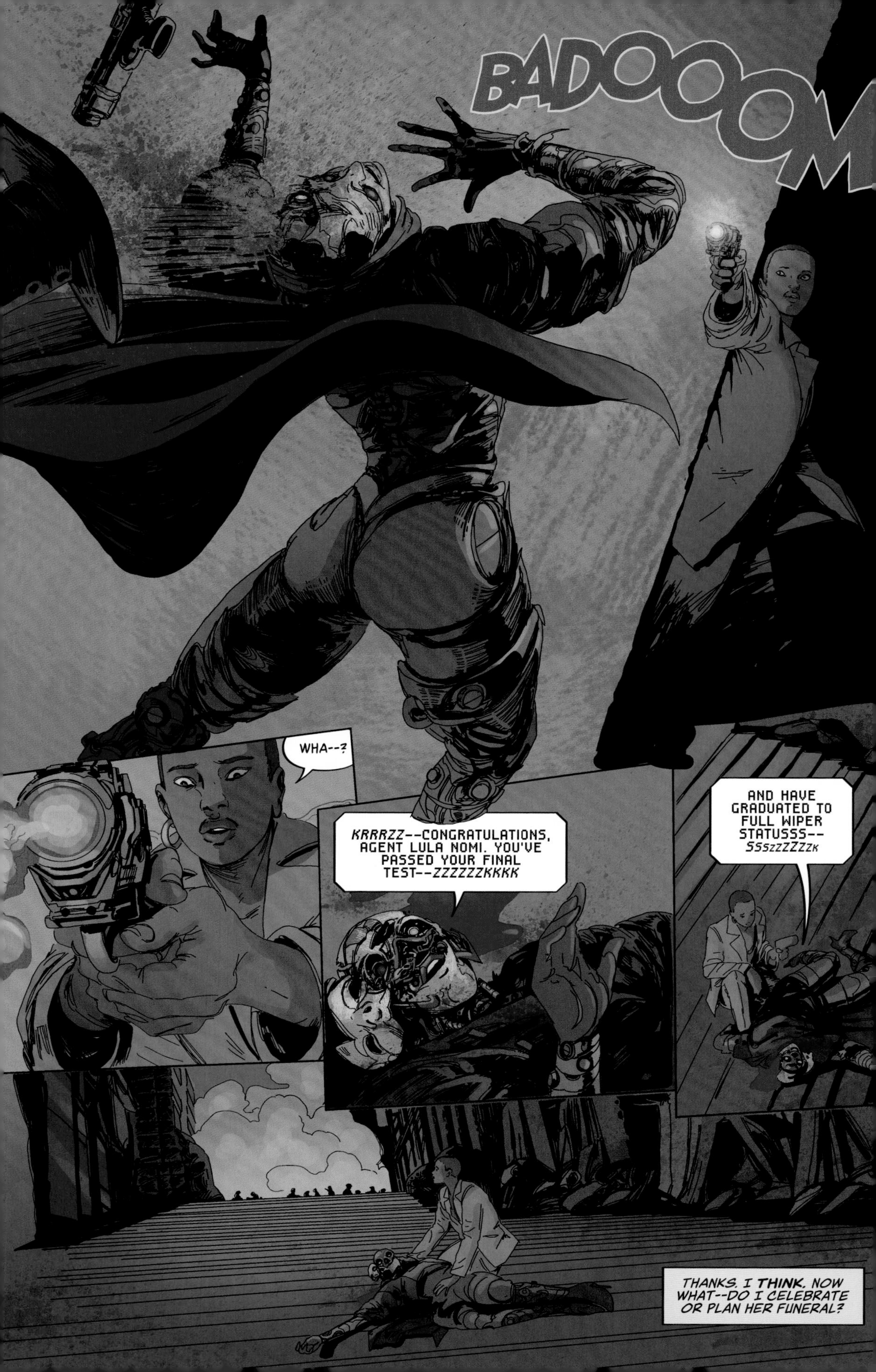
BADOOOOM
WHA--?
KRRRZZ--CONGRATULATIONS, AGENT LULA NOMI. YOU'VE PASSED YOUR FINAL TEST--ZZZZZZKKKK
AND HAVE GRADUATED TO FULL WIPER STATUSSS--SSSZZZZZZK
THANKS. I THINK. NOW WHAT--DO I CELEBRATE OR PLAN HER FUNERAL?

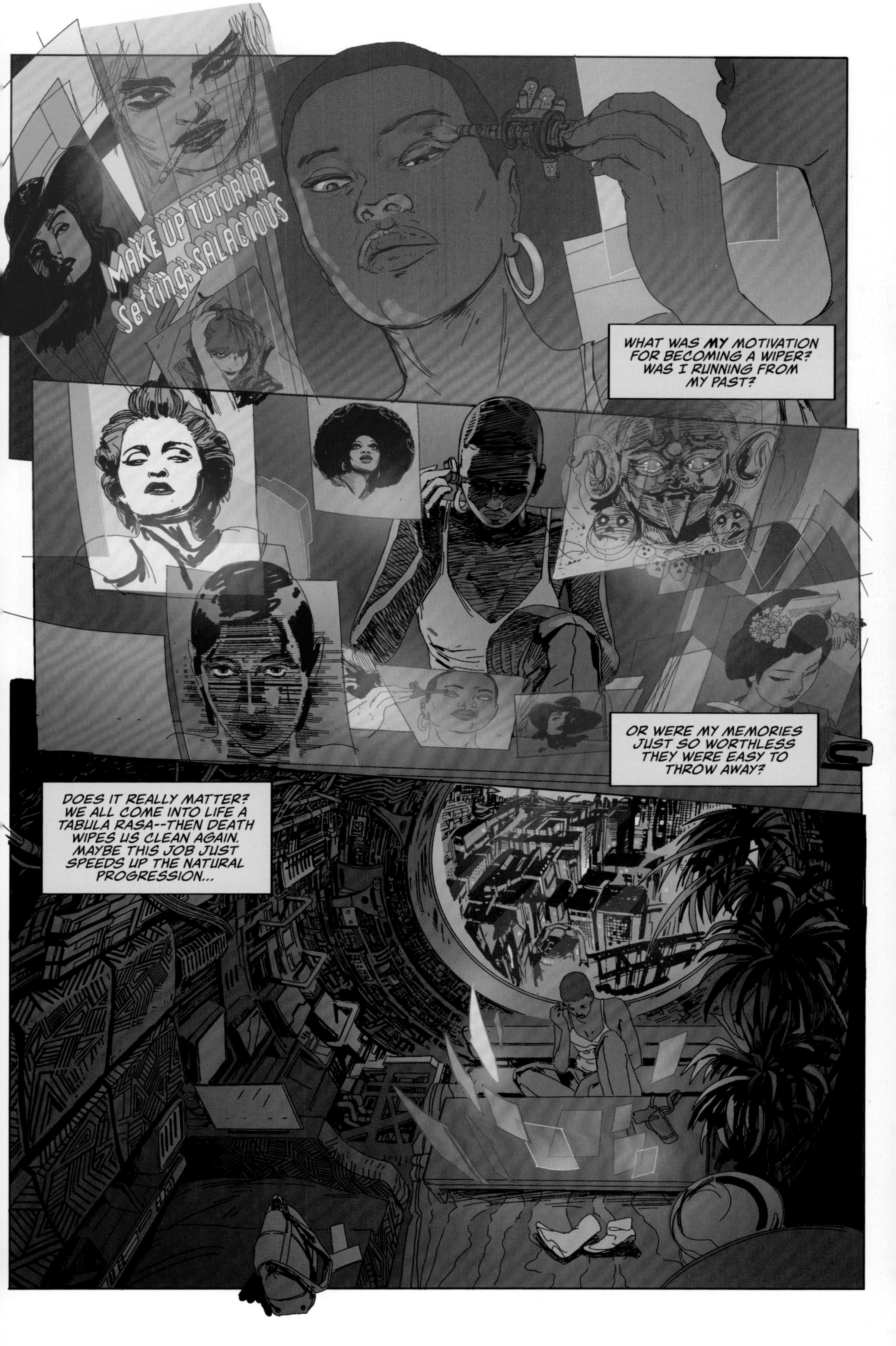
MAKE UP TUTORIAL
Setting: SALACIOUS
WHAT WAS MY MOTIVATION FOR BECOMING A WIPER? WAS I RUNNING FROM MY PAST?
OR WERE MY MEMORIES JUST SO WORTHLESS THEY WERE EASY TO THROW AWAY?
DOES IT REALLY MATTER? WE ALL COME INTO LIFE A TABULA RASA--THEN DEATH WIPES US CLEAN AGAIN. MAYBE THIS JOB JUST SPEEDS UP THE NATURAL PROGRESSION...

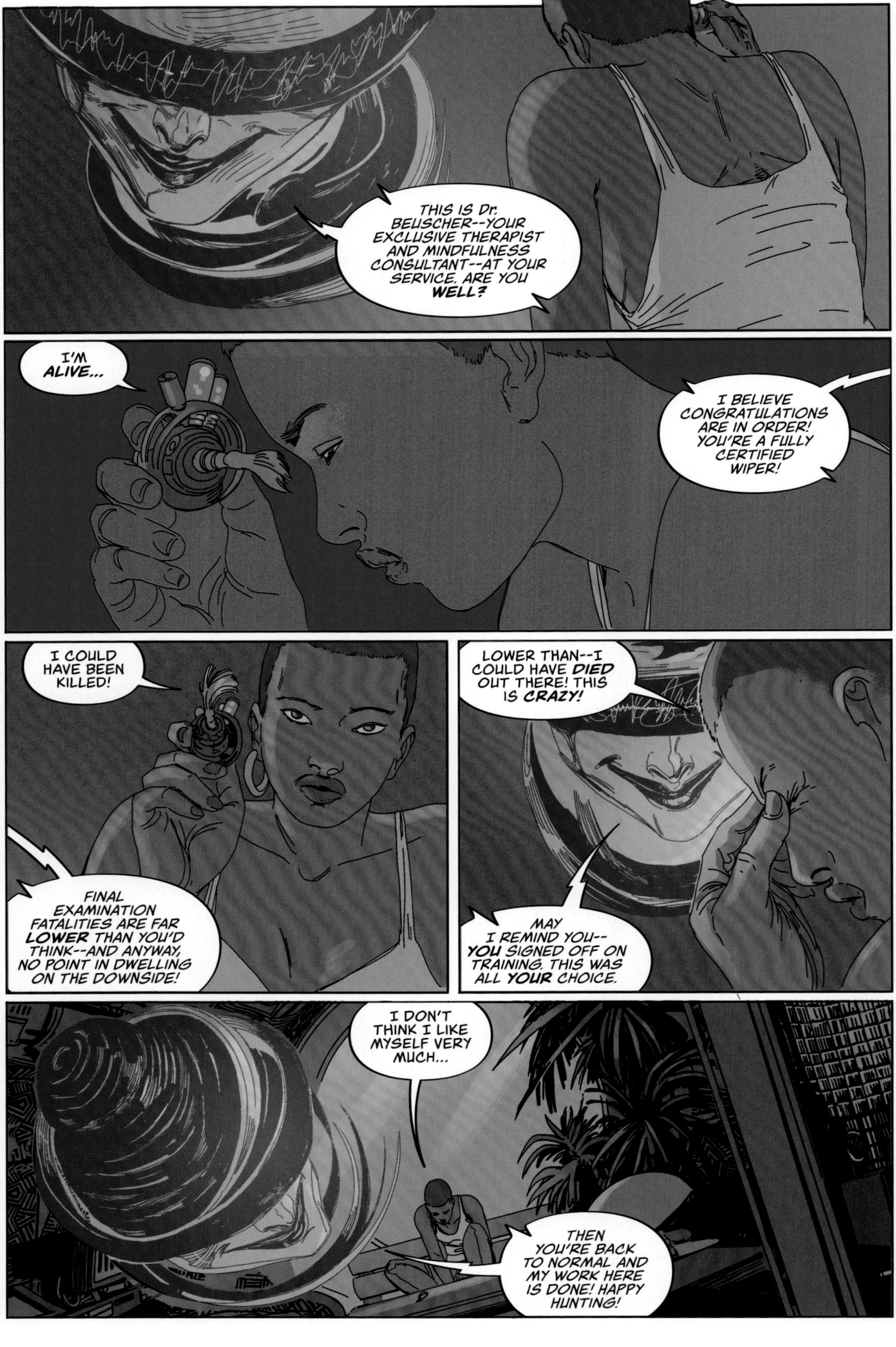
THIS IS Dr. BEUSCHER--YOUR EXCLUSIVE THERAPIST AND MINDFULNESS CONSULTANT--AT YOUR SERVICE. ARE YOU WELL?
I'M ALIVE...
I BELIEVE CONGRATULATIONS ARE IN ORDER! YOU'RE A FULLY CERTIFIED WIPER!
I COULD HAVE BEEN KILLED!
FINAL EXAMINATION FATALITIES ARE FAR LOWER THAN YOU'D THINK--AND ANYWAY, NO POINT IN DWELLING ON THE DOWNSIDE!
LOWER THAN--I COULD HAVE DIED OUT THERE! THIS IS CRAZY!
MAY I REMIND YOU--YOU SIGNED OFF ON TRAINING. THIS WAS ALL YOUR CHOICE.
I DON'T THINK I LIKE MYSELF VERY MUCH...
THEN YOU'RE BACK TO NORMAL AND MY WORK HERE IS DONE! HAPPY HUNTING!

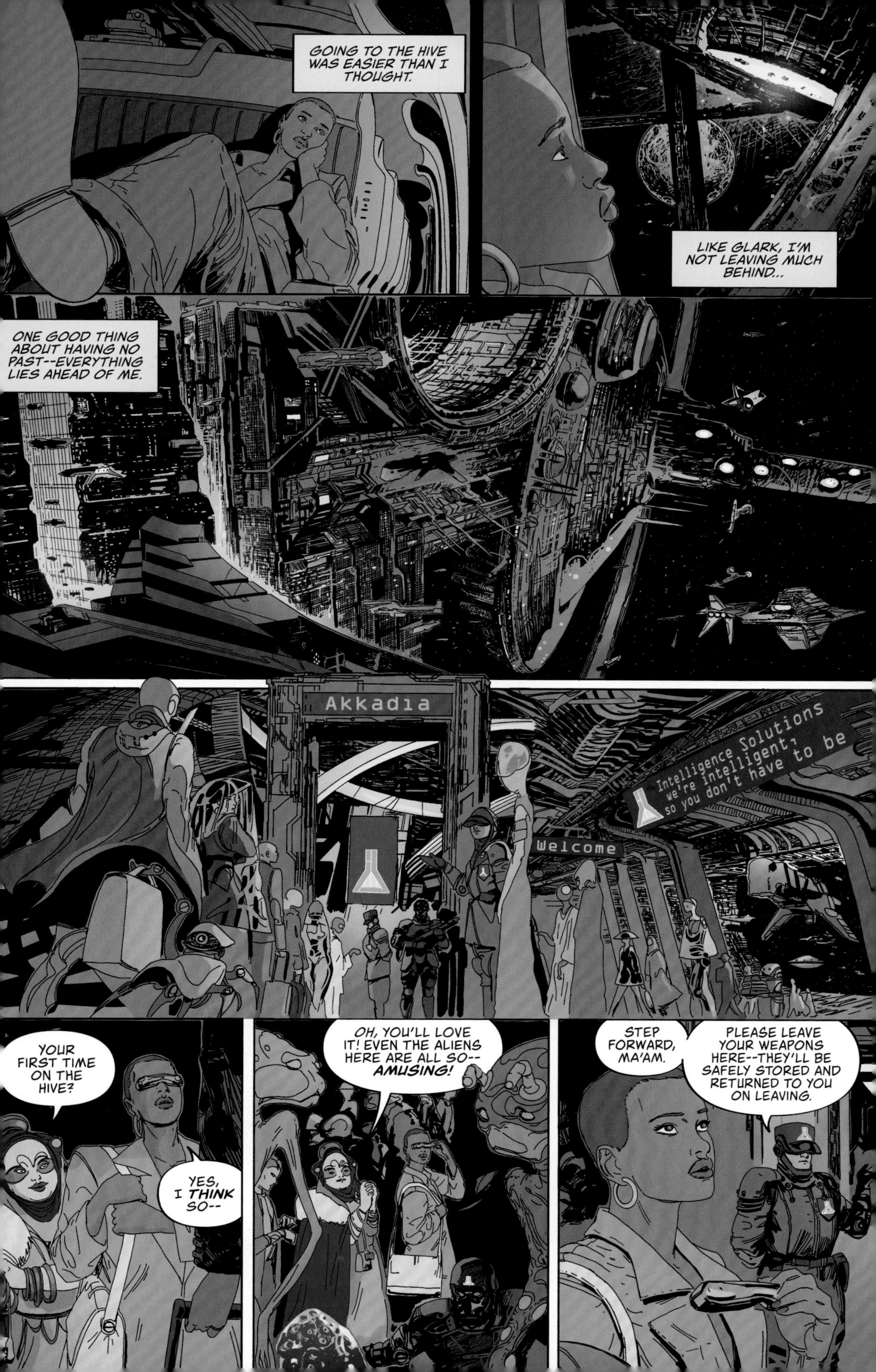
GOING TO THE HIVE WAS EASIER THAN I THOUGHT.
LIKE GLARK, I'M NOT LEAVING MUCH BEHIND...
ONE GOOD THING ABOUT HAVING NO PAST--EVERYTHING LIES AHEAD OF ME.
Akkadia
Intelligence Solutions
we're intelligent, so you don't have to be
Welcome
YOUR FIRST TIME ON THE HIVE?
YES, I *THINK* SO--
OH, YOU'LL LOVE IT! EVEN THE ALIENS HERE ARE ALL SO-- ***AMUSING!***
STEP FORWARD, MA'AM.
PLEASE LEAVE YOUR WEAPONS HERE--THEY'LL BE SAFELY STORED AND RETURNED TO YOU ON LEAVING.

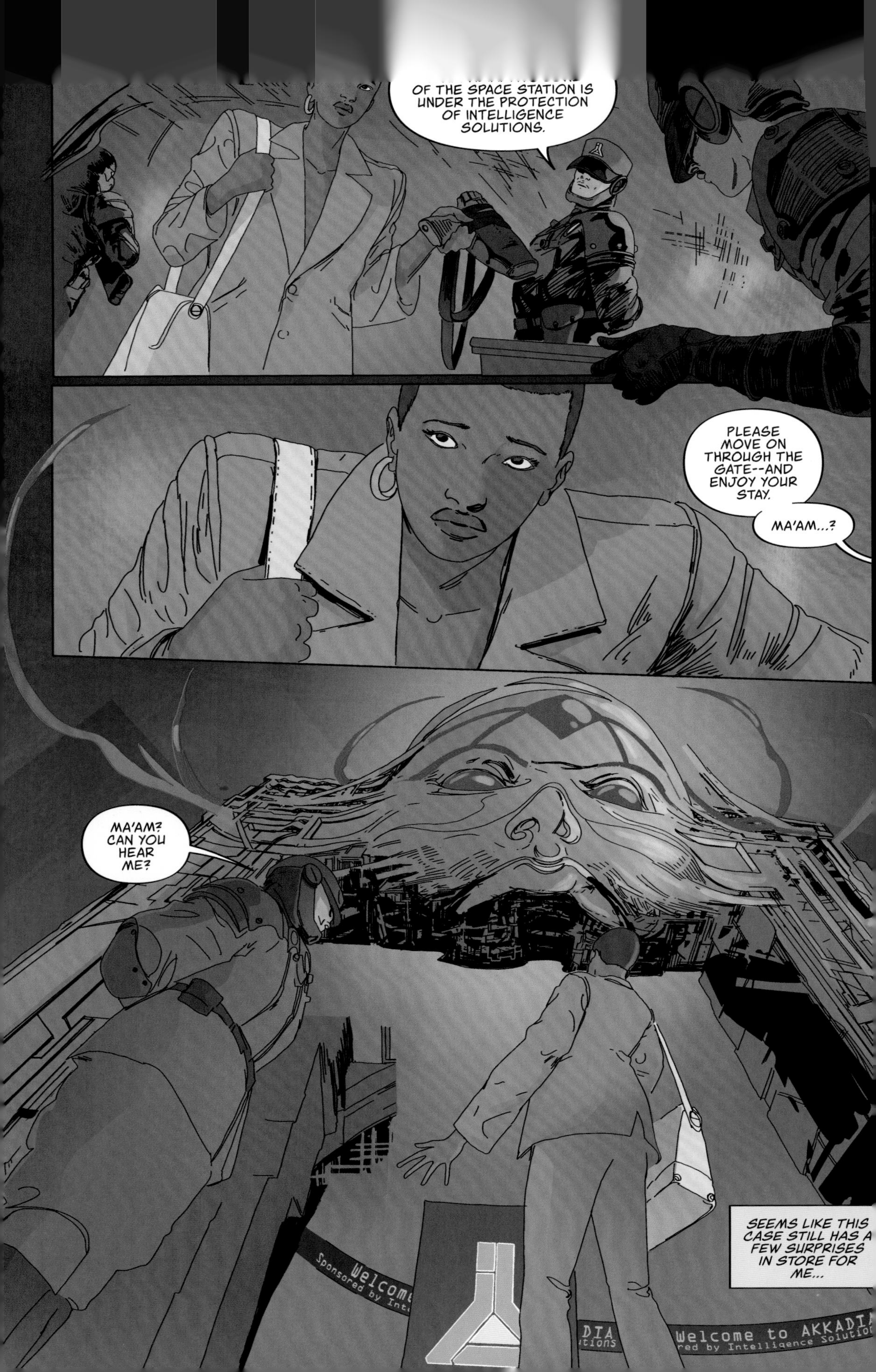
OF THE SPACE STATION IS UNDER THE PROTECTION OF INTELLIGENCE SOLUTIONS.
PLEASE MOVE ON THROUGH THE GATE--AND ENJOY YOUR STAY.
MA'AM...?
MA'AM? CAN YOU HEAR ME?
SEEMS LIKE THIS CASE STILL HAS A FEW SURPRISES IN STORE FOR ME...
Welcome to AKKADIA

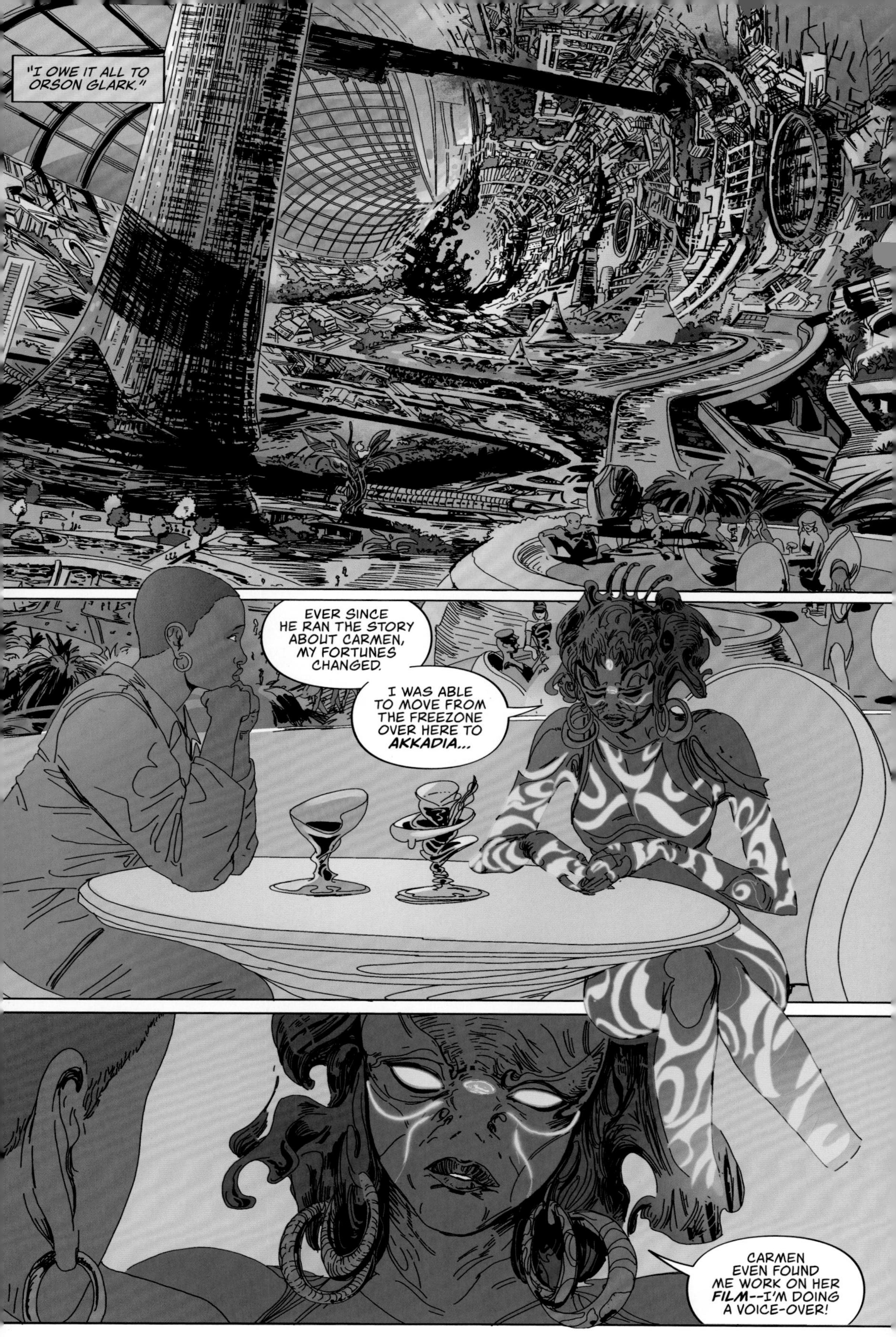
"I OWE IT ALL TO ORSON GLARK."
EVER SINCE HE RAN THE STORY ABOUT CARMEN, MY FORTUNES CHANGED.
I WAS ABLE TO MOVE FROM THE FREEZONE OVER HERE TO AKKADIA...
CARMEN EVEN FOUND ME WORK ON HER FILM--I'M DOING A VOICE-OVER!

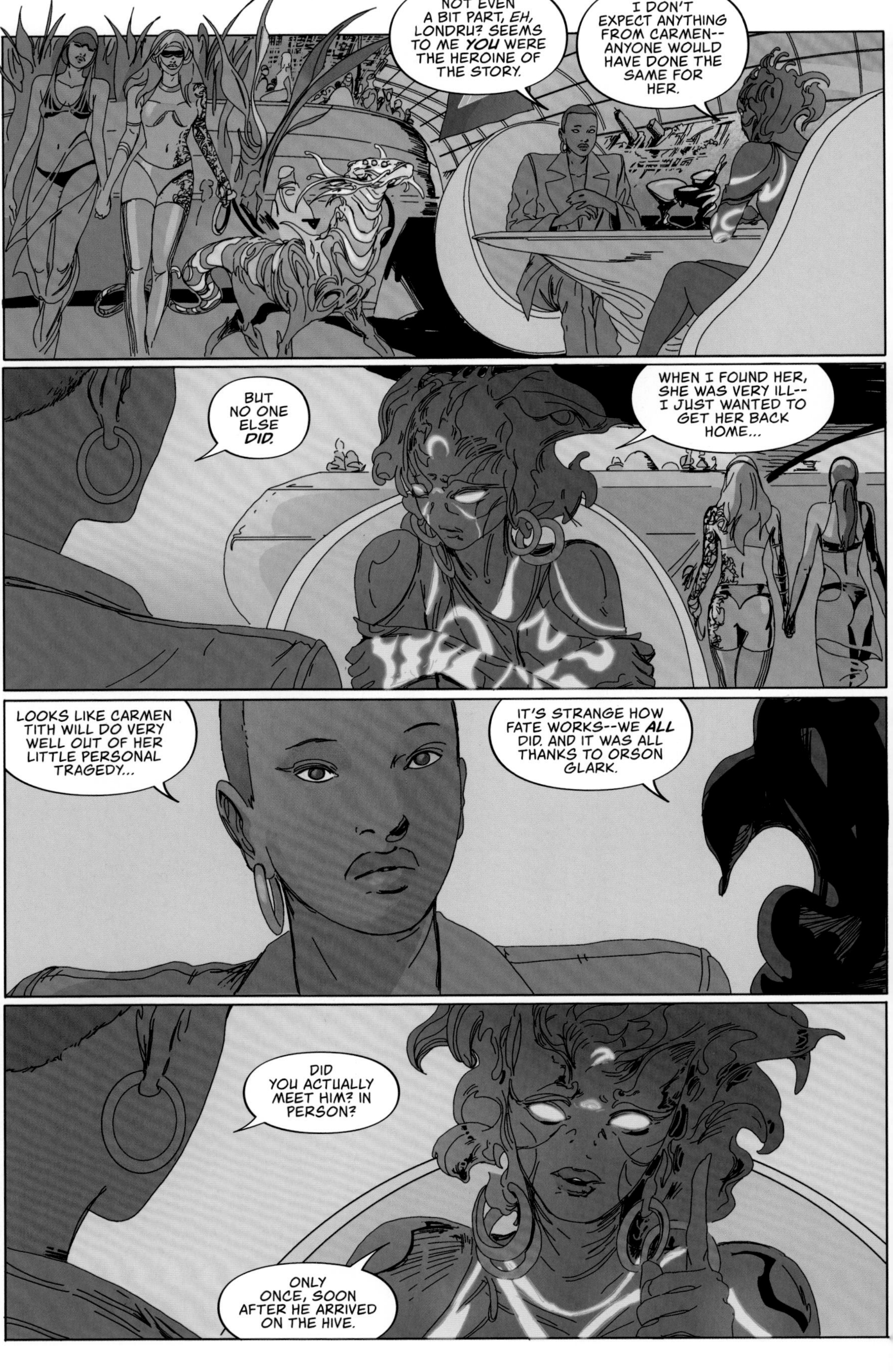
NOT EVEN A BIT PART, EH, LONDRU? SEEMS TO ME YOU WERE THE HEROINE OF THE STORY.
I DON'T EXPECT ANYTHING FROM CARMEN-- ANYONE WOULD HAVE DONE THE SAME FOR HER.
BUT NO ONE ELSE DID.
WHEN I FOUND HER, SHE WAS VERY ILL-- I JUST WANTED TO GET HER BACK HOME...
LOOKS LIKE CARMEN TITH WILL DO VERY WELL OUT OF HER LITTLE PERSONAL TRAGEDY...
IT'S STRANGE HOW FATE WORKS--WE ALL DID. AND IT WAS ALL THANKS TO ORSON GLARK.
DID YOU ACTUALLY MEET HIM? IN PERSON?
ONLY ONCE, SOON AFTER HE ARRIVED ON THE HIVE.

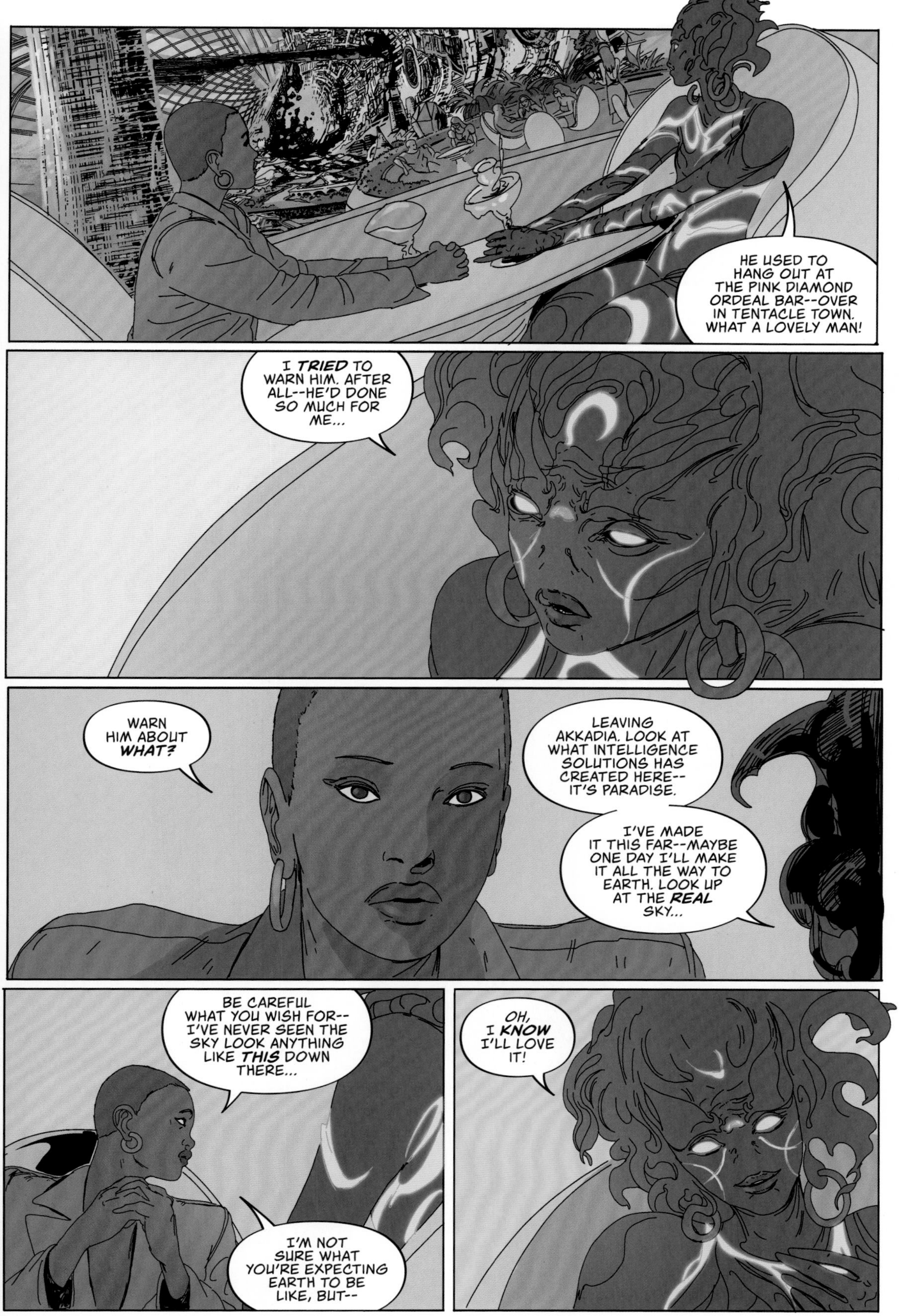
HE USED TO HANG OUT AT THE PINK DIAMOND ORDEAL BAR--OVER IN TENTACLE TOWN. WHAT A LOVELY MAN!
I TRIED TO WARN HIM. AFTER ALL--HE'D DONE SO MUCH FOR ME...
WARN HIM ABOUT WHAT?
LEAVING AKKADIA. LOOK AT WHAT INTELLIGENCE SOLUTIONS HAS CREATED HERE-- IT'S PARADISE.
I'VE MADE IT THIS FAR--MAYBE ONE DAY I'LL MAKE IT ALL THE WAY TO EARTH. LOOK UP AT THE REAL SKY...
BE CAREFUL WHAT YOU WISH FOR-- I'VE NEVER SEEN THE SKY LOOK ANYTHING LIKE THIS DOWN THERE...
I'M NOT SURE WHAT YOU'RE EXPECTING EARTH TO BE LIKE, BUT--
OH, I KNOW I'LL LOVE IT!

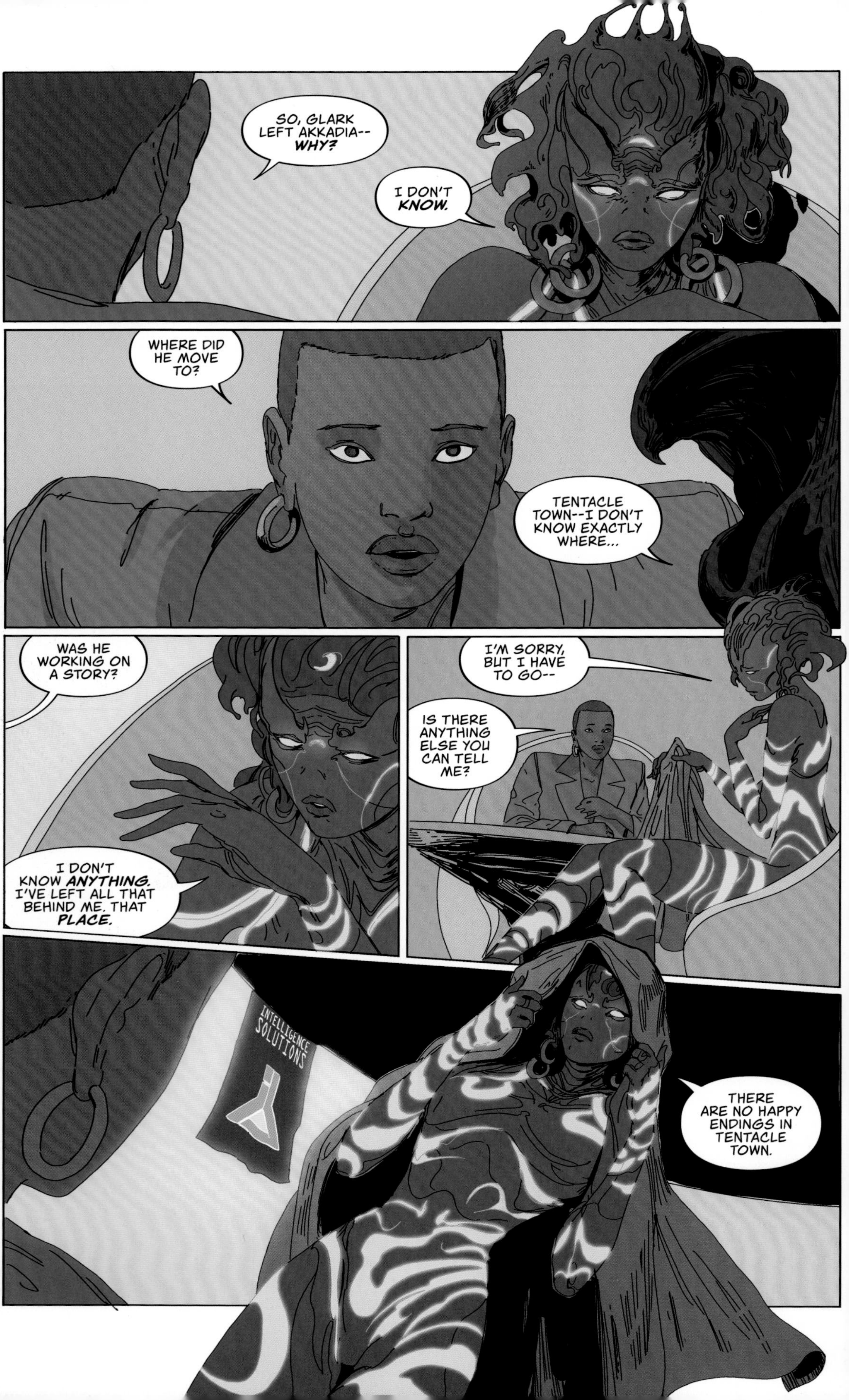
SO, GLARK LEFT AKKADIA-- *WHY?*
I DON'T *KNOW.*
WHERE DID HE MOVE TO?
TENTACLE TOWN--I DON'T KNOW EXACTLY WHERE...
WAS HE WORKING ON A STORY?
I DON'T KNOW *ANYTHING.* I'VE LEFT ALL THAT BEHIND ME. THAT *PLACE.*
I'M SORRY, BUT I HAVE TO GO--
IS THERE ANYTHING ELSE YOU CAN TELL ME?
INTELLIGENCE SOLUTIONS
THERE ARE NO HAPPY ENDINGS IN TENTACLE TOWN.

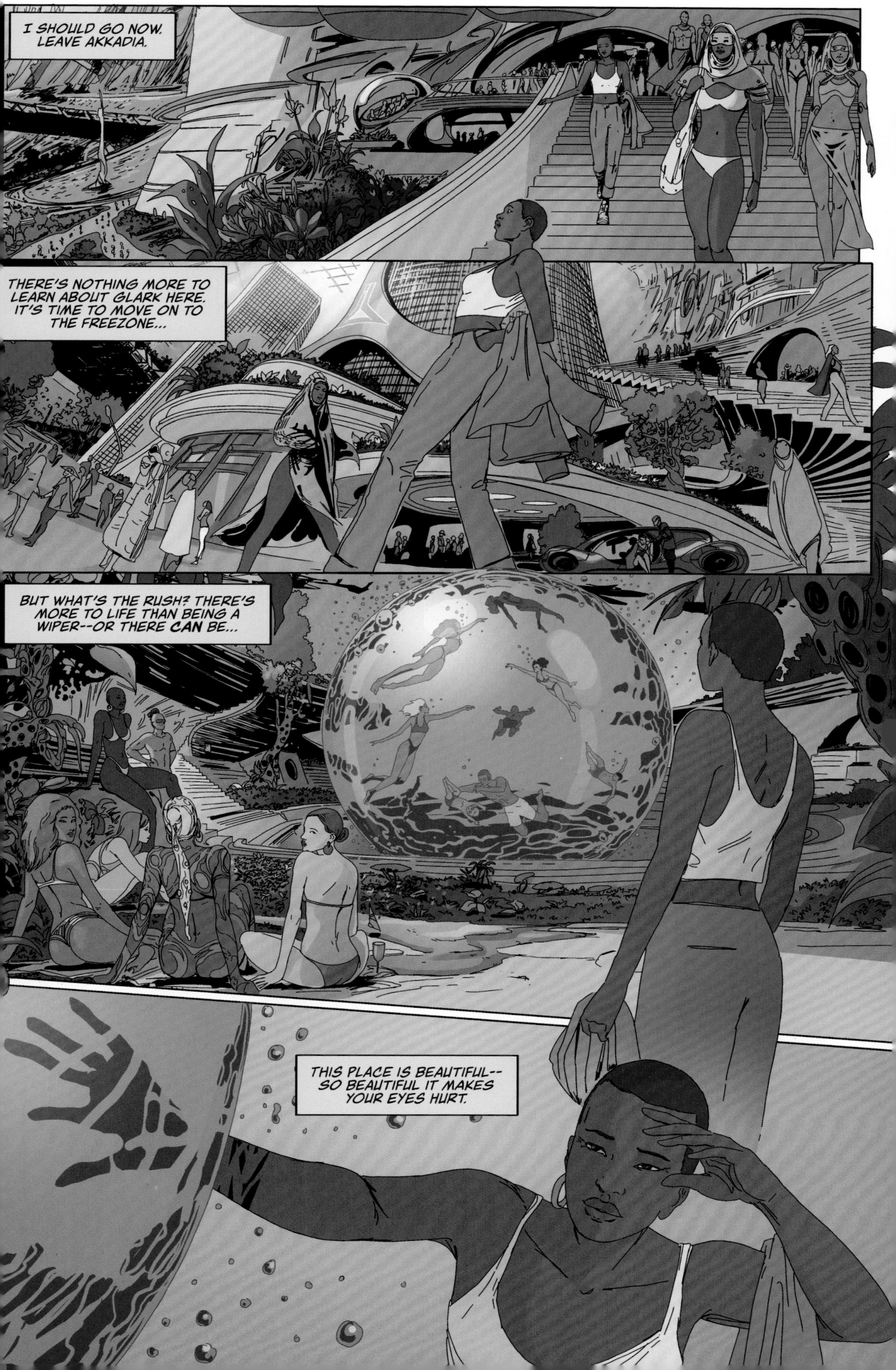
I SHOULD GO NOW. LEAVE AKKADIA.
THERE'S NOTHING MORE TO LEARN ABOUT GLARK HERE. IT'S TIME TO MOVE ON TO THE FREEZONE...
BUT WHAT'S THE RUSH? THERE'S MORE TO LIFE THAN BEING A WIPER--OR THERE CAN BE...
THIS PLACE IS BEAUTIFUL-- SO BEAUTIFUL IT MAKES YOUR EYES HURT.

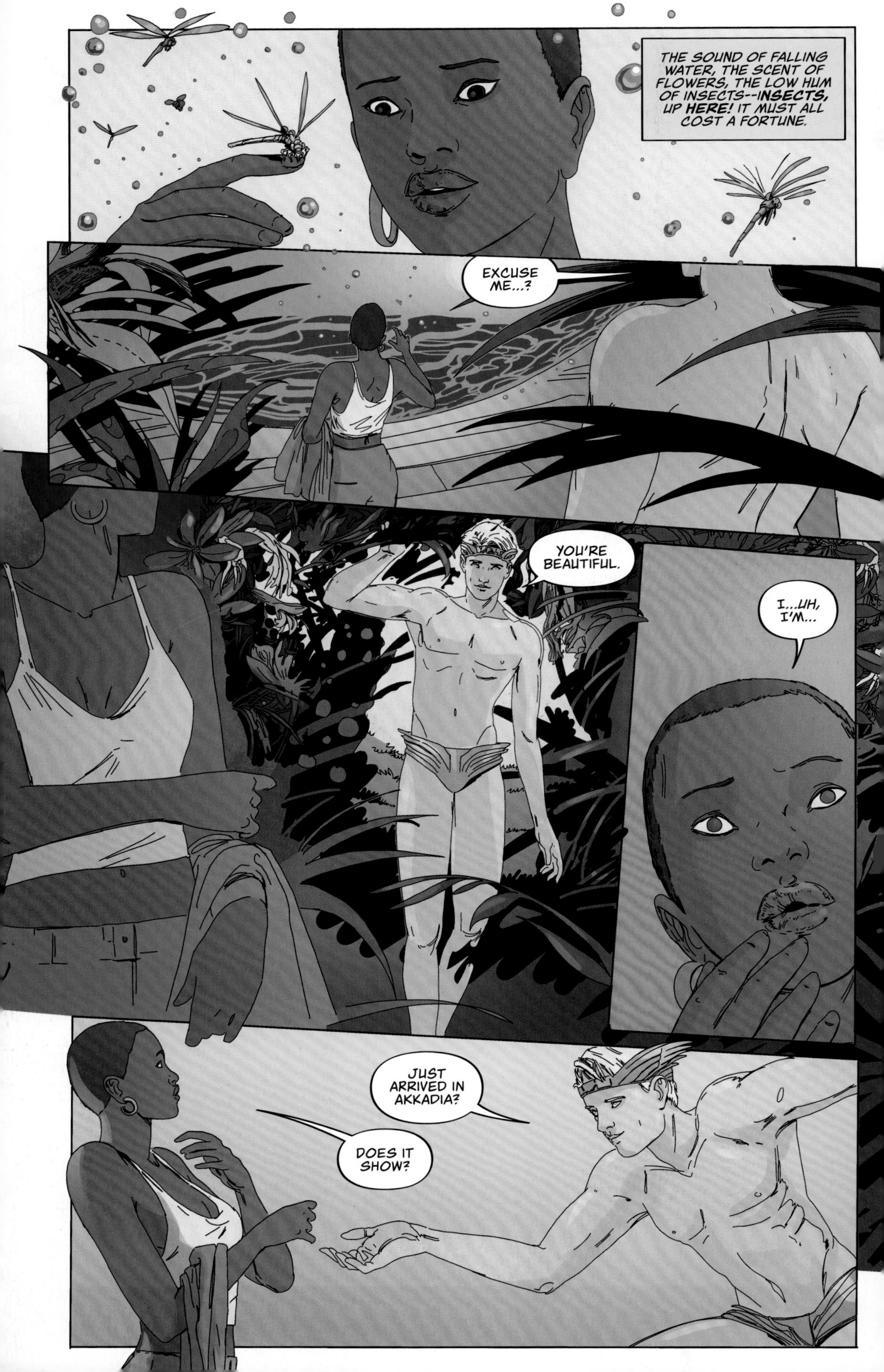
THE SOUND OF FALLING WATER, THE SCENT OF FLOWERS, THE LOW HUM OF INSECTS--INSECTS, UP HERE! IT MUST ALL COST A FORTUNE.
EXCUSE ME...?
YOU'RE BEAUTIFUL.
I...UH, I'M...
JUST ARRIVED IN AKKADIA?
DOES IT SHOW?

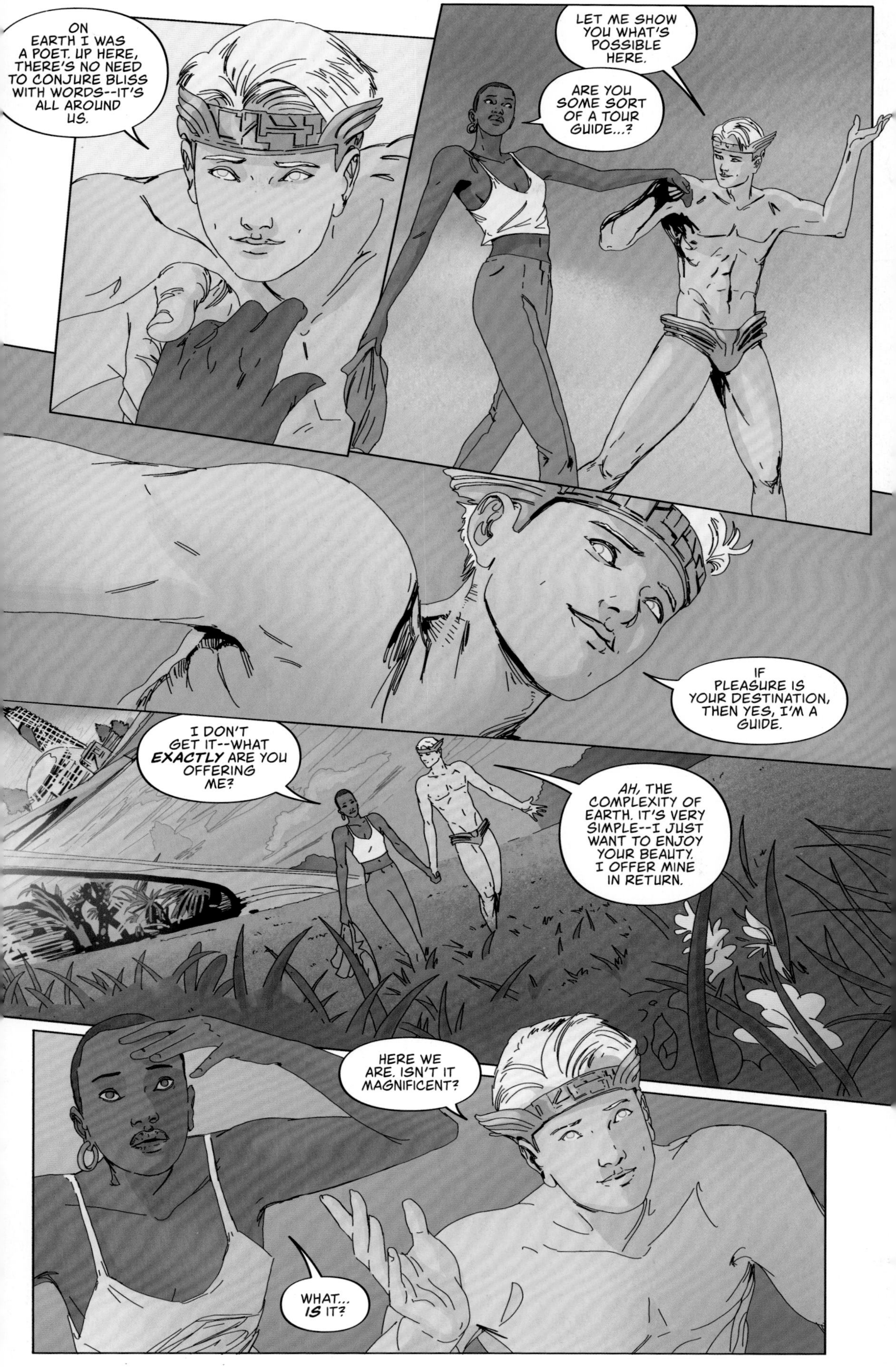
ON EARTH I WAS A POET. UP HERE, THERE'S NO NEED TO CONJURE BLISS WITH WORDS--IT'S ALL AROUND US.
LET ME SHOW YOU WHAT'S POSSIBLE HERE.
ARE YOU SOME SORT OF A TOUR GUIDE...?
IF PLEASURE IS YOUR DESTINATION, THEN YES, I'M A GUIDE.
I DON'T GET IT--WHAT EXACTLY ARE YOU OFFERING ME?
AH, THE COMPLEXITY OF EARTH. IT'S VERY SIMPLE--I JUST WANT TO ENJOY YOUR BEAUTY. I OFFER MINE IN RETURN.
HERE WE ARE. ISN'T IT MAGNIFICENT?
WHAT... IS IT?

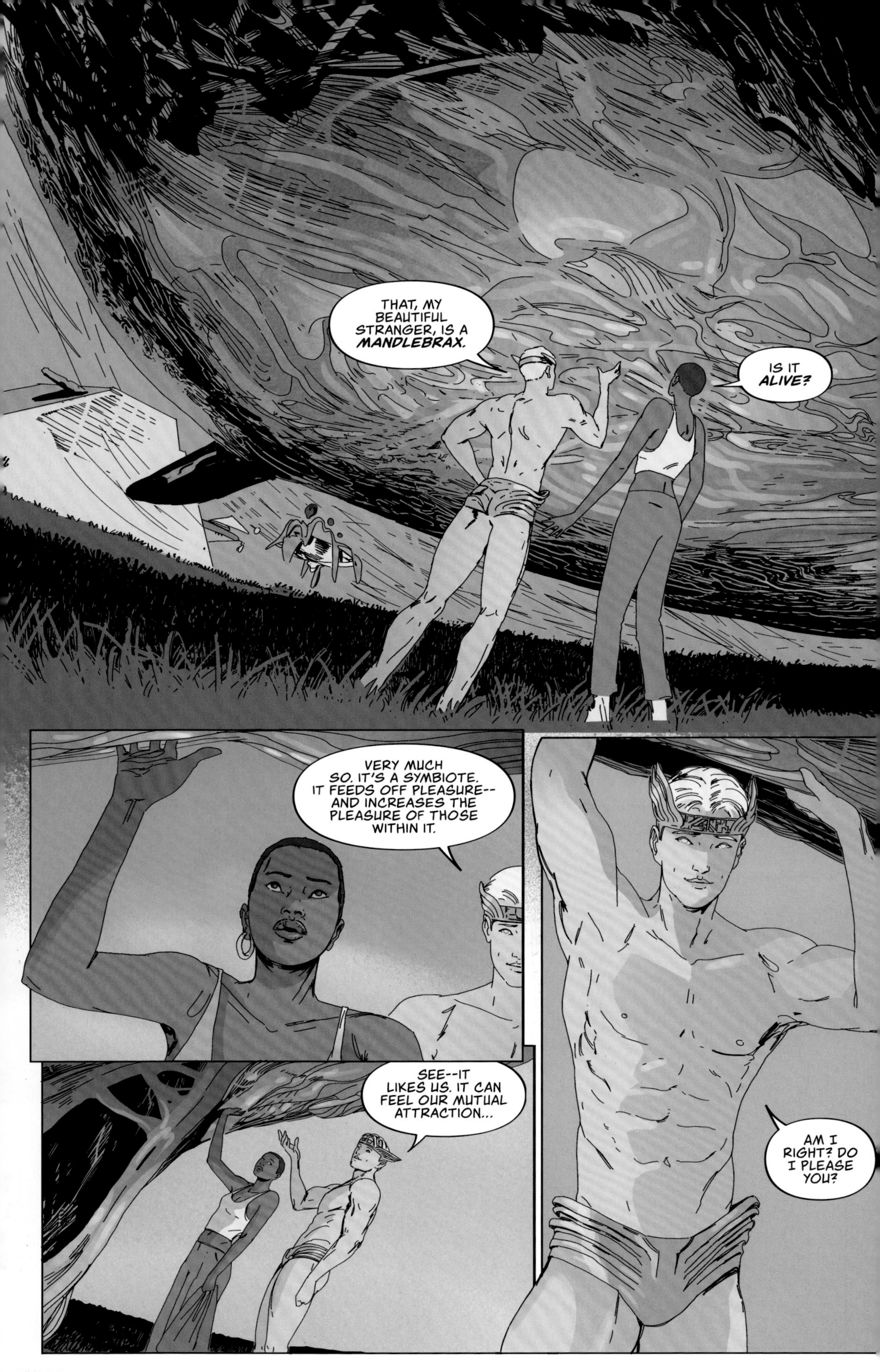
THAT, MY BEAUTIFUL STRANGER, IS A MANDLEBRAX.
IS IT ALIVE?
VERY MUCH SO. IT'S A SYMBIOTE. IT FEEDS OFF PLEASURE-- AND INCREASES THE PLEASURE OF THOSE WITHIN IT.
SEE--IT LIKES US. IT CAN FEEL OUR MUTUAL ATTRACTION...
AM I RIGHT? DO I PLEASE YOU?

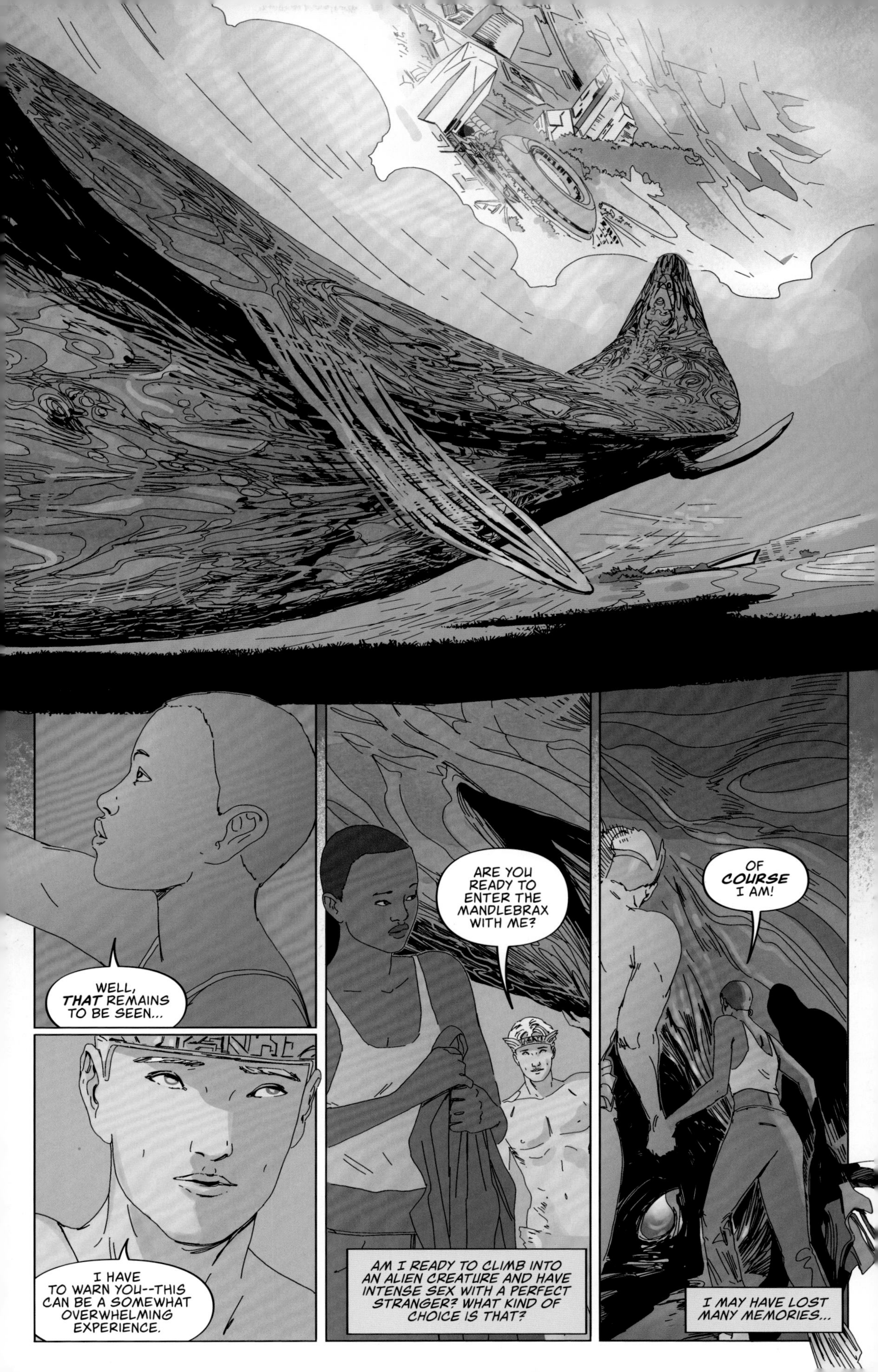
WELL, THAT REMAINS TO BE SEEN...
I HAVE TO WARN YOU--THIS CAN BE A SOMEWHAT OVERWHELMING EXPERIENCE.
ARE YOU READY TO ENTER THE MANDLEBRAX WITH ME?
AM I READY TO CLIMB INTO AN ALIEN CREATURE AND HAVE INTENSE SEX WITH A PERFECT STRANGER? WHAT KIND OF CHOICE IS THAT?
OF COURSE I AM!
I MAY HAVE LOST MANY MEMORIES...

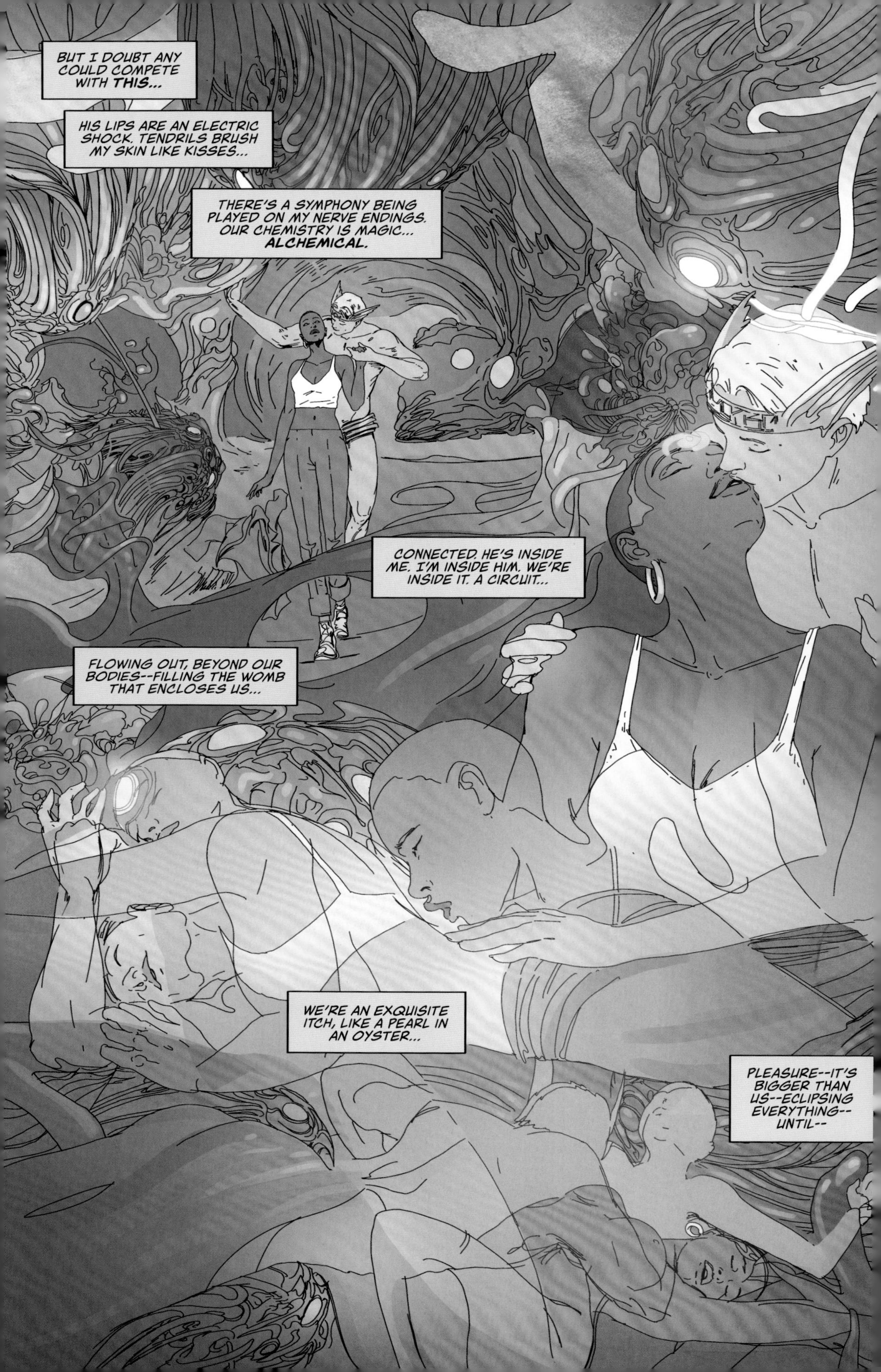

BUT I DOUBT ANY COULD COMPETE WITH THIS...
HIS LIPS ARE AN ELECTRIC SHOCK. TENDRILS BRUSH MY SKIN LIKE KISSES...
THERE'S A SYMPHONY BEING PLAYED ON MY NERVE ENDINGS. OUR CHEMISTRY IS MAGIC... ALCHEMICAL.
CONNECTED. HE'S INSIDE ME. I'M INSIDE HIM. WE'RE INSIDE IT. A CIRCUIT...
FLOWING OUT, BEYOND OUR BODIES--FILLING THE WOMB THAT ENCLOSES US...
WE'RE AN EXQUISITE ITCH, LIKE A PEARL IN AN OYSTER...
PLEASURE--IT'S BIGGER THAN US--ECLIPSING EVERYTHING--UNTIL--

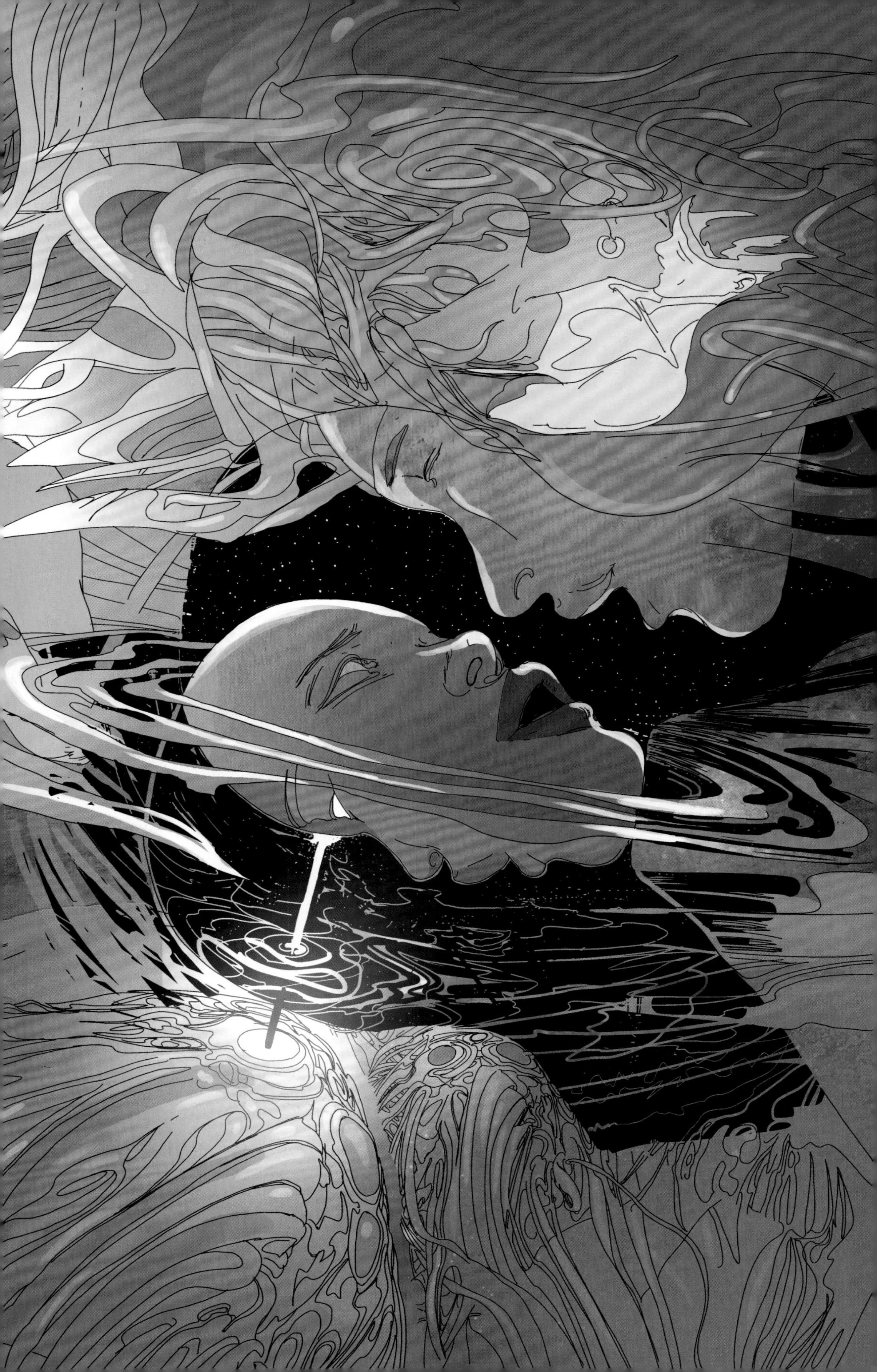

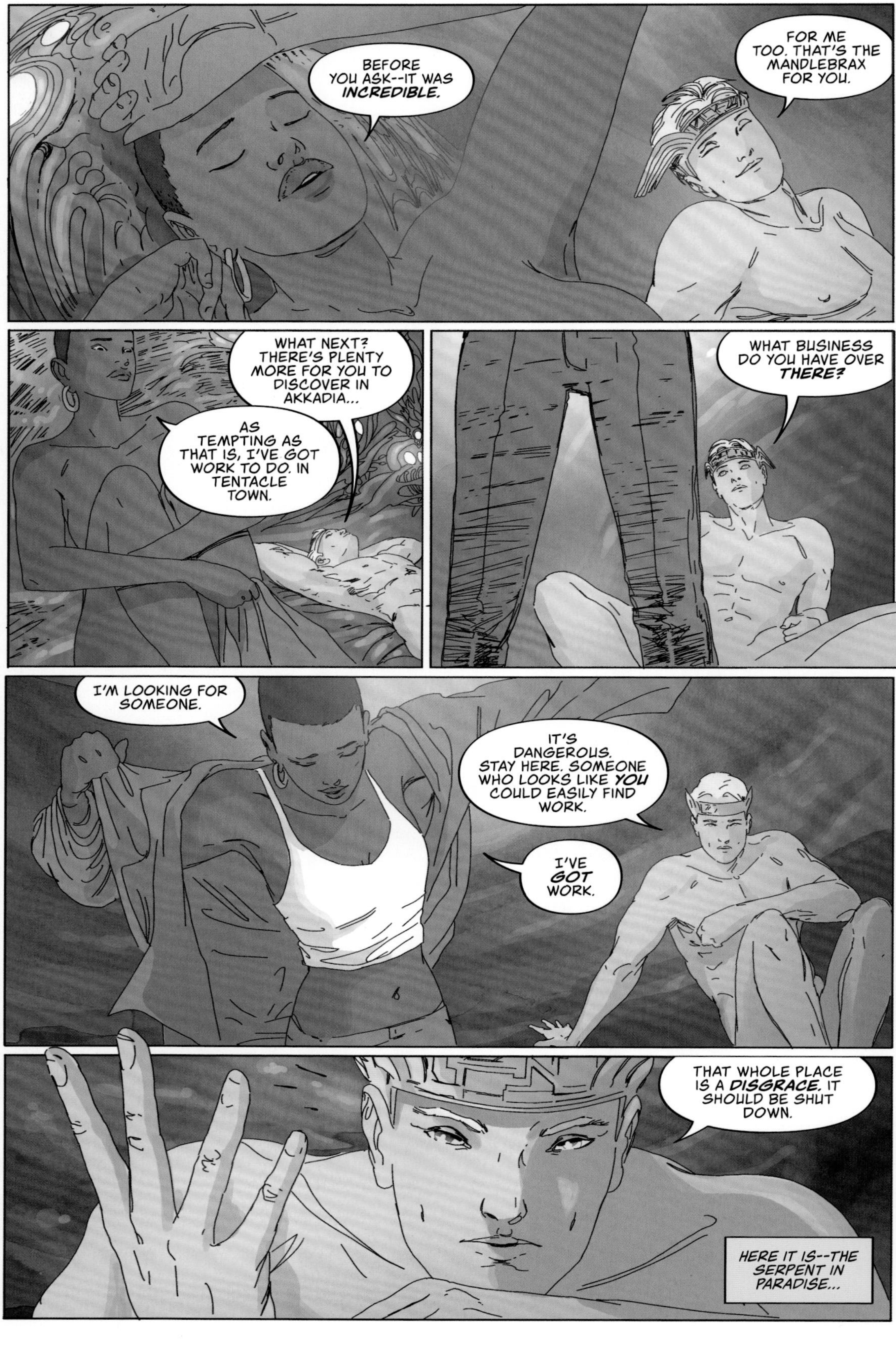
BEFORE YOU ASK--IT WAS INCREDIBLE.
FOR ME TOO. THAT'S THE MANDLEBRAX FOR YOU.
WHAT NEXT? THERE'S PLENTY MORE FOR YOU TO DISCOVER IN AKKADIA...
AS TEMPTING AS THAT IS, I'VE GOT WORK TO DO. IN TENTACLE TOWN.
WHAT BUSINESS DO YOU HAVE OVER THERE?
I'M LOOKING FOR SOMEONE.
IT'S DANGEROUS. STAY HERE. SOMEONE WHO LOOKS LIKE YOU COULD EASILY FIND WORK.
I'VE GOT WORK.
THAT WHOLE PLACE IS A DISGRACE. IT SHOULD BE SHUT DOWN.
HERE IT IS--THE SERPENT IN PARADISE...

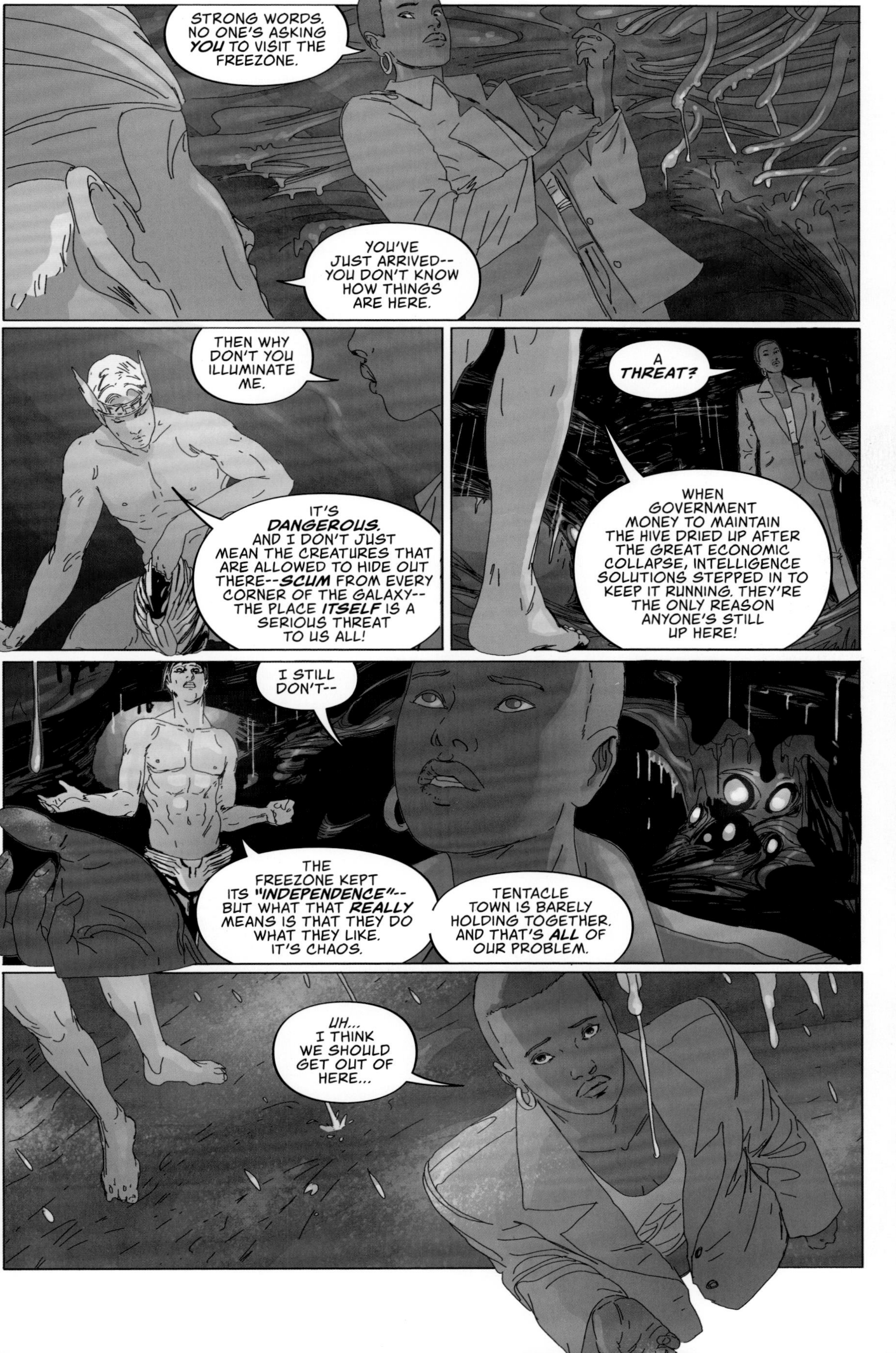
STRONG WORDS. NO ONE'S ASKING YOU TO VISIT THE FREEZONE.
YOU'VE JUST ARRIVED-- YOU DON'T KNOW HOW THINGS ARE HERE.
THEN WHY DON'T YOU ILLUMINATE ME.
IT'S DANGEROUS. AND I DON'T JUST MEAN THE CREATURES THAT ARE ALLOWED TO HIDE OUT THERE--SCUM FROM EVERY CORNER OF THE GALAXY-- THE PLACE ITSELF IS A SERIOUS THREAT TO US ALL!
A THREAT?
WHEN GOVERNMENT MONEY TO MAINTAIN THE HIVE DRIED UP AFTER THE GREAT ECONOMIC COLLAPSE, INTELLIGENCE SOLUTIONS STEPPED IN TO KEEP IT RUNNING. THEY'RE THE ONLY REASON ANYONE'S STILL UP HERE!
I STILL DON'T--
THE FREEZONE KEPT ITS "INDEPENDENCE"-- BUT WHAT THAT REALLY MEANS IS THAT THEY DO WHAT THEY LIKE. IT'S CHAOS.
TENTACLE TOWN IS BARELY HOLDING TOGETHER. AND THAT'S ALL OF OUR PROBLEM.
UH... I THINK WE SHOULD GET OUT OF HERE...

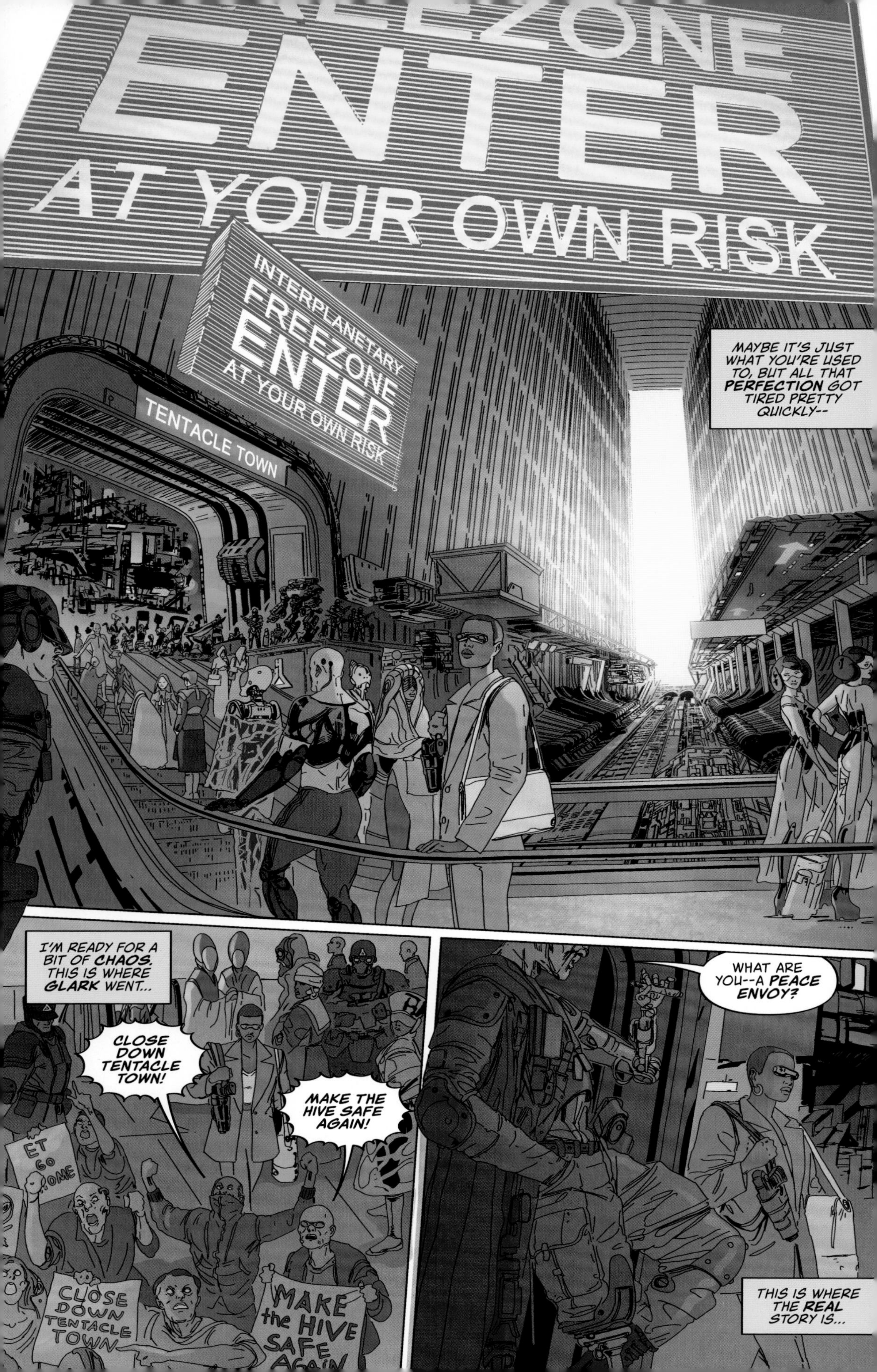

FREEZONE
ENTER
AT YOUR OWN RISK
INTERPLANETARY FREEZONE ENTER AT YOUR OWN RISK
TENTACLE TOWN
MAYBE IT'S JUST WHAT YOU'RE USED TO, BUT ALL THAT PERFECTION GOT TIRED PRETTY QUICKLY--
I'M READY FOR A BIT OF CHAOS. THIS IS WHERE GLARK WENT...
CLOSE DOWN TENTACLE TOWN!
MAKE THE HIVE SAFE AGAIN!
ET GO HOME
CLOSE DOWN TENTACLE TOWN
MAKE the HIVE SAFE AGAIN
WHAT ARE YOU--A PEACE ENVOY?
THIS IS WHERE THE REAL STORY IS...

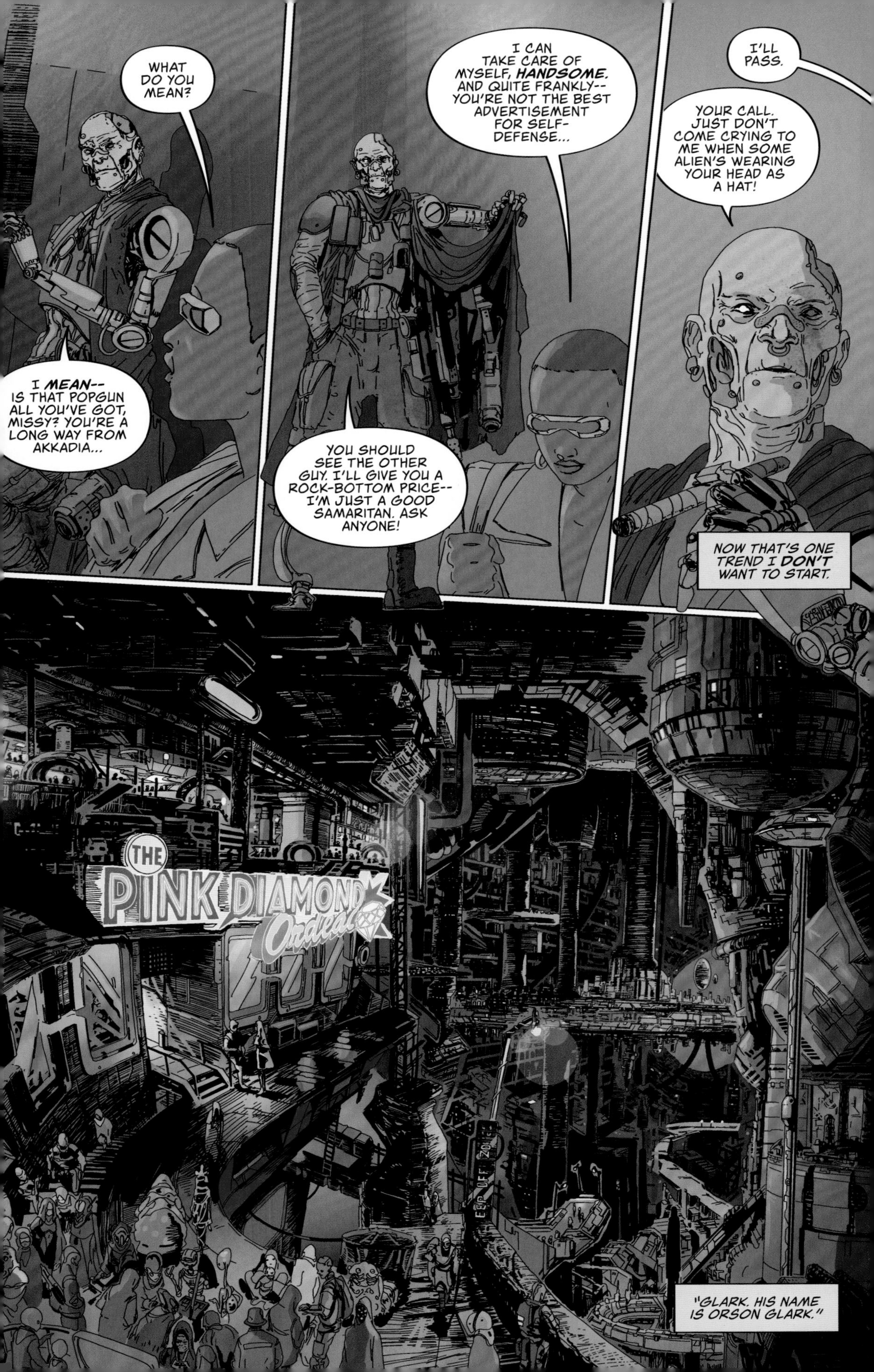
WHAT DO YOU MEAN?
I MEAN-- IS THAT POPGUN ALL YOU'VE GOT, MISSY? YOU'RE A LONG WAY FROM AKKADIA...
I CAN TAKE CARE OF MYSELF, HANDSOME. AND QUITE FRANKLY-- YOU'RE NOT THE BEST ADVERTISEMENT FOR SELF-DEFENSE...
YOU SHOULD SEE THE OTHER GUY. I'LL GIVE YOU A ROCK-BOTTOM PRICE-- I'M JUST A GOOD SAMARITAN. ASK ANYONE!
I'LL PASS.
YOUR CALL. JUST DON'T COME CRYING TO ME WHEN SOME ALIEN'S WEARING YOUR HEAD AS A HAT!
NOW THAT'S ONE TREND I DON'T WANT TO START.
THE PINK DIAMOND Ordeal
"GLARK. HIS NAME IS ORSON GLARK."

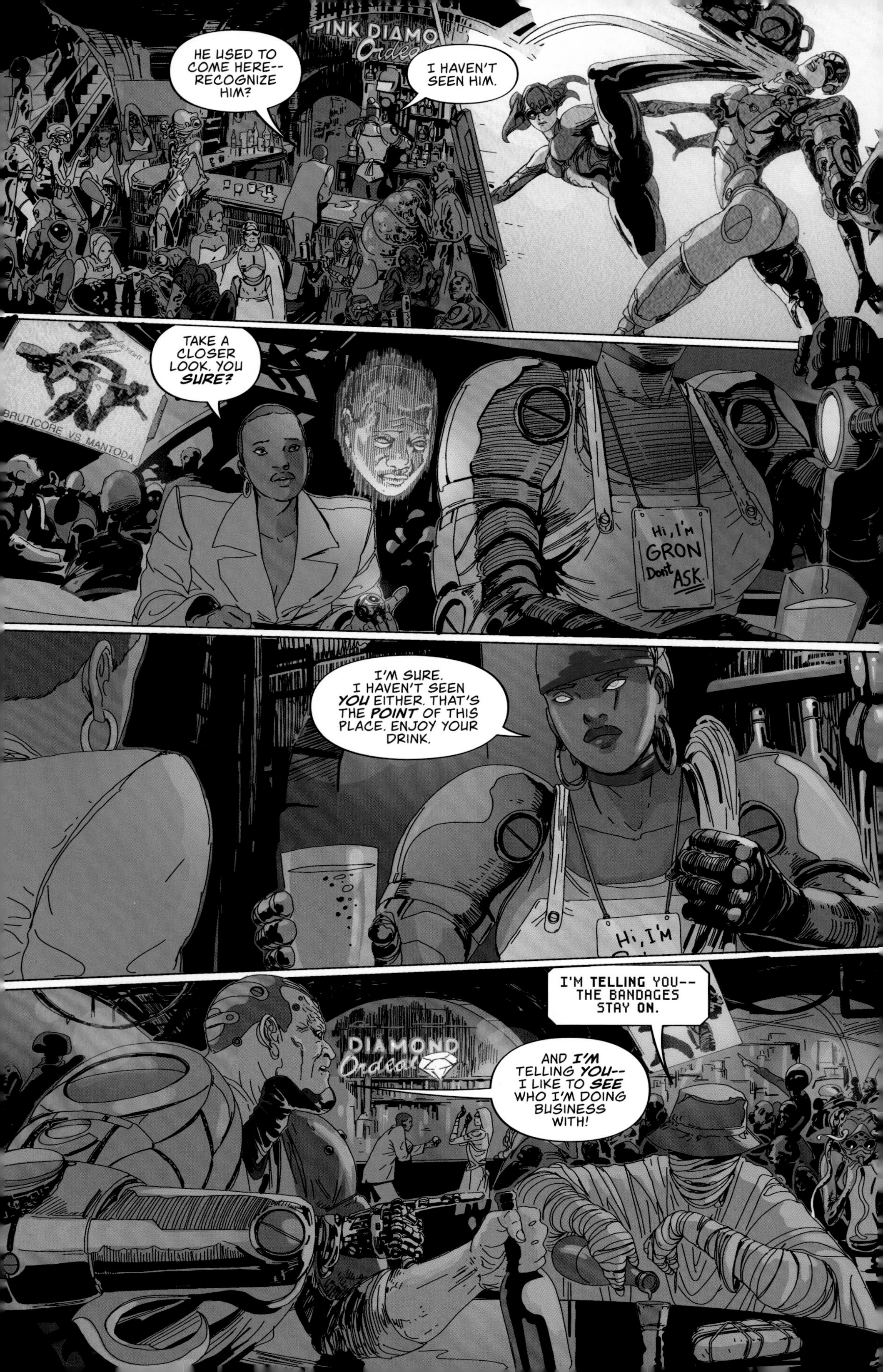
PINK DIAMO
Ordeal
HE USED TO COME HERE-- RECOGNIZE HIM?
I HAVEN'T SEEN HIM.
BRUTICORE VS MANTODA
TAKE A CLOSER LOOK. YOU SURE?
Hi, I'm GRON Don't ASK.
I'M SURE. I HAVEN'T SEEN YOU EITHER. THAT'S THE POINT OF THIS PLACE. ENJOY YOUR DRINK.
Hi, I'M
DIAMOND
Ordeal
I'M TELLING YOU-- THE BANDAGES STAY ON.
AND I'M TELLING YOU-- I LIKE TO SEE WHO I'M DOING BUSINESS WITH!

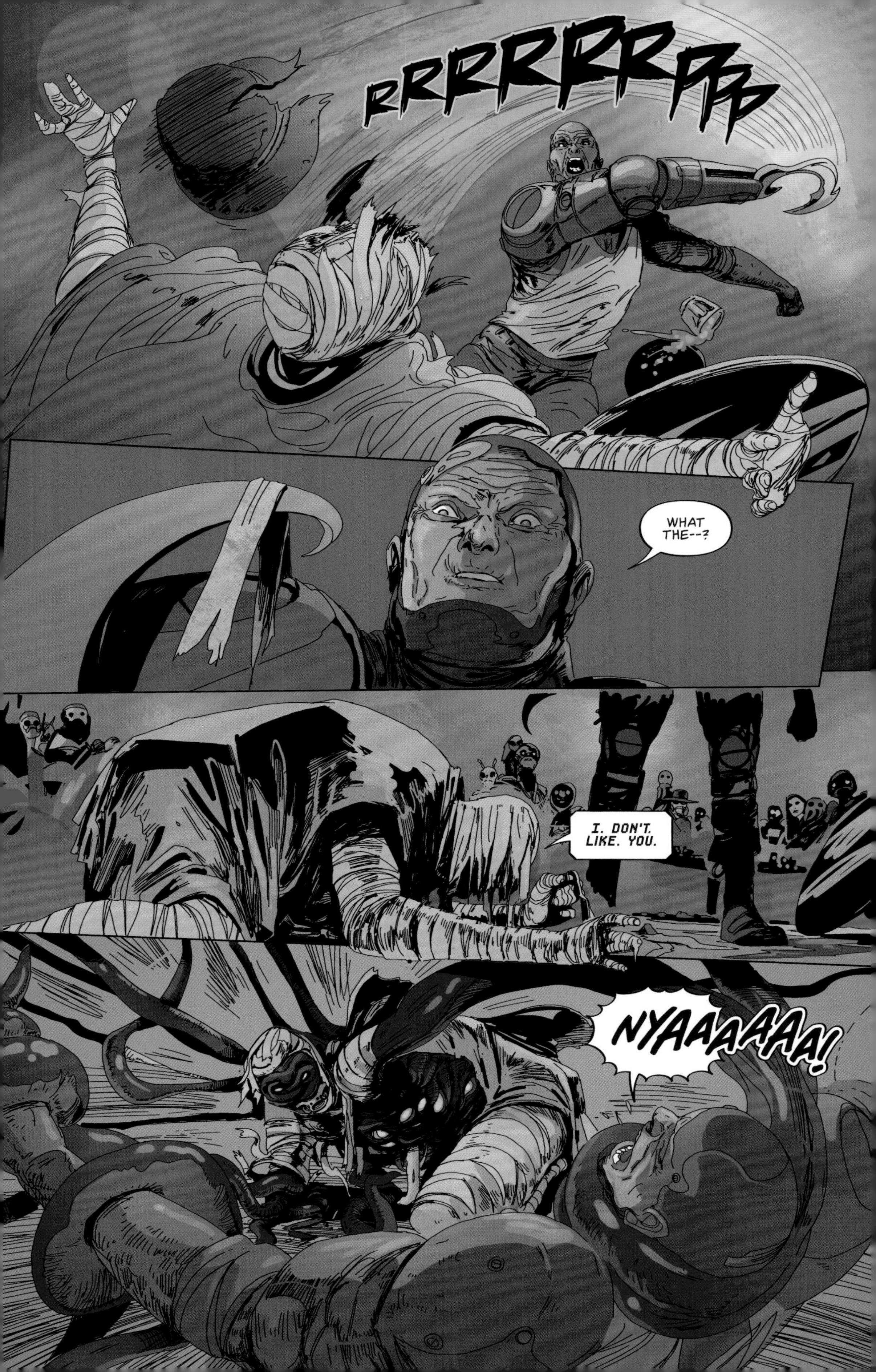
RRRRRRRPPP
WHAT THE--?
I. DON'T. LIKE. YOU.
NYAAAAAAA!

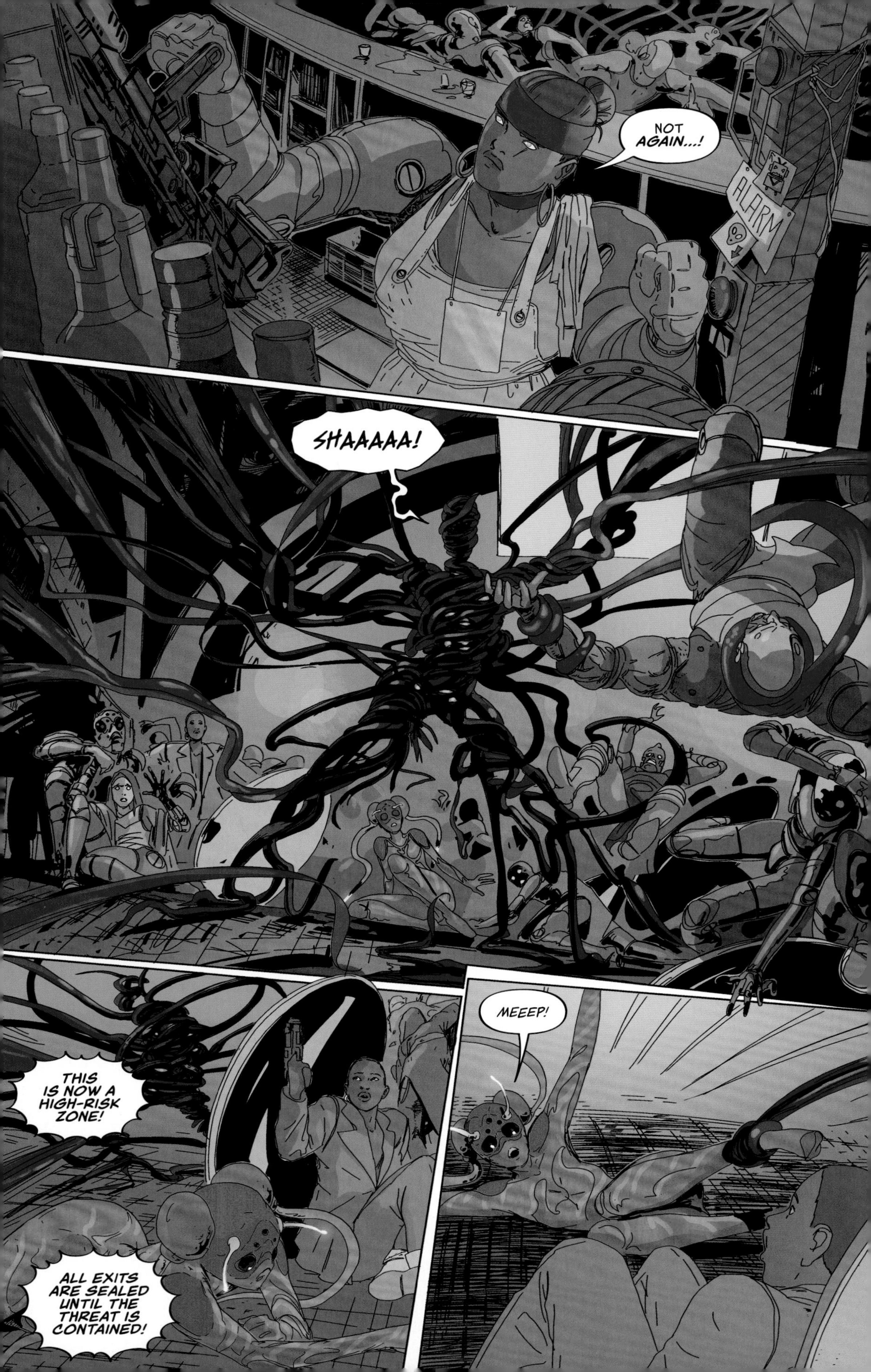
NOT AGAIN...!
SHAAAAA!
THIS IS NOW A HIGH-RISK ZONE!
ALL EXITS ARE SEALED UNTIL THE THREAT IS CONTAINED!
MEEEP!

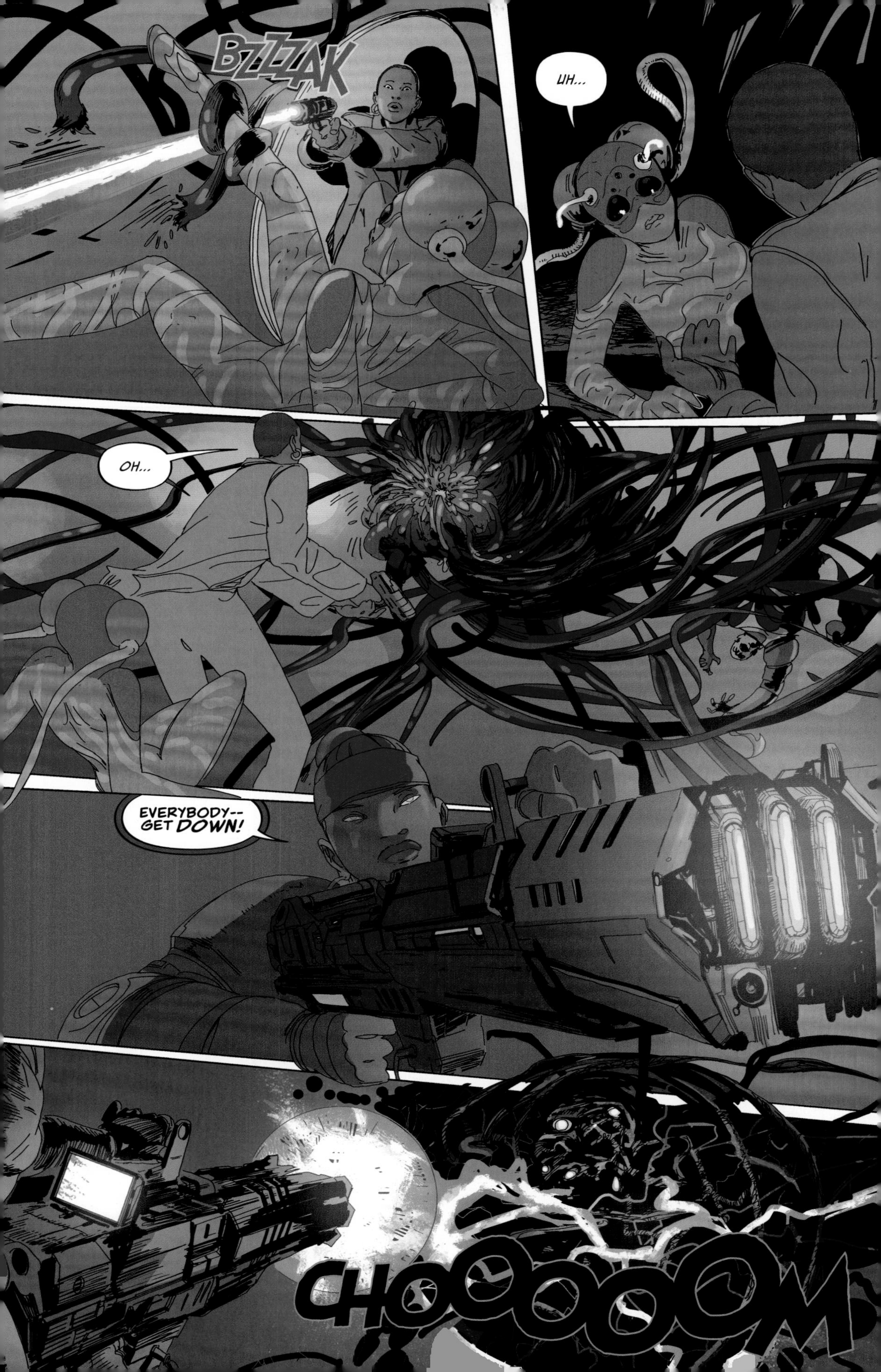
BZZZAK
UH...
OH...
EVERYBODY--
GET DOWN!
CHOOOOOOM

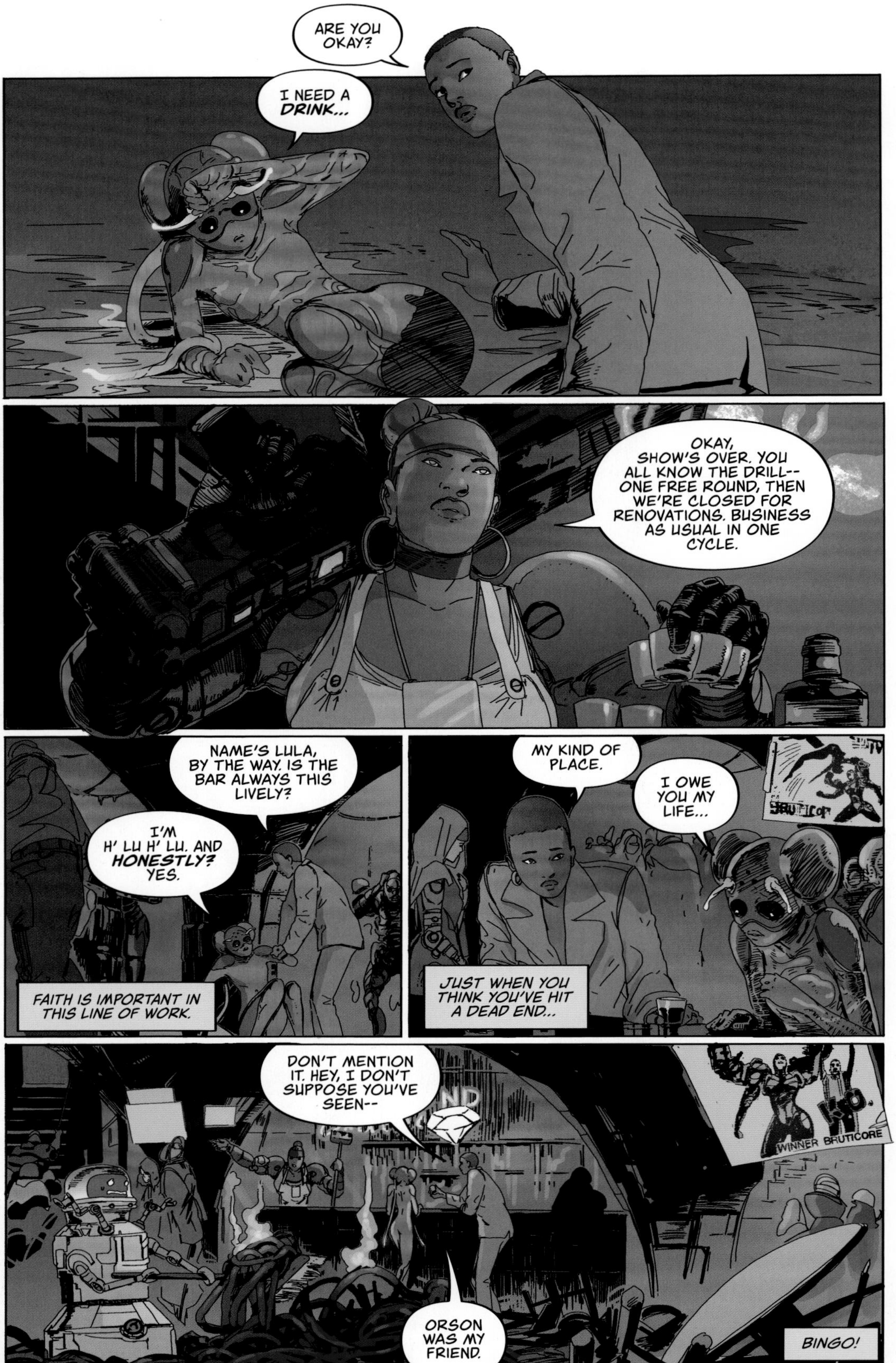

ARE YOU OKAY?
I NEED A **DRINK...**
OKAY, SHOW'S OVER. YOU ALL KNOW THE DRILL-- ONE FREE ROUND, THEN WE'RE CLOSED FOR RENOVATIONS. BUSINESS AS USUAL IN ONE CYCLE.
NAME'S LULA, BY THE WAY. IS THE BAR ALWAYS THIS LIVELY?
I'M H' LU H' LU. AND ***HONESTLY?*** YES.
FAITH IS IMPORTANT IN THIS LINE OF WORK.
MY KIND OF PLACE.
I OWE YOU MY LIFE...
JUST WHEN YOU THINK YOU'VE HIT A DEAD END...
DON'T MENTION IT. HEY, I DON'T SUPPOSE YOU'VE SEEN--
WINNER BRUTICORE
ORSON WAS MY FRIEND.
BINGO!

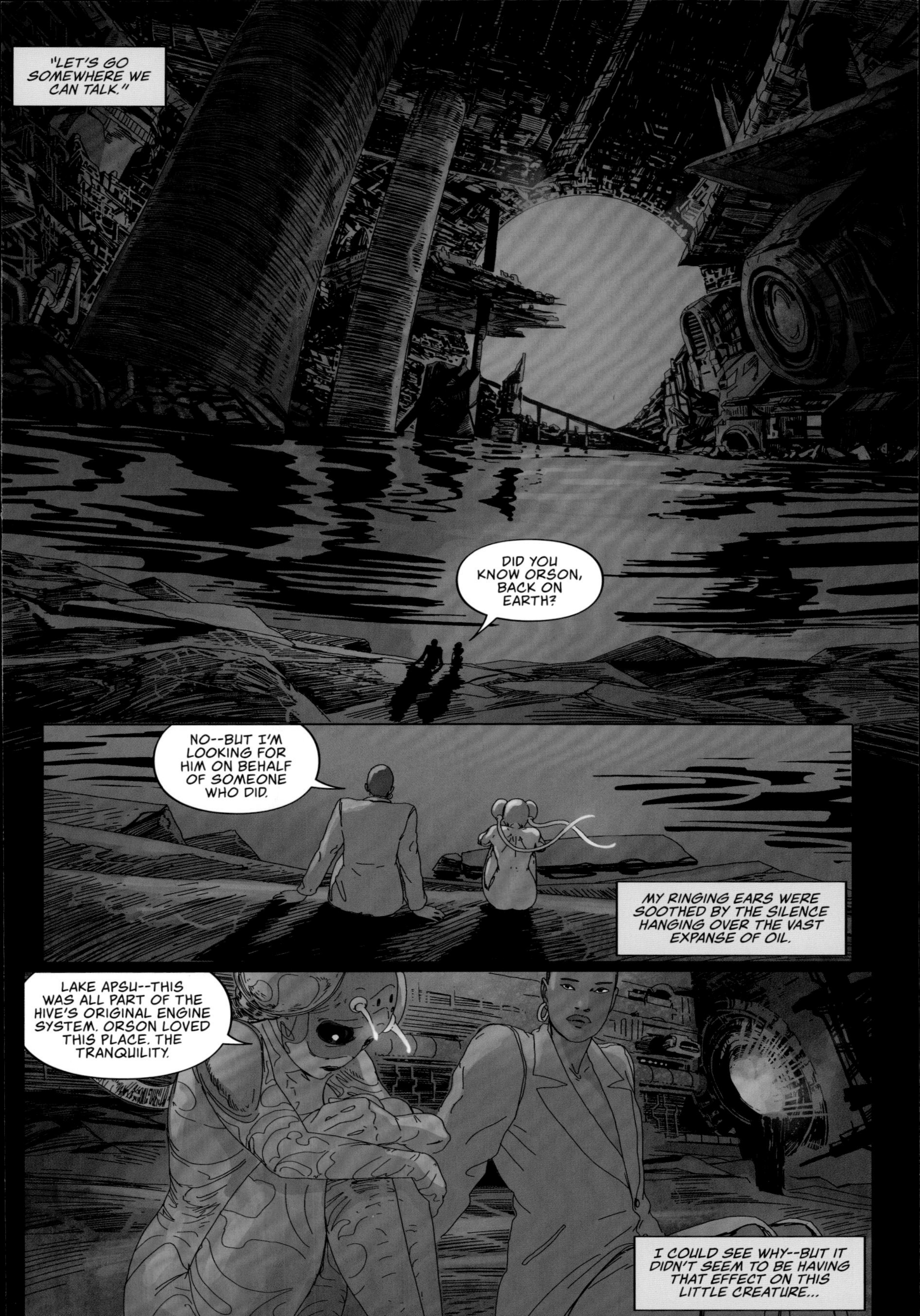
"LET'S GO SOMEWHERE WE CAN TALK."
DID YOU KNOW ORSON, BACK ON EARTH?
NO--BUT I'M LOOKING FOR HIM ON BEHALF OF SOMEONE WHO DID.
MY RINGING EARS WERE SOOTHED BY THE SILENCE HANGING OVER THE VAST EXPANSE OF OIL.
LAKE APSU--THIS WAS ALL PART OF THE HIVE'S ORIGINAL ENGINE SYSTEM. ORSON LOVED THIS PLACE. THE TRANQUILITY.
I COULD SEE WHY--BUT IT DIDN'T SEEM TO BE HAVING THAT EFFECT ON THIS LITTLE CREATURE...

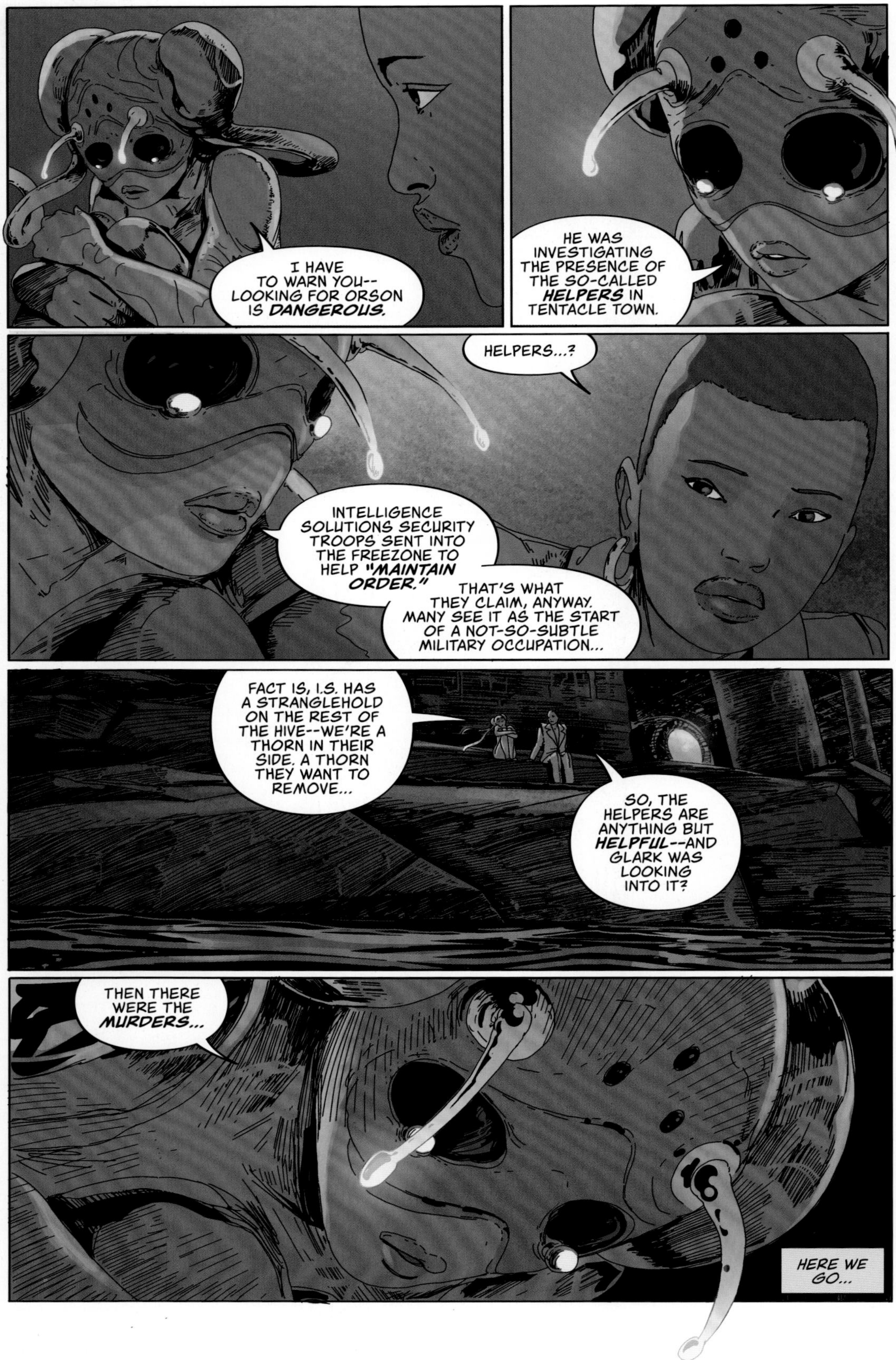
I HAVE TO WARN YOU-- LOOKING FOR ORSON IS **DANGEROUS.**
HE WAS INVESTIGATING THE PRESENCE OF THE SO-CALLED **HELPERS** IN TENTACLE TOWN.
HELPERS...?
INTELLIGENCE SOLUTIONS SECURITY TROOPS SENT INTO THE FREEZONE TO HELP **"MAINTAIN ORDER."**
THAT'S WHAT THEY CLAIM, ANYWAY. MANY SEE IT AS THE START OF A NOT-SO-SUBTLE MILITARY OCCUPATION...
FACT IS, I.S. HAS A STRANGLEHOLD ON THE REST OF THE HIVE--WE'RE A THORN IN THEIR SIDE. A THORN THEY WANT TO REMOVE...
SO, THE HELPERS ARE ANYTHING BUT **HELPFUL**--AND GLARK WAS LOOKING INTO IT?
THEN THERE WERE THE **MURDERS...**
HERE WE GO...

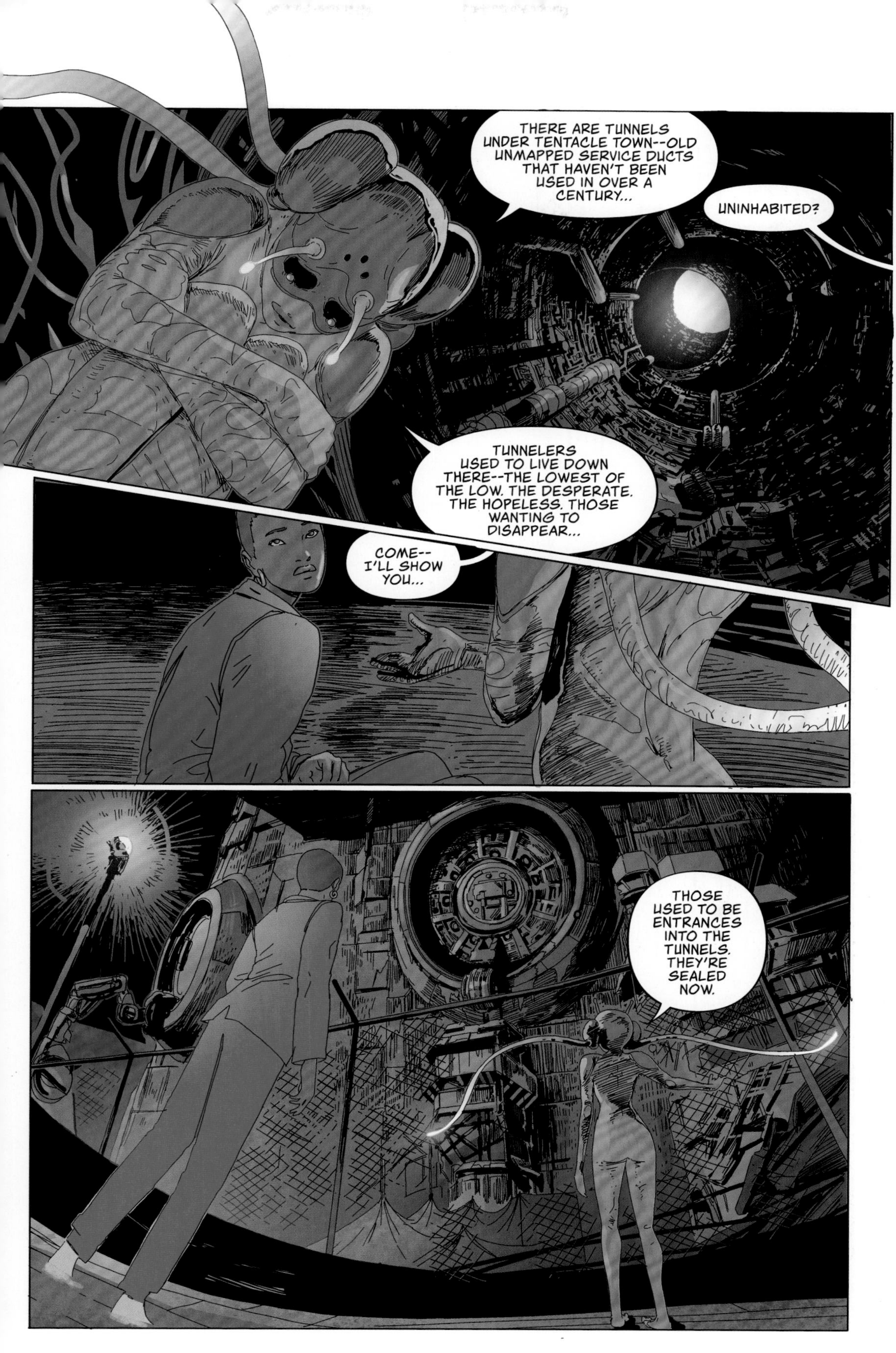
THERE ARE TUNNELS UNDER TENTACLE TOWN--OLD UNMAPPED SERVICE DUCTS THAT HAVEN'T BEEN USED IN OVER A CENTURY...
UNINHABITED?
TUNNELERS USED TO LIVE DOWN THERE--THE LOWEST OF THE LOW. THE DESPERATE. THE HOPELESS. THOSE WANTING TO DISAPPEAR...
COME-- I'LL SHOW YOU...
THOSE USED TO BE ENTRANCES INTO THE TUNNELS. THEY'RE SEALED NOW.

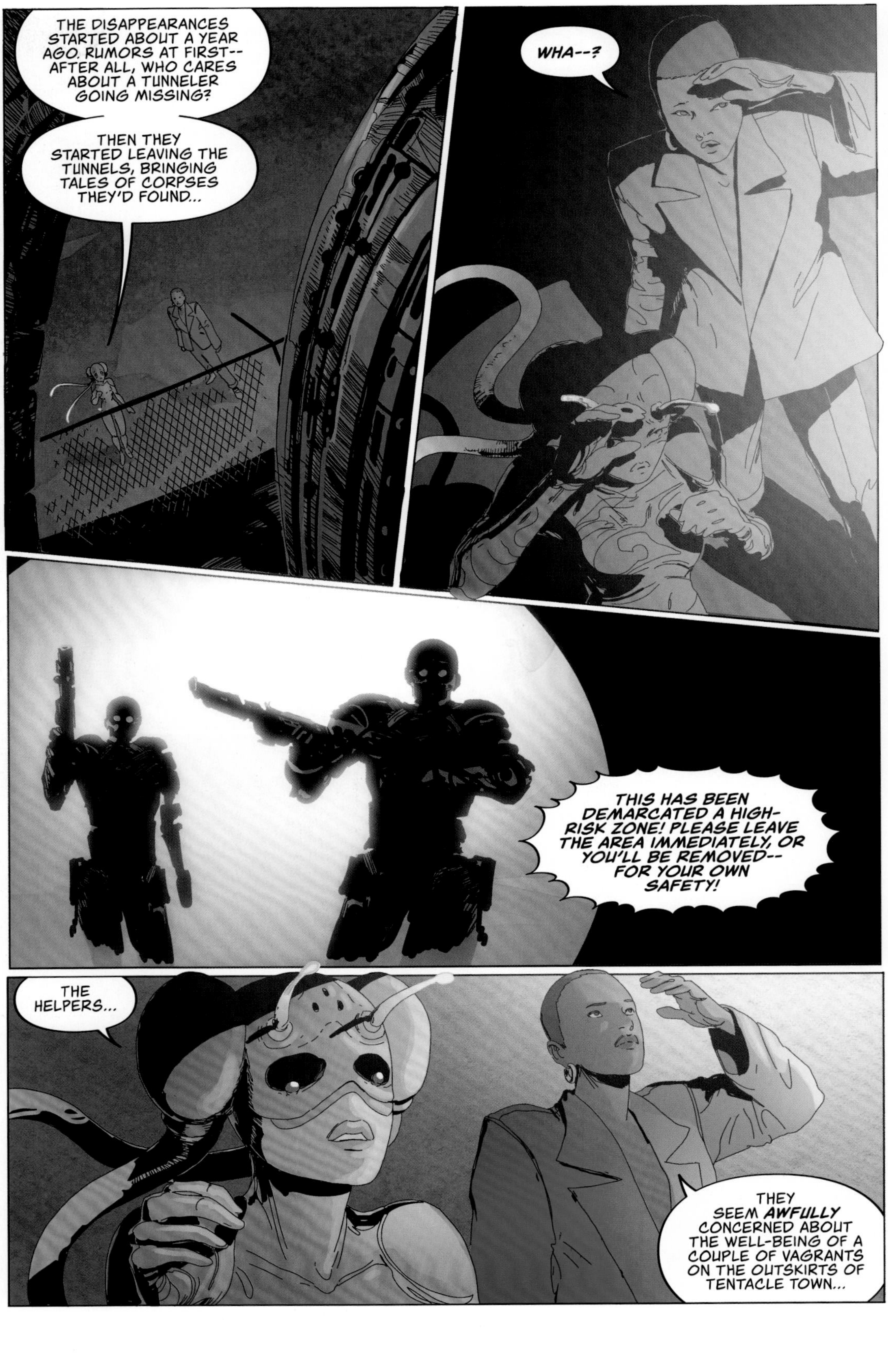
THE DISAPPEARANCES STARTED ABOUT A YEAR AGO. RUMORS AT FIRST-- AFTER ALL, WHO CARES ABOUT A TUNNELER GOING MISSING?
THEN THEY STARTED LEAVING THE TUNNELS, BRINGING TALES OF CORPSES THEY'D FOUND...
WHA--?
THIS HAS BEEN DEMARCATED A HIGH-RISK ZONE! PLEASE LEAVE THE AREA IMMEDIATELY, OR YOU'LL BE REMOVED-- FOR YOUR OWN SAFETY!
THE HELPERS...
THEY SEEM AWFULLY CONCERNED ABOUT THE WELL-BEING OF A COUPLE OF VAGRANTS ON THE OUTSKIRTS OF TENTACLE TOWN...

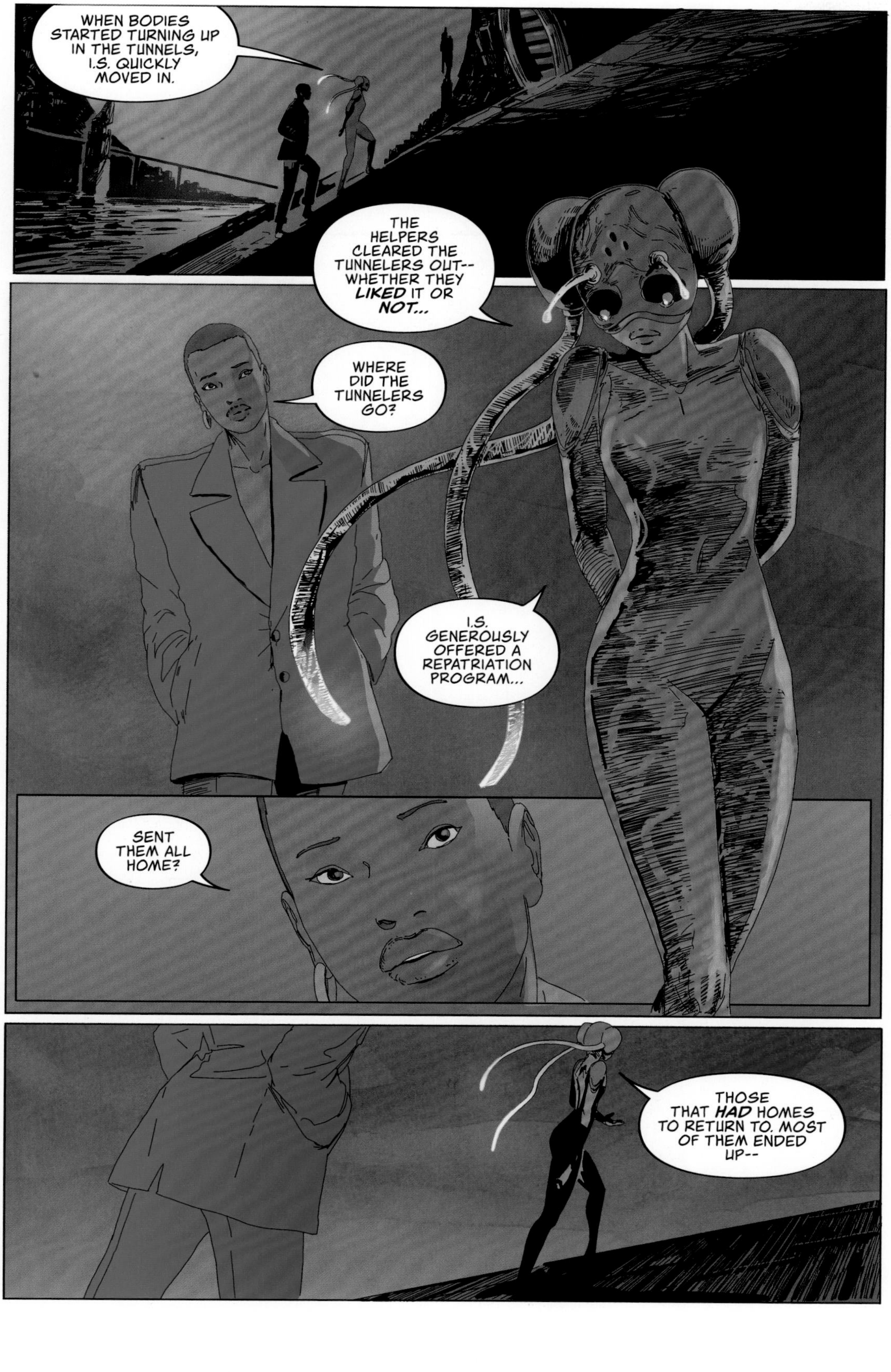
WHEN BODIES STARTED TURNING UP IN THE TUNNELS, I.S. QUICKLY MOVED IN.
THE HELPERS CLEARED THE TUNNELERS OUT-- WHETHER THEY **LIKED** IT OR **NOT...**
WHERE DID THE TUNNELERS GO?
I.S. GENEROUSLY OFFERED A REPATRIATION PROGRAM...
SENT THEM ALL HOME?
THOSE THAT **HAD** HOMES TO RETURN TO. MOST OF THEM ENDED UP--

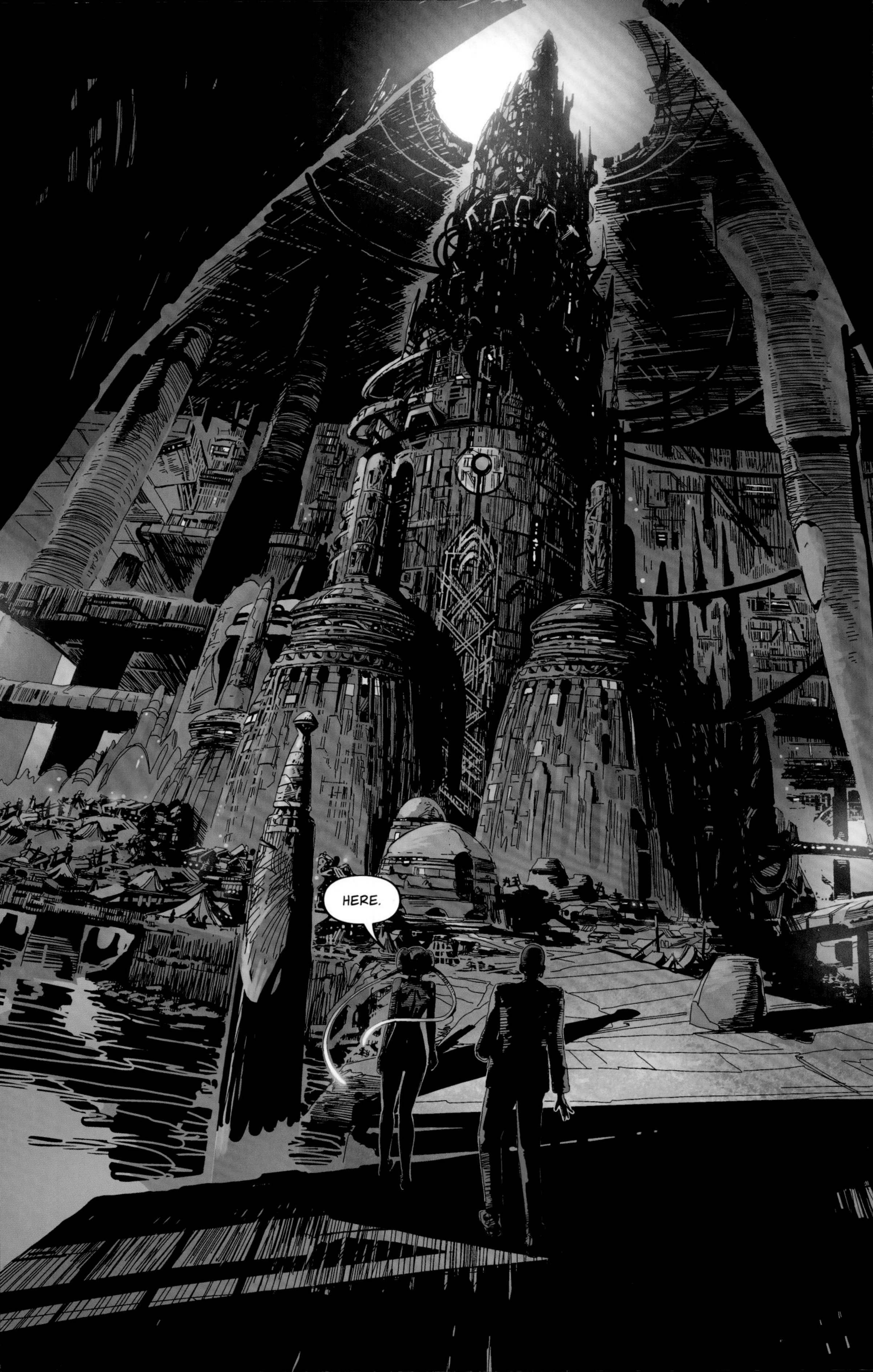
HERE.

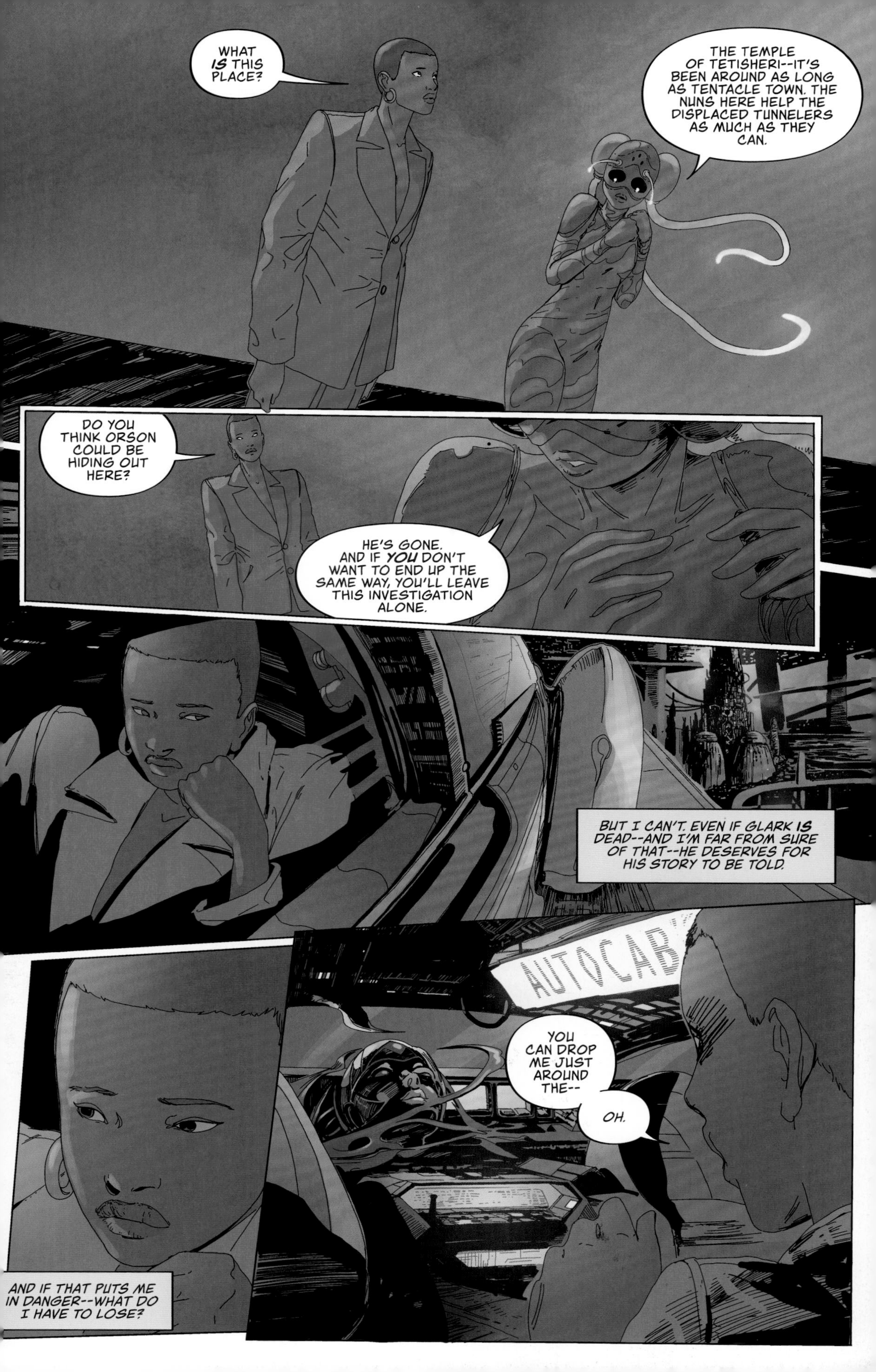
WHAT IS THIS PLACE?
THE TEMPLE OF TETISHERI--IT'S BEEN AROUND AS LONG AS TENTACLE TOWN. THE NUNS HERE HELP THE DISPLACED TUNNELERS AS MUCH AS THEY CAN.
DO YOU THINK ORSON COULD BE HIDING OUT HERE?
HE'S GONE. AND IF YOU DON'T WANT TO END UP THE SAME WAY, YOU'LL LEAVE THIS INVESTIGATION ALONE.
BUT I CAN'T. EVEN IF GLARK IS DEAD--AND I'M FAR FROM SURE OF THAT--HE DESERVES FOR HIS STORY TO BE TOLD.
AUTOCAB
YOU CAN DROP ME JUST AROUND THE--
OH.
AND IF THAT PUTS ME IN DANGER--WHAT DO I HAVE TO LOSE?

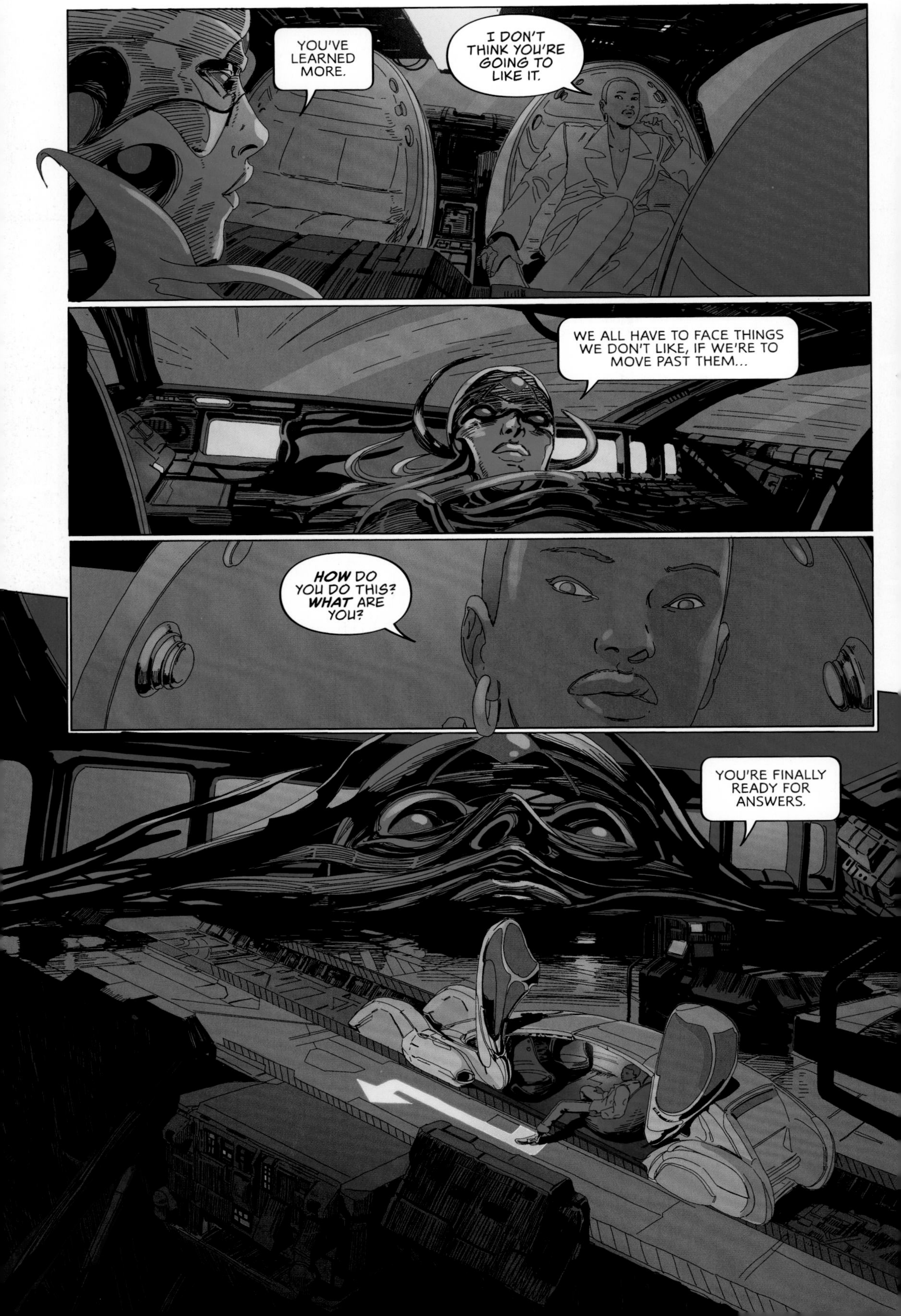
YOU'VE LEARNED MORE.
I DON'T THINK YOU'RE GOING TO LIKE IT.
WE ALL HAVE TO FACE THINGS WE DON'T LIKE, IF WE'RE TO MOVE PAST THEM...
HOW DO YOU DO THIS? WHAT ARE YOU?
YOU'RE FINALLY READY FOR ANSWERS.

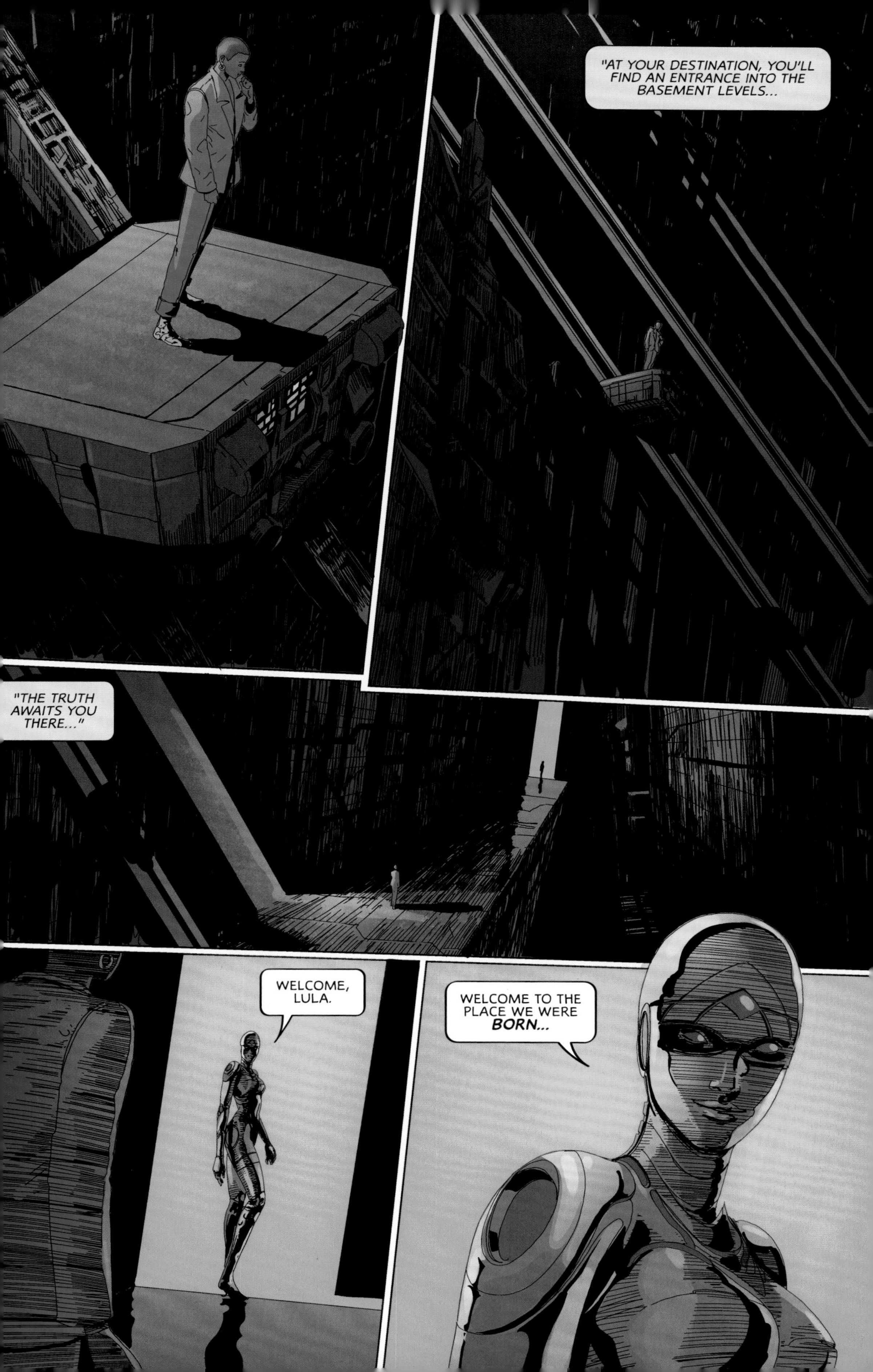
"AT YOUR DESTINATION, YOU'LL FIND AN ENTRANCE INTO THE BASEMENT LEVELS...
"THE TRUTH AWAITS YOU THERE..."
WELCOME, LULA.
WELCOME TO THE PLACE WE WERE BORN...

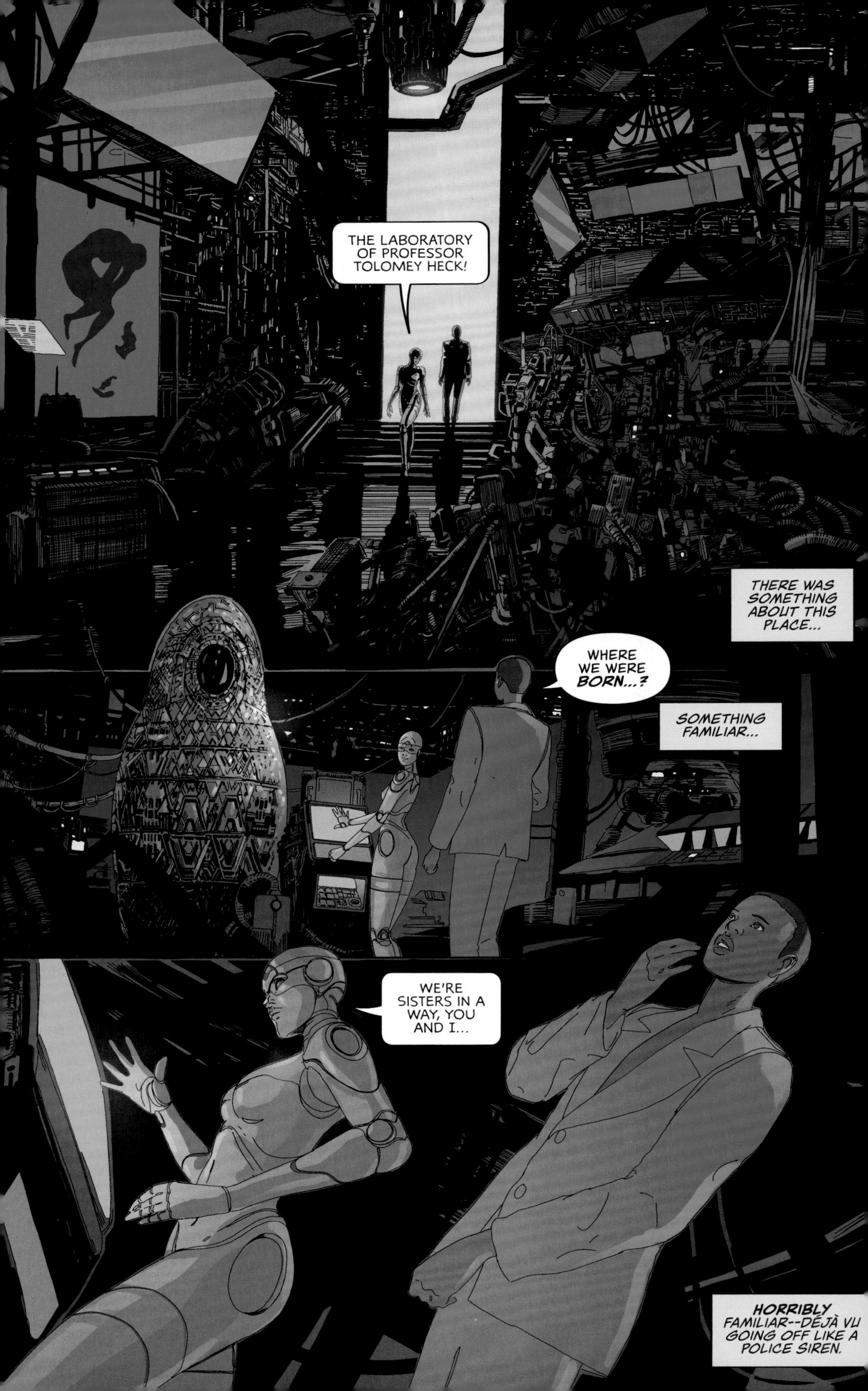
THE LABORATORY OF PROFESSOR TOLOMEY HECK!
THERE WAS SOMETHING ABOUT THIS PLACE...
WHERE WE WERE BORN...?
SOMETHING FAMILIAR...
WE'RE SISTERS IN A WAY, YOU AND I...
HORRIBLY FAMILIAR--DÉJÀ VU GOING OFF LIKE A POLICE SIREN.

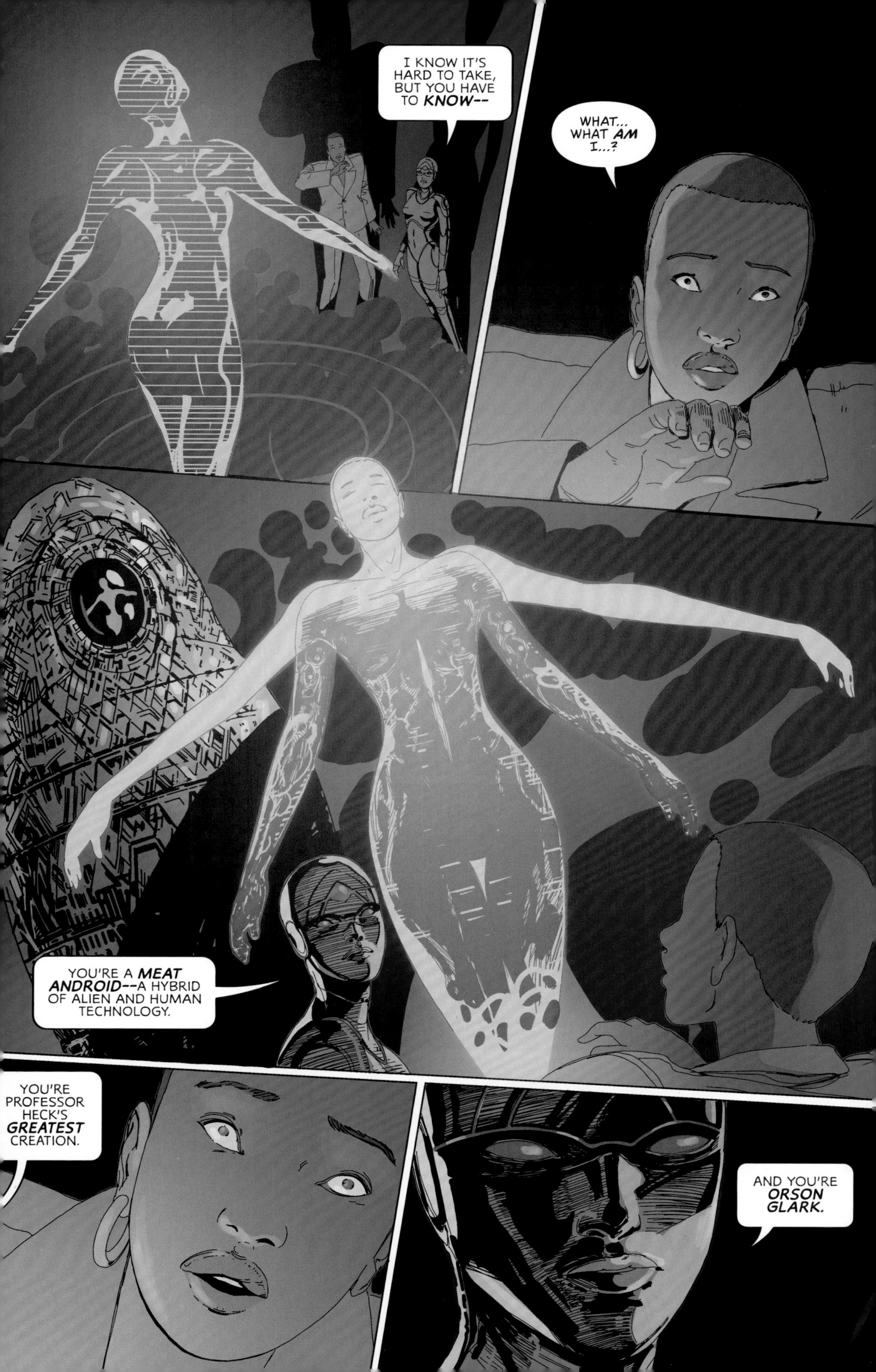
I KNOW IT'S HARD TO TAKE, BUT YOU HAVE TO KNOW--
WHAT... WHAT AM I...?
YOU'RE A MEAT ANDROID--A HYBRID OF ALIEN AND HUMAN TECHNOLOGY.
YOU'RE PROFESSOR HECK'S GREATEST CREATION.
AND YOU'RE ORSON GLARK.

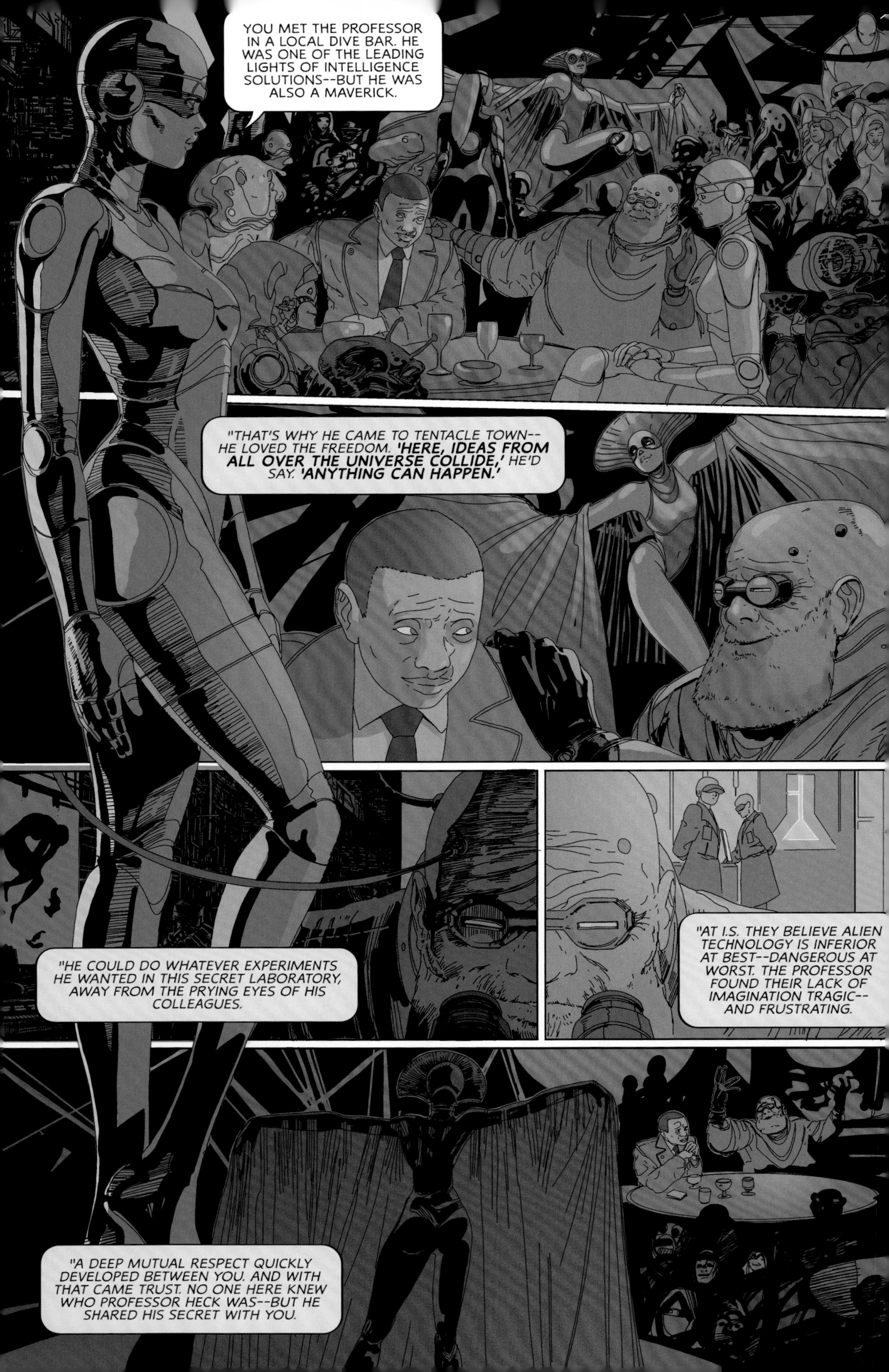
YOU MET THE PROFESSOR IN A LOCAL DIVE BAR. HE WAS ONE OF THE LEADING LIGHTS OF INTELLIGENCE SOLUTIONS--BUT HE WAS ALSO A MAVERICK.
"THAT'S WHY HE CAME TO TENTACLE TOWN--HE LOVED THE FREEDOM. 'HERE, IDEAS FROM ALL OVER THE UNIVERSE COLLIDE,' HE'D SAY. 'ANYTHING CAN HAPPEN.'
"HE COULD DO WHATEVER EXPERIMENTS HE WANTED IN THIS SECRET LABORATORY, AWAY FROM THE PRYING EYES OF HIS COLLEAGUES.
"AT I.S. THEY BELIEVE ALIEN TECHNOLOGY IS INFERIOR AT BEST--DANGEROUS AT WORST. THE PROFESSOR FOUND THEIR LACK OF IMAGINATION TRAGIC--AND FRUSTRATING.
"A DEEP MUTUAL RESPECT QUICKLY DEVELOPED BETWEEN YOU. AND WITH THAT CAME TRUST. NO ONE HERE KNEW WHO PROFESSOR HECK WAS--BUT HE SHARED HIS SECRET WITH YOU.

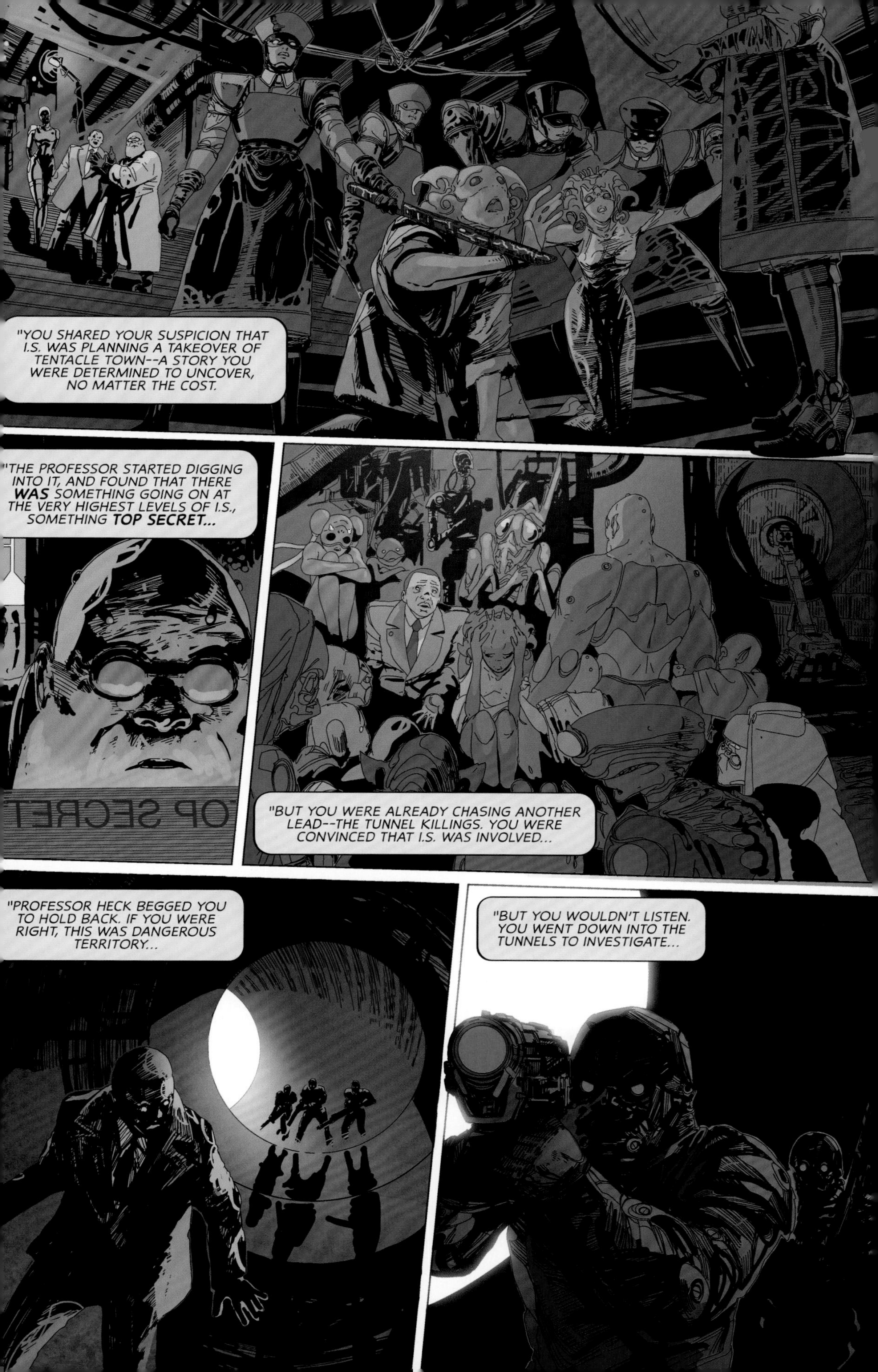
"YOU SHARED YOUR SUSPICION THAT I.S. WAS PLANNING A TAKEOVER OF TENTACLE TOWN--A STORY YOU WERE DETERMINED TO UNCOVER, NO MATTER THE COST.
"THE PROFESSOR STARTED DIGGING INTO IT, AND FOUND THAT THERE WAS SOMETHING GOING ON AT THE VERY HIGHEST LEVELS OF I.S., SOMETHING TOP SECRET...
OP SECRET
"BUT YOU WERE ALREADY CHASING ANOTHER LEAD--THE TUNNEL KILLINGS. YOU WERE CONVINCED THAT I.S. WAS INVOLVED...
"PROFESSOR HECK BEGGED YOU TO HOLD BACK. IF YOU WERE RIGHT, THIS WAS DANGEROUS TERRITORY...
"BUT YOU WOULDN'T LISTEN. YOU WENT DOWN INTO THE TUNNELS TO INVESTIGATE...

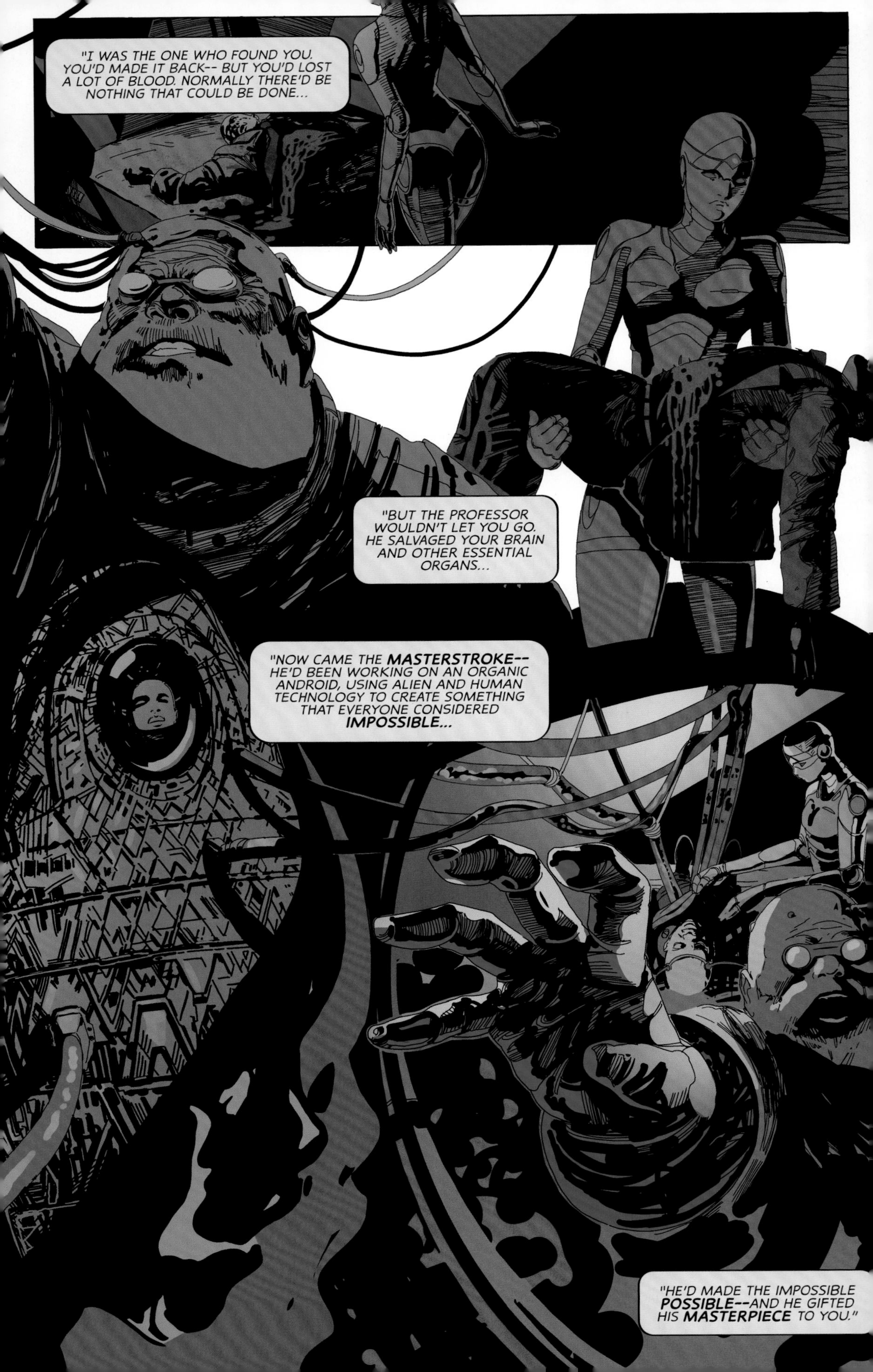
"I WAS THE ONE WHO FOUND YOU. YOU'D MADE IT BACK-- BUT YOU'D LOST A LOT OF BLOOD. NORMALLY THERE'D BE NOTHING THAT COULD BE DONE...
"BUT THE PROFESSOR WOULDN'T LET YOU GO. HE SALVAGED YOUR BRAIN AND OTHER ESSENTIAL ORGANS...
"NOW CAME THE **MASTERSTROKE**-- HE'D BEEN WORKING ON AN ORGANIC ANDROID, USING ALIEN AND HUMAN TECHNOLOGY TO CREATE SOMETHING THAT EVERYONE CONSIDERED **IMPOSSIBLE...**
"HE'D MADE THE IMPOSSIBLE **POSSIBLE**--AND HE GIFTED HIS **MASTERPIECE** TO YOU."

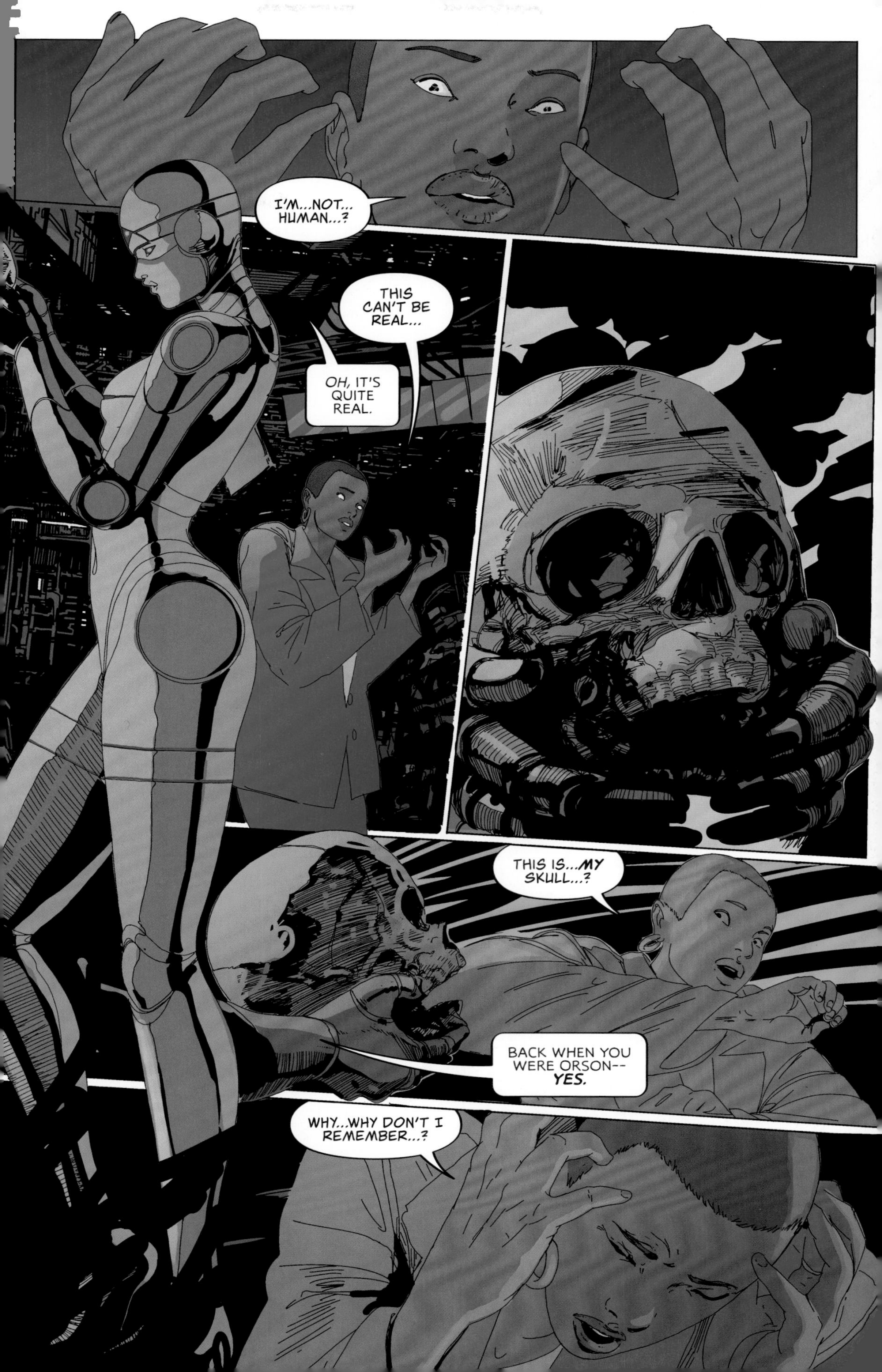
I'M...NOT... HUMAN...?
THIS CAN'T BE REAL...
OH, IT'S QUITE REAL.
THIS IS...MY SKULL...?
BACK WHEN YOU WERE ORSON-- YES.
WHY...WHY DON'T I REMEMBER...?

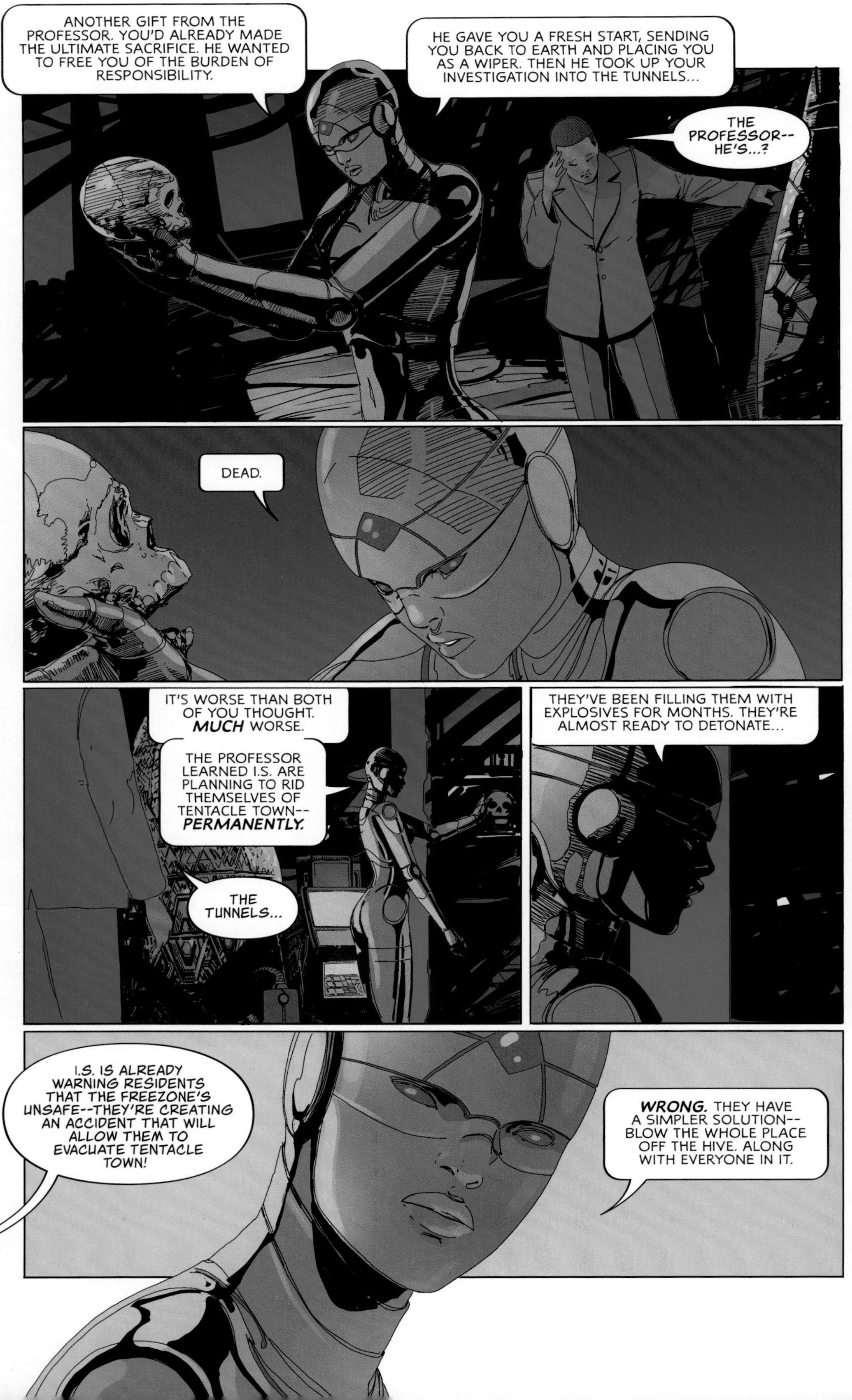
ANOTHER GIFT FROM THE PROFESSOR. YOU'D ALREADY MADE THE ULTIMATE SACRIFICE. HE WANTED TO FREE YOU OF THE BURDEN OF RESPONSIBILITY.
HE GAVE YOU A FRESH START, SENDING YOU BACK TO EARTH AND PLACING YOU AS A WIPER. THEN HE TOOK UP YOUR INVESTIGATION INTO THE TUNNELS...
THE PROFESSOR-- HE'S...?
DEAD.
IT'S WORSE THAN BOTH OF YOU THOUGHT. **MUCH** WORSE.
THE PROFESSOR LEARNED I.S. ARE PLANNING TO RID THEMSELVES OF TENTACLE TOWN-- ***PERMANENTLY.***
THE TUNNELS...
THEY'VE BEEN FILLING THEM WITH EXPLOSIVES FOR MONTHS. THEY'RE ALMOST READY TO DETONATE...
I.S. IS ALREADY WARNING RESIDENTS THAT THE FREEZONE'S UNSAFE--THEY'RE CREATING AN ACCIDENT THAT WILL ALLOW THEM TO EVACUATE TENTACLE TOWN!
WRONG. THEY HAVE A SIMPLER SOLUTION-- BLOW THE WHOLE PLACE OFF THE HIVE. ALONG WITH EVERYONE IN IT.

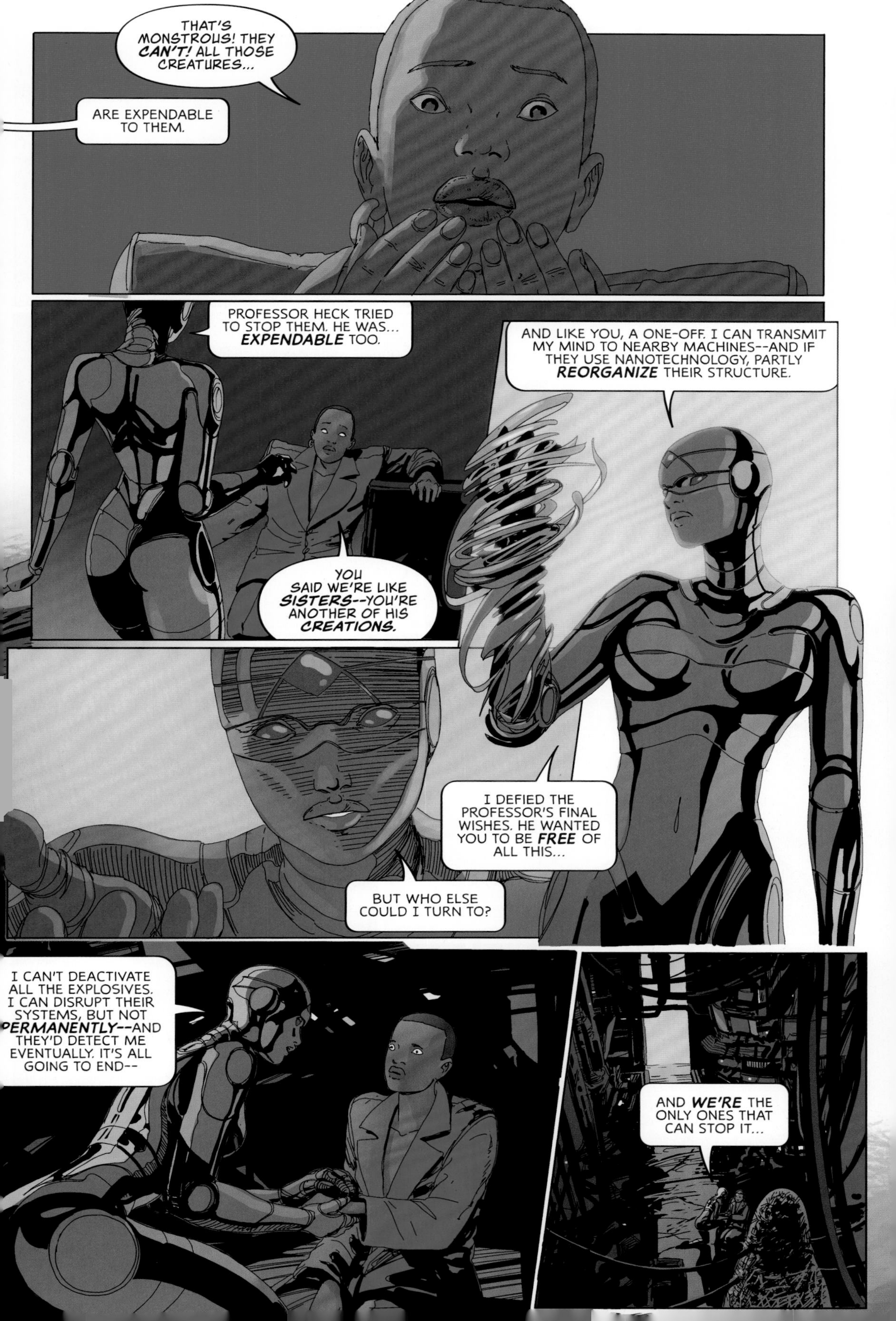
THAT'S MONSTROUS! THEY CAN'T! ALL THOSE CREATURES...
ARE EXPENDABLE TO THEM.
PROFESSOR HECK TRIED TO STOP THEM. HE WAS... EXPENDABLE TOO.
YOU SAID WE'RE LIKE SISTERS--YOU'RE ANOTHER OF HIS CREATIONS.
AND LIKE YOU, A ONE-OFF. I CAN TRANSMIT MY MIND TO NEARBY MACHINES--AND IF THEY USE NANOTECHNOLOGY, PARTLY REORGANIZE THEIR STRUCTURE.
I DEFIED THE PROFESSOR'S FINAL WISHES. HE WANTED YOU TO BE FREE OF ALL THIS...
BUT WHO ELSE COULD I TURN TO?
I CAN'T DEACTIVATE ALL THE EXPLOSIVES. I CAN DISRUPT THEIR SYSTEMS, BUT NOT PERMANENTLY--AND THEY'D DETECT ME EVENTUALLY. IT'S ALL GOING TO END--
AND WE'RE THE ONLY ONES THAT CAN STOP IT...

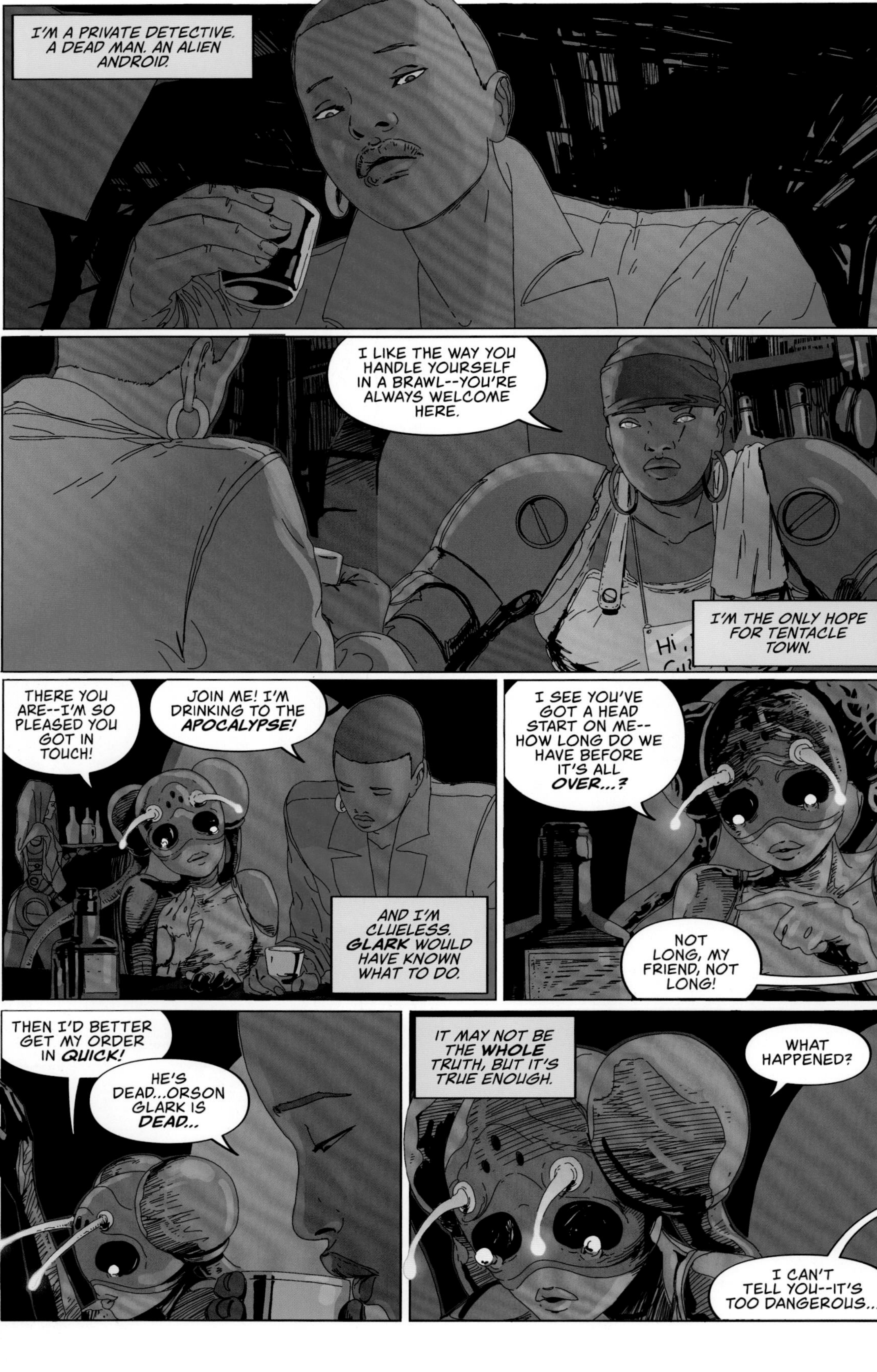
I'M A PRIVATE DETECTIVE. A DEAD MAN. AN ALIEN ANDROID.
I LIKE THE WAY YOU HANDLE YOURSELF IN A BRAWL--YOU'RE ALWAYS WELCOME HERE.
I'M THE ONLY HOPE FOR TENTACLE TOWN.
THERE YOU ARE--I'M SO PLEASED YOU GOT IN TOUCH!
JOIN ME! I'M DRINKING TO THE APOCALYPSE!
AND I'M CLUELESS. GLARK WOULD HAVE KNOWN WHAT TO DO.
I SEE YOU'VE GOT A HEAD START ON ME--HOW LONG DO WE HAVE BEFORE IT'S ALL OVER...?
NOT LONG, MY FRIEND, NOT LONG!
THEN I'D BETTER GET MY ORDER IN QUICK!
HE'S DEAD...ORSON GLARK IS DEAD...
IT MAY NOT BE THE WHOLE TRUTH, BUT IT'S TRUE ENOUGH.
WHAT HAPPENED?
I CAN'T TELL YOU--IT'S TOO DANGEROUS...

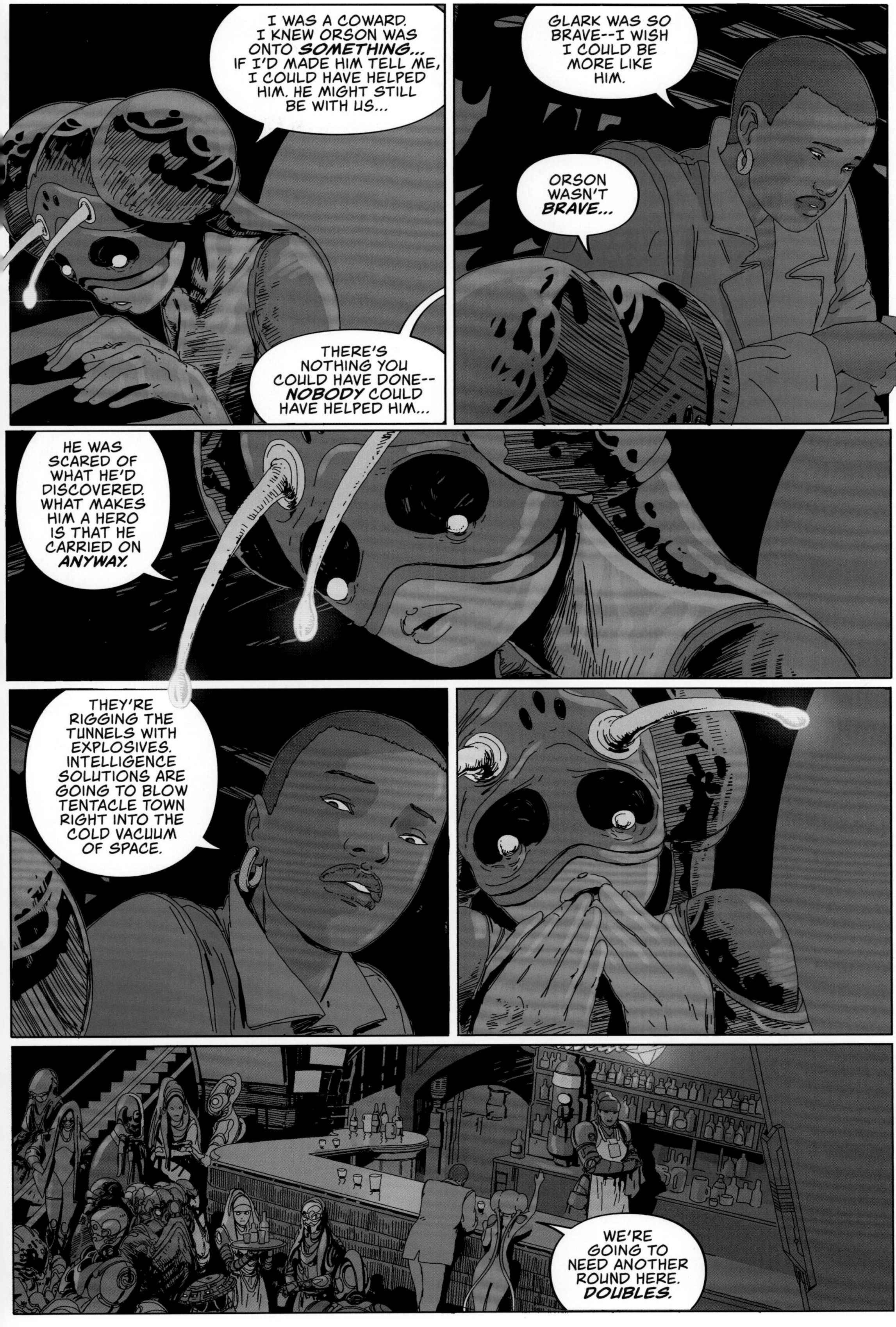
I WAS A COWARD. I KNEW ORSON WAS ONTO **SOMETHING...** IF I'D MADE HIM TELL ME, I COULD HAVE HELPED HIM. HE MIGHT STILL BE WITH US...
GLARK WAS SO BRAVE--I WISH I COULD BE MORE LIKE HIM.
ORSON WASN'T **BRAVE...**
THERE'S NOTHING YOU COULD HAVE DONE-- **NOBODY** COULD HAVE HELPED HIM...
HE WAS SCARED OF WHAT HE'D DISCOVERED. WHAT MAKES HIM A HERO IS THAT HE CARRIED ON **ANYWAY.**
THEY'RE RIGGING THE TUNNELS WITH EXPLOSIVES. INTELLIGENCE SOLUTIONS ARE GOING TO BLOW TENTACLE TOWN RIGHT INTO THE COLD VACUUM OF SPACE.
WE'RE GOING TO NEED ANOTHER ROUND HERE. **DOUBLES.**

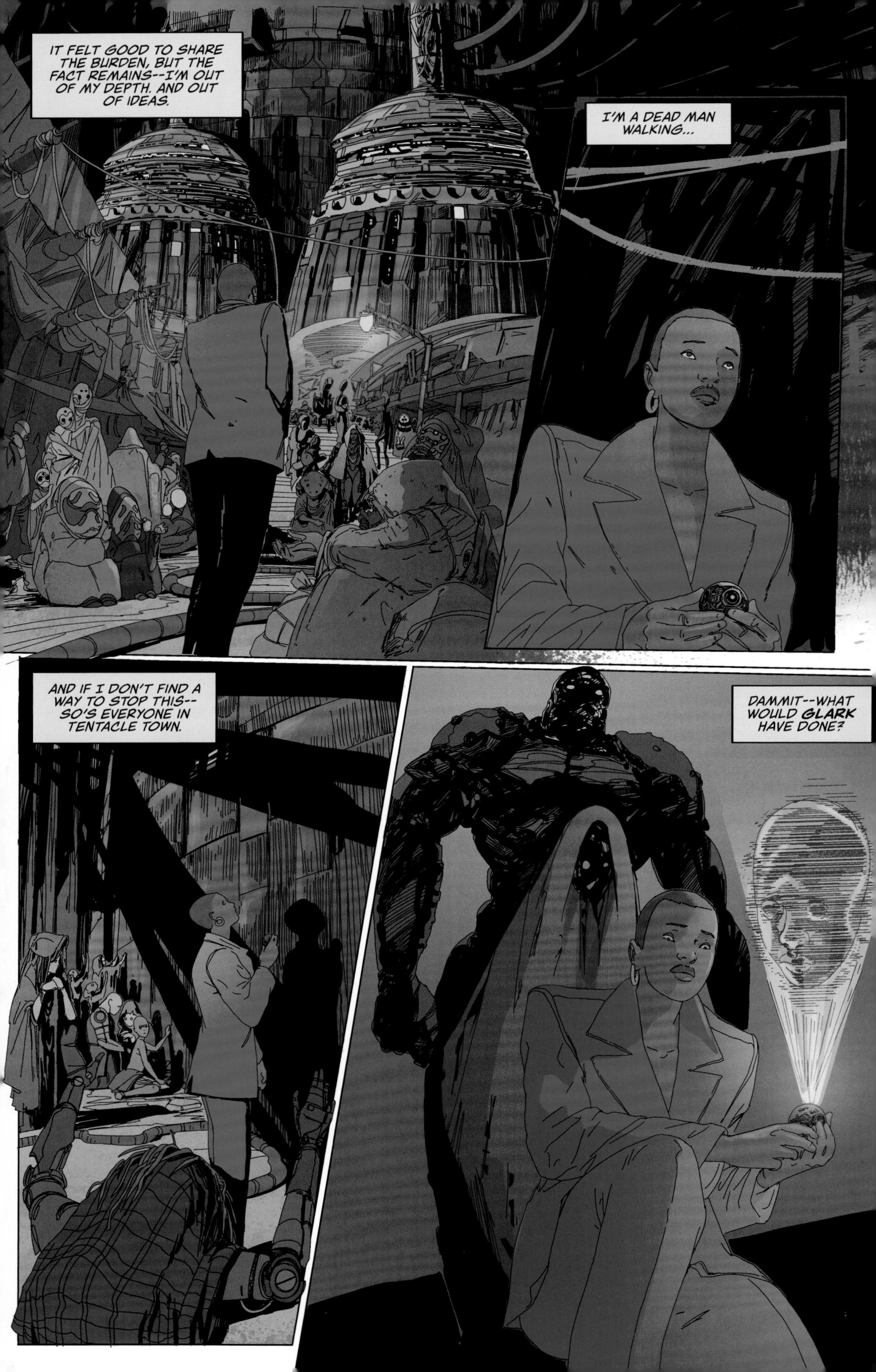
IT FELT GOOD TO SHARE THE BURDEN, BUT THE FACT REMAINS--I'M OUT OF MY DEPTH. AND OUT OF IDEAS.
I'M A DEAD MAN WALKING...
AND IF I DON'T FIND A WAY TO STOP THIS--SO'S EVERYONE IN TENTACLE TOWN.
DAMMIT--WHAT WOULD GLARK HAVE DONE?

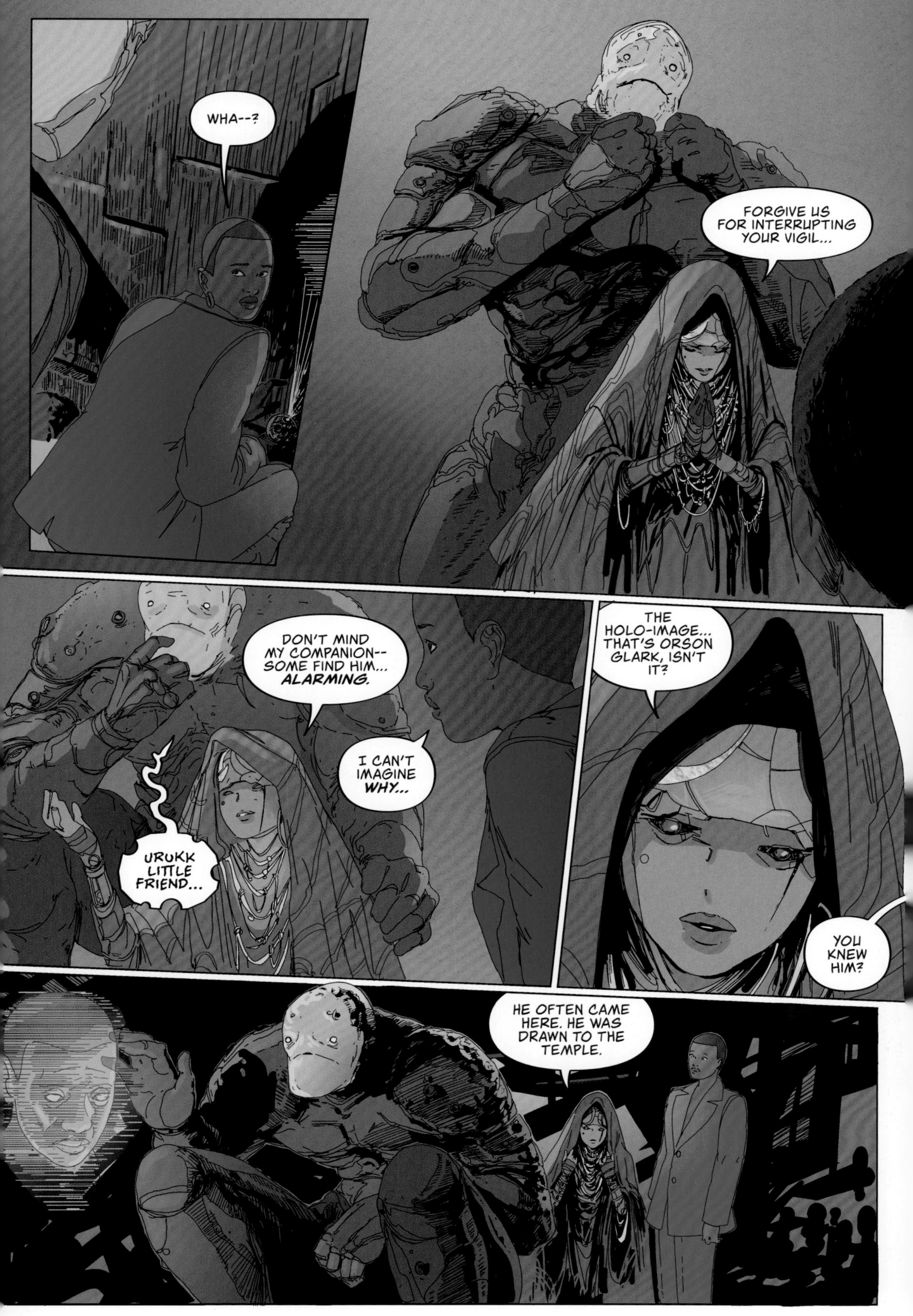
WHA--?
FORGIVE US FOR INTERRUPTING YOUR VIGIL...
DON'T MIND MY COMPANION--SOME FIND HIM... ALARMING.
I CAN'T IMAGINE WHY...
URUKK LITTLE FRIEND...
THE HOLO-IMAGE... THAT'S ORSON GLARK, ISN'T IT?
YOU KNEW HIM?
HE OFTEN CAME HERE. HE WAS DRAWN TO THE TEMPLE.

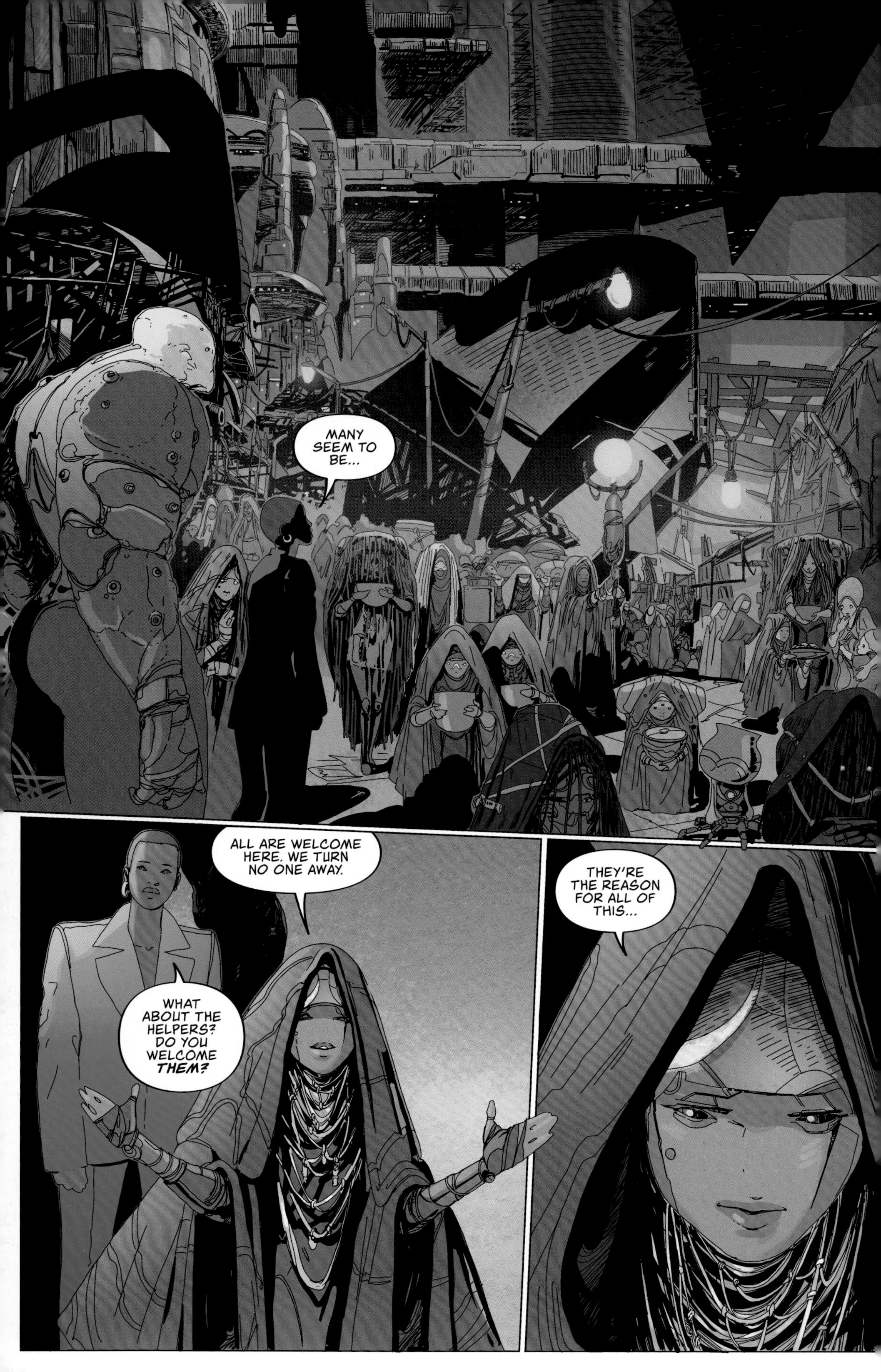
MANY SEEM TO BE...
ALL ARE WELCOME HERE. WE TURN NO ONE AWAY.
WHAT ABOUT THE HELPERS? DO YOU WELCOME *THEM?*
THEY'RE THE REASON FOR ALL OF THIS...

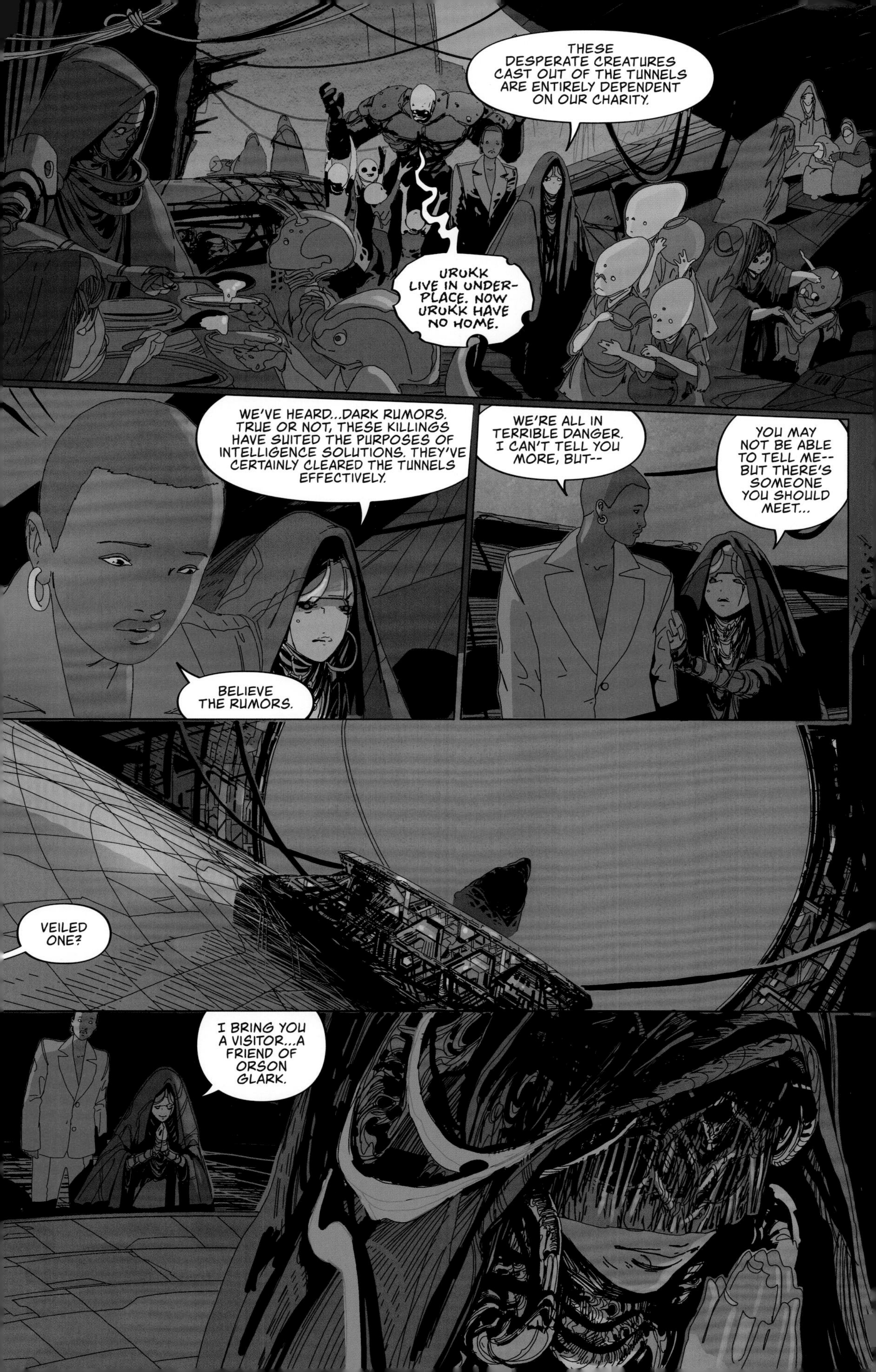
THESE DESPERATE CREATURES CAST OUT OF THE TUNNELS ARE ENTIRELY DEPENDENT ON OUR CHARITY.
URUKK LIVE IN UNDER-PLACE. NOW URUKK HAVE NO HOME.
WE'VE HEARD...DARK RUMORS. TRUE OR NOT, THESE KILLINGS HAVE SUITED THE PURPOSES OF INTELLIGENCE SOLUTIONS. THEY'VE CERTAINLY CLEARED THE TUNNELS EFFECTIVELY.
BELIEVE THE RUMORS.
WE'RE ALL IN TERRIBLE DANGER. I CAN'T TELL YOU MORE, BUT--
YOU MAY NOT BE ABLE TO TELL ME--BUT THERE'S SOMEONE YOU SHOULD MEET...
VEILED ONE?
I BRING YOU A VISITOR...A FRIEND OF ORSON GLARK.

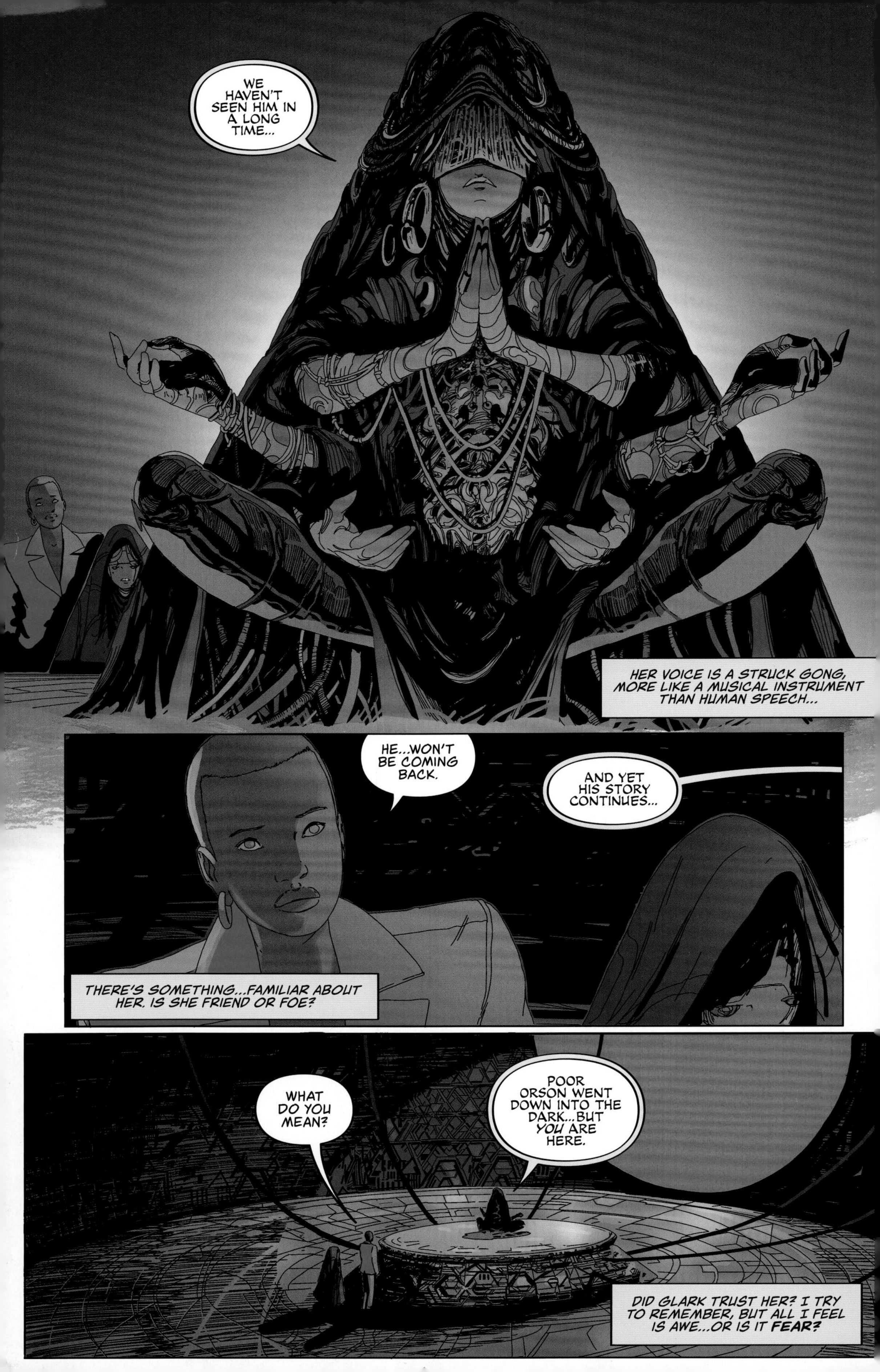
WE HAVEN'T SEEN HIM IN A LONG TIME...
HER VOICE IS A STRUCK GONG, MORE LIKE A MUSICAL INSTRUMENT THAN HUMAN SPEECH...
HE...WON'T BE COMING BACK.
AND YET HIS STORY CONTINUES...
THERE'S SOMETHING...FAMILIAR ABOUT HER. IS SHE FRIEND OR FOE?
WHAT DO YOU MEAN?
POOR ORSON WENT DOWN INTO THE DARK...BUT *YOU* ARE HERE.
DID GLARK TRUST HER? I TRY TO REMEMBER, BUT ALL I FEEL IS AWE...OR IS IT **FEAR?**

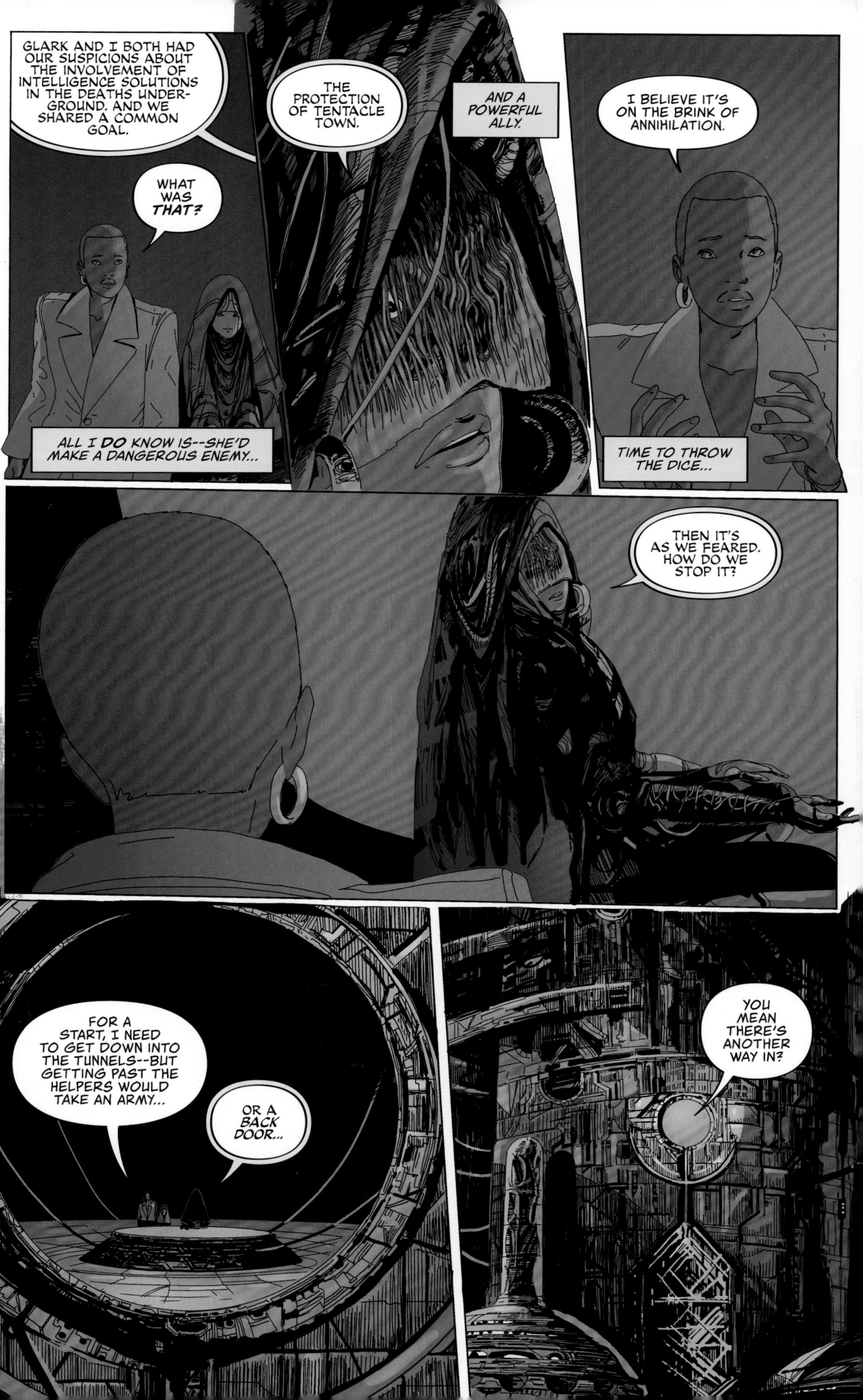
GLARK AND I BOTH HAD OUR SUSPICIONS ABOUT THE INVOLVEMENT OF INTELLIGENCE SOLUTIONS IN THE DEATHS UNDERGROUND. AND WE SHARED A COMMON GOAL.
WHAT WAS THAT?
ALL I DO KNOW IS--SHE'D MAKE A DANGEROUS ENEMY...
THE PROTECTION OF TENTACLE TOWN.
AND A POWERFUL ALLY.
I BELIEVE IT'S ON THE BRINK OF ANNIHILATION.
TIME TO THROW THE DICE...
THEN IT'S AS WE FEARED. HOW DO WE STOP IT?
FOR A START, I NEED TO GET DOWN INTO THE TUNNELS--BUT GETTING PAST THE HELPERS WOULD TAKE AN ARMY...
OR A BACK DOOR...
YOU MEAN THERE'S ANOTHER WAY IN?

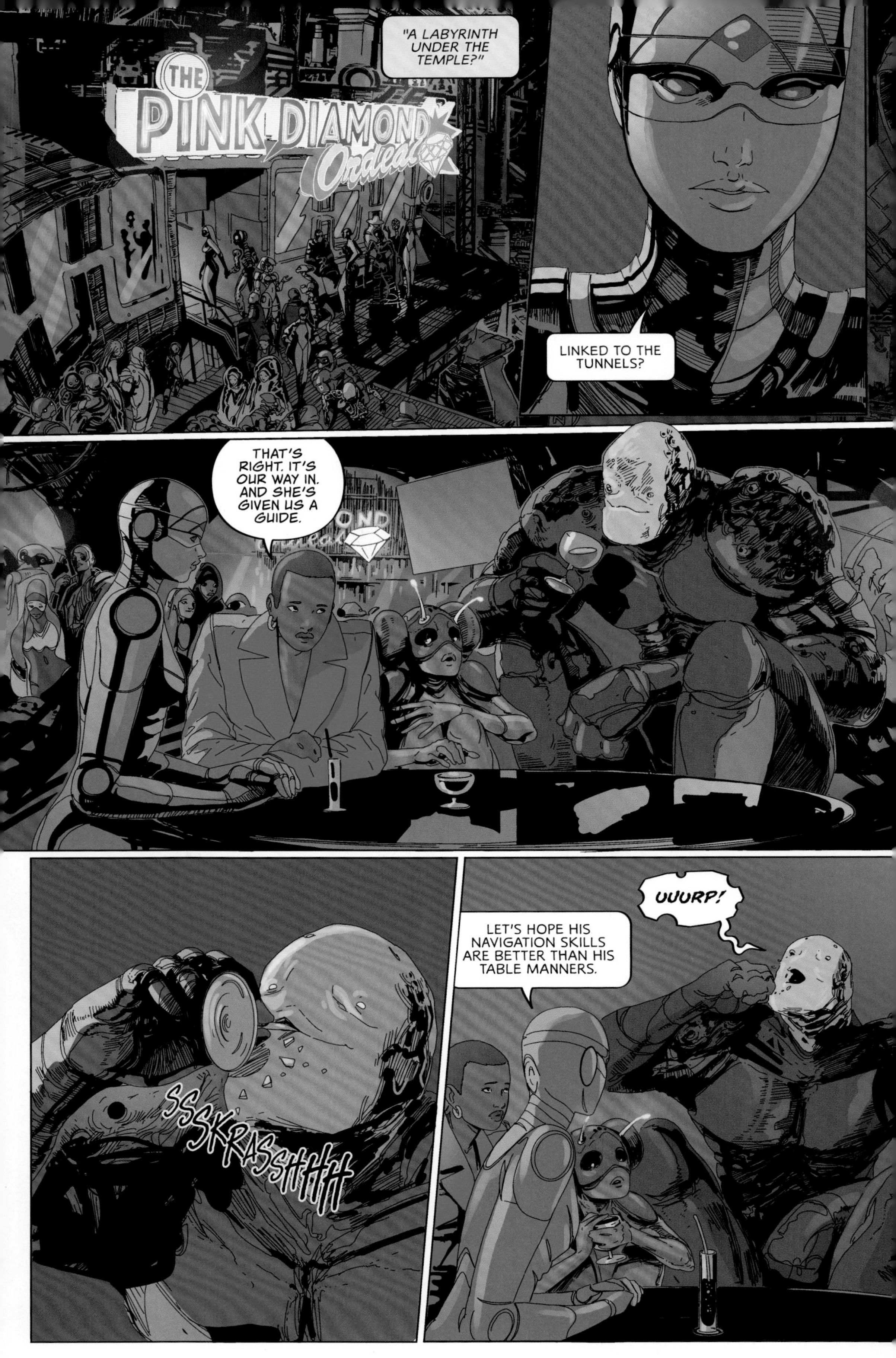
"A LABYRINTH UNDER THE TEMPLE?"
THE PINK DIAMOND Ordeal
LINKED TO THE TUNNELS?
THAT'S RIGHT. IT'S OUR WAY IN. AND SHE'S GIVEN US A GUIDE.
SSSKRASSHHHH
UUURP!
LET'S HOPE HIS NAVIGATION SKILLS ARE BETTER THAN HIS TABLE MANNERS.

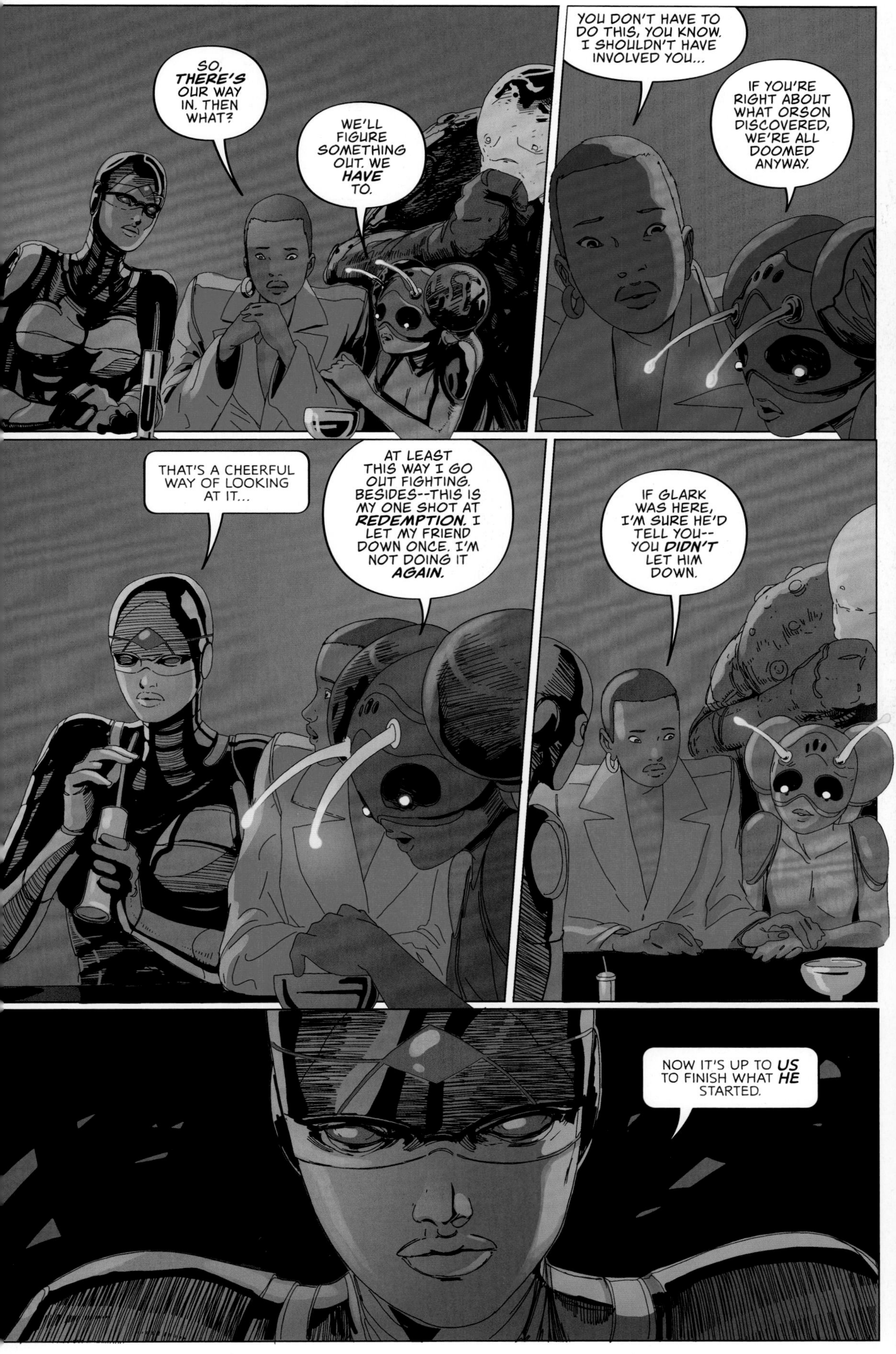
SO, THERE'S OUR WAY IN. THEN WHAT?
WE'LL FIGURE SOMETHING OUT. WE HAVE TO.
YOU DON'T HAVE TO DO THIS, YOU KNOW. I SHOULDN'T HAVE INVOLVED YOU...
IF YOU'RE RIGHT ABOUT WHAT ORSON DISCOVERED, WE'RE ALL DOOMED ANYWAY.
THAT'S A CHEERFUL WAY OF LOOKING AT IT...
AT LEAST THIS WAY I GO OUT FIGHTING. BESIDES--THIS IS MY ONE SHOT AT REDEMPTION. I LET MY FRIEND DOWN ONCE. I'M NOT DOING IT AGAIN.
IF GLARK WAS HERE, I'M SURE HE'D TELL YOU--YOU DIDN'T LET HIM DOWN.
NOW IT'S UP TO US TO FINISH WHAT HE STARTED.

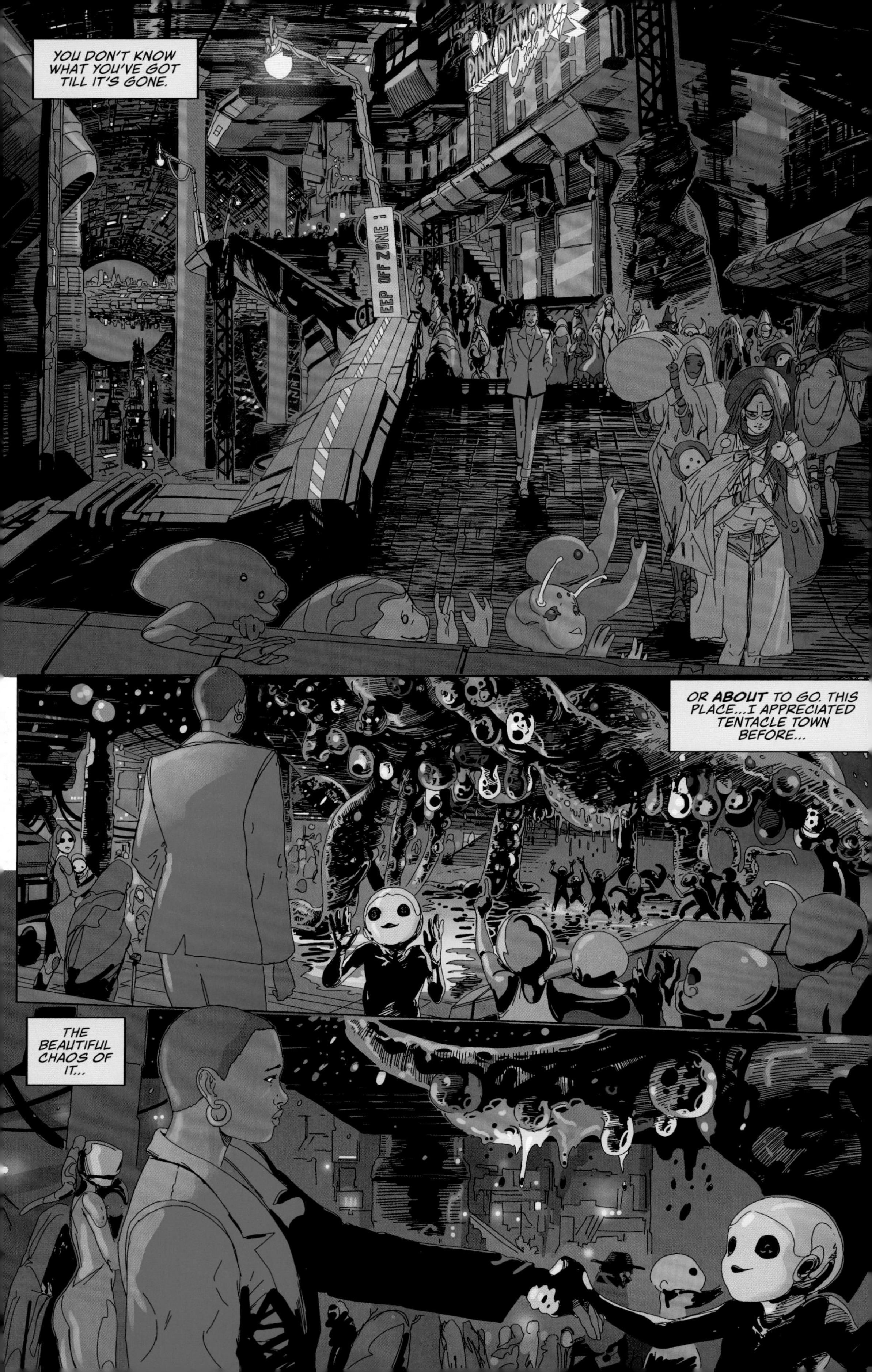
YOU DON'T KNOW WHAT YOU'VE GOT TILL IT'S GONE.
PINK DIAMOND
EEP OFF ZONE
OR ABOUT TO GO. THIS PLACE...I APPRECIATED TENTACLE TOWN BEFORE...
THE BEAUTIFUL CHAOS OF IT...

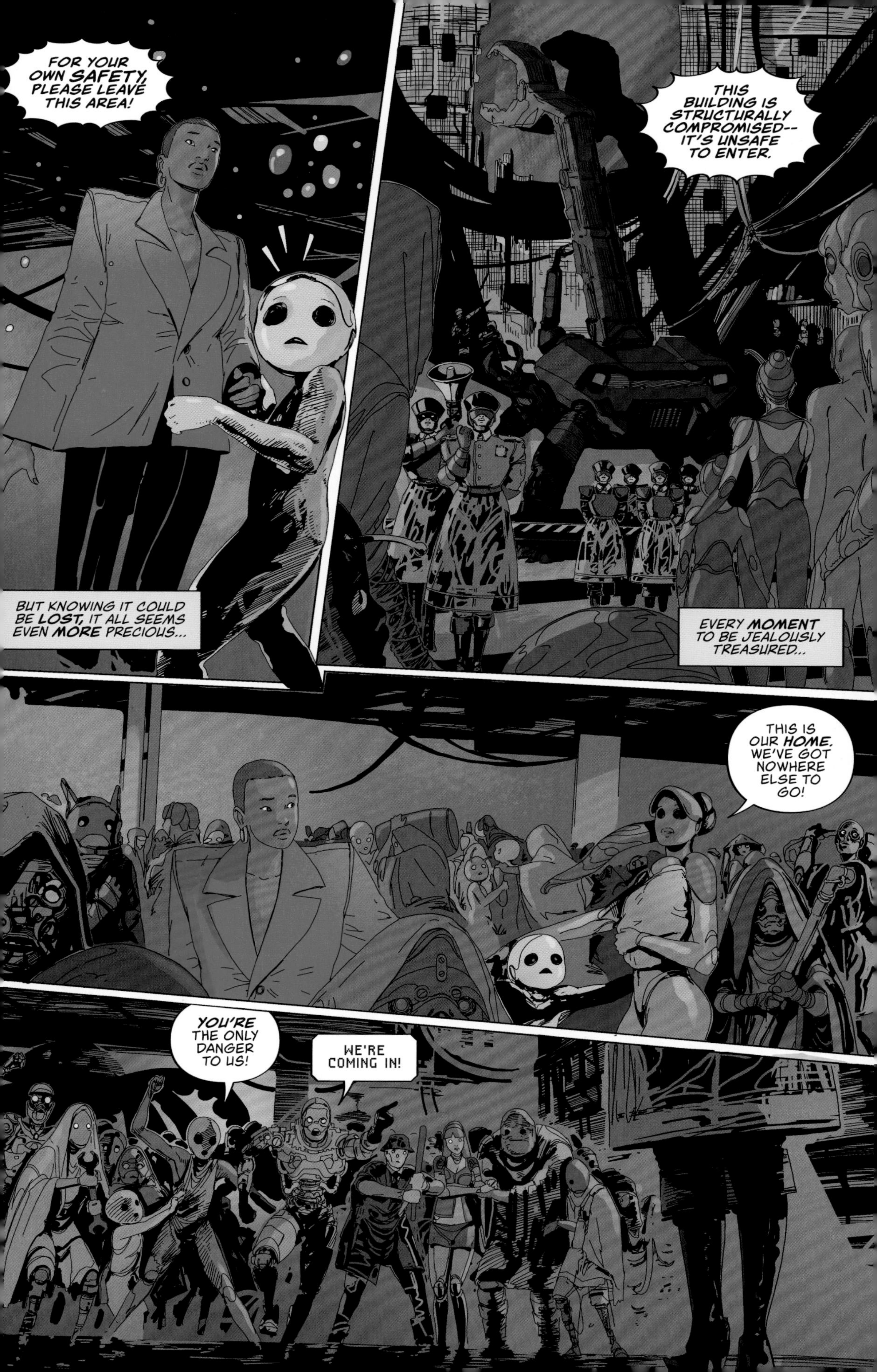
FOR YOUR OWN SAFETY, PLEASE LEAVE THIS AREA!
BUT KNOWING IT COULD BE LOST, IT ALL SEEMS EVEN MORE PRECIOUS...
THIS BUILDING IS STRUCTURALLY COMPROMISED-- IT'S UNSAFE TO ENTER.
EVERY MOMENT TO BE JEALOUSLY TREASURED...
THIS IS OUR HOME. WE'VE GOT NOWHERE ELSE TO GO!
YOU'RE THE ONLY DANGER TO US!
WE'RE COMING IN!

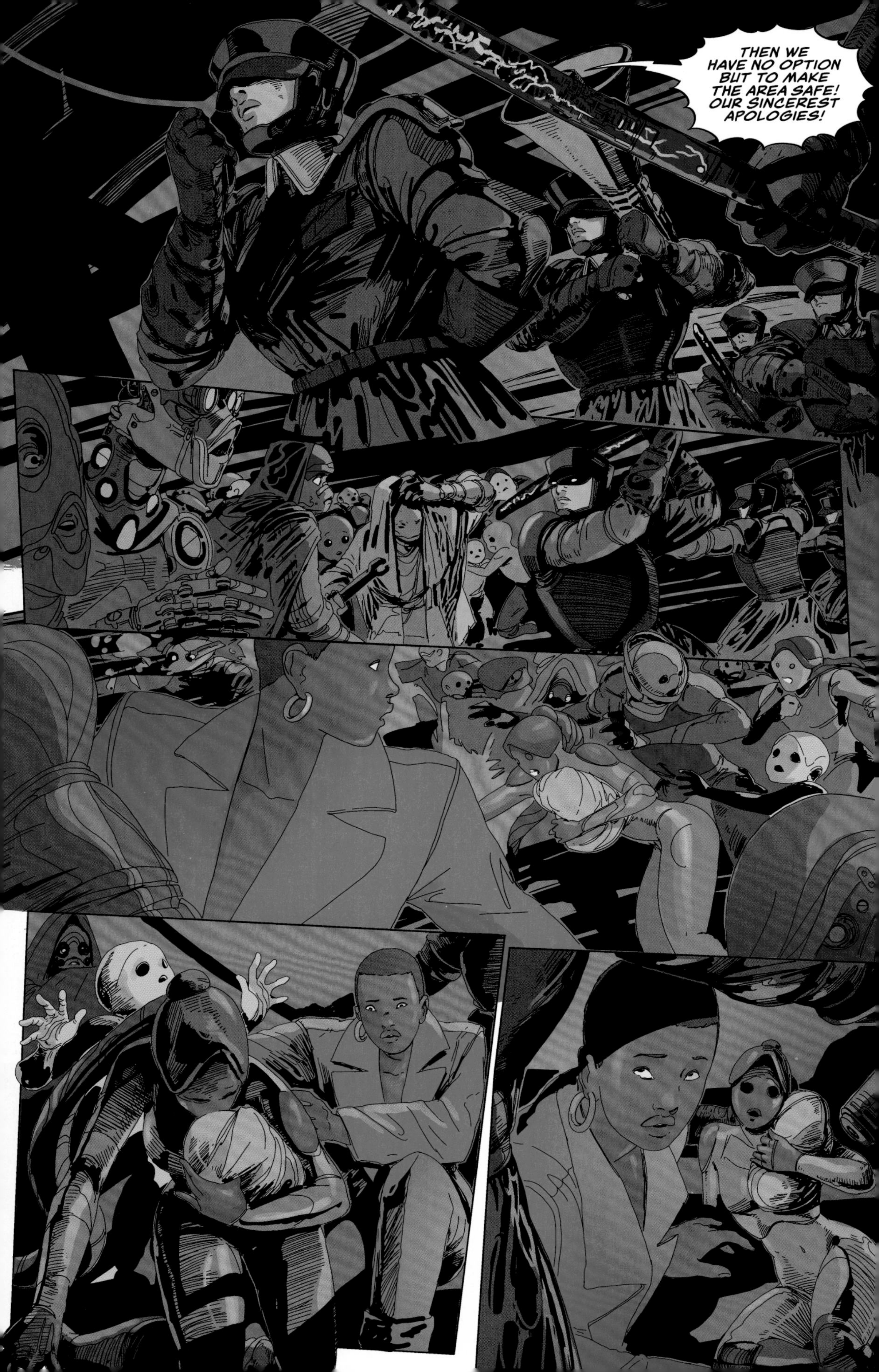
THEN WE HAVE NO OPTION BUT TO MAKE THE AREA SAFE! OUR SINCEREST APOLOGIES!

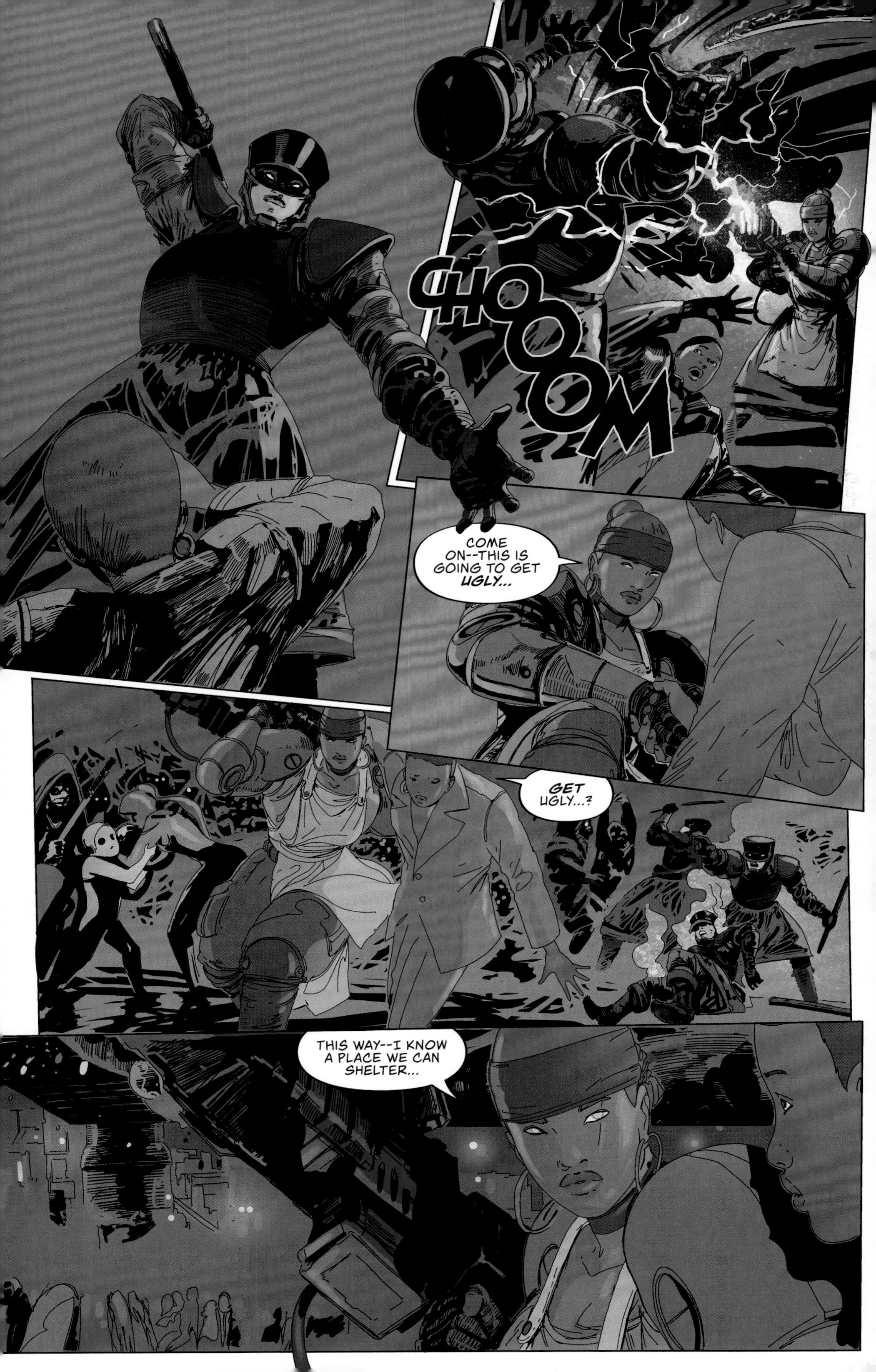
CHOOOOM
COME ON--THIS IS GOING TO GET UGLY...
GET UGLY...?
THIS WAY--I KNOW A PLACE WE CAN SHELTER...

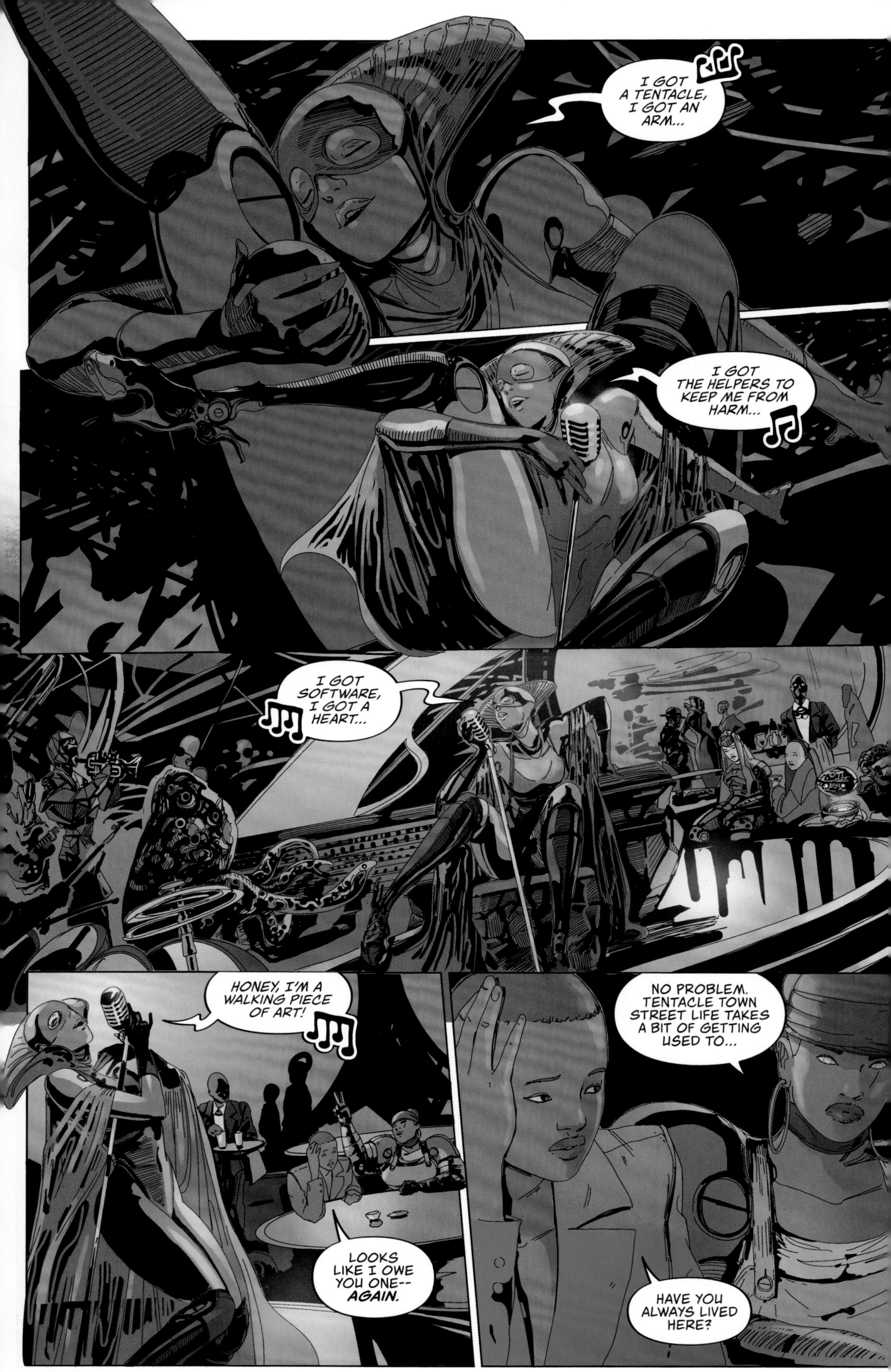
I GOT A TENTACLE, I GOT AN ARM...
I GOT THE HELPERS TO KEEP ME FROM HARM...
I GOT SOFTWARE, I GOT A HEART...
HONEY, I'M A WALKING PIECE OF ART!
LOOKS LIKE I OWE YOU ONE-- **AGAIN**.
NO PROBLEM. TENTACLE TOWN STREET LIFE TAKES A BIT OF GETTING USED TO...
HAVE YOU ALWAYS LIVED HERE?

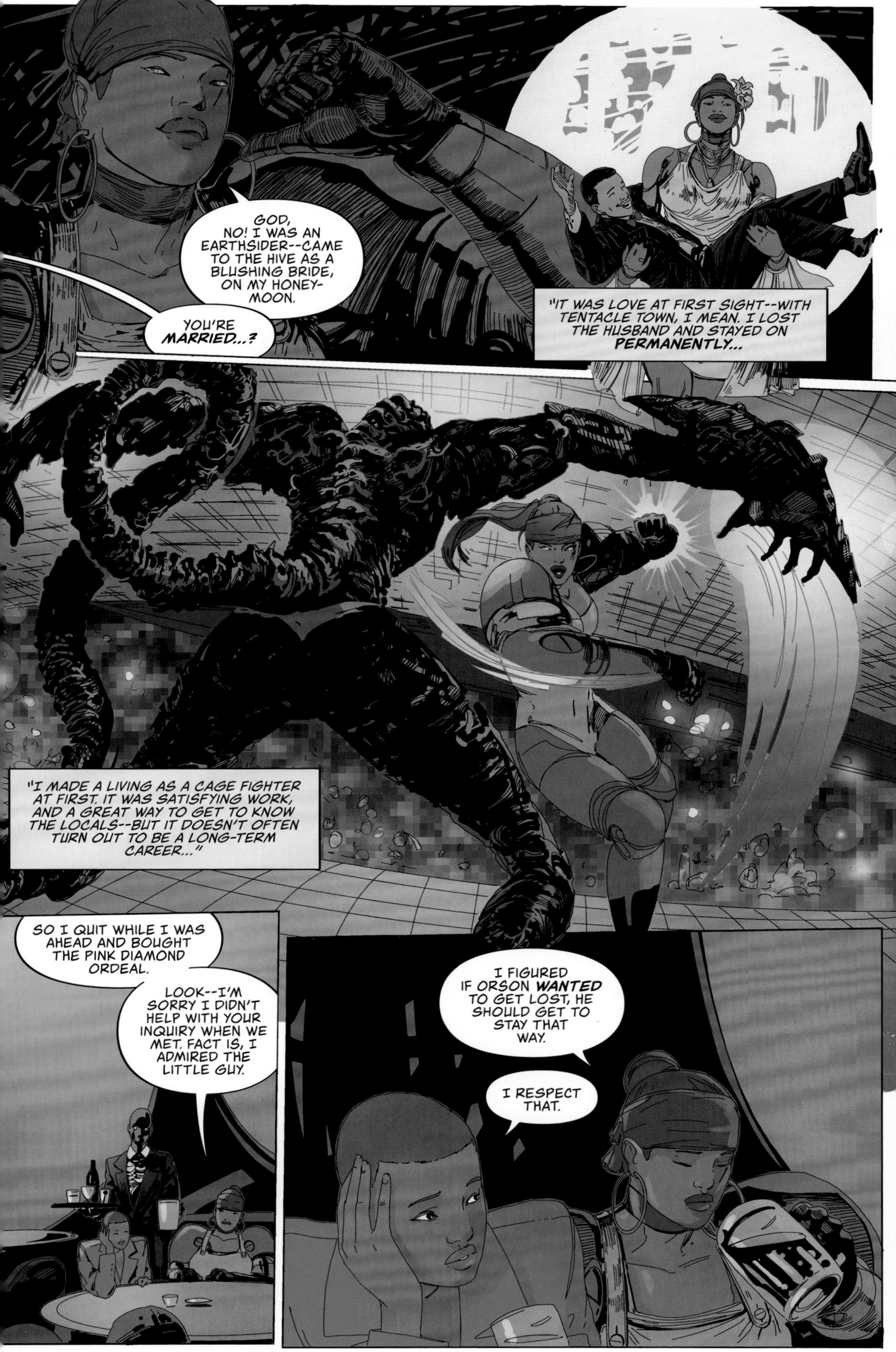
GOD, NO! I WAS AN EARTHSIDER--CAME TO THE HIVE AS A BLUSHING BRIDE, ON MY HONEY-MOON.
YOU'RE MARRIED...?
"IT WAS LOVE AT FIRST SIGHT--WITH TENTACLE TOWN, I MEAN. I LOST THE HUSBAND AND STAYED ON PERMANENTLY...
"I MADE A LIVING AS A CAGE FIGHTER AT FIRST. IT WAS SATISFYING WORK, AND A GREAT WAY TO GET TO KNOW THE LOCALS--BUT IT DOESN'T OFTEN TURN OUT TO BE A LONG-TERM CAREER..."
SO I QUIT WHILE I WAS AHEAD AND BOUGHT THE PINK DIAMOND ORDEAL.
LOOK--I'M SORRY I DIDN'T HELP WITH YOUR INQUIRY WHEN WE MET. FACT IS, I ADMIRED THE LITTLE GUY.
I FIGURED IF ORSON WANTED TO GET LOST, HE SHOULD GET TO STAY THAT WAY.
I RESPECT THAT.

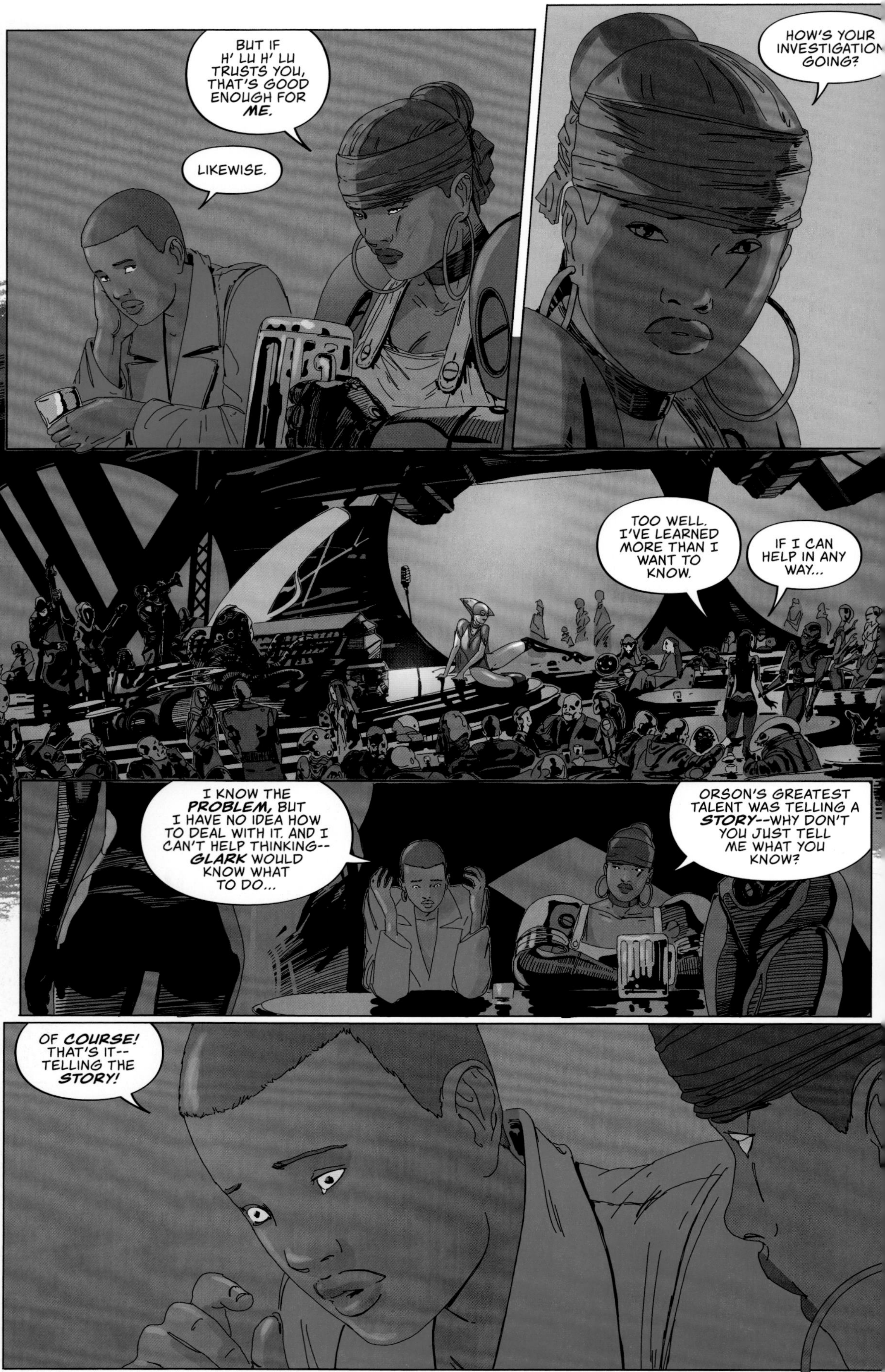
BUT IF H' LU H' LU TRUSTS YOU, THAT'S GOOD ENOUGH FOR ME.
LIKEWISE.
HOW'S YOUR INVESTIGATION GOING?
TOO WELL. I'VE LEARNED MORE THAN I WANT TO KNOW.
IF I CAN HELP IN ANY WAY...
I KNOW THE PROBLEM, BUT I HAVE NO IDEA HOW TO DEAL WITH IT. AND I CAN'T HELP THINKING-- GLARK WOULD KNOW WHAT TO DO...
ORSON'S GREATEST TALENT WAS TELLING A STORY--WHY DON'T YOU JUST TELL ME WHAT YOU KNOW?
OF COURSE! THAT'S IT-- TELLING THE STORY!

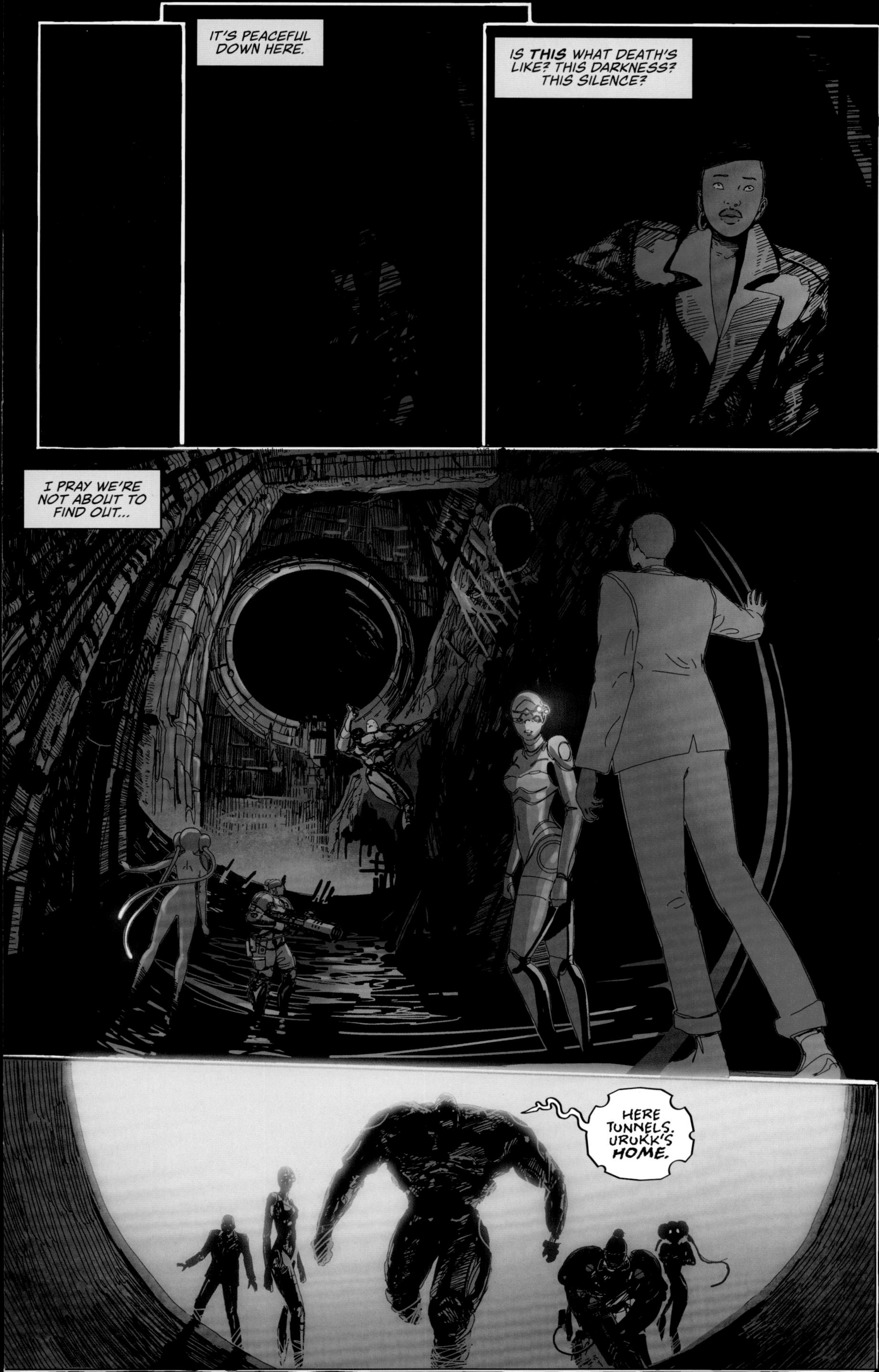

IT'S PEACEFUL DOWN HERE.
IS THIS WHAT DEATH'S LIKE? THIS DARKNESS? THIS SILENCE?
I PRAY WE'RE NOT ABOUT TO FIND OUT...
HERE TUNNELS. URUKK'S HOME.

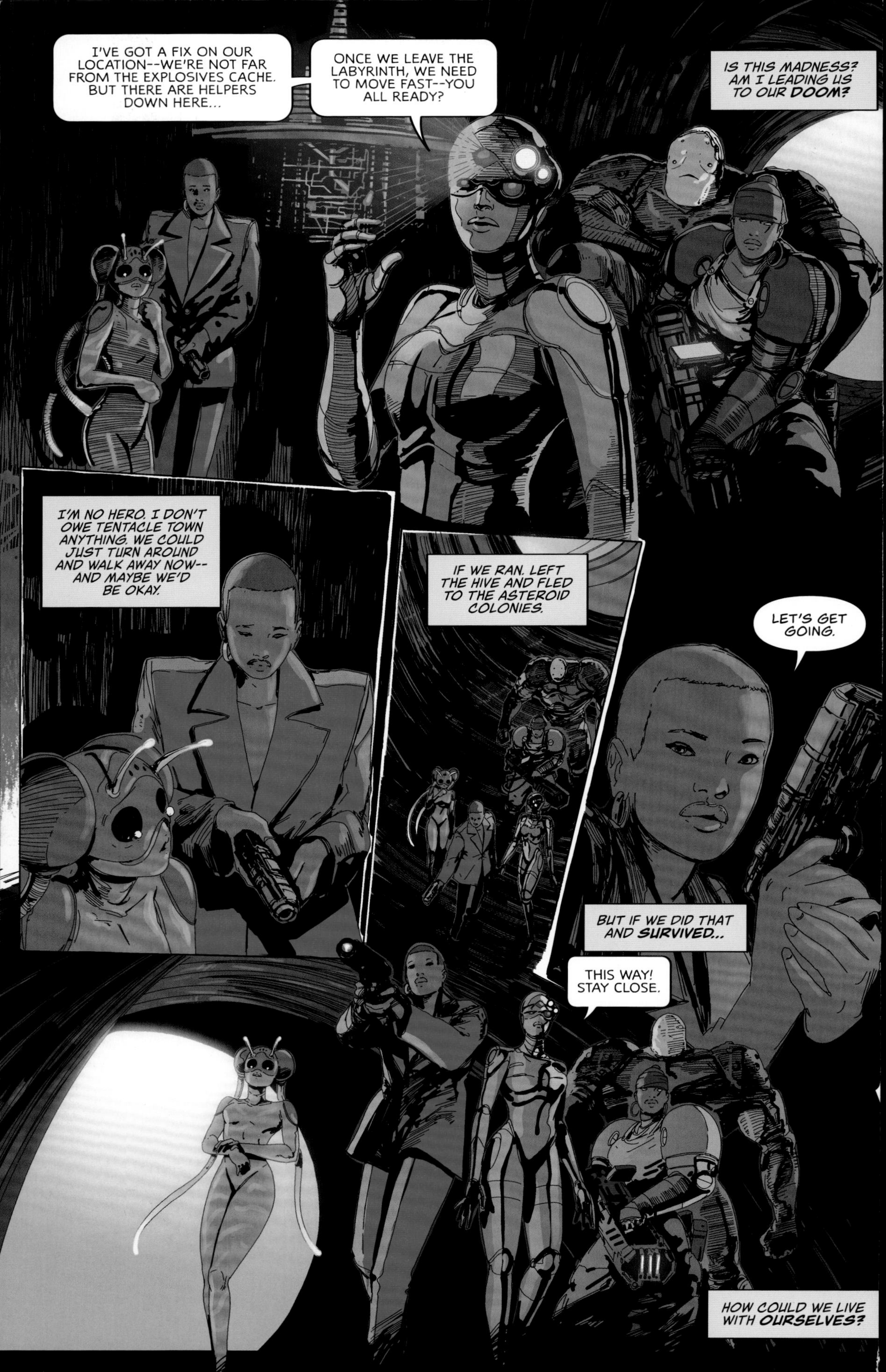

I'VE GOT A FIX ON OUR LOCATION--WE'RE NOT FAR FROM THE EXPLOSIVES CACHE. BUT THERE ARE HELPERS DOWN HERE...
ONCE WE LEAVE THE LABYRINTH, WE NEED TO MOVE FAST--YOU ALL READY?
IS THIS MADNESS? AM I LEADING US TO OUR DOOM?
I'M NO HERO. I DON'T OWE TENTACLE TOWN ANYTHING. WE COULD JUST TURN AROUND AND WALK AWAY NOW--AND MAYBE WE'D BE OKAY.
IF WE RAN. LEFT THE HIVE AND FLED TO THE ASTEROID COLONIES.
LET'S GET GOING.
BUT IF WE DID THAT AND SURVIVED...
THIS WAY! STAY CLOSE.
HOW COULD WE LIVE WITH OURSELVES?

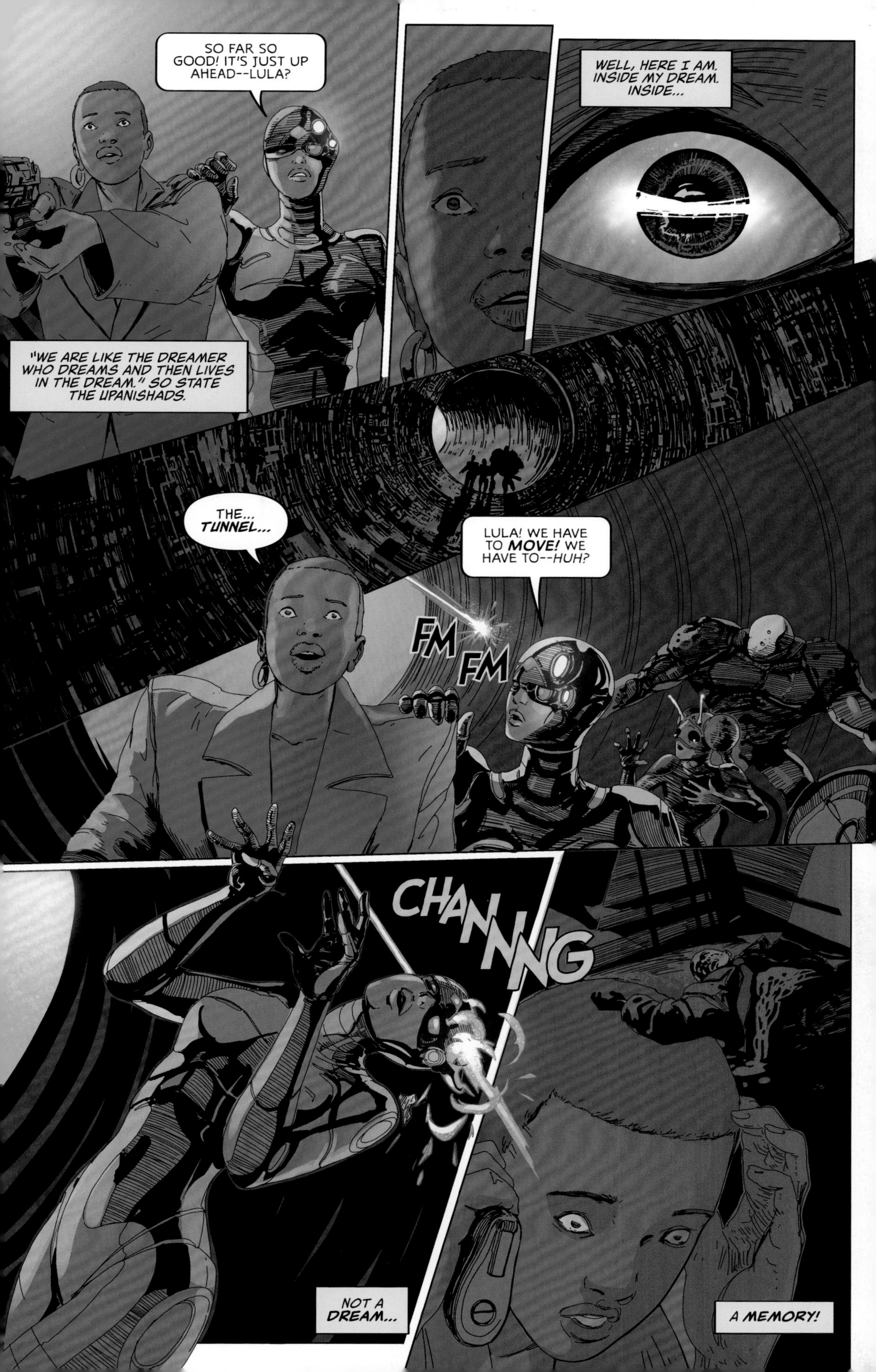
SO FAR SO GOOD! IT'S JUST UP AHEAD--LULA?
WELL, HERE I AM. INSIDE MY DREAM. INSIDE...
"WE ARE LIKE THE DREAMER WHO DREAMS AND THEN LIVES IN THE DREAM." SO STATE THE UPANISHADS.
THE... TUNNEL...
LULA! WE HAVE TO MOVE! WE HAVE TO--HUH?
FM
FM
CHANNNG
NOT A DREAM...
A MEMORY!

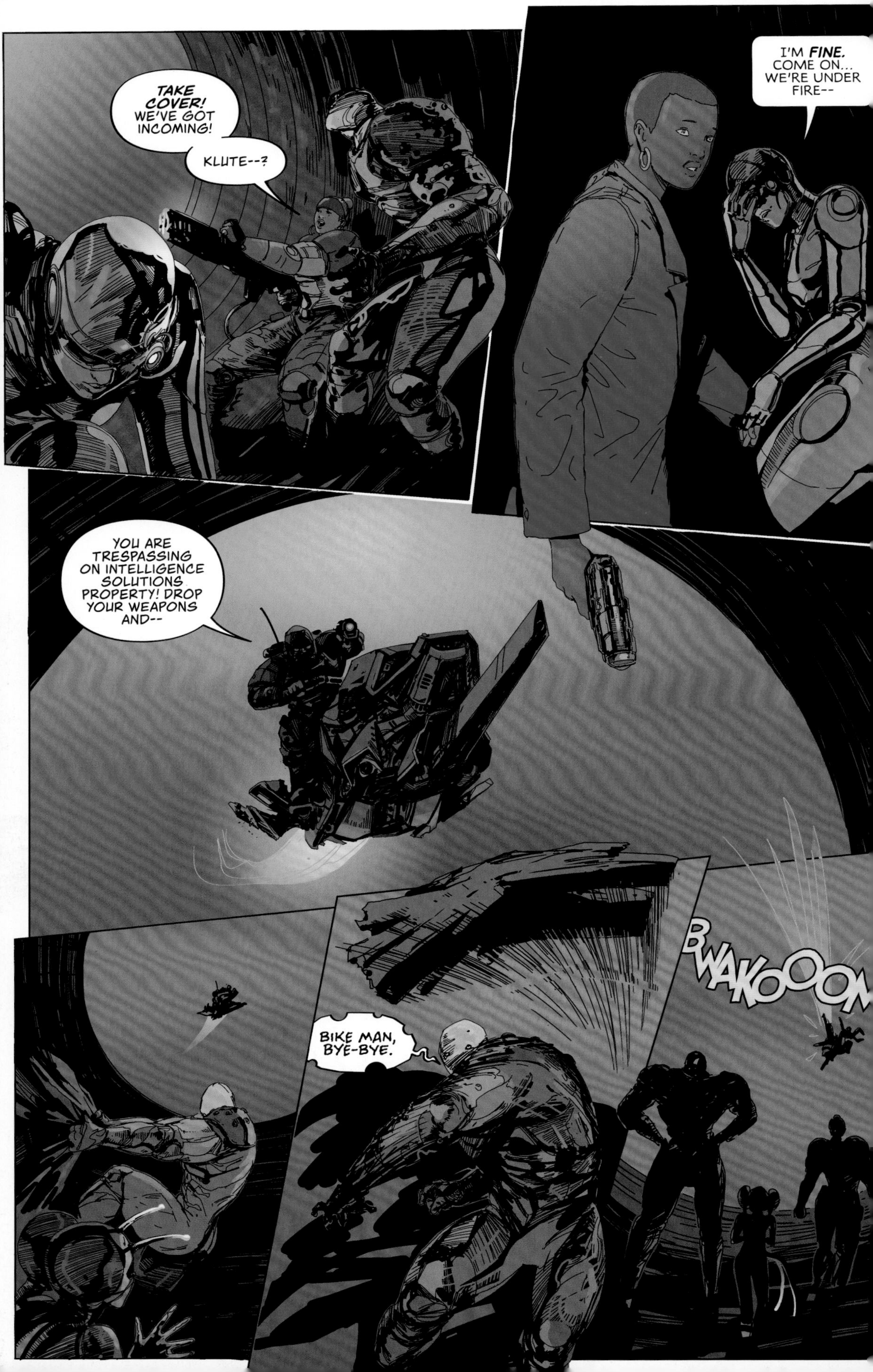
TAKE COVER! WE'VE GOT INCOMING!
KLUTE--?
I'M FINE. COME ON... WE'RE UNDER FIRE--
YOU ARE TRESPASSING ON INTELLIGENCE SOLUTIONS PROPERTY! DROP YOUR WEAPONS AND--
BWAKOOOM
BIKE MAN, BYE-BYE.

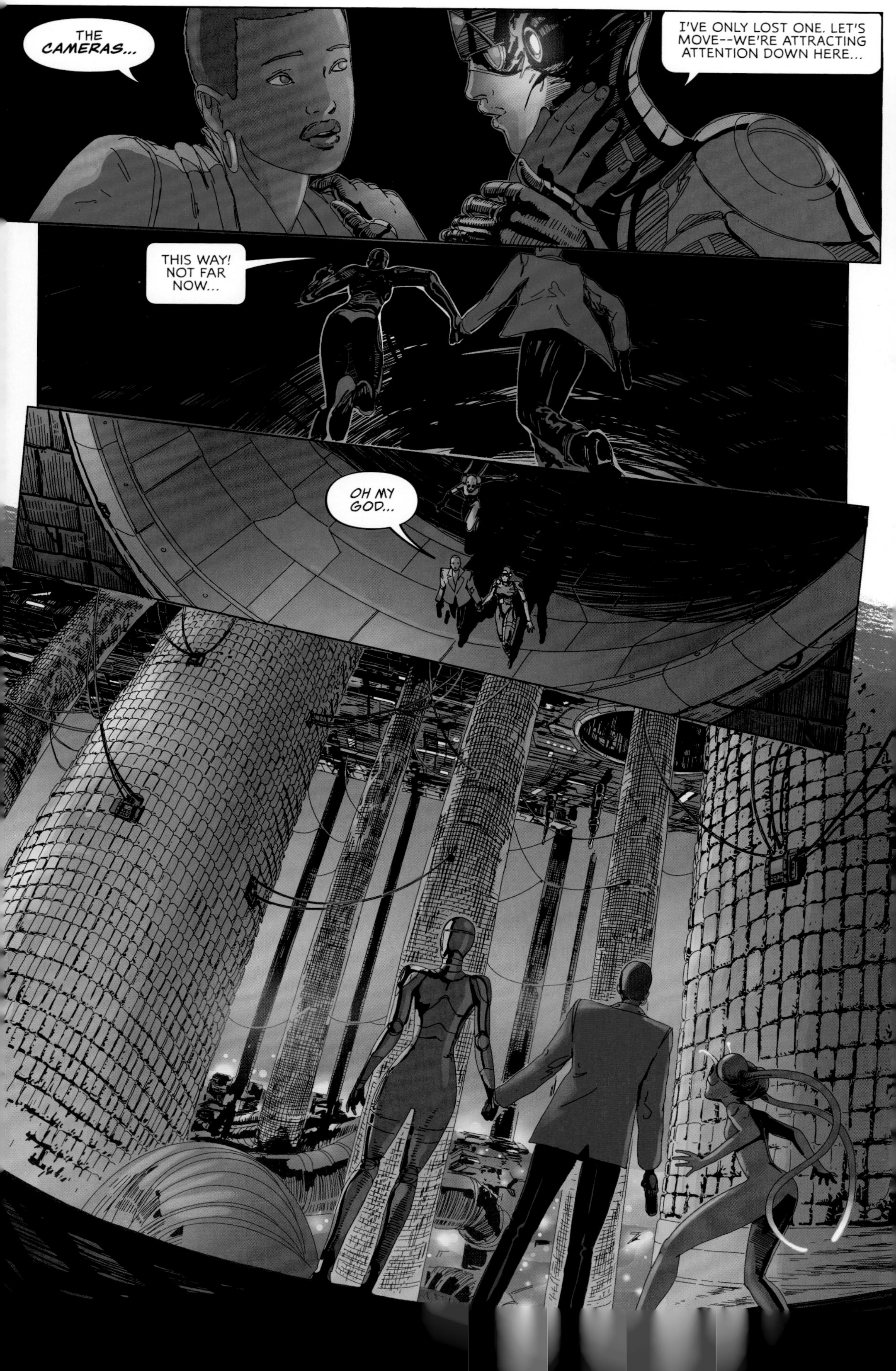
THE CAMERAS...
I'VE ONLY LOST ONE. LET'S MOVE--WE'RE ATTRACTING ATTENTION DOWN HERE...
THIS WAY! NOT FAR NOW...
OH MY GOD...

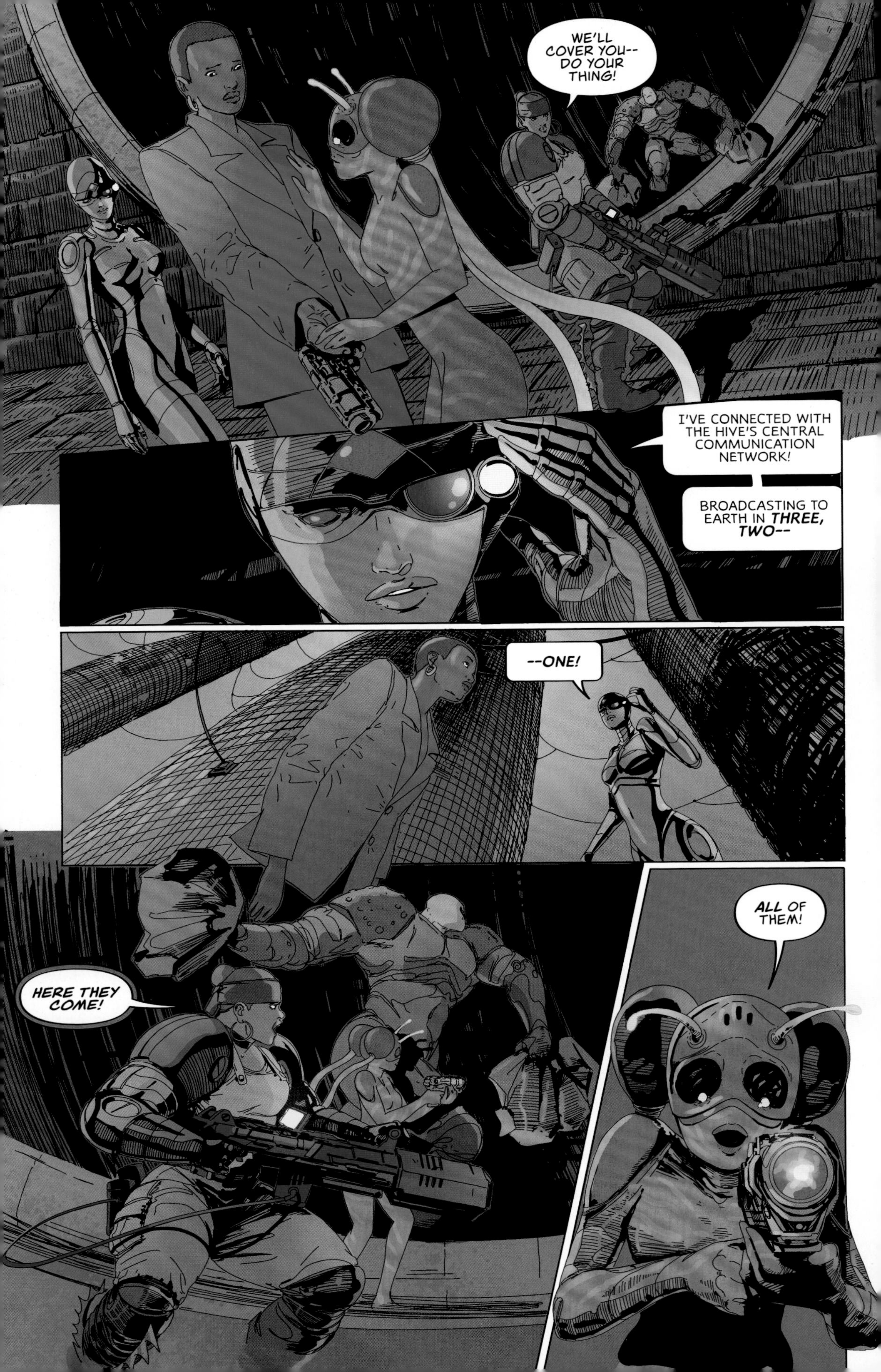
WE'LL COVER YOU-- DO YOUR THING!
I'VE CONNECTED WITH THE HIVE'S CENTRAL COMMUNICATION NETWORK!
BROADCASTING TO EARTH IN THREE, TWO--
--ONE!
HERE THEY COME!
ALL OF THEM!

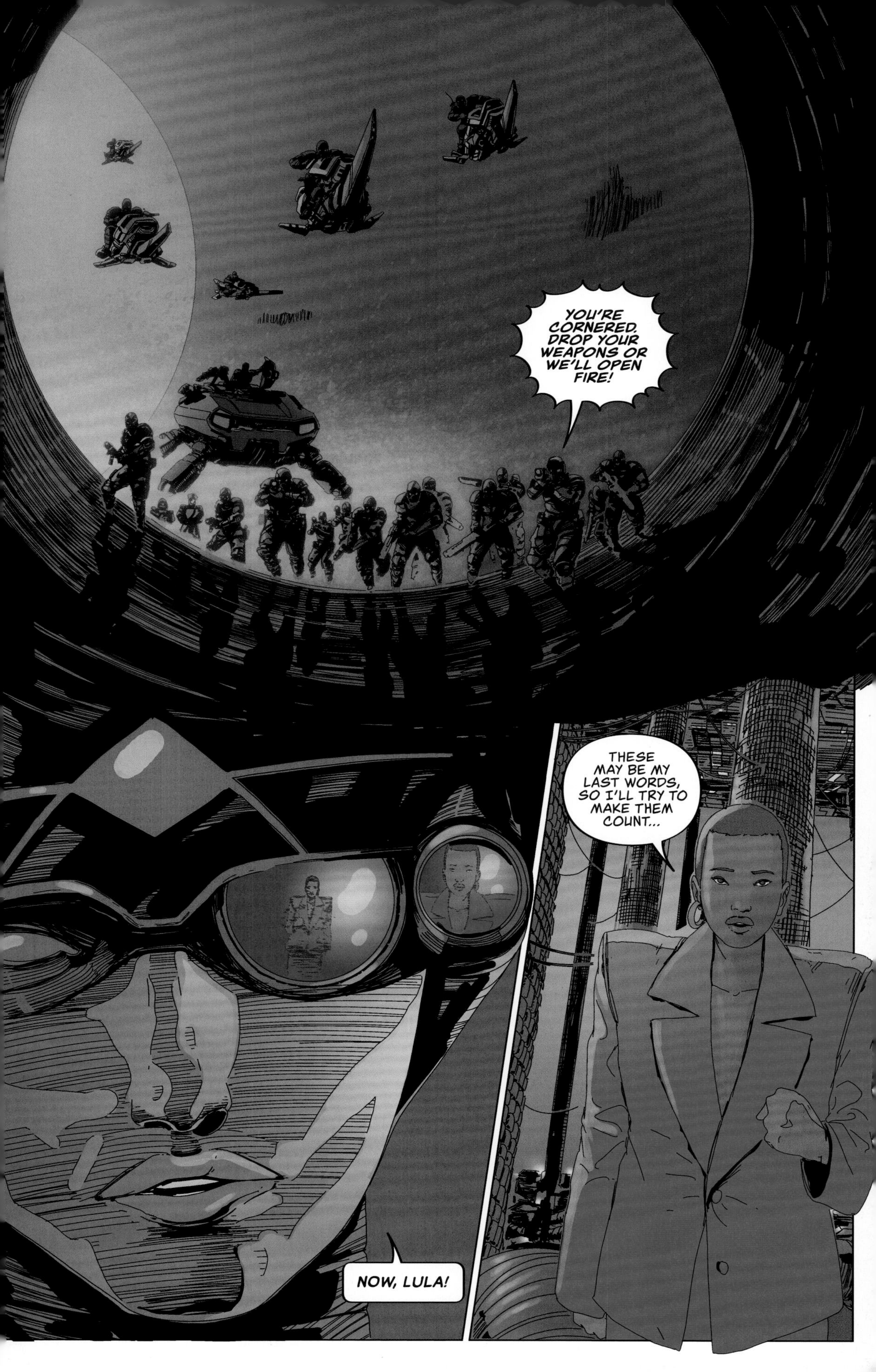
YOU'RE CORNERED. DROP YOUR WEAPONS OR WE'LL OPEN FIRE!
THESE MAY BE MY LAST WORDS, SO I'LL TRY TO MAKE THEM COUNT...
NOW, LULA!

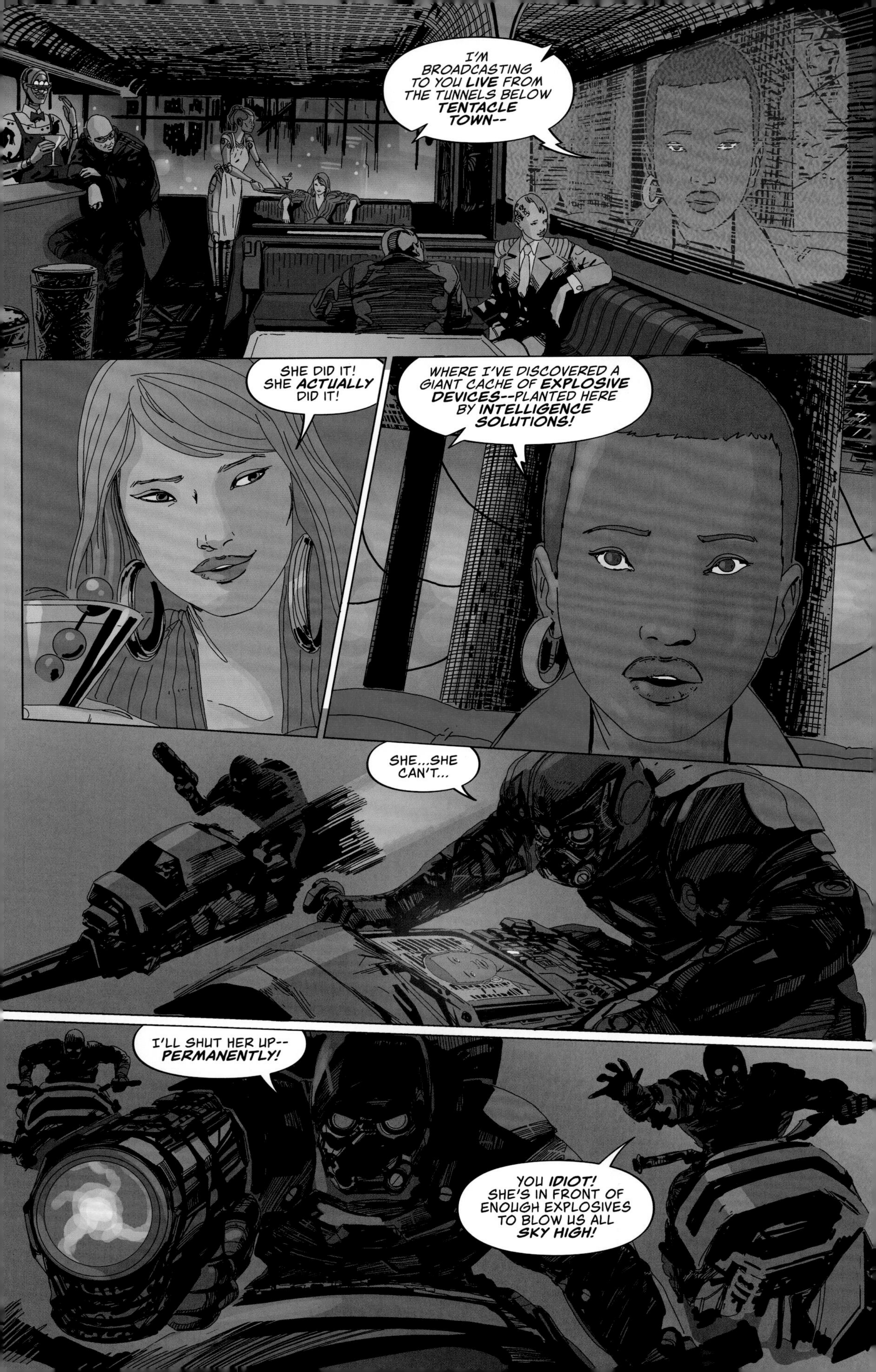
I'M BROADCASTING TO YOU LIVE FROM THE TUNNELS BELOW TENTACLE TOWN--
SHE DID IT! SHE ACTUALLY DID IT!
WHERE I'VE DISCOVERED A GIANT CACHE OF EXPLOSIVE DEVICES--PLANTED HERE BY INTELLIGENCE SOLUTIONS!
SHE...SHE CAN'T...
I'LL SHUT HER UP-- PERMANENTLY!
YOU IDIOT! SHE'S IN FRONT OF ENOUGH EXPLOSIVES TO BLOW US ALL SKY HIGH!

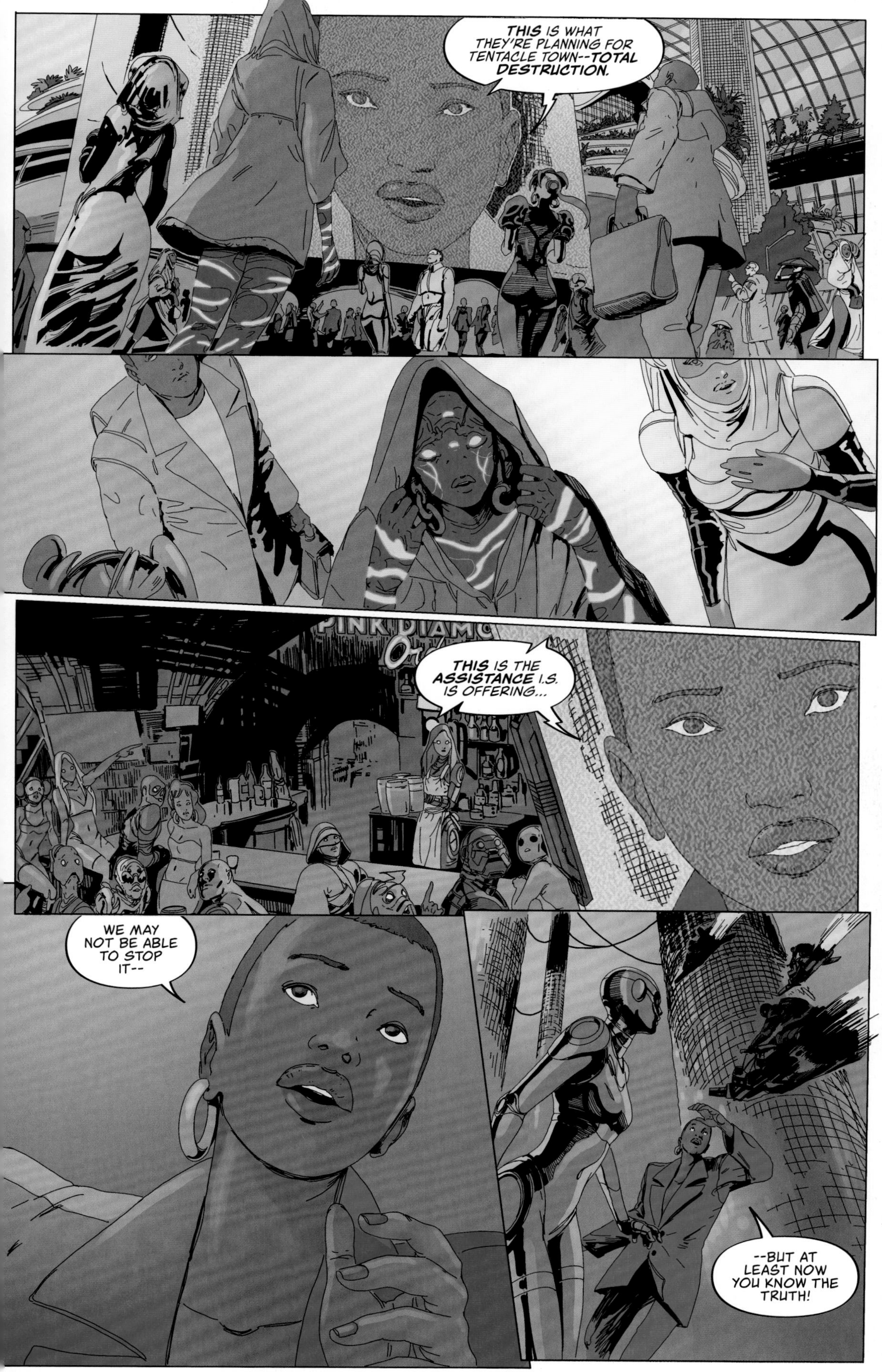
THIS IS WHAT THEY'RE PLANNING FOR TENTACLE TOWN--TOTAL DESTRUCTION.
PINK DIAMO
THIS IS THE ASSISTANCE I.S. IS OFFERING...
WE MAY NOT BE ABLE TO STOP IT--
--BUT AT LEAST NOW YOU KNOW THE TRUTH!

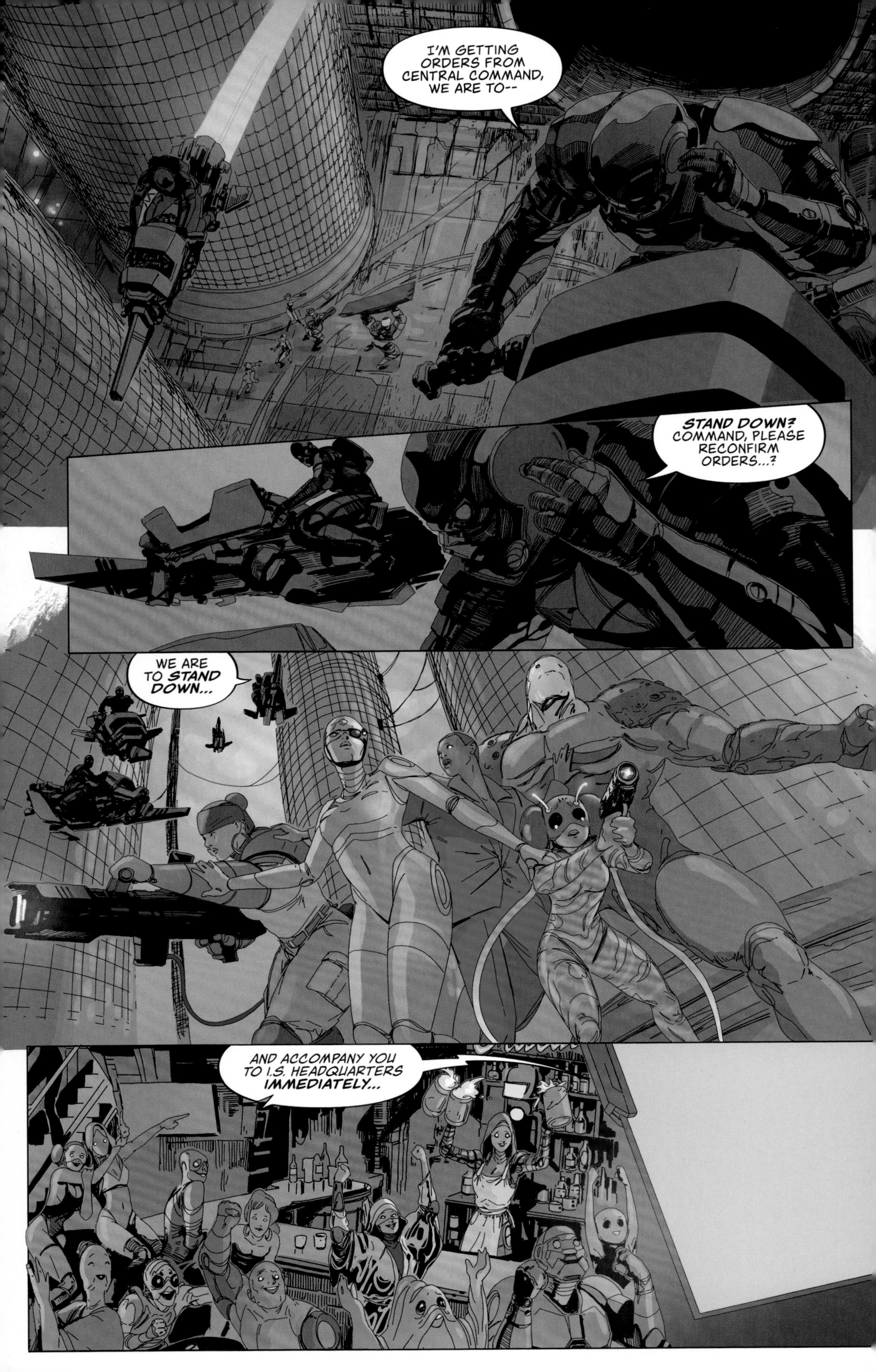
I'M GETTING ORDERS FROM CENTRAL COMMAND, WE ARE TO--
STAND DOWN? COMMAND, PLEASE RECONFIRM ORDERS...?
WE ARE TO STAND DOWN...
AND ACCOMPANY YOU TO I.S. HEADQUARTERS IMMEDIATELY...

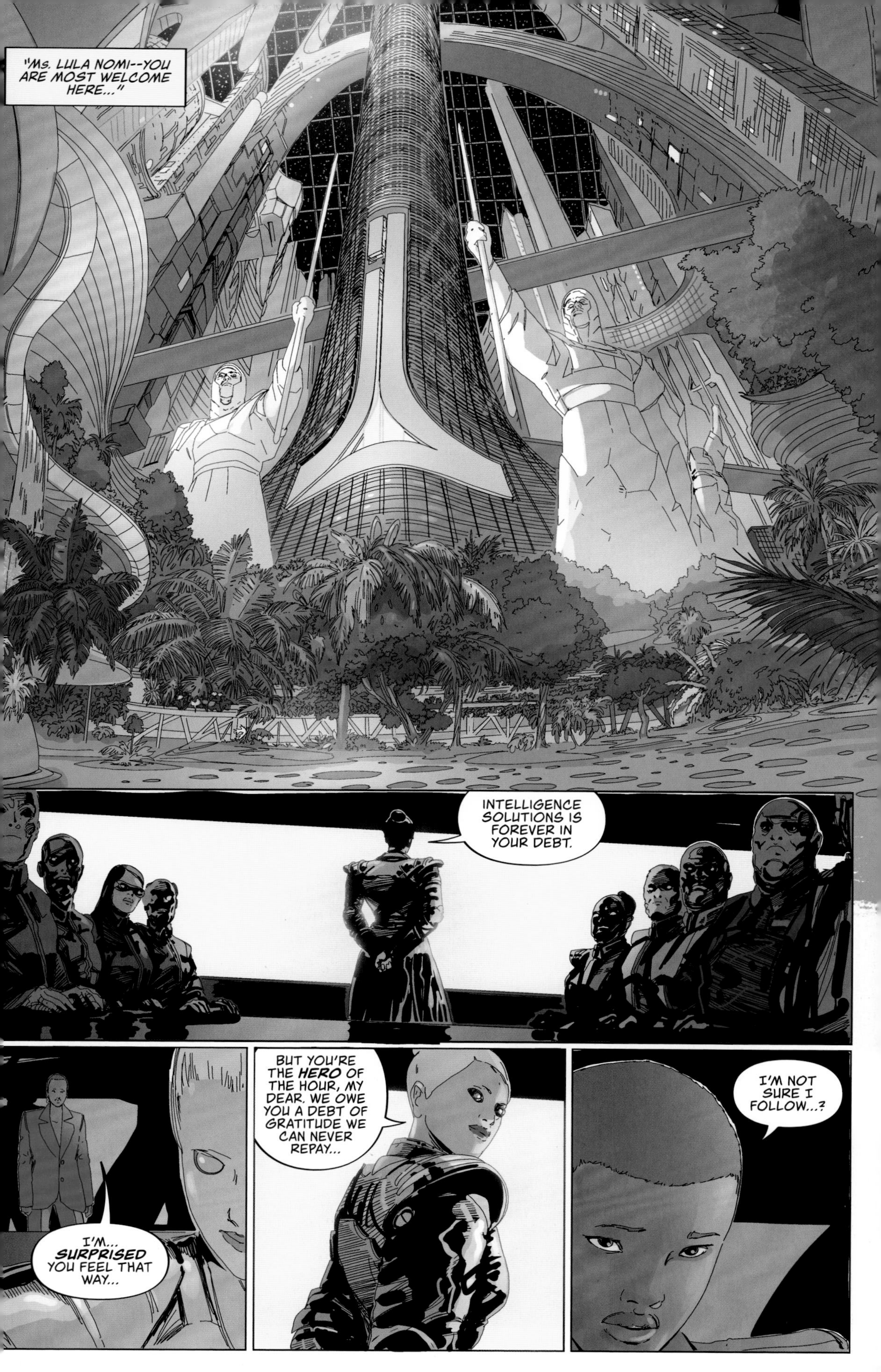
"Ms. LULA NOMI--YOU ARE MOST WELCOME HERE..."
INTELLIGENCE SOLUTIONS IS FOREVER IN YOUR DEBT.
I'M... SURPRISED YOU FEEL THAT WAY...
BUT YOU'RE THE HERO OF THE HOUR, MY DEAR. WE OWE YOU A DEBT OF GRATITUDE WE CAN NEVER REPAY...
I'M NOT SURE I FOLLOW...?

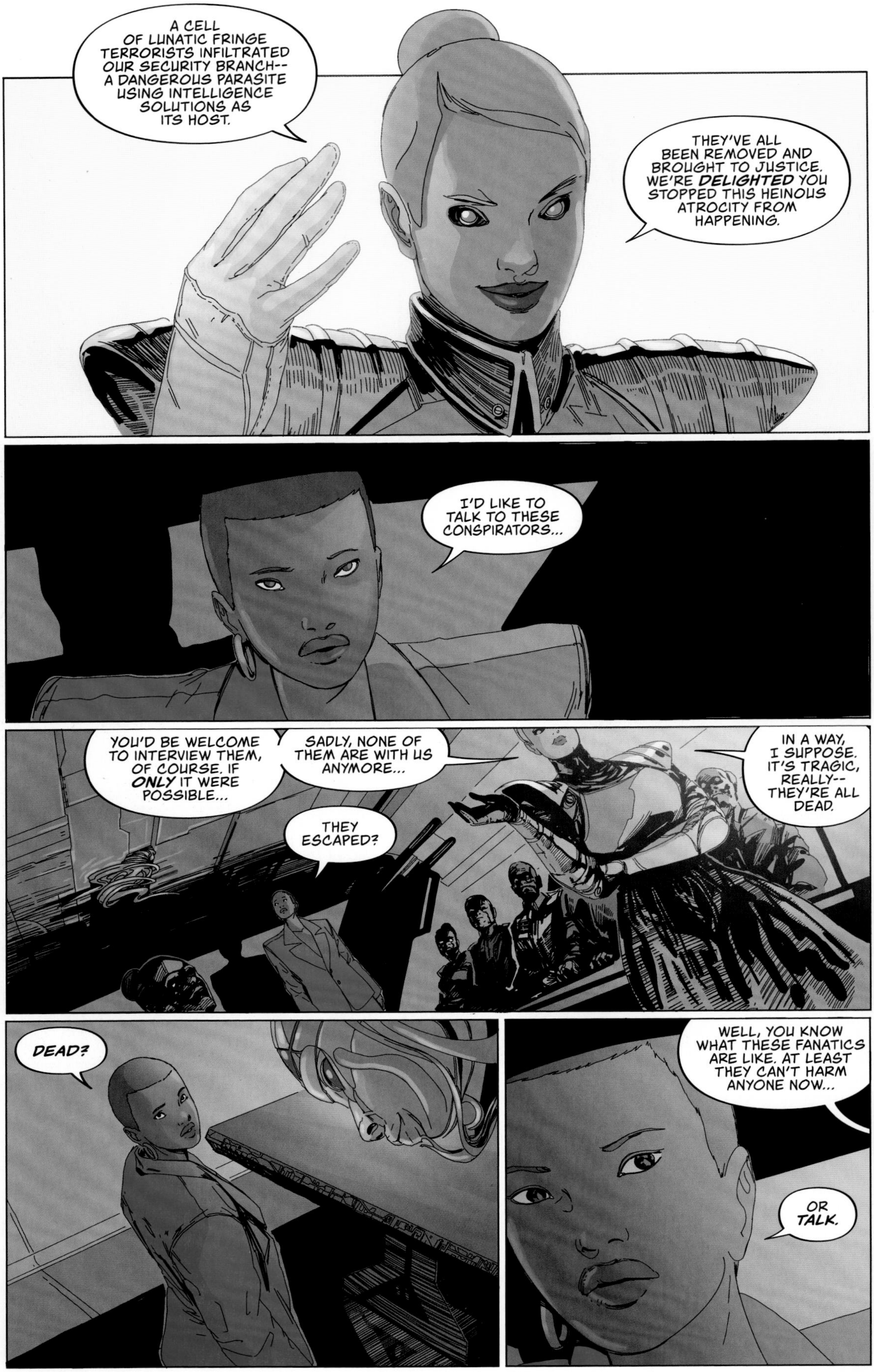

A CELL OF LUNATIC FRINGE TERRORISTS INFILTRATED OUR SECURITY BRANCH-- A DANGEROUS PARASITE USING INTELLIGENCE SOLUTIONS AS ITS HOST.
THEY'VE ALL BEEN REMOVED AND BROUGHT TO JUSTICE. WE'RE DELIGHTED YOU STOPPED THIS HEINOUS ATROCITY FROM HAPPENING.
I'D LIKE TO TALK TO THESE CONSPIRATORS...
YOU'D BE WELCOME TO INTERVIEW THEM, OF COURSE. IF ONLY IT WERE POSSIBLE...
SADLY, NONE OF THEM ARE WITH US ANYMORE...
THEY ESCAPED?
IN A WAY, I SUPPOSE. IT'S TRAGIC, REALLY-- THEY'RE ALL DEAD.
DEAD?
WELL, YOU KNOW WHAT THESE FANATICS ARE LIKE. AT LEAST THEY CAN'T HARM ANYONE NOW...
OR TALK.

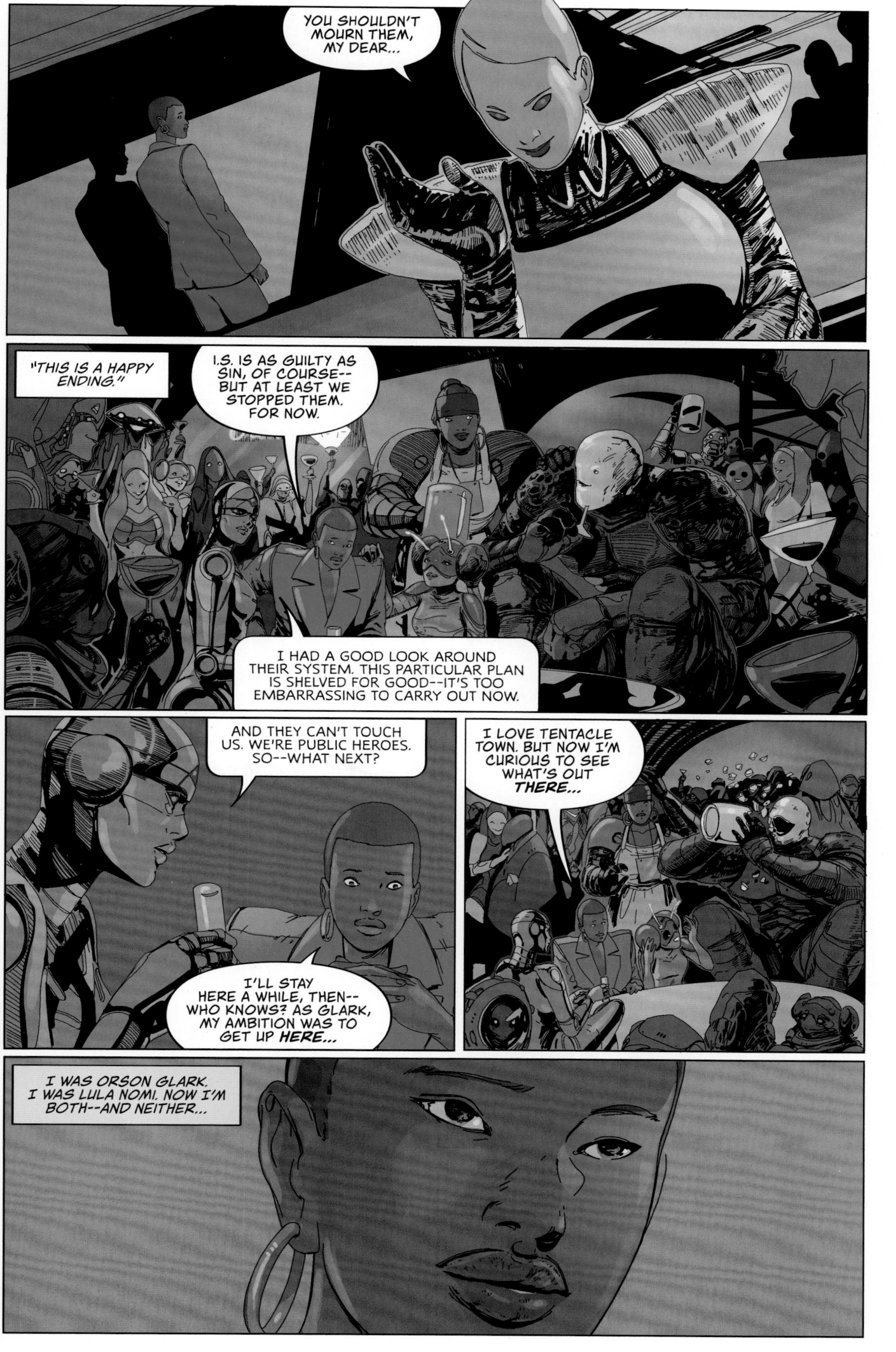
YOU SHOULDN'T MOURN THEM, MY DEAR...
"THIS IS A HAPPY ENDING."
I.S. IS AS GUILTY AS SIN, OF COURSE-- BUT AT LEAST WE STOPPED THEM. FOR NOW.
I HAD A GOOD LOOK AROUND THEIR SYSTEM. THIS PARTICULAR PLAN IS SHELVED FOR GOOD--IT'S TOO EMBARRASSING TO CARRY OUT NOW.
AND THEY CAN'T TOUCH US. WE'RE PUBLIC HEROES. SO--WHAT NEXT?
I'LL STAY HERE A WHILE, THEN-- WHO KNOWS? AS GLARK, MY AMBITION WAS TO GET UP *HERE...*
I LOVE TENTACLE TOWN. BUT NOW I'M CURIOUS TO SEE WHAT'S OUT *THERE...*
I WAS ORSON GLARK. I WAS LULA NOMI. NOW I'M BOTH--AND NEITHER...

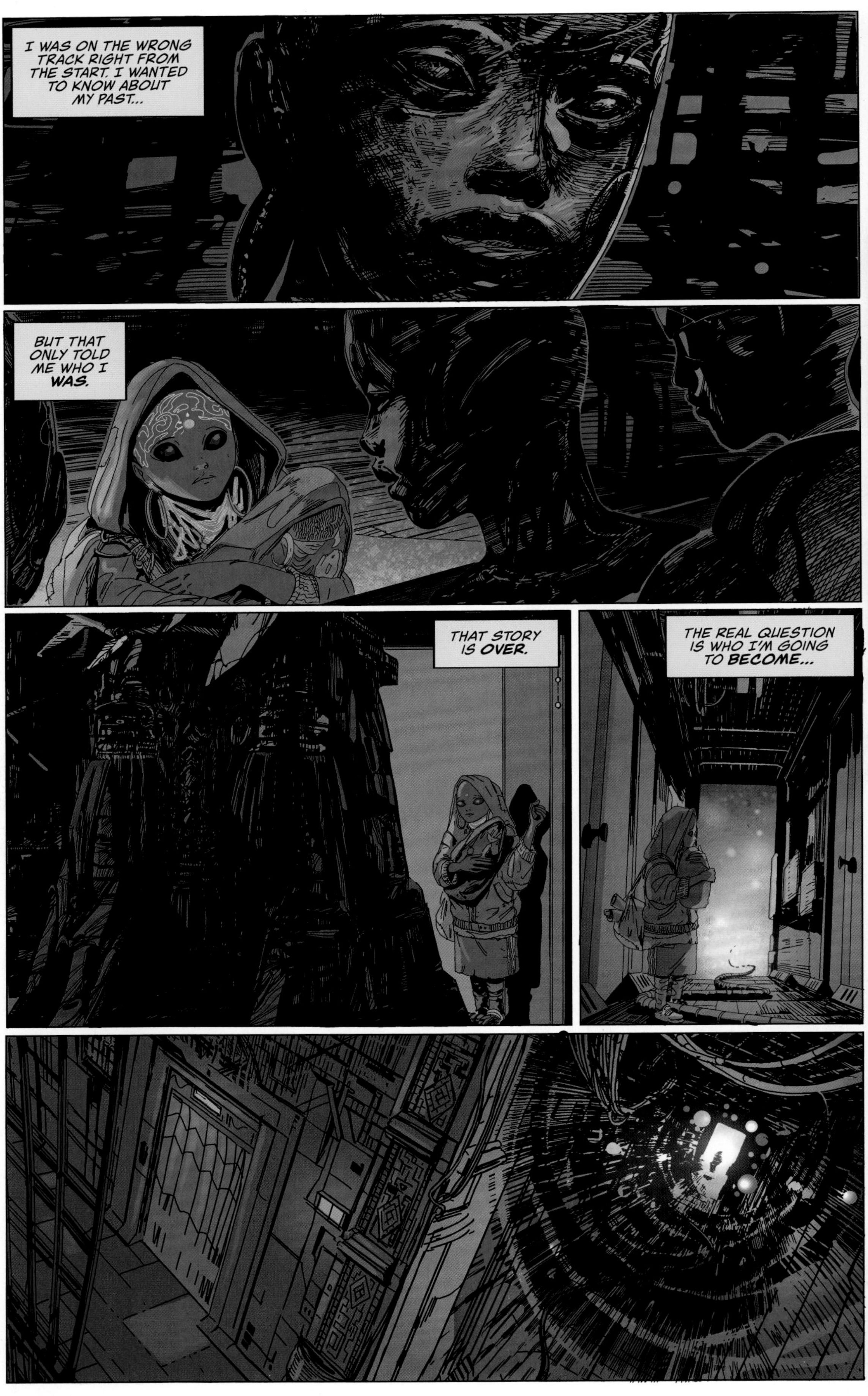
I WAS ON THE WRONG TRACK RIGHT FROM THE START. I WANTED TO KNOW ABOUT MY PAST...
BUT THAT ONLY TOLD ME WHO I **WAS.**
THAT STORY IS **OVER.**
THE REAL QUESTION IS WHO I'M GOING TO **BECOME...**

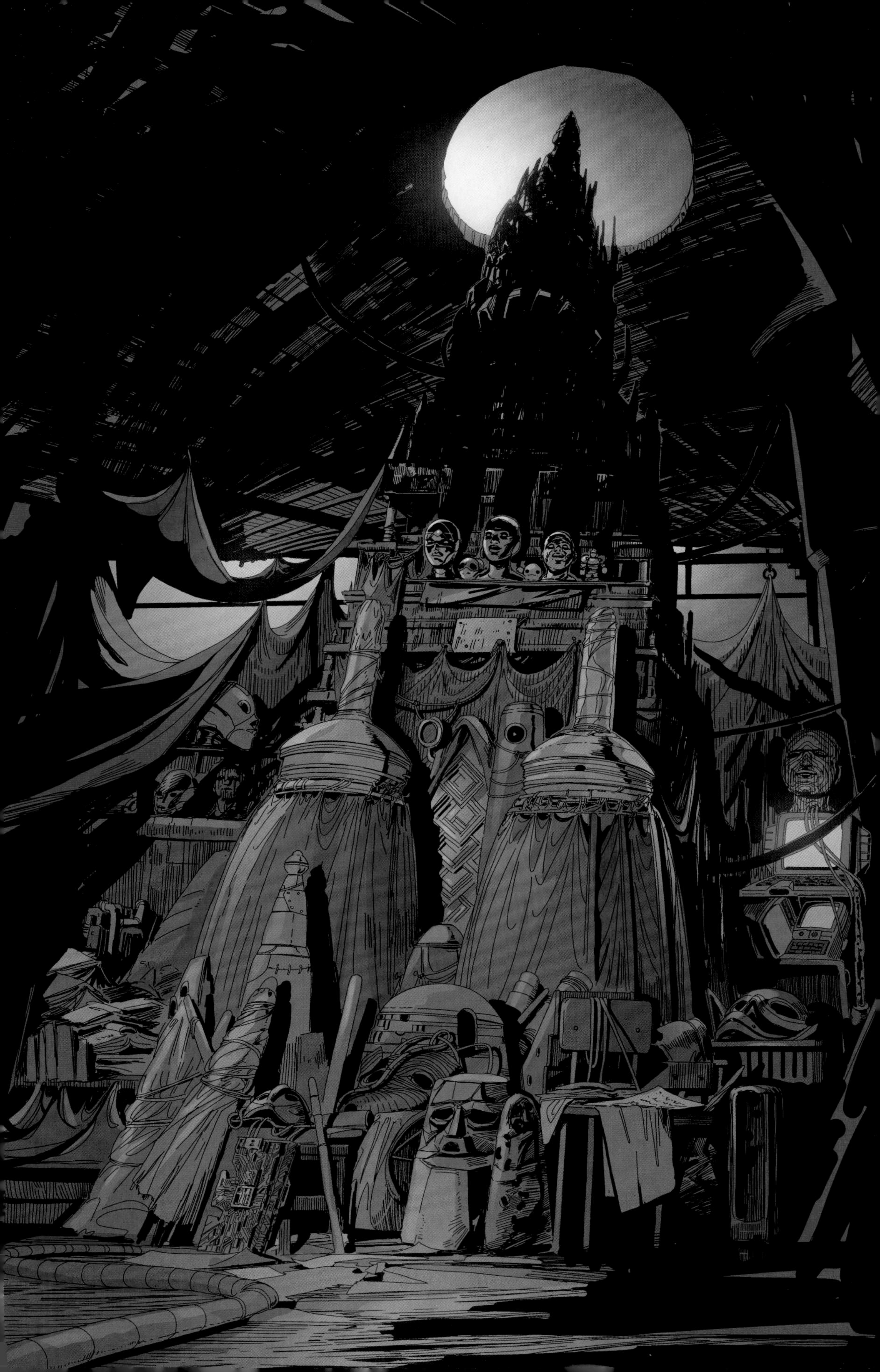

WIPER™

SKETCHBOOK

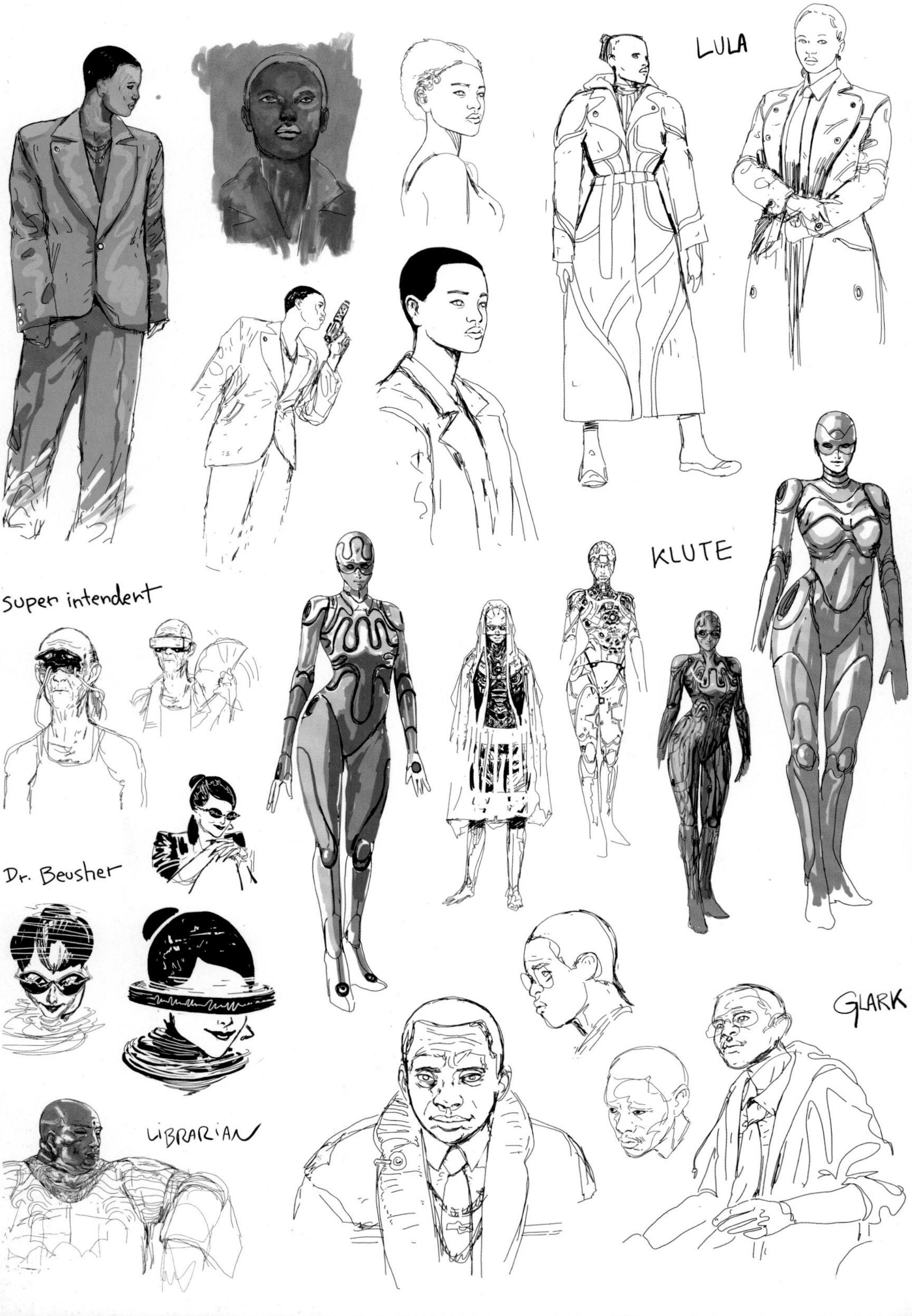

LULA
KLUTE
super intendent
Dr. Beusher
GLARK
LIBRARIAN